HUSTLING THE MOB

THE MAFIA, MALWARE, AND MURDER

DON SPILLANE

Tea Leaf Productions
Huntington Beach, California

Hustling the Mob: The Mafia, Malware, and Murder
© 2024, Don Spillane. All rights reserved.
Published by Tea Leaf Productions,
19744 Beach Blvd, # 368
Huntington Beach CA 92648

ISBN 978-0-9903283-7-7 (paperback)
ISBN 978-0-9903283-1-5 (Kindle)
ISBN 978-0-9903283-2-2 (EPUB)
ISBN 978-0-9903283-3-9 (Audiobook)
Library of Congress Control Number: 2024913660

https://www.donspillane.com
don@donspillane.com

Publishing consultant: David Wogahn, AuthorImprints.com

DEDICATION

I dedicate this book to my wife Carol and sister Joan.
They provided much needed love, support, patience and
encouragement.

AUTHOR'S NOTE

Ten percent of the net proceeds from book sales will be donated to the Alzheimer's Association, https://alzfdn.org

Our story about murder and crime unfolds in the summer of 1996 when the internet and wi-fi were in their infancy. Communications took place in far different world from 2024. I understand it's possible the more technically inclined may find a fault and hope the reader will grant me license if the historical data is not quite exact.

ACKNOWLEDGMENTS

I could not have completed this novel without encouragement and expertise from the following people. My editor, Thornton Sully, www.awordwithyoupress.com; David Wogahn, www.authorimprints.com; and Barbara Villasenor of Oceanside, CA were instrumental in helping me transform a raw manuscript into the version I now offer for your entertainment. My friends, Martin Merriman and his partner Beth were indispensable in providing technical details with humor, intelligence, know-how and a disregard of their valuable time.

CHAPTER 1

The best laid plans…

**Santa Monica, California
Tuesday, August 13, 1996**

Show time approached.

Joshua sat in the dark behind the heavily tinted windows of the rented Ford Windstar van and glanced intermittently between the computer on his lap and the entrance to the two-story building they'd staked out over the previous week. Using his Nokia 9000 with a new SIM card, he was hacking the alarm system for the offices occupied by Whitlock, Katz, and Dixon, accountants to the rich and famous. His fingers raced over the keys, pausing as a beep alerted him that he was successful and could shut down the alarms should they be activated.

His partner, Sarah, sat in the passenger seat and filtered out the sound, meditating—her eyes closed, using controlled yoga breathing to calm herself, preparing for the task at hand. Something in her subconscious alerted her to Joshua's intrusion.

She opened her eyes. "What are you thinking?"

He smiled. "The first time we met. It was…" His reply went unfinished. "Hang on." He pointed to a black Aston Martin DB7 that appeared as the garage door rolled open. He consulted his list.

"That's Dixon, the last one out."

The driver, presumably Dixon, but shielded from view by tinted windows, floored it on the empty street. The tires left a strip of rubber, and the back end weaved a little before the oversteer was corrected. The tuned exhaust snarled and echoed between the buildings, becoming a distant growl as the taillights faded to pinpricks. A flash of brake lights announced a turn, and it disappeared.

"A hundred to one he's taking the Incline to Coast Highway. He's on his way to his place in Malibu. We'll give him a few minutes. Wouldn't want him turning up because he forgot his drugs and catches you with your knickers down. Just an expression," he added hastily, catching her look. "Moving on. Quick recap. You have the ID card to get in the front door?"

"Right here." She lifted the photo ID badge from around her neck. "Let's hope it works."

"You certainly look the part. Nice suit."

"Well, I am supposed to be a VP from London. Did you see the jewels?" She held out her hand to show a gold band together with a diamond engagement ring on her wedding finger. "Cubic Zirconia. That's 150 bucks. The real thing would be twenty grand or more."

Joshua smirked. "I didn't know you were married. Maybe that's the reason we never got together."

"Screw you!" she answered acidly. "Boy, it makes a nice change to be dressed to the nines. Better than the grungy cleaner's outfit for that Brussels job. I could have done better with the shoes though; these heels are going to be a bitch."

"Should you get stopped, the driver's license and credit cards will pass as genuine. If there's a problem with the alarms, I'll take care of them from here. You're looking for anything relating to Leon and Kirov. All set with the camera?"

She nodded. "Of course."

"Good. The radios are working. Finally, you've got to be out before the cleaners arrive." He peered at his watch. "That gives you forty-five minutes or so."

She grimaced. "Time will be tight but should be OK. Fingers crossed for a group-two lock." They hugged awkwardly in the confines of the van as she kissed him lightly on the cheek.

"Good luck," he muttered.

"I'm off." Sarah opened the door and strode towards her rendezvous with Whitlock, Katz, and Dixon.

She swiped her cloned security card through the front entrance lock, a buzzer sounded, and she pushed the door open. Their LA contact had supplied them with *Realistic TRC-222* hand-held radios. She pressed the talk button.

"I'm in."

Joshua acknowledged her with a squawk from his radio.

She walked briskly up the stairs towards the executive offices, stopped outside an office with Dixon's name printed on the glass panel, flexed her fingers inside her surgical gloves, and tried the door handle. She cautiously opened the door and momentarily stood still, feeling her surroundings. The streetlight streaming through the windows provided enough light for her to see there was no threat.

It was a large, luxuriously furnished office; several red-and-black patterned Afghan rugs thrown over the thick dark green carpet provided a pleasing contrast. On one side, a couch and four plush chairs around a coffee table embraced a small meeting area. She faced a wall of glass with French doors leading to the building's spacious balcony. A silk curtain hung over the glass, suspended from brass-colored rings on a golden curtain rod. Although partially drawn, there was enough to show the motif embroidered down one side. Sarah pondered, *Hmmmm . . . Azure Dragon of the East?* She tilted her head to one side, considering. *I'd have thought a Red Dragon; that's the powerful one. Disappointing.*

Sarah gave the gallery of framed photos hanging on the wall a cursory glance, dismissing the multiple pictures of Dixon posing with celebrities as a vanity project. An imposing desk stood on the opposite side of the room, heavy dark wood from a bygone age.

The minutes ticked by as she sat in a leather chair and surveyed the desktop. *Wow, even the dog gets a portrait.* She used the Minox to photograph a silver framed picture of Dixon with his arm around his model wife and children. Protecting the well-polished glass top was a black cushioned pad on which stood a computer keyboard and monthly desk calendar. She briefly examined a Tiffany Damascene Harp lamp standing on one side. *That's got to be twenty grand. This guy's loaded.* With a glance at the computer monitor, she thought, *Dixon would have a fit if he knew Joshua was monitoring his hard drive in real-time.*

She pushed the keyboard to one side and closely examined the scribbled notes written randomly on the desktop calendar. *Well, I'll be. He's a doodler. Look at this. He's written down all kinds of stuff.* She dangled the chain attached to the Minox until it just touched the calendar, the exact length needed for the picture to be in perfect focus. After taking photographs, she moved the keyboard back to its original position and turned her attention to the desk pad. Peeling back one corner, the camera's flash illuminated handwritten notes showing numbers of file passwords and usernames. She took several shots, sighing, *everything but the safe combination. He must have that written down somewhere.*

The clock in her subconscious counted the minutes down—*tick tock, tick tock*—giving urgency to her actions. She used a flashlight to rifle through the bottom drawer observing several celebrity names but nothing on Leon or Ivan Kirov. Similarly, the next two drawers contained nothing of interest. The locked center desk drawer proved no obstacle but only contained assorted office materials. She crouched over and shone her flashlight in the back of the drawer, reaching in to pull out two plastic bags, each half full of a fine white powder. Pursing her lips in disapproval, she put them back where she found them, closing then relocking the drawer. The chiming of a French wall clock reminded her she was taking too long; the safe was the big target. Swinging around in the chair, she faced a credenza, scanning likely files proved to be a vain hope.

"He writes everything else down but not the number I want," she complained to herself.

Her attention now turned to the large print of Monet's *Water Lilies* hanging on the wall above the credenza. She ran her hand carefully around the frame, seeking an alarm and, satisfied there were no wires, called Joshua on the radio.

"No wires. You see anything else?"

Joshua was sure the safe was not alarmed. "Nothing," crackled the response over the radio.

After releasing the catch, the hinged painting swung out. Concealed behind it was a steel safe, the door set flush to the wall. She sighed with relief; the make and model were familiar and well within her capabilities. Checking her surroundings, she shivered as a sudden chill came over her. *It's just stage fright,* she thought

"I'm ready to go. I'm turning my radio off, so I'll be out of contact until I finish. Be patient. You never know what snags we'll meet. Look at what happened in Rome."

"Got that. All clear here."

She used an amplifier to magnify the sounds inside the safe lock. The amplifier had been customized to her specifications by a friendly engineer who had incorporated a magnetized base. A nearby plug and an extension cord enabled her to power it up. There was a distinct clunking sound as she secured the amplifier against the safe door beside the combination wheel. The sound amplification was such, even wearing headphones, a ringing telephone or a squawk on the radio could permanently damage her hearing. She turned off the radio and became isolated from the outside world. Confirming everything was working properly, she knelt on the credenza and began to manipulate the combination dial.

Finding the contact points was the first step. Her mind was focused as she turned the dial multiple times, left and right, listening for the tiny click made by the levers dropping into the notched wheels inside the lock. These noises spoke to her, giving up their secrets until, using a graph, she identified the three correct numbers making up the combination. This gave her six possible sequences to try. She pushed down on the handle, and the safe door opened on her second attempt.

Christ, only fifteen minutes left; I'd better get a move on.

Laying three blue folders from the safe on Dixon's desk, she photographed the pages in each using her Minox with a flash. The first two contained fewer than five pages but were a treasure trove of banking records. Drug sales were listed on spreadsheets detailing initials, amounts, and dates but no identifying names. She opened the last folder and saw the name "Leon" penciled on the front page. Without pausing to read them, she photographed each of half a dozen pages showing itemized banking, drug sales, and real estate investments.

Just five more minutes, and I'll wrap up.

Turning back to the safe, she opened a flat blue box marked "Tiffany." A gold emerald and diamond necklace sparkled in the light.

"Wow!" she whispered out loud. Shaking her head, she reluctantly put it back. *Another time.*

At the back of the safe, a .38 two-shot Derringer with over-and-under barrels raised her eyebrows but went untouched. Another look at her watch. *Time to go.*

The Monet print swung back into place with a click as the catch engaged. Sarah packed up her equipment and gave a last check for traces of her illicit entry. Satisfied there were none, she closed the office door quietly and turned to leave. Lights suddenly shot on outside the office. Two cops were advancing down the corridor, weapons drawn.

What the fuck!

Her brain went into overdrive, scouring for escape options that weren't there. *Oh, God, I'm royally screwed.* Her heart sank to her boots. "Don't shoot," she pleaded.

Brussels, Belgium
Two weeks earlier: Wednesday, July 31

Having netted 850,000 euros from their last three thefts, Joshua and Sarah were riding high until an unexpected problem cropped up. An auditor at a bank in Brussels discovered a 285,000-euro deficit. The account holder, Geert Goossens, on being told of the deficit, denied there was a problem.

"These funds were legally transferred under a power of attorney. I'm involved in a business transaction."

His excuse didn't wash with the sceptical bank auditor who, later chastised by a senior partner for losing the business, reported the matter to the police. Goossens was arrested, held without bail, and charged with money laundering and tax evasion.

London, England

Later that day, while in his London apartment, Joshua received a message, from a source within Belgian intelligence, through an internet relay chat using multiple proxies.

"The police didn't like what they saw on Goossens' bank records. They've set up a task force to investigate this and any other similar cases."

Joshua, now worried that both the criminals and the police would be on Sarah's trail, decided it was time for her to move but wasn't sure where. He picked a newsagent at random and purchased a number of prepaid phone cards. Within walking distance from his flat, he found a payphone that hadn't been vandalized. There, using one of the prepaid cards, he made an international call to his Uncle Sonny. Long rumored in the family to work for various intelligence services, Sonny declared he was a consultant to a technology company. No one believed him, nor did his demeanor encourage further questions. Only Joshua knew the truth.

Sonny was a Cockney, born of Russian-Jewish parentage, and raised on the streets where Jack the Ripper once roamed. From these humble beginnings, he rose to become a successful jeweler and spent lunchtimes meeting clients in The Old Mitre, a historic pub in Hatton Garden, the world-renowned diamond market. It was here he was approached by a friend who asked him to attend a meeting later the same day.

The meeting was a request by Mossad for his help on an organized crime case. A warm relationship developed to eventually include Britain's MI6, kissing cousins with the CIA. His knowledge of organized crime in the diamond and precious metals markets prompted inquiries from various governments at a ministerial level.

Sonny eventually moved to Israel where, relaxing in his favorite armchair, he took a sip of Cabernet as he thumbed through a tattered Torah scroll. His phone rang, eliciting from him a grunt of exasperation.

"What the hell…" he muttered to himself as he put the scroll to one side and picked up his phone; the caller ID said UNAVAILABLE.

"Who is this, please?"

"It's Joshua."

"Joshua, this is unexpected. You caught me in the middle of something."

"This is urgent. You're my last resort. Sarah has a big problem in Brussels."

"This is the same woman you recruited against my advice?"

"Yes, the one who's consistently risked her neck on jobs for you."

"Oh, yeah. Trouble in Brussels, eh? Wouldn't by any chance be the tens of thousands of euros I hear you both pocketed recently?"

"I think there's a leak. Someone's been talking and she's been compromised."

"That's just great, isn't it? I suppose now I'll see her picture posted every time I buy stamps."

"Let's not get too critical here," Joshua said. "We got the financial information you wanted on Yassine, that Moroccan living in Molenbeek, didn't we?"

Sonny went quiet. "OK." he admitted reluctantly. "You did get results." He heaved himself out of the chair with a heavy sigh. "What do you need?"

Joshua explained the situation, summing it up nicely, "The best way to protect her is to move her as soon as possible. Please tell me you have some ideas."

"Give me a minute."

The week previously, Joshua, together with Sarah, had staged a successful coup. Working in concert, Sarah burgled a house in a Brussels suburb and cracked the safe of a known terrorist while, at the same time, Joshua hacked the group's network. As a result, Sonny received detailed records of the group's funding sources. After this success, with time in hand and resources available, Joshua and Sarah pursued the opportunities found during the pursuit of Yassine. Their hunches proved correct on this freelance venture as they hacked thousands of euros from bank accounts held by three criminals.

The minutes ticked past, Joshua could hear papers rustling and heavy breathing, but, other than that, it was silent. His nervousness turned to a smile as a picture of Sonny crossed his mind: a short, slight man, balding with a neatly trimmed beard and moustache. His spectacles were round, suggestive of John Lennon, but it was his dress that made him memorable. Somewhat hippy, always with a *kippah*, Sonny wore brightly colored vests over tie-dyed T-shirts. Harem pants and sandals completed the festive look. He loved to smoke marijuana and painted Kabbalah scenes with various paints he compounded using natural pigments. As a hobby, he spent hours of his time repairing worn Torah scrolls. His peers regarded him as a highly intelligent man who could demonstrate a caustic wit when it came to arguing his side. Most spies crave anonymity, but not Sonny; his colorful character excelled as a spymaster. Naturally cautious, it was unlikely he'd be exposed, but he knew nothing could be taken for granted in the spy game.

"This is almost too much of a coincidence." Sonny's words jarred Joshua back to the present.

"Recently, I received some information on drug and arms activity in the Caribbean. There's a money launderer and cocaine dealer who thinks he's under the radar. He exchanges guns for drugs with the Mexican cartels and recently expanded his customer base to include Hamas. That move brought him to my firm's attention. One of his customers is a Russian, Ivan Kirov, who's hiding from various US government agencies and keeping a very low profile. We believe they're both doing business with a California company, and we would like to learn more."

"Tell me about the money launderer."

"Ah, yes. Leon. He's in Grand Cayman. We know he invests money into lots of dodgy deals. I could use some help with any information that could be used to discredit him. We have a small window of opportunity to kill the arms deal. My informants tell me they haven't reached an agreement yet. There are rockets in the package which could end up killing a lot of our people. Hell, maybe even ignite a war. You two are off the hook in Belgium but you'd better sort out Leon and Kirov, sharpish."

There was silence as Joshua considered the possibilities.

Sonny went on, "Think about the benefits for a moment. This gets Sarah to California, out of harm's way, and we maybe get a peek at what Kirov and Leon are up to. This is a win-win situation. What do you think?"

Joshua didn't hesitate. "You had me at money launderer. Usual rates and conditions?"

Sonny snorted his disgust. "Listen. I'm not too happy with this last stunt. The hundreds of thousands of euros that went into your safety deposit box in some unknown bank. Just outrageous. And it's not the first time. You put me in a very awkward situation."

"How many millions of dollars did we save your company by identifying the Molenbeek faction?" Joshua broke in. "We're private consultants, and we get results. We just relieved some undesirables from their ill-gotten gains, that's all."

"Just remember, you may be doing valuable work, but I don't want to know about any of your private ventures. You must be more discreet. It's a fine line you're treading, and discovery might mean all kinds of unpleasant consequences. Got it?"

"Got it. Usual terms and conditions?" Joshua laughed the warning off.

"I'm fucking serious," snapped Sonny. "Leon and Kirov are not to be sneezed at. They're connected to drug cartels and the Mob, some very unpleasant and dangerous people. My partners aren't any picnic either. If they find out about your extracurricular activity . . ." He was silent a moment, letting the point sink home. "Do not underestimate the danger here. From all sides."

Joshua was apologetic. "All right, all right," he grumbled. "We'll be careful, I promise."

"I'll send the information about California, and I'll honor our payment agreement. Keep me posted." Sonny hung up in a huff.

An hour later, Joshua received an encrypted relay chat message on his Nokia 9000 cellphone offering surprisingly little information about Leon and Kirov. Sonny suggested Joshua start with Whitlock, Katz, and Dixon, an accounting firm in Los Angeles where Kirov was believed to be a client of Dixon. He also received several faxed surveillance pictures which didn't show too well on his monochrome screen. They appeared to be mostly drug cartel middle management, macho types brandishing a number of different automatic weapons, Kalashnikovs being a clear favorite. He squinted to read the names handwritten underneath their respective images, but Leon was not identified. The photos identified an active Kirov, mugging for the camera, playing Al Capone with an Uzi machine gun.

A real cowboy. Joshua was unimpressed.

There was one photo that attracted his interest, however. It showed a tall white man, maybe six feet tall, mid-thirties, muscular build, dressed in jeans, a plain black T-shirt, and with something resembling a .45 automatic strapped to his hip. Under the photograph was written, 'Matthew—IRA.' The photo caught him in the act of mopping the sweat off his forehead, a cowboy hat held loosely in his hand. The skin peeling off his face and nose heralded an Irishman in the tropical sun. Sonny's notes revealed Matthew spent time with Leon before making frequent trips by private aircraft throughout the US, South America, and Europe. Recently he had been in Turkey where he was reportedly meeting with representatives of Hamas.

Joshua called Sonny back from a different payphone. "Hey, what do you know about Matthew? The IRA guy."

"I don't know anything more right now. I'm waiting for a reply from a couple of sources. By the way, did you happen to catch the headline news recently about an attempt to buy off a couple of Hollywood studios' union officials?"

"Yeah, I saw that. The DA indicted a Mob guy called Moran."

"Exactly. Moe Moran screwed up. His boss, Tony Nunzio…"

"New Jersey Nunzio? Don't he and his pals run waste management and construction companies out of Newark?"

"Yes, that Tony Nunzio. Word on the street is Moran had a life sentence hanging over him and started negotiating an immunity deal with the Feds in return for testifying against Nunzio. Matthew was handpicked to take care of business. Next thing you know, Moran's at Gladstones on Coast Highway in Malibu with a couple of civilians; he's finishing up his crab salad, and he gets a call on his cellphone. One of our informants said his face went white, he became agitated and immediately left the meeting, gabbling something about a family emergency. He's still missing but they did find his Rolls Royce. It turned up at the Long Beach docks inside a container bound for Nigeria. My guess is he's in a hole in the Mojave Desert."

"Waste management at its finest," responded Joshua, chuckling. "Where was Matthew at the time?"

"When the LAPD questioned him, Sonny mimicked a tough guy's voice, *'I'm just a tourist. Went to Disneyland. Here's the ticket stubs. There all afternoon. Yeah, on my fucking own.'* He threatened to lawyer up. There was no evidence linking him to Moran's disappearance, so they had to let him go. Look, Josh, this is a very capable bad guy who's managed to avoid any jail time. He's done contracts, and no one's come close to nailing him for even one. He was well respected for his talents with explosives when he was with the IRA. We're not talking about an Individual Retirement Account here; we're talking Irish Republican Army. You'd better keep an eye out for him. Good luck!" He rang off and got back to his Cabernet.

Joshua found another public payphone where, using a different prepaid card, he rang a contact with Belgian intelligence.

"Pierre, what have you got for me?"

Pierre said, "There's a tip-off from an anonymous source about hackers for hire. They've got the names Joshua and Sarah. The informant said they like to travel around Europe by rail and have used Eurostar in the past. That's all the information I've got right now."

Joshua connected an acoustic coupler between his laptop and the payphone. He used multiple internet proxies to send an encrypted instant chat message to Sarah in Brussels.

"I've got something from our uncle." Sarah would know he meant Sonny. "You need to come home. There's an issue with that first one. Remember?"

"Yeah." She messaged back, hesitant, thinking *that must be that prick, Goossens.*

"A task force has been set up, you know what that means; plus, there's always the possibility of blowback from his friends. It's time to get you out of there."

"Shit."

"There's some activity in a nice sunny place but come here first, stay a few days, relax a little, and it will give us time to make some plans."

He promised to send her a chat message within the hour containing details of her travel documents and times of trains.

CHAPTER 2

*Goossens takes an international trip.
In California, a mobster makes a deal.*

**Brussels, Belgium
Thursday, August 1st**

Goossens thanked his lucky stars that the fool of a politician, a degenerate gambler, had overridden protests from the arresting officers and granted his bail. It had cost a 20,000-euro bribe but he learned the last few days had seen police intelligence sources investigating rumors of a hacker for hire. He had returned home, packed a bag, and gone to a cousin's house. From there, he called one of his contacts, a technician in the Belgian police department.

"It's possible there's a partner," he was told, "a woman called Sarah, maybe based in London, occasionally using Eurostar but that's not confirmed. What's going on? We hear the Russians are looking for you."

Goossens said carelessly, "A small admin matter that's about to be solved. I'll be in touch. Bye."

He pulled the chip out of the phone and destroyed it, replacing it with a new one. He called a contact at passport control, requesting a check for a single woman possibly named Sarah. The EU open border policies stifled that line of inquiry. A contact at Eurostar proved fruitful, finding a lone single woman traveler booked under a different name on the last train to London that same day. Goossens' gut instincts told him there was a possibility this might be Sarah. He reserved a seat just one coach car away, figuring, even if his instincts were wrong, he would at least postpone a certain jail sentence by fleeing to London.

To travel incognito he selected a forged passport he'd used in the past, patting a false goatee-style beard and mustache into place to match the photograph. Wearing a trilby hat pulled low over his face, he more resembled a visiting professor than an arch-criminal. He boarded the train and immediately engrossed himself in a newspaper. He was able to hide behind the open pages and monitor everyone coming and going without being suspected. After the train left the station, he waited half an hour then took a walk through the train. In the next carriage, Goossens saw the unsuspecting Sarah working on her laptop, her fingers fairly flying over the keyboard, and knew he had found his prey.

That's got to be the bitch that stole my money. There were too many witnesses, so he restrained an impulse to confront her there and then. *You wait, I'll get mine.*

A tall, muscular man met Sarah at London's Waterloo Station. When Goossens saw them embrace, he realized he had hit the jackpot; this was another one of the team. Keeping in the background he watched them, observing the man was distracted by the woman as they talked up a storm. Amid the sea of people arriving and departing the station, Goossens maneuvered himself close enough to hear Joshua tell the cabbie their destination. He hailed a taxi.

"Is there a pub on Leman Street in Whitechapel?" he asked the cabbie in heavily accented English.

"Yes, sir. Several. There's The Brown Bear at the end of the street, there's . . ."

Goossens interrupted him. "Drop me off there, please."

Whitechapel, London, England

Joshua's rented flat was above a vacant furniture store in a row of old retail shops anchored at one end by The Brown Bear pub. The entrance from the street opened onto a short, narrow hallway with a linoleum floor. A single bulb hanging from an electrical cord offered adequate lighting for the narrow set of uncarpeted stairs leading up to the flat's front door. Beyond the front door, the main living area contained a separate dining room, living room, a large kitchen, and a toilet. Three bedrooms and a full bathroom were another floor up. The high ceilings in the living areas gave an airy feel to the place even though the rooms were small. A ghastly gold-colored flock wallpaper covered the walls; the vertical fleur-de-lis pattern was off-center, provoking a nauseous effect. Nevertheless, the flat came furnished with inexpensive furniture and hunt-scene prints on the walls, offering a temporary but secure refuge until their next move.

Sarah dropped her backpack and suitcase on the floor and, with a sigh of relief, plopped down in one of a pair of blood-colored leather armchairs. The flat had been modernized with central heating, making it warm and cozy. Joshua returned from the kitchen holding a bottle of red wine. He opened it expertly, poured two glasses, and held one out to her. She took it. They toasted each other, clinking glasses, "Cheers."

He contemplated her wan and drawn complexion over the rim of his glass. "These jobs sure are stressful. How are you feeling?"

"Pretty good, considering. We got clean away. It was a nice job."

"We're not out of the woods yet, not by a long shot. We need to move addresses and cover our tracks. We'll rest up tomorrow and then be ready to move the day after."

"Are you worried about Goossens?"

"No. He's in jail. I am worried about his friends and more worried about the leak."

"Sonny has no idea how or who?"

"No. He sort of blew it off. Moaned about the money."

"He knows about the money then?"

He hesitated, not wanting to worry her. "He knows something's fishy, but he doesn't know the details yet. Anyway, he warned me off. But, and it's a big but, he did give us another job. I want to get you there in the next few days."

"What other job?"

"In a minute. While we're here, keep your gun handy, just in case. We don't have to go anywhere. We'll finish up tomorrow and move to Roz's place. It's a bit more upscale, and we'll be perfectly safe there."

"You don't think we're safe here? Now you've got me worried."

"We're fine," Joshua said soothingly. "Just being prudent. Go and get some sleep."

Putting her hand in front of her mouth, she yawned. "I must admit I'm tired and could do with a break. This next job must be the last one for a little while." She took a liberal swallow of wine.

"You know how sharp we must be, and I don't feel at the top of my game right now. A couple of days will help me recharge, but in the long run I, we," she gave him a questioning look, "need a rest. Before that, are you ever going to tell me about this other job?"

She looked over at him and thought him very handsome with his shock of blonde curly hair and muscular build. Tall, maybe six two, with a touch of Robert Redford in his looks. Her emotions ran the gamut as she tried to balance work with the growing feeling inside that she'd like to make him more than a partner in crime.

Unaware of her thoughts, Joshua linked his hands behind his head, sat back in his chair, and briefly considered the ceiling. "We need to get you to Los Angeles." He moved forward in his chair, grinning. "Sonny has a job for us there. Get some sun and beach, and let's see how you feel then."

Her face lit up. "That's a great idea. Give me a little time to spend our money. And going to California will throw any problems with Brussels into a dead end."

"That's settled then." They embraced. "God, it's good to know you're safe and here." He disentangled himself from her.

She drained her wine, "I'm going to bed. I couldn't relax on the train."

Wishing him good night, she went upstairs to bed. The rain beat on the windows, causing her to snuggle under the comforter, troubled by thoughts of Goossens and their two other marks. *California can't come too soon. At times like this, I sometimes wish I had a more ordinary life.* She fell asleep dreaming of having kids with Joshua.

Meanwhile, Goossens, caught in the open by a sudden rain shower, was cold and wet.

Shit English weather, he thought as he shivered in his measly coat, shrinking back into the shadow of the shop doorway as Joshua drew the curtains in the flat opposite him. He was surprised they hadn't seen him following them but, satisfied he had discovered their hideout, he walked down Leman Street away from their apartment. As he approached a railway bridge, he saw a cab dropping off a customer. He shouted to get the driver's attention and opening the rear door, he said, "Bayswater Road. I'll tell you where to drop me off."

"Right you are, Guvna," said the driver, a heavy-set man with a ready smile, Buddy Holly-style black glasses, and the quick wit of a Cockney cabbie. He turned and spoke to Goossens through the open compartment window.

"Comfortable back there, sir? Put your seatbelt on if you wouldn't mind." He watched as Goossens fastened his seatbelt.

"On our way then." He set off smoothly. "See the football, did you, sir? Wouldn't be an Arsenal fan, would you?"

Not wanting to get into a conversation, Goossens said, "My English is not so good."

"No problem, sir."

They rode in silence to the Bayswater Road where Goossens paid off the cabbie and walked to Lancaster Mews. Here, known only to himself, he kept a small house as a hideout.

Los Angeles, California

Six thousand miles away in Los Angeles, another in a series of apparently unconnected events started when the repeater chimed on Ara Danielian's Vacheron Constantin watch. He was in his Ventura Boulevard restaurant, Le Gourmet, soothing the new chef who was nervous and worried about the following day's special.

"Look, we've been over this a thousand times. Just stick to what we agreed, and all will work out. I've done this many times and…"

"But, Ara," interrupted the chef and stopped as Ara raised his hand.

"Enough now," he said with authority. "I'm already running late. I've got a quick call to make. Then I'm leaving for a meeting at Studio Z. Just do what I'm telling you."

He went to a small room near the rear exit that served as an office. From there, shielded from the noise of the kitchen, he made his telephone call to Ben Weiner, an attorney whose main client was Anthony Nunzio. The same Nunzio mentioned by Sonny earlier. His Los Angeles protégé, Vincent (Big Vinnie) Esposito ran La Cucina di Papa in Van Nuys, an innocuous restaurant on Van Owen Street. From there it was convenient for a quick trip over Benedict Canyon to Studio Z Recording Studios in Beverly Hills, one of Nunzio's West Coast interests.

Nunzio used Vincent to oversee Studio Z recording studios where they were able to launder money, facilitate the drug business, and take financial advantage of artists when they could get away with it. Over the years, the musicians constantly demanded a wide variety of drugs and Big Vinnie controlled the supply. Drug revenue often exceeded the studio rental intake but, as Nunzio pointed out, the real money came from production credits and copyrights on recordings themselves. Taking full advantage, both Nunzio and Vinnie were often shown as producers or even composers on a number of the recordings produced through the studios. Over time, this amounted to millions of legal dollars as they took a share of the royalties.

"Have you got all the information on the airport deal we discussed the other day?" asked Ara, idly doodling green daffodils on a yellow pad lying in front of him. He was using the green ink from his Mont Blanc fountain pen to make the leaves more realistic.

"Yes," said Weiner. "It looks good. What are you doing on the Studio Z deal? We could avoid some taxes."

"Yes, if we can do a 1031 exchange. I'm only getting started on putting the word out. There's interest but nothing solid yet. I'm hoping we don't have to take a haircut on the price."

"Why's that? I thought it was a good earner."

"It was for the last twenty years, but we're being outmuscled by the Crips and the Bloods these days."

"Can you believe it? All our activities have been impacted." Weiner sighed, "It's not like the old days."

"You'd better believe it. Nunzio's unhappy with the downturn in revenue and when you add in the Moran union fiasco . . ." He left his sentence unfinished.

"What now?"

"How about lunch, say the day after tomorrow? Maybe two o'clock here at Le Gourmet? Bring the numbers, and let's see about making an offer. I may even have something on the studio by then, you never know."

"That's good for me."

"Great."

Ara put the phone down. He finished his shading of the daffodil, pulled his cuff back to see the time, frowned, shrugged into a grey silk jacket, and walked out of the restaurant. He drove to his appointment with a smile of satisfaction, cocooned in the style and comfort offered by his 1964 S3 Bentley Continental.

Ara was a deal maker for the Mob. Armenian by heritage, moderately wealthy, always dressed impeccably, and muscular from years of lifting weights. He acted ten years younger than his sixty-two years. Of average height, heads turned when he walked into the room; he had presence. With a full head of white hair and a tanned face, Ara attracted more than his share of attention from the opposite sex. Over the past few years, he had a steady girlfriend but wasn't averse to discreet dalliances when the fancy took him. A flirtation with a shop assistant, a chance encounter in a grocery store, a smile in a coffee shop often turned into a seduction ending at the Beverly Hills Hotel or some other appropriate spot.

With his love of good food and background in the New York food industry, it was natural for Ara to start a restaurant when he landed in Los Angeles. His investors were invisible but said to be Mob affiliated. The French restaurant, Le Gourmet, on Ventura Boulevard in Sherman Oaks quickly became a top LA venue. He followed this with another success in Beverly Hills, Enzo's, serving exquisite Italian fare. His bonhomie approach to life, expertise in the kitchen, and his nose for what the public wanted created a publicity buzz. The celebrity world loved his panache, and the fascination of rumored Mob connections never hurt business. Enzo's was a noisy and bustling Italian restaurant with an open kitchen, counter bar, and a brick pizza oven. This was countered at Le Gourmet where an atmosphere of calm, muted conversation and mouth-watering food offered an oasis away from the hustle and bustle of everyday life.

On a social level then, the success of his restaurants allowed Ara access to many Hollywood celebrities, their attorneys, agents, and general hangers-on. This particularly applied to the recording industry where the Mob was always in the background. Ara augmented his restaurant income by being the "person who gets things done" for Ben Wiener. When persuasion was needed, Ara, despite his nickname 'Iron Arms,' represented the soft approach. The hard approach was handled through Weiner and New Jersey.

Ara drove over Benedict Canyon and made his way to Studio Z on Santa Monica Boulevard in Beverly Hills. He gave a smile to the two valet attendants as he swept past them and parked across two parking bays.

"Make sure no one goes near the car," he said sternly, handing the valet a twenty.

"Thank you, señor, no problem."

Ara walked into the rear of the building and acknowledged the security guard. He ran up the stairs and walked down a bright corridor where, every few steps it seemed, framed gold records hung on the walls. He came to a reception area where a stunning black woman, a former beauty queen, held court behind an antique desk. Charlene Jones was wearing a red silk dress, showing plenty of cleavage, and held herself with heaps of confidence.

"Good afternoon, Ara, I hope you're having a good day. Barry's expecting you, go right on in." Her southern drawl, slow and sexy, sounded like a black panther daring you to take another step.

"Thank you, Charlene, you're looking particularly lovely today." Ara gave her a very frank appraisal, baring gleaming white teeth. His smile was similarly predatory, but more the original great white shark.

"Thank you, Ara. You're such a flirt."

The telephone rang, interrupting the conversation. "Studio Z Studios, how may I help you?" She fluttered him on his way with long red fingernails.

Ara walked into a large office on the street side of the building through the open door. It was cool and quiet with no traffic noise from the street. The glare from the sun was muted by a dark window tint.

"Finally," said Barry. "We wondered if you were ever going to get here."

Barry Goldman managed and operated a recording studio that was legendary in the music business. Gold and platinum records recorded in these studios decorated walls by the acre throughout the world. Jack, his sidekick, was the resident sound engineer and occupied the couch opposite Barry's desk. The decor was glass, chrome, leather, and suede. Expensive, just like the rest of the building which was designed for the comfort of world-famous celebrities and musicians on a 24/7 basis.

Barry was slim and fit. He favored jeans, hand-tooled Lucchese alligator cowboy boots, and fancy shirts. Today it was a white shirt with hand-embroidered flowers running down each side of the buttons. With his blond hair and weathered good looks, he appeared to be in better shape than most celebrities despite his own rock 'n roll lifestyle. He reclined in a beige leather chair with his boots on the glass desk.

Ara, always the perfect gentleman, greeted them both with a smile. "I got held up by the chef and then the traffic on Benedict Canyon, sorry about that. How are you, Jack?"

Jack acknowledged Ara with a smile and a head nod as Ara continued. "I've put the word out to a couple of players about selling Studio Z, but I've heard nothing yet."

Barry took his boots down and leaned forward, his elbows on the desk.

"As you know, none of this makes us happy. We did hear of someone selling his studio in Memphis and may be looking to move out here." He grimaced, "It's just disappointing that it's come to this."

Ara was straight with them. "Look, I'm sorry, but we must move on. Under its current set up there's no way the studios can continue and make a profit. Substantial investment is needed in electronic upgrades, the soundboards to start. You know this." He frowned. "You've had a good run in a business that's changed over the past few years. We'd have to put a few million into the studios and there's no guarantee on return." He held back when Jack interrupted him.

"Successful musicians are building out their home studios now. They can develop projects on their equipment before finalizing the recordings in the studios. If, and that's a big if, they use the studios for the final cuts. That rehearsal and composition time was good for us. Losing it cut into the time a band uses the studio, and we lose studio rental income."

"No one's blaming you two," admitted Ara. "You're victims of changing times. Both of you have a good future. I think you should count yourselves lucky because you've got a great compensation package." He studied them as he awaited their confirmation.

Barry spoke up. His face showed his disappointment.

"Yes, Ara, and I'm sorry if we sound ungrateful. You've been generous, and we're thankful."

Jack said. "Absolutely," nodding his head in agreement.

"My hope," Barry continued, "is that this Memphis guy, I think his name is Richard Lee or something similar, will want to buy."

"He just sold a studio in Memphis and has the cash, apparently," interjected Jack.

Ara thoughtfully sat back, steepling his fingers. "Do we know how to contact this Lee character, then?"

"I've left him a voicemail with your number, so expect a call from him," said Barry.

"If he's willing to pay the price we're asking, then he'll buy the studios, and everyone will be happy."

Ara could see the reality. Although still luxurious, the bloom was starting to go off, the lush furnishings slightly jaded and out of style. The décor needed freshening up. New investment and new faces were needed to take Studio Z into the future. "I'm going to my office." He turned and walked out the door, thinking, *you're a dwindling format doomed to failure. You just want to keep your jobs.*

He left Barry and Jack in his wake, commiserating with each other as he made his way to his own office, stopping only to flirt with Charlene once more.

He unlocked the door to his office, pushed it open, and walked over to his desk. Unlike the comparative luxury of Barry's office, Ara's room was simple but elegant. Decorated in peach with one wall a rich green, the mouldings and door were a bright gloss white, making a nice contrast. The office was well lit despite the dark tinted windows. As with all the offices facing the busy street, double glazing reduced the traffic noise to a whisper. Furnishings were functional, sparse even, with only a leather office chair behind a smart working desk and two comfortable occasional chairs in front for guests. The glass top of his desk was bare but for a telephone and a fax machine. There was no computer.

Ara didn't go in for gold records on the walls, preferring to admire David Hockney's work. Comparatively rare prints, *Apples, Pears & Grapes* hung on the wall behind his desk while *Colored Flowers Made of Paper and Ink* decorated the wall facing him. The art complimented the antique Mohajeran Sarouk carpet lying across the hardwood floor. Although this office offered privacy and confidentiality, he preferred his meetings take place in the early afternoon at one of his restaurants. There, he could wine and dine prospects and cut deals in complete privacy.

He passed the time looking through a Patek Phillipe catalog, intending to reward the chef for critically praised menu improvements and increased sales at Enzo's. His phone rang, it was Charlene.

"I have Vincent on the phone."

"Put him through." Ara licked his finger and turned the page.

"Hi, Ara. Having a good day?" said Vinnie, his nasal voice harsh in Ara's ear.

"Hello to you too, Vincent. How can I help you?"

"There's a party coming up at Star's Encino house. I'd like to get Bruno an invitation. Do you think you can swing it?"

"Will there be much demand?" Ara referred to the cocaine and heroin that Bruno would be taking to the party.

"Are you kidding? I lay in extra for this kind of do."

"I'll let you know when I have the invitation—just one?"

"No, he'll be taking a friend who will be carrying a piece but has a permit."

"OK, Vincent, I'll call you and let you know where to pick up the invitations."

"Thanks for the courtesy. I'll call you after the event to schedule coming by with your cut."

They finished the call cordially, and Ara spent most of the afternoon contacting an agent of Star's to organize Bruno's invitation. He was able to negotiate the exclusive use of a room for drug sales in return for several free ounces of cocaine. He called Vincent, explained the deal, and gave him a contact number for the setup. Afterward, Ara sat at his desk and carefully considered making minor adjustments to the menu at Le Gourmet. At last, satisfied with the changes, he decided to visit the restaurant and advise the chef of his recommendations.

I'll pick up my dry cleaning on the way. Maybe see if that long-legged piece will come to dinner and try one of the new desserts. He felt a stirring in his loins.

CHAPTER 3

Joshua takes care of business.

Whitechapel, London, England
Thursday, August 1st

While Ara contemplated his chances of getting laid, eight hours away in London, Sarah caught up on her sleep while Joshua shook himself awake and made a fresh pot of coffee. Half an hour later, showered and feeling refreshed, he made himself comfortable in front of his computer. His raid on Whitlock, Katz, and Dixon started with a search of their corporate web page. On the "About Us" tab, Joshua obtained the names, photos, email addresses, phone numbers, and biographies of the senior staff for their California, New York, and London offices. He learned they were an accounting firm specializing in the entertainment field and renowned for their tax avoidance planning. He also noted that Barbara Fielder, the Vice President for Marketing in the New York office, was a recent transfer from the London office. Joshua got up from his chair, stretched, and walked in circles around the living room pondering his next move.

His opening gambit used a pawn in this chess match against Leon and Dixon. Joshua composed an email addressed to Ursula Burnett, listed on the web page as a secretary to Dixon's partner Jerome Katz. The email address showed it was from the Federal Trade Commission. Ursula didn't notice that the actual sending email address looked genuine but was in fact bogus. The subject line just contained the words "Pending Consumer Complaint" and was designed to immediately capture the reader's attention. The body of the letter went on to outline that a complaint had been made about unfair business practices. Details were to be found in the attached document.

Ursula frowned when she saw the email in her inbox. *What the hell?* she thought. *I'd better have a look at this before Jerry comes back from his meeting.* She clicked on the attachment and opened it.

She immediately thought, *This has been sent in error.*

The attachment, an MS Excel document, outlined a series of statistics whereby the Flynn Accounting Company of New York accused the Fortescue Corporation in Miami of anti-competitive practices. She frowned and sat with her hand over her mouth as she read the document through for a second time. *Why's there no cover letter? I don't think we've ever had any dealings with this Flynn company, and I've certainly never heard of the Fortescue Corporation. Must be a mistake. I'd better let Jerry deal with this when he gets back.*

Ursula showed Jerry Katz the email as soon as he returned from his meeting.

He said, "It's obviously a mistake. To my knowledge, we've never had any dealings with either of these companies. Just ignore it, and we'll get in touch with the FTC if we receive another email from them."

In London, Joshua saw the email attachment had been opened with a smile of satisfaction. He had successfully lured Ursula into downloading a malware-infected file. It resembled an innocent email, but he had inserted a macro in the MS Excel attachment. When Ursula downloaded the attachment, the malware had installed itself within her computer's data files. He kept it deliberately simple to avoid any suspicion that the email was phishing. Now, it lay there, submerged in a collection of zeros and ones, awaiting the command to activate.

Friday, August 2: 6:00am London time / (August 1) 10:00pm Los Angeles time

Joshua waited impatiently. Sleep was impossible. He paced the room until the first hint of light turned the room grey. Dixon's offices were some six thousand miles away where it was late evening, and the building was almost certainly empty. Feeling nervous and excited at the same time, he activated the malware.

Several hours later, Joshua turned to see a very drowsy Sarah standing at the foot of the stairs, rubbing the sleep from her eyes.

"You're up early," he remarked.

"God, is that the time? No wonder I'm still so sleepy."

She was distracting in a robe that left very little to the imagination. He turned to face his computer screen lest his expression reveal his lewd thoughts.

"Do you want to hear the good news or the bad news?" he said cockily.

She yawned. "Coffee, then bad news, always."

"Fresh coffee in the kitchen. The bad news is our target has a safe containing information we need to see. This is stuff not on a computer."

"That's the bad news? I like it!" Sarah said eagerly, turned on by the thought of burglary. "Can't wait to hear the good news."

Choosing a plain white mug, she poured herself a cup of coffee and walked over to stand behind him. She crouched down to see the screen, her head close to his. Joshua briefly closed his eyes, inhaling her just-woke-up scent.

He pushed those thoughts to the back of his mind. "I finally got admin credentials for Dixon's network and can now read his hard drive as he uses it. I went everywhere looking for our Kirov. Nothing on him, but I did find a reference to Leon in an email which said, in part, 'file in my office safe.' You're going to have to locate the safe and copy those files."

He sat back in his chair, disappointed at this new wrinkle, "Nothing on Kirov at all."

"Wow. Nice job." She drew back, cupping her hands around the mug of coffee. "What about my cover if we can get in front of Dixon's safe?"

Joshua gave an evil laugh, "Heh, heh, heh. ID is no problem. I accessed some HR files. Look at these." Sarah put her head near his, again studying the series of faces Joshua pulled up on his screen in quick succession. For an unknown reason, her thoughts acquired a Jamaican accent. *Joshua's smell be good, Mon.* She drew in another silent breath. *Hairy-chested musk. Yummee.*

"Look at this one. She even looks a little like you."

Sarah came back to earth with a bump. "You think so?" She studied the picture critically. Joshua glanced sidewise at her and saw her pert nipples as her robe fell open. He quickly averted his gaze.

"We could use her ID."

"Be nice to be a boss instead of the usual blue-collar type."

Sarah stood up and gathered her robe around her, unsuccessfully concealing her nakedness. Joshua desperately ignored this distraction, blandly staring her directly in the eye.

"I'll have no problem dealing with their security in real time. We should get you on your way to Los Angeles, although I won't join you for a day or so." He shrugged. "In the meantime, we'll use a local contact in Santa Monica to put IDs together and any other stuff we'll need. When you get to LA you can scout Dixon's office and work out the best strategy to get the information from the safe."

"Agreed."

Sarah shivered as a cool draft made her aware of her scant attire.

"Let me get showered and dressed, and we can figure out our plans for LA."

They spent the rest of the day relaxing, but the topic of conversation was mostly about work. As night fell, the flat became warm and cozy. Sarah curled up with a book in a vain attempt to read, while her mind was alive to the possibilities in Los Angeles.

Joshua saw her fidgeting. "You need to relax. See those headphones over there? Put them on and listen to some music."

"Is that an order?" All thoughts of his masculine aroma were now banished from her mind.

"Of course not. I need to concentrate, and you're distracting me."

"No, I'm OK here. I'll be as quiet as a mouse. Promise." She took a beat. "Squeak, squeak."

"This is serious stuff and needs my full attention. If this isn't done right, we could end up dead."

"Squeak, squeak," was all she offered.

He shook his head in mock surrender and continued to massage and coordinate the information he had gathered so far about Dixon and his partners, Whitlock and Katz.

While Joshua worked, and Sarah finally dozed, Goossens tried the street door leading to their flat. Closed with two single-cylinder deadbolt locks, he deftly opened the first lock with professional picks. To his delight, the second deadbolt was unlocked so he cautiously opened the door and closed it behind him. It was pitch black. He pulled on a headband with a battery-powered light that lit up the stairs in front of him. Carefully putting his weight down ever so slowly, one step at a time, his left hand used the handrail for support. A cocked .45 automatic in his right hand pointed steadily at the center of the door at the top of the stairs where revenge lay. Despite all his precautions, it was an old building, and he winced each time a step gave a small creak.

Upstairs, a small alarm bell tinkled by the side of the computer. A large WELCOME mat, set inside the downstairs front door, disguised an alarm pressure plate underneath. Anyone stepping on it sounded the bell beside Joshua's computer.

"Hold tight," Joshua said. "We have company."

He put the phone down and from a shelf under the desk took up a Heckler and Koch MP5K submachine gun with a pistol grip and a noise suppressor. Sarah had fallen asleep but was instantly alert. She tiptoed into the kitchen, reappearing seconds later, her Sig Saur P 229 9mm automatic at the ready. Assuming a combat position beside the front door, her finger extended along the barrel with the safety off; she was set.

Joshua cocked the submachine gun as quietly as possible. Switching from safety to auto, he slipped off his loafers and moved silently to the flat's front door. As he got there, he listened with his ear to the door. He could faintly hear someone creeping up the stairs.

He whispered to Sarah, "At least one on the stairs. Maybe halfway up."

Joshua knew the steps leading to the flat well; he trod them many times a day. Suspecting any possible assailant would aim high, Joshua knelt on one side of the door, waiting. He motioned Sarah to the light switch and pointed the gun at the door handle. She instantly understood her role, changing her position, ready to open the door and switch on the light at Joshua's signal. Seconds passed. Joshua could sense the visitor taking his or her time, cautiously judging their next step. Towards the top of the stairs, one of the steps always gave a very distinct, groaning creak. The agonizing silence was broken by Goossens gingerly putting his weight down on that very step. It didn't disappoint.

Joshua nodded to Sarah who switched on the hall light and flung open the door in one smooth motion. There was a deafening bang and a blinding flash as Goossens fired wildly, distracted by the sudden light and noise. The bullet flashed between Sarah and Joshua, embedding itself in the ceiling.

Missed was his last thought as Joshua fired a controlled burst from the submachine gun down the stairs. The silencer reduced the gunfire noise to a minimum; it couldn't be heard beyond the front door. There had been no cry, just the sound of a body falling heavily down the stairs followed by silence. From the top step, a whiff of cordite hit Joshua's nostrils, his ears still ringing from Goossens's shot.

He kept the body covered, "Go check the street from the roof."

Sarah quickly accessed the stairs to the roof and peered cautiously over the false mansard frontage. *Nothing. Not even a drunk. Anyone waiting in the shop doorways? Anyone in a parked car?* It was very quiet, no traffic or pedestrians. and no obvious danger from hidden accomplices.

Joshua walked down the stairs and kicked Goossens's gun to one side. *Hope he doesn't have company.*

Sarah returned to the top of the stairs and stood looking down at Joshua.

"All clear," she said.

He opened the front door a crack, peeked up and down the street, and listened. Still all quiet. He closed the door and approached the body. "Yeah. Nothing down here either. He was on his own. Let's see who it is." He wrestled the body on its back where it let out a large groan.

He cried out in amazement. "It's Goossens."

"Are you sure? Isn't he supposed to be in jail?"

He bent over the dying man. "How the hell did you get out of jail? How did you find us?"

Goossens coughed up blood, hate in his eyes. "You stole from me, and I want my money back," he said weakly.

Joshua was indifferent, "You stole from someone else. There's no difference. How did you find us?"

"Followed her." He jerked his head toward Sarah at the top of the stairs. "All the way here and you never knew." His face contorted, "Amateurs," he hissed, coughing blood, choking, suddenly unable to speak, his eyes registering his hate. He coughed up more blood. His breathing grew labored. Suddenly, Goossens was dead.

Joshua stood up and stared down at the corpse in disgust. He walked back up the stairs.

"Get your stuff together and get out now. Leave this mess to me, and let's get you on your way to Los Angeles as soon as possible. Skip off to Roz's safe house in West London. I'll join you as soon as I've taken care of things here."

Sarah started to protest, but he shushed her. Knowing it was the best decision, she packed and left for the safe house by taxi.

With Sarah gone, Joshua remained calm. First things first: how to deal with Goossens's body at the bottom of the stairs? Knowing it had the possibility of being traced and wouldn't endear him to Sonny, he nonetheless called him anyway.

Sonny picked up the phone, gathering his wits, his eyes too unfocused to read the caller ID as he struggled to become fully awake, "Who is it?"

He heard Joshua say, "I need some help. I'm in London and had an unexpected visitor. Our friend from Brussels. He's still here but can't come to the phone. if you get my meaning."

That got Sonny's attention in a hurry. "But you're OK?"

"It was a near thing, but I got lucky. I'm on a time deadline here, can you help or not?" Joshua said impatiently.

"Yes. Yes, of course. But Brussels? How did they get on to you in London?"

Joshua cut him off. "So, no help then?"

"Wait. Wait. Don't be so impatient, you just woke me up. Let me think." He took a few moments, rubbing his face to become fully awake. "London, hmmm. Let me check something, it'll take a few seconds." Joshua could hear his computer keyboard clacking away.

"Here we go. I've got just the right person for you, and it's someone you've already met. Do you remember that meeting I sent you to in Whitechapel? The man?" Not hearing any word from Joshua, he prompted him, "Well dressed?"

"Yes. Yes, of course."

"Get in touch. He runs The Ship, on the High Street, and can arrange anything. You'll have to pay upfront in cash. Of course, that's no problem for you," Sonny said, his voice heavy with sarcasm.

Joshua grimaced as the barb went home. Sonny was still pissed about the money. "Thanks, I'll make it up to you."

Sonny retorted, "You're right, you'll make it up. You owe me big time." Sonny's venom fell on deaf ears; Joshua had already disconnected the call.

Joshua made a call to the pub and asked for Isaac.

"He's not here but will be back shortly. Did you want to leave a message?"

"No thanks," he said and hung up.

He weighed up the chances of the body at the foot of the stairs being discovered if he went to see Isaac personally. Deciding it was worth the risk, he nevertheless prepared to disappear at the first sign of trouble.

The nature of his work meant Joshua traveled light. Leaving the corpse where it was, he went upstairs and stuffed a backpack with his computer, followed by six cellphones, spare SIMs, and prepaid phone cards. There was a hidden pocket where Joshua stashed four spare passports showing his photo but in different names and 20,000 euros in 1,000-euro stacks, shrink-wrapped in plastic for protection. They were concealed by clean underwear, light clothing, and other travel necessities neatly placed on top. It wouldn't stand a hard search but was good for a cursory inspection. A Fairbairn-Sykes fighting knife hidden in his right boot provided a wicked weapon in his hands.

His other belongings, including the HK MP5K, two additional magazines, and combat gloves, were tucked into a compact wheely suitcase he placed beside his desk. He decided the rug in the living room was best suited to the task at hand and manhandled it down the stairs. Blood had trickled from Goossens's mouth down his chin. His shirt front was marred by a neat line of bullet holes that had stitched him from chest to naval as he'd fallen backwards down the stairs.

Joshua was sweating. *Damn, dead weight is right. Goossens's body feels like it weighs 350 pounds.* The oppressive burden made it a monumental struggle to get it rolled in the carpet. *That will have to do for now. Should be enough to soak up any remaining blood.* Despite manhandling the body, he had avoided getting any blood on his clothes, but his shoes and hands were a mess.

He returned upstairs where he cleaned himself up. The white face reflected in the mirror showed the tiredness he felt after the killing, the feeling of exhaustion as the adrenaline rush subsided. He recognized the reaction from the previous times he'd been in a kill-or-be-killed scenario.

Joshua knew that his destination, The Ship, was a haven for old-school gangsters, men with extensive criminal records. Everyone would be suited and booted, blue jeans and sneakers would be frowned upon. He slipped into a smart silk, double-breasted jacket over a black T-shirt and grey slacks, with a military-style raincoat as a precaution against the possibility of rain. The weight of the P229 in a shoulder holster felt comforting. He went down the stairs, squeezed around the body, opened the door carefully, and stood in the shadows, watching, listening. It was quiet. He locked the door with both deadbolts.

If I'd locked that the first time, Goossens wouldn't have gotten in so easily. He shook his head, angry at himself for the mistake.

It took him 15 minutes of brisk walking to reach Aldgate tube station. He stashed the backpack and suitcase in a luggage locker, and another 15 minutes found him in front of The Ship. Joshua knew the owner's customers called it Isaac's, the name of the current landlord.

The pub was in the center of a terraced set of shops with a mixture of owners and renters living in the flats above. The Ship occupied the ground floor; the three stories above were Isaac's living accommodations. Joshua walked into the front door and shut the door behind him. He saw the pub was quite small, maybe sixty feet long by thirty feet wide, being, in effect, a long narrow room. Patrons sitting on one of the stools in front of the bar could admire themselves in an ancient mirror inscribed: *Watney's Best Bitter.* From the red carpet to the heavily embossed Regency stripe wallpaper, the interior was outdated and ancient. He shivered; it was colder than expected. Four people eyeballed him, one behind the bar and three seated behind a table at the far end of the pub. This table was round, and from it Isaac held court, playing robber baron rather than the fabled King Arthur.

Isaac was a strange little man. Jewish, with rather large ears sticking out of either side of his bony skull, his hairpiece sat looking like a dead grey squirrel. He was thin, almost emaciated, seemingly frail, and, with a milky white complexion, he had a strong resemblance to a cadaver. This appearance belied the truth—the young good-looking barman, Alfred, could attest to Isaac's sexual prowess with a fetish for pretty boys and golden showers.

A well-known fence, Isaac preferred buying stolen goods in bulk. A hijacked truckload of liquor would be sold on to his outstanding network of contacts, anywhere from London to Newcastle. Taking no part in the actual theft itself, he bought the stolen goods at a substantial discount. As far as possible he tried to keep his hands clean, working through trusted third parties. He encouraged his contacts to meet at the pub, a Mecca for all types of career criminals.

Isaac, meticulous as usual, dressed in a beautiful light blue wool suit with thin white pinstripes, his snow-white shirt almost matched his complexion, which in the bar's bright lighting seemed paler than usual. His jewelry was not subtle. A heavy gold sovereign ring adorned the pinky of his left hand, and a gold identity bracelet jangled around his wrist. Smoke drifted upwards from a small cigar in the ashtray beside him. Careful to avoid any ash on his suit, he picked it up and took a puff, blowing the smoke toward the ceiling. He leaned forward and knocked the ash into the ashtray as his reptilian eyes flickered at Alfred and then back to the two men at the table. He smiled. It made him look like a grinning skull.

"Gentlemen, you'll have to excuse me. I think our business is done. Albie will deal with the merchandise, just deliver it to his metal yard."

He stood, as did the two men, then shook hands, and he wished them good night. Joshua felt the keen looks of interest directed his way as he stood aside to let them pass but, apart from a nodded acknowledgment, nothing was said. Isaac waved Joshua forward and they sat, close together, at the round table.

"Drink?" Isaac asked.

"Yes, fine." He did not want to seem impolite by refusing the invitation.

"Scotch, OK?"

"Yes, that would be good."

"Alf, give us a drink," Isaac said with a wave of his hand.

Alf reached for the Johnny Walker Black Label, poured two generous drinks, brought them over to the table, and returned to polishing glasses behind the bar, just within hearing range.

"Cheers. I was surprised to see you of all people walk in the door," remarked Isaac.

"Cheers." Joshua felt the smooth, peated whiskey warm his throat and chest. "Until an hour or so ago, I had no intentions of being here. Do you remember our last meeting?"

"Very well indeed, Sonny sent you my way. How is he, by the way? Still in touch?"

"I just got off the phone with him, and he's sending me your way again. You helped last time, but this is more serious. A body needs to disappear now, and I mean now. Can you help?"

Isaac's stony look was impenetrable. "Just the body, nothing else, car for instance?"

"I don't think there's a car, but the body must disappear for good. There's a gun too."

"Where is it now?"

"Leman Street down by The Brown Bear. I'll have to let them in because the doors are locked."

"Let me make a call and see what I can do."

Isaac got up from the table and walked through the door leading to a private room behind the bar. He returned a few minutes later.

"OK, two friends are going to help you out. They'll pick you up here in ten minutes. You take them to the location. They'll do the business, and everything will be hunky dory." He spread his hands expansively and smiled. It wasn't a nice smile, but Joshua didn't mind, a huge problem was solved.

"How much?"

"Five grand."

Joshua reached inside his jacket and produced a wad of neatly wrapped banknotes held together by an elastic band. He counted off ten 500-euro notes, laid them in front of Isaac, and put the remainder back in his pocket.

"That's the five grand right there. Check it."

Isaac's smile widened, "I don't think I need to count it. Euros, too. Nice one."

They continued to make small talk as they waited for the clean-up crew to arrive.

By midnight, the body had been rolled up in the carpet and loaded in the back of a Ford Transit van. Carrying its grisly load, the two men drove away to an appointment with a distant crematorium where they had an "arrangement" for body disposal.

After they left, Joshua sighed in relief as he examined the hallway at the bottom of the stairs. There was no sign that a bloody corpse had recently occupied the space. Even the bullet from Goossens's wild shot from the stairs had been retrieved; the hole concealed by a dab of spackle and a spot of matching paint. Isaac's crew had been very thorough.

He had cleaned the rest of the flat as best he could with bleach and hydrogen peroxide. *At least there should be no fingerprints,* he thought, as he took a last look around. *Forensics is so sophisticated these days it's hard not to leave something incriminating behind. Hopefully, they won't link the flat to Goossens's disappearance.* He cringed at the thought.

He went to a nearby phone booth and called his contact in the Brussels magistrate's office.

"I'm glad you're there," whispered the voice on the other end of the phone. "Goossens got bail. He's out for revenge, and you'd better be on your guard."

"I'm not worried. He doesn't know where I am. How did he get bail?" He tossed Goossens's bullet in his hand; an onlooker might be reminded of George Raft. He brought it close to his eye, carefully examining it while his informant rattled on.

"Looks like a murky affair. Highly irregular circumstances, and the anti-corruption police began an immediate investigation. Documents were found showing a senior government minister ordering Goossens's release in return for a 20,000-euro bribe. Apparently, this was the tip of the iceberg; they've found proof of multiple similar bribes. Unfortunately, the minister committed suicide before he could be questioned. Confidential memos were found mentioning a Joshua and a Sarah as hackers for hire. Meanwhile, Goossens disappeared, and no one knows where he's gone."

"I heard he's wanted by some Russians," Joshua said casually, solidifying his bluff. The striation marks of the bullet intrigued him as he waited for an answer.

"The rumor is he owes for a missing heroin shipment."

"Ouch. Russians can be nasty bastards." He tossed the bullet and caught it in his hand again.

"He'll lose his nuts if they get hold of him," agreed the informant.

"Thanks for the information. Something will be appearing in your mailbox soon." Joshua returned to his flat.

Saturday, August 3

As dawn broke, Joshua walked to Aldgate tube, collected his luggage, and took a cab to Eaton Square. From there he walked to Eaton Place where he dropped the bullet down a convenient drain before he rang the doorbell to the safe house. A barred viewing slot slid back, and a woman's face, from her eyebrows to just below her mouth, became visible.

"Ah, Joshua, we're expecting you and have been worried. Just a minute." He heard two double deadbolts being withdrawn, and the door swung open. He gave Rebecca, the housekeeper, a peck on the cheek, observing the Baretta by her side.

"Mind that doesn't go off," he grinned.

She cackled, "If it does, you'll only lose your testicles."

There was no snappy response; he was too busy rushing through to the living room where Sarah was waiting. They embraced.

"Oh, my God," she sobbed. "Goossens!" She pulled back from him. "He followed me, that bastard. I didn't have a clue. How are you?" She grasped his arms and gazed up into his eyes.

"I'm good. Little shaken up, and I need to get some sleep. Your mascara's running, by the way." He took a tissue out and offered it.

She sniffed. "Thanks," and blew her nose. "What's happening now, I've been so worried."

"It's all taken care of. I'll call the landlord to let him know we left early, and the keys are inside. We're paid through the end of the month, and I've left it clean. I wrapped Goossens in the rug, so we'll have to pay him for that."

"How did Goossens get on to us?"

"Bribed a politician. Someone's been talking because our names came up as being hackers for hire."

"Who?"

"Don't know, all very odd, but someone's been talking. Evidently, the information was in a document from a Belgian intelligence source."

"So, we're busted."

"We'll have to be more careful in the future. Only use public phones and landlines and do more changing of IDs, locations, and, whenever possible, use internet relay chat with proxies. Let's remember to keep the batteries and SIM cards out of cellphones until they're needed for a call, and destroy everything afterwards." He gave a huge sigh. "I'm beat. Let's go to bed, get some rest, and I'll take care of the landlord later.

Turning to Roz, he said, "Can you dispose of these?" He handed her several cellphones he'd recently used.

"No problem," she replied, taking them from him.

He hugged Sarah, and she kissed him lightly on the cheek. He kissed her back, then pulled away, breaking the spell. Going to his bedroom, he climbed into a comfortable double bed and instantly fell asleep.

CHAPTER 4

Sarah and Joshua prepare for action.

**Los Angeles, California
Wednesday, August 7 - Thursday, August 8**

A few days after Goossens's shooting, Sarah sat awaiting her flight to Milan in the passenger waiting area at Heathrow. She wasn't looking forward to the days ahead. *God, it's going to be a long trip to get to Los Angeles,* she groaned, looking at her itinerary. *Milan to Montreal, stay overnight. Then a rented car to Toronto for another overnight stay before a final flight to Los Angeles. Got to watch my back all the way. I hate planning this shit, but Mr. Computer loves it. Good for him.* Her thoughts were interrupted by the loudspeaker announcing her flight.

Finally arriving at LAX, she took a cab to Santa Monica where she booked a comfortable suite in a boutique hotel on Santa Monica Boulevard, a couple of blocks from Dixon's Wilshire Boulevard offices. Other than the physical convenience, her room offered internet access for non-confidential work, and there were plenty of payphones in the neighborhood which would assist her secret work. Too tired to enjoy the sunshine or the sights, leaving her suitcase unpacked, she threw off her clothes and climbed into bed, falling asleep in seconds.

A rolling motion brought her awake with a jolt. She could make out the faint silhouette of the swag lamp swinging in the early light seeping through the curtains.

"Shit, an earthquake!"

Her heart pounding, she scrambled for the bathroom, switched on the lights, and stood braced in the door frame. A shiver ran through her body as a cool draft of air caught her nakedness by surprise. The rolling motion continued and something glass shattered in the bathroom sink.

The lights flickered for a few seconds, and she was plunged into darkness. Gritting her teeth, anticipating the worst, she couldn't see her hand in front of her face. Minutes later the lights came back on and, as suddenly as it started, it was over. She remained in position for a few minutes in case of aftershocks. Then, sitting on the bed she switched on the TV where the quake was reported as 3.9, centered under West Los Angeles. Not worthy of comment among native Angelenos. *Welcome to LA, motherfucker,* she thought. *Dixon must sense my presence.*

Still tired despite sleeping for seven hours straight, she decided to go back to bed. Closing her eyes, she lay there dozing, but it was no good; changing time zones prevented her resuming her sleep. Rolling on her back, linking her hands behind her head, and staring blankly at the ceiling, she went over the conversations she'd had with Joshua in London. Goossens was pushed to the back of her mind as she considered the work ahead. How to infiltrate an international accounting firm, Whitlock, Katz, and Dixon, whose focus was anything and everything Hollywood.

I wonder what make of safe is in Dixon's office. More than likely a regular office-safe combo lock. Let's hope it doesn't offer much of a challenge.

Closing her eyes, Sarah relaxed and touched herself under the sheet while erotic fantasies of Joshua went through her mind. She knew her attraction to him was growing despite the lack of serious flirting. Or maybe because of it.

Perhaps I should take more initiative.

She teased herself to climax, dropping off to sleep almost instantly and waking with a start half an hour later. Feeling languid, moaning, and sighing, she dragged herself to the bathroom, turned on the light, and groaned out loud on seeing the broken glass in the sink. She gingerly picked up the pieces and dropped them in a wastebasket, grateful there wasn't more damage. Another groan came as she looked at the face staring back at her from the mirror. *Christ, I look worse than I feel.* She yawned, bringing tears to her eyes, and stood, head hung down, leaning against the sink, gathering her wits for a few moments. She raised her head and looked once more at the beast looking back at her from the mirror.

"No wonder I'm single," she muttered to herself.

She was very white without the olive skin normally associated with Mediterranean complexions. Turning her head from side to side, her reflection disturbed her.

"Fuck, I look old."

While in London, she had cut and dyed her normally long dark brown hair and had it styled into her current blond bob. Her weight tended to vary depending on her emotional mood; presently, she was happy and slim. She pushed her 'B' cup breasts together, released them with a sigh, and wished they were bigger. Her teeth were white and evenly spaced but her nose had a small bump from a childhood accident, marring its perfection. Even in heels she was petite, had an IQ of 145, and with big blue eyes was a nice package. Despite her present scary look, when dressed up, men of any culture found her very attractive. She showered and wrapped herself in a light cotton robe, retrieved the hotel guide, and ordered a massage. Afterward, feeling hungry, she ate a plate of fruit.

Rejuvenated, Sarah settled herself at the table and got to work on her laptop, first reviewing the file she had downloaded from Joshua in London. A couple of hours later, she sat back, flexing her fingers and rolling her shoulders to ease the tension in her neck. She had memorized the important details of each of the company's top people. Dixon, forty-eight years old according to his biography but looking younger, cultivated an exotic lifestyle exhibited through extensive use of the corporate jet. Married with three children, he lived with his trophy wife in nearby Malibu. He also had a mistress, who resembled Jennifer Anniston, no doubt selected for her talents as an "exotic dancer."

Sarah shut down the computer and pushed the lid shut. *Time to check out Dixon's.* For her venture outdoors, Sarah dressed in blue jeans, grinning as she struggled into a black Rolling Stones T-shirt; their trademark lolling red tongue on the front. Wearing it made her feel good, bringing back memories of a great concert. *Almost two years ago now.* She wasn't wearing a bra, just the T-shirt pulled down over her breasts, together with jeans. She picked up a pair of black Converse Chuck Taylor All Stars sneakers and grunted as she bent over to lace them up. A cellphone was clipped to her belt. *After all, everyone has one these days,* she thought. *I'll use it for general calls only and won't care if they can be traced.* Swinging a small backpack containing other necessities on her shoulder, she wriggled to make it comfortable, ruffled her hair in the mirror, thinking *Mirror,*

Mirror, on the wall, feeling anything but the fairest of them all.

Sarah walked the few blocks from her hotel to Dixon's office building to get a feel for the neighborhood. A coffee shop was open for business on the north side of Wilshire Boulevard and slightly diagonal to his building on the south side. She ordered the house special brew and sat at a waist-high counter running across the front window. There were half a dozen stools, two of them occupied by a couple smitten with each other, uninterested in the world beyond their little universe. Sarah sat on the end stool, farthest away from them, and concentrated on the entrance to the target building, clearly visible from this vantage point.

Whitlock, Katz, and Dixon occupied an attractive two-story office building in the sixteen-hundred-block of Wilshire Boulevard in Santa Monica. Built in the early 1990s with two floors and a typically white stucco exterior, its large dark, green-tinted windows concealed the interior from prying eyes. A balcony, running across most of the second floor, curved out, making room for a large patio. Various big multi-colored umbrellas peeked over the patio wall providing shade when staff dined alfresco. Parking was accessed through a roll-up gate beside the building's front door.

If I'm here in the mornings and at lunchtime for a couple of days, I'll get to see who's going in and out. Must find a way to keep watch. Can't stay here for hours on end, people will wonder what I'm doing.

Downing her coffee, she crossed the street to walk around the block to seek vantage points from which to watch the building's entrance. Walking by Dixon's building, she noted the absence of security cameras either over the front door or by the parking entrance. The single mesh gate enabled her to see a dozen cars parked inside. Turning the street corner, she walked down to the alley at the rear of the building where a large blue trash container piled high with heaps of plastic bags awaited the arrival of the next pickup.

"Perfect," muttered Sarah, "time to go dumpster diving."

This statement was immediately followed by a disgusted "Fuck" at the sight of a security camera on a power pole, its lens covering the back of the building. She decided to call it a day and strolled back to her hotel to make notes in preparation for the break-in.

Thursday, August 8

The next morning Sarah returned to the coffee shop to watch the Dixon's office building from the same vantage point. Three women congregated outside of the doors in conversation when one broke off to cross the street while the other two entered the building. A minute later, the same woman came into the coffee shop where she joined a line of four waiting to place their orders. Sarah's eyes zoomed in on the identity pass around the woman's neck. She turned on her stool, picked up her backpack, and joined the line behind her. They made eye contact and the woman smiled.

Sarah smiled right back and said, "Another day in paradise, right?"

"Only when I get my coffee," came the reply, as the line shuffled forward. "You a Stones fan?" she asked, looking at Sarah's T-shirt.

"Big time, saw them a couple of years ago at the Rose Bowl."

"I was there too. In the boonies, but it was a good show."

"I'll say. Your turn," Sarah pointed towards the cashier.

"Oh, thanks." The woman turned and placed her order, paid, and waited for her latte at the other end of the counter. Sarah paid for another muffin and turned to walk back to her stool; in so doing, the woman from Dixon's had to step out of her way.

"Nice speaking with you," said Sarah.

"You, too." The woman returned a friendly grin.

"Do you work in that building over there?" Sarah pointed at the Dixon building.

"As a matter of fact, I do."

"Great balcony. Must be nice dining under the umbrellas. Is it a good place to work?" Sarah asked casually.

"Yes, lots of nice perks. They bring in a chef once a week. Pretty cool."

"Latte for Glenda." A shout from the barista interrupted the conversation.

"Whoops, must go." Glenda picked up the cup and with a smile and a "bye" left the coffee shop.

Sarah watched her cross the road and walk in the front door of Dixon's office building. She was ecstatic. *Wow! Contact on the second day. I'd better come back here at five and see what's going on.*

Finished with her coffee and a second muffin, she shouldered her backpack and returned to her hotel room where she studied the photos sf executives in the Los Angeles office. Joshua's file confirmed she had spoken to Glenda, executive assistant to Dixon. Sarah then visited the Santa Monica library's newspaper section looking for articles on Dixon's company. There was nothing of importance. On the way back to her hotel, she rented a Ford Windstar with dark-tinted windows, perfect for observation purposes. It had been a busy day, and she saw it was time to return to the coffee shop.

Between five and five-thirty that evening, she counted thirteen people leaving the building. The license plates of the cars in which six men and four women left the parking structure were noted, but she couldn't do much about the three women on foot. Just after six, Sarah saw Glenda being picked up by a car driven by a man, *probably her husband*, whose license plate joined the others on her notepad. She sat there for a few more minutes, finished her coffee, and waved a cheery goodbye to the owner.

Sarah walked half a block to the van she had rented where she continued to watch Dixon's building entrance. *It's not tax time*, she reasoned, *they're probably only working till 7 pm.* She was proven right when at 6:30 pm a Maserati bellowed its way down Wilshire.

So much for conservative accountants, but good taste. Sarah noted the time and license plate.

Fortunately, she only had to wait another fifteen minutes for the last car to leave, an Aston Martin, which she figured was probably Dixon himself. Half an hour later she casually sauntered past Dixon's office building. Both the parking garage and the offices appeared empty, and a walk around the block didn't reveal anything out of the ordinary. She returned to her hotel room distracted by worries for Joshua's safety; she was still waiting for him to be in contact.

Friday, August 9

Joshua had acted like a fugitive, traveling by train, ferry, and car on a circuitous route from England to Ireland through France into Switzerland. He watched his back all the way but could not see anybody suspicious. Nor did his sixth sense report anything out of the ordinary. He arrived in Los Angeles late in the morning having used and discarded several false passports and IDs to throw any prospective pursuers off the scent.

Sarah's computer beeped. "I've arrived and to prove it, I'm here." Joshua's internet chat message was a little too chirpy.

She messaged back. "How come so cheerful?"

"Just feeling in a positive frame of mind. When and where can we meet?"

She considered the time, "Do you have transport?"

"Not yet."

"I have a van, let me pick you up. Where are you staying?"

"Well, coincidence of coincidences, I'm at the Beverly Wilshire. Pick me up in 20 minutes a block west of the hotel on Wilshire. You'll be coming towards me, and I'll be walking west towards you."

"You dog," Sarah fumed, "the Beverly Wilshire indeed," but Joshua had already ended the chat.

She picked him up on schedule and during their trip to Hollywood, he updated her on the Goossens situation. They parked on a side street off Sunset Boulevard and walked into a courtyard surrounded on three sides by mid-1920s Spanish-style buildings. Comfortable in the shade of an old oak tree, they talked over recent events while enjoying a ploughman's lunch at The Cat and Fiddle.

"That Brussels deal was too close for comfort, we have to be more careful," said Sarah. "Did you find out how the Belgians got our details?"

"No. Sonny is looking into it but he's as baffled as we are." He sighed in exasperation. "The leak allowed Goossens to follow you and then us."

He took a sip of beer. "Not as good as a pint of Ruddle's Best Bitter, but close." Two more swallows and the glass was empty; he put it down with a sigh. "Anyway, Goossens is dead. It should end there. Everyone thinks the Russians are looking for him so his disappearance will be put down to them. We've been cautious with cellphone and computer use and used different IDs, so I think we're good. Let's get this job done, then take some time to disappear completely."

Sarah's blue mood lightened a little, "That would be nice. In the meantime, let's hope you're right, and Brussels doesn't follow us around."

She updated him on her progress with Dixon. He congratulated her on her budding connection with Glenda.

"The more we know, the better off we are."

"No shit, Sherlock," answered Sarah sarcastically.

"Next move?" His eyes crinkled at the corners as though he knew what she was going to say.

She surprised him. "The dumpster with the trash is at the rear of the building, but it means disabling at least one camera. Also, it's stuffed to the brim with plastic bags of trash. We should ask ourselves if we should shut down the security camera or wait until we make our other move."

Joshua took a couple of seconds while he thought through all the possibilities.

"No, it's sure to be shredded. Dixon's emails told us there's something in the safe, so let's see what comes from there."

"Agree. In the meantime, even though the street parking sucks, I'll use the van and the coffee shop for the next few days to see the pattern of the employees knocking off work. Once we know the time the building's sure to be clear, we'll give it a shot. What about you?"

"Just arrived in town and getting myself acclimated. For now, I'll monitor Dixon's email and be your support when you decide to pull the trigger. Any thoughts on how you're getting inside?"

"I'd like to get hold of that access card Glenda wears around her neck." She frowned. "Stealing it is out of the question. It wouldn't be long before it was missed and canceled."

"She swipes it through a reader to get into the building, doesn't she?"

"Yes. I'm sure it allows access to the parking as well."

He sat quietly, thinking. "Is there any way you can borrow it for a few minutes?"

"I have no idea. We're not exactly bosom buddies. Let's say yes. What do you have in mind?"

He said slowly, "Maybe we could copy it. I'm going to pay our friend the Printer a visit later today. He runs a legit printing business in Marina Del Rey but dabbles in the dark side for the right people at the right price. Anything we're likely to need, fake IDs, guns, passports, the whole schmear. Let's see what he can come up with."

"So, he can make me up a false ID?"

Joshua hesitated, then said, "Yes. That's the reason for the visit. As for Dixon's, I can take care of the alarms, but that's a last resort. If we can swing it, having a valid ID and access card is a much better way to go."

"I'll leave that up to you."

"Let's meet later, after I've seen the Printer."

Sarah dropped him off in Beverly Hills and returned to her hotel after agreeing to meet him at Palisades Park in Santa Monica later that afternoon.

Joshua's newly rented Honda pulled up in front of an untidy building whose neighbors were a strip center on one side and a used car sales lot on the other. He had told Sarah he was going to Marina Del Rey, but this nearby location was a less salubrious neighborhood on Lincoln, well north of Washington Boulevard. He looked over at two homeless men, trash scattered around them. Empty bottles of Old Thunderbird testified as to why they lay sprawled unconscious beside the wall enclosing the strip center. He shook his head in disgust.

The sign over the door simply said *Printing—Satisfaction Guaranteed.* The windows on either side of the door held examples of custom indoor and outdoor signage. He pushed open the door. A bell tinkled, causing a man to look up from the newspaper he was reading. He brushed back a lock of thick hair from his thin face and looked at Joshua.

"Can I help you?"

What followed was a series of coded sentences between the two to establish and confirm identities. Satisfied, the Printer, whose real name was Alejandro Rivas, said, "Come out back, I've got some new stuff you might want to look at, and I'm sure we can get anything else you want within a couple of days."

He took Joshua into a back room and unlocked a padlocked steel gate leading to a security door protected by an electronic lock. He entered the combination and a green light accompanied by an audible beep announced the door was unlocked.

"Come on in." Alejandro led the way.

Joshua walked in the door and saw two trestle tables covered in white cloth. Alejandro pulled the covers off, revealing one table covered in a mix of revolvers, automatics, and several Uzi machine guns. The other table was covered by electronic equipment including computers and multiple cellphones.

He was stunned. "Wow."

After making his purchases, he made his way to Santa Monica for the pre-arranged meeting with Sarah. Half an hour passed before her van pulled up. She opened his door and moaned, "This had better be good. I should have realized when we set the meeting that I would be at Dixon's counting people going in and out."

"Stop whining," he snapped. "I've spent most of the afternoon with the Printer, trying to make this break-in safer for you."

'Yeah? Well, I've been cooped up in a hot van watching Dixon's building for the past couple of hours. That's no picnic, you know." She relapsed into silence, looking straight ahead through the windshield, clearly in a snit.

Joshua reached over the back seat and pulled a leather gym bag from the back seat. He pushed it onto her lap.

"I think you're going to like this."

Still sulking. "What is it?"

"Open it and see."

She pulled the zipper to open the bag and revealed a small, plain cardboard box. "Oh yes, I can do a lot with this." The sarcasm dripped off her tongue.

"Stop being a bitch and open the box."

Not understanding her frustration, he repeated himself. "Open the box."

She glared at him and lifted the lid of the box. "What the hell is this?"

She was looking at a piece of electronic equipment about the size of a shoe box but only a couple of inches deep. One end had a numbered keyboard with a minimal screen above it. At the rear was a fold down antenna and halfway along was a slot containing a blank plastic card.

"It's a battery driven wireless card terminal," he explained. "The Printer got hold of a prototype from a Norwegian firm. Don't ask me how, but he did. It's brilliant work. He reprogrammed the firmware so it will copy the magnetic strip on Glenda's swipe card and store the information until you're ready to make a duplicate."

"It's very bulky. Heavy too." She complained, lifting it from the box for closer examination.

"Keep it in this bag. Tell her you're going to the gym for all I care." He was tired of her petulance.

"I still have to get her security card. She has it on a lanyard around her neck."

"That's your job. I got you what you wanted, and I don't have to worry about the alarms. Deal with it."

She sneered. "And what about the fake IDs?"

Joshua, detesting her tone, hesitated. "Yes. We're good there. We'll use Barbara Fiedler's ID, the VP from the London office who transferred to New York."

She jumped in. "Perfect. We can show her credentials on Glenda's security pass. Also have him make up credit cards, driver's license, the works. If there's a problem, I can bluff my way through."

"Here's an idea. Now we have access to Dixon's email, when we know the day of the deed, why don't I send

Glenda an email from Barbara? I could mention she's in Los Angeles on other business but might stop by for a visit. How's that?"

"Wow. Brilliant. I'll have to go shopping in Santa Monica and pick out something appropriate." She cheered up at the thought.

"We'll make you look as good as the real Barbara. The Printer gave me extra SIM cards as well. Just don't forget to use landlines whenever possible. If you must use the cellphone, get rid of it after one call, and make sure you destroy the SIM card."

They parted on relatively good terms, but he was still miffed at her. *She can be such an ass,* he thought as he drove away.

In a somewhat happier mood on the drive back to her hotel, Sarah thought resignedly, *Jeez, his eyes say yes but there's no follow-through. Some romantic I'm hooked up with here.*

On the other side of town at Roscoe's Chicken and Waffles, a restaurant on Crenshaw in mid-city Los Angeles, sat three budding African American entrepreneurs, Dewayne, Jayden, and Jamal. Facing them was Gabriel, a wealthy black real estate investor together with his right-hand man, R. J., also an African American. Gabriel put the brothers at ease right away, recognizing they were young and nervous.

"I've known your father, Henry, a long time. He's someone I respect. As you know, we've been going to the same church these past twenty years or so. To cut to the chase, R.J. tells me you'd like me to bankroll you guys in the recording business." He gave them a quizzical look. "How much do you want me to invest?"

Jayden said, "We'll put up $500,000. If you match that, it gets us off to a good start."

"And, what's my return?"

Dewayne broke into the conversation, waving a cassette tape. "Nothing guaranteed. Here's five artists we think are worth recording. Listen and see if you want to make a deal."

Gabriel saw the brothers were hungry and R.J. had spoken well of them. His attention turned to Jayden, who said, "Our dream is to be a prominent recording studio in Los Angeles. If you like these tapes, we've got plenty of people with songs, most are rap. We'll cater to the artists most popular at our DJ events. Our intention is to sell records at the events and see if we can't build from there. We just heard that Studio Z came on the market. That's our dream, but first we'd like to work towards renting small studios while moving slowly into ownership."

"How much are they asking for Studio Z?" R.J. inquired.

Dewayne admitted, "We heard $10 mill, which not only buys out the lease but includes the building as well."

"Studio Z sounded like a good idea right up until I heard ten million." Gabriel gave a wry chuckle. "Way too rich for my blood. Let me think about your proposal on the investment. I'll listen to the tapes and get back to you within the next couple of days. One last thing. I heard there's a lot of competition and aggravation between the West and East Coast rappers these days. How do you fit in there?"

Jayden laughed. "We're way too small and not involved at all. That's between Death Row Records here in LA and Bad Boy Records in New York."

"Good. That's what I was thinking. I have no interest in getting into what I see as an escalating and dangerous situation."

"We're in agreement on that. We're interested in making lots of money and avoiding any aggravation."

"OK. Let me think things over, and R.J. will be in touch if we're interested."

The meeting ended and after the three brothers left, Gabriel turned to R.J.

"Studio Z. Doesn't the Mob have a hand in there?"

"Big Vinnie Esposito is behind the scenes, running it for New Jersey. I heard they've stuck with an old format, you know, haven't changed with the times. Word on the street is its losing money hand over fist and you know how the Mob is about their money. Ten mill." He made a face. "With all that fixup? Pretty hefty price."

Gabriel rubbed his chin for a few moments, contemplating the meeting before he snapped back to the present, "Moving on. I'll listen to the tape in the car and make up my mind about the record deal." With that, the subject was dropped from their immediate conversation.

Meanwhile, the three brothers were in an excited state as they drove away from the appointment.

"If we could get a few investors like Gabriel together we could buy Studio Z," speculated Jamal.

Dewayne was sceptical. "We'd need more than a few investors. The ten million asking price is for starters. The place needs fixing up too. That's probably another four or five million, right there."

"Too right," interjected Jayden. "Even if we could buy it, which we can't, we'd still have to make enough money to pay the debt. In the final analysis, we're looking at closer to $20 million."

Jamal sighed, "I was just thinking out loud. I suppose it would be hard trying to figure out how to run a big studio when we haven't got the experience."

Dewayne was more optimistic. "Yeah, but we'd learn. Get help along the way. We're going to be dealing with studio rentals when we record our acts, that will give us experience. The big record labels or even forming a label of our own will all come in time. Let's continue to focus on finding an experienced business partner."

They rode without talking, Tu Pac's "California Love" blasting on the stereo, each dreaming of their future success.

Pulling to a stop at a traffic light, Jayden turned to Dewayne, "Are you going to the party at Star's house?"

"Damn right."

"Not thinking of letting me go as well?"

"Bobbie," Dewayne named an executive at Atlantic Records, "was insistent that I go there without you." He gave a mocking laugh. "Ha, ha, hardy, ha, ha."

Jamal burst out laughing and Jayden grinned back.

"Bitch," was all he said as he stepped on the gas.

They were heading to their father's company, Henry's Trucking, where they worked as drivers.

CHAPTER 5

Sarah accepts an invitation.

**Los Angeles, California
Friday, August 9–Monday, August 12**

After leaving Joshua at Palisades Park, Sarah checked her watch and decided to go to the coffee shop opposite Dixon's office building to look for likely prospects. By a stroke of good fortune, Glenda was seated at the window bar nursing a coffee. She saw Sarah come in the door and smiled. Sarah smiled back, bought a hot latte, and sat on an adjacent stool, being careful not to crowd her and leaving an empty stool between them.

"Hi there, I'm Glenda." A hand was offered.

Sarah took it saying, "I'm Sarah. You work over there." She pointed at the Dixon building.

"For my sins," sighed Glenda. She took a drink of coffee. "You're the Stones fan."

"Still can't get no satisfaction. That be me," answered Sarah.

"Off to the gym?"

Sarah hefted her gym bag and said, "Got all my kit. The Y beckons."

Glenda screwed up her face. "I hate working out almost more than dealing with these entertainment types."

"Really. That's what do you do?"

"Their accounting, payrolls, and their money management. We're an accounting firm."

"You're an accountant." It was a statement and not a question.

"No, nothing so grand. I'm the executive assistant to El Presidente." She laughed and finished her coffee. "Listen, there's a bar down the street, and I'm going there to catch the happy hour. I haven't had a drink for a while and fancy one. How about you? Jose Cuervo is half price. Still wanna go to the Y?" She raised a questioning eyebrow.

"Well, now you twist my arm. I'm in. I can work out anytime."

Ten minutes later they found themselves sitting at a booth in a noisy bar. The waitress arrived, and Glenda ordered tequila shooters. *Fuck,* thought Sarah, *she's a serious drinker. If I match her shot for shot, she'll put me under the table.* Groaning inwardly, she thought, *Looks like tomorrow is going to be hangover day.*

"By the way, you still have your security thingy around your neck. Is that a job requirement?" Sarah remarked casually. She had placed her gym bag alongside Glenda's purse at the end of the table.

Glenda laughed. "Oops. Forgot I had it on."

She took the lanyard from around her neck and reached over Sarah's bag to drop it into her purse. The tequila arrived and more was ordered. Glenda, her tongue quickly loosened by the liquor, turned out to be fun and good company, a warm-hearted woman whose husband didn't excite her anymore. She insisted on calling Dixon "Mr. Dick." Sarah continued to offer a sympathetic ear, gleaning any useful information Glenda dropped. When asked, she offered her "just moved into town" story, followed up with a fictitious upbringing.

"Would you excuse me? I gotta pee like a racehorse." Glenda left the table and disappeared into the pub crowd.

Taking advantage of the moment she'd been waiting for, Sarah rifled through Glenda's purse, retrieved her identity card, and, using her bag as cover, passed it through the magnetic tape reader. A green light and an electronic beep indicated a successful capture as the card's information was recorded. She carefully returned it to Glenda's purse.

After a few minutes, Glenda rejoined her. "Phew, I sure needed that," she exclaimed.

Later, fueled by even more tequila, she mentioned how Mr. Dick, now relegated to "The Dick," was very careless with confidential material. He frequently lost files and passwords and then blamed her. Laughing, she told Sarah about pasting a list of passwords under his desk pad to save from changing them every time they were lost.

"He even left the safe door in his office open and went home. Came running into the office in a complete panic. Stupid ass," she said indignantly, gulping her fourth drink, her words slurring. "I'd already found it open, so I closed it up and put back the stupid painting covering it. I'll admit, he did say thank you, but it's not the point."

"Was there anything valuable worth stealing?" Sarah asked, also slurring slightly, the tequila was beginning to have an effect.

"No, just his dusty old files."

The biggest revelation came towards the end of the evening. "I won't have to put up with him very much longer. He might be a partner but there's some questions about his ethics. The other partners want him gone. My lips are sealed." She made a zipper movement across her lips. "What's the time? My husband's going to kill me," she muttered drunkenly, rummaging in her bag for her car keys. A rumpled white envelope fell onto the floor. Sarah picked it up and handed it to Glenda, who ripped it open. The puzzled look on her face quickly turned to an expression of horror.

"Shit, shit, shit. I forgot. I should go to this tomorrow night." She showed Sarah an invitation to a private party announcing the launch of a new album.

"Hanging with the celebs, eh?"

"Sort of. Our company gets these invites all the time. I won't be able to go to this one. My husband will hit the roof if I'm out again. I'll go next time." She hesitated, looking attentively at Sarah, "I know we just met, but would you like to go? This invitation will go to waste otherwise, and if you can go . . ." she left the sentence hanging in the air.

"Are you sure I could? You'd give me your invitation?"

"Yes, why not? You're fun, and this will be right up your alley. Not too dressy, good food, great music, and you never know who you might meet. Could get me fired, but my boss is out of town, so what the hell? Interested?"

"I'll say, are you kidding? I'm there. It's tomorrow evening, should I take a date?"

"No, not necessary, loads of available men. Here you go." Glenda handed Sarah the envelope and invitation, together with her business card.

"Give me a call from the party and let me know how it's going."

They finished the evening with Glenda, facing a DUI if she drove, taking a cab home to face the wrath of her husband. Meanwhile, Sarah staggered back to her hotel, hoping she wasn't being followed. Arriving back at her room, Sarah took the card reader from her bag. Her lack of coordination, due to her intake of tequila, forced her to make several attempts at commanding the reader's memory to write a new card. Finally, she pressed a button and, with a sigh of relief, was presented with a clone, an identical card containing Glenda's information.

This should give me access to anywhere in the building. Sarah's mind was animated by the possibilities as she lay on the bed before falling asleep.

Joshua picked up his hotel phone when it rang and noted it was almost midnight.

Sarah greeted him. "Hi there, I'm calling from a nearby payphone."

"It's a bit late. I wasn't expecting to speak to you tonight. Is everything OK?"

"I wasn't planning on calling but I managed to clone Glenda's swipe card." She described her accomplishment.

"That was very friendly of her," Joshua said dryly.

"There's more. She gave me an invitation to a party tomorrow night. She can't go."

"A party? Whose party?"

"Star's."

"You're kidding! Score! Be loads of celebs there. Can I come?"

"No, this is a solo deal. Pays you back for the Beverly Wilshire," Sarah said smugly.

"I'm bummed. But moving on, now you have a swipe card; when are we going to have a look inside Dixon's safe?"

Sarah summed up her plan. "Like we said, there's no sense making concrete plans. It's imperative we confirm everyone's gone by about seven, seven-thirty. A couple more days of observation should give us the pulse of the place. In the meantime, I'll just get friendlier with Glenda and see what information I can get."

"I'll think of you while you're at the party, shaking your *tuchus* at every Tom, Dick, and Harry. In the meantime, I'll continue to monitor Dixon's computer. Nothing interesting yet. Let's meet, you can give me the cloned card, and I'll go to the print shop. I'll have him put your photo on the card identifying you as that new hire, Barbara Fiedler. He can run up a fake New York driver's license with some bogus credit cards as well. It will all stand any computer check by a cop."

"Sounds good, but we need a lot more preparation before doing the job. At this point, I don't even know if there's a cleaning crew. Every little hitch must be anticipated and smoothed out beforehand."

"I agree. Getting the cloned card gets you in and out without tampering with the alarms. The system will show entry by Glenda, but with your abilities, no one should ever know you were ever there, let alone tampering with the safe."

"I should get back to my room. I stepped out to make this call. Let's talk later."

"Have fun at the party," Joshua said, "I'm jealous as hell. Call me after."

"Sweet payback for the hotel. Enjoy yourself. All alone." Her tone mocked him, and she wore a smile of satisfaction.

Saturday, August 10

It was a swanky do for a couple of hundred people to celebrate the release of Star's latest record, already charting on Billboard. A ten thousand square foot Spanish-style house in the foothills of Encino provided the venue. South of the Boulevard towards Mulholland, set on two acres with a view over the lights of the San Fernando Valley, the estate provided privacy and refuge. A hedge of drought-resistant old-growth oleander offered an impenetrable hedge around the property. If eaten, its highly poisonous properties were offset by the beautiful pink, red, yellow, and white flowers growing in profusion.

Sarah arrived as a passenger in a Lincoln Town car hired for the occasion. They were stopped at the entrance to the driveway leading to the house by a guardhouse manned by two security guards checking invitations. Two more guards stood by the open gates, watching with neutral but observant expressions. One of them turned, the vent in his jacket momentarily exposing a holstered gun on his hip.

Probably a Glock. I'll bet it's the 19 model with a 15-round magazine. Her mind automatically stored the details away.

They were waved through the gates and as they rounded the curve at the top of the driveway, a magnificent mansion came into view. The interior and exterior lights had been turned on, making it look even more impressive. Moments later, the driver pulled up, got out, and opened her door while she stepped out of the car.

She smiled at him. "Thank you."

"I'll be waiting over there," the driver pointed behind them to the forecourt where the valet service was running ragged, tasked with parking numbers of luxury cars because many guests were arriving at the same time.

A quick look around at the other guests confirmed her decision to dress casually was the right one. Anticipating the typically cool Southern California evening, she'd opted for warmth with a multi-colored silk throw around her shoulders as a barrier against any breeze. A silk, cream-colored, long-sleeved blouse contrasted well with the black skirt draped over knee-length leather, stiletto-heeled boots. The outfit made her look curvy; leaving the top couple of buttons on her blouse undone gave her a casual and sexy look.

This house was certainly built for parties, she mused, showing her invitation at the front door to one of the numerous muscled attendants, all dressed alike in blue blazers, white shirts, red ties, and chinos. He nodded her to enter. Sarah followed her fellow guests through a series of rooms, each furnished with large divans, armchairs, coffee tables, and throw rugs over marble floors where other guests were mingling as they recognized and greeted one another. Art on the wall, most of it original African American works, made for a more formal look than Sarah had expected.

She walked through the final door into a room big enough to be called a ballroom. High ceilings with ten-foot glass doors around three walls gave the room a light, airy feeling despite the heavy, ornate, curving ironwork decorating each one. A black lacquered Baldwin grand piano stood in one corner with a group of guests, mainly admiring ladies, watching a guy tinkling a recognizable Gershwin song on the keys.

What's his name again? Sarah had the name of the pianist on the tip of her tongue. *Come on, you know his name.* But it had slipped her mind, lost. For the moment anyway.

There were two well-stocked bars at either end of the room, surrounded by guests impatiently waiting to order. An outer circle of guests, already served and grasping their glasses, stood gossiping with friends and acquaintances. They watched the band setting up on stage and made comments, generally approving the content of Star's latest album. To liven up the action, when everyone was fed and had a couple of shots of liquor inside them, Star intended to belt out a few songs with several prominent musicians rumored to be performing with her.

The doors to one side of the ballroom were wide open, leading down steps to the pool and spa area. Standing on the far side of the pool, a cabana with a red tile roof, changing rooms, and a lounge area, featured bamboo architecture. Strolling mariachis, their harmonies echoing through the still night, provided a nice backdrop against the hum of conversation. Shrieks of laughter occasionally punctuated the general noise created by a hundred or so people as the Jack Daniels took hold. Guests crowded around the little individual food carts dotting the patio. Thai, Chinese, Middle Eastern, Indian, American burgers and hot dogs, it was all available. Another bar was serving drinks at a breakneck pace. The cocaine being snorted in one of the upstairs bedrooms was in the care of Bruno, a made member of Big Vinnie's crew. His presence was enough to discourage other dealers from crashing the party if they valued their health.

Meanwhile, Sarah pushed her way through the scrum surrounding one of the free bars. Finally getting the barman's attention, she was forced to shout her order over the din of the surrounding conversation. Receiving a large glass of red wine and leaving a ten-dollar tip in return, she struggled back through the mostly obliging crowd, managing to avoid spilling her drink. One of those "Excuse me, coming through. Excuse me. Excuse me" type trips.

She managed to find a little space on the fringe of the gathering where she took in her surroundings and had a tentative sip of wine.

This is very nice, she held the glass up to the light and then to her nose, smelling the bouquet. *They've rolled out the expensive stuff.*

Taking a large mouthful, she enjoyed the taste as a warm glow spread through her chest, and she relaxed. Choosing quantity as well as quality, Sarah quickly emptied her glass, discarded it on a nearby empty table, and picked up a full glass of red wine from a passing waiter's tray.

Time to check things out.

Sarah found herself trying to fit in where everyone seemed to know everyone else. People who knew each other from business and social circles had broken into groups. Many of these people were "A" list celebrities. Breaking into those groups was far too intimidating. Feeling awkward, she nodded and smiled to people who nodded and smiled in return, but they still continued their mission to another group. Spotting a familiar face from the firm's webpage, she avoided them by turning in another direction.

To her annoyance, there were droves of much younger wannabee starlets, grown-up men fawning over them. She pushed through the crowd, pausing to look around, sipping her wine, looking for a connection. Out of the corner of one eye she saw the mariachis packing up their instruments as a drum riff sounded from the band in the ballroom. Guitars joined in and the beat announced the rhythm and blues number, "Baby, Please Don't Go." The crowds on the patio thinned noticeably as guests flocked to the ballroom. There was plenty of space for dancing, the bars were doing a roaring trade, and the band was in a groove. The party was in full swing.

Sarah continued to seek out possible hook-ups. Then she saw him. A black man, maybe mid-twenties. He was sipping his wine and gazing reflectively at the mixture of black and white people dancing to the band now playing a Chuck Berry number, complete with duck walk.

She went up to him and smiled. "Hi there, I'm Sarah, and I don't know you but you're standing here all alone, and I thought I'd introduce myself." She held out her hand.

He smiled back and took her hand in his.

"Hi, I'm Dewayne. Sarah, you said?"

"Yes."

"Are you in the business?" His handshake felt warm with a firm without being macho grip.

"Yes and No. I'm a guest of Star's accountancy firm. They handle mostly entertainment-related clients. But no, not directly in the business as such. How about you?"

She took a sip of wine and appraised him. He wasn't half bad looking although he could do with some fashion advice. He was about her age, she guessed. She saw him glance at her cleavage. A twinge ran through her nether regions reminding her she hadn't been laid in a while.

"I'm in the DJ business and produce records," he said in an offhanded manner.

"How interesting. Have you worked with anyone I'd know?"

"Probably not," he said shyly. "The truth is that my brothers and I have done very well being DJs, but we see our future in artist management and record production, especially with rap. We want to take advantage of it because it's only going to get bigger. But, what about you? What do you do? Excel all day long?"

She ignored the obvious pun. "No, nothing like that, I've only just arrived in town. This is pretty good wine." She held the glass up to the light, changing the subject.

"I was hoping there'd be champagne, but I guess the last case has come and gone. I'm not a lover of wine, to tell you the truth." He took a sip from his glass and pulled a long face. "This is a little too strong for me, and, if I'm not careful, I'll end up with a headache."

She was curious. "How did you get invited here?"

"Here?" He thought for a moment, "A friend from Atlantic Records got me an invitation. He was supposed to show up but bailed at the last minute. It was unfortunate because you need someone here who's going to introduce you around. Most of these people here," he extended his arm to encompass the various guests, "know one another. So, it's difficult; you can't just break in, especially with celebrities. You know what I mean?"

"Yeah. I'm in the same boat. I had the impression this party would be more fun." She took his arm. "Things might be looking up. I see some seats over there, right by the Mexican food cart. Let's sit down, have a snack, and get better acquainted. Interested?"

"Best offer I've had all evening," he said eagerly. "Let's go."

They snacked at an empty table set by the pool with a spectacular view of the San Fernando Valley lights. The band played on in the ballroom, a vocalist now warming up the crowd with a soft jazzy refrain. Dewayne stopped a passing waiter, tipped him handily, and five minutes later he was presented with an uncorked bottle of Perrier Jouet and two champagne flutes.

"Found it lying around, sir," said the waiter.

"Thank you." He placed another twenty-dollar bill on the waiter's tray.

"Sir. Thank you." The waiter scurried off and was soon lost amid the crowd still making their way to the ballroom.

Sarah was impressed with Dewayne's nerve and attitude but said little, doing what she did best: listening. He uncorked the champagne with a minimum of fuss and poured her a glass.

"Thank you. Are you getting a lot of DJ work?"

"We're doing well. My father owns a trucking business. He bought the three of us a house on the understanding we'd drive long distance for him for three years. That time's nearly up, and we had a meeting recently where we discussed the company's future."

"How did that go?"

"Dad's not wanting to retire just yet, you understand. We drive and he deals with a lot of the government administration; there's always loads of paperwork. When we part company, he may well sell up if it's too difficult. Right now, my brother Jayden and I alternate days driving trucks up to San Francisco and back. Then most evenings are devoted to DJ work. Now you know something about me, what about you?"

Sarah didn't hesitate and launched into her current legend. Despite a growing attraction to Dewayne, the story was a pack of lies but would pass scrutiny.

"What about this Whitlock and partners accounting company? They sponsored all this, didn't they?"

"I don't know much about it," she said carelessly. "A friend gave me the invitation." She lowered her voice, "Confidentially, I heard Dixon's on his way out, partners don't trust him." She winked, "Know what I mean?" It was an offhand remark, a bad joke. Later, she wondered why she'd said it. Dixon definitely saw it as a bad joke. He had arrived unexpectedly and was walking around making sure the event was going as planned. He overheard every word of her conversation but chose not to confront her and assigned one of the security personnel to find out who she was.

She continued to chat with Dewayne, personal questions were deflected and, apart from being single and new to Los Angeles, Dewayne learned very little else. In the meantime, she continued to encourage him to talk about his experiences as a DJ. Sarah was all-world at listening and encouraging the other person to talk. Sometime afterwards, Dewayne came to realize that he knew nothing about her, nothing. He wasn't sure if Sarah was even her real name. She had fooled them all.

She looked at him directly and posed a question. "What's your dream? What would you like to achieve?"

"I think, we think—I must include my brothers—our goal is ownership of a major recording studio. The DJ work is fun. Full of drinking, drugs, money, and sex. It's just not the future for us." He considered her, grinning, and thought, *I'm impressed, here's someone who actually listens to what I have to say.*

She gave him a flirtatious look; *he has a very nice smile.*

He hesitated. "Are you sure you want me to go on?"

"Duh. Of course. You haven't told me about the studio yet."

Visibly excited at being able to share his dream with a stranger, he took the plunge. "With a recording studio, we'll provide the facilities for the musicians to do their thing. We've had various people asking us if we know where they can record. For the right investor, it's a good opportunity. And . . ." he laughed, "we may do even better with the drinking, drugs, money, and sex. Anyway, that's the dream, who knows?"

"What will it take to make this happen?" she asked.

"There's something going on right now. A major opportunity, in fact. We just heard from an industry source that a certain recording studio's coming up for sale." Dewayne's talk made him and his brothers seem a lot bigger financially than they were, but he was looking to impress. "Just word of mouth, you understand, nothing formal. We've got a certain amount of cash but need an investor to complete the deal."

"With the building and studio business being collateral?" She was sharp.

"Exactly," he agreed.

"What are local banks saying?"

"It's complicated. You'd think with our trucking company we'd be able to swing it but nooooooo." He did a great Belushi imitation making her choke on her drink.

She's a little tipsy, he decided, but went on, "Rap will only grow, especially in the black community and a big segment of the white population too. Eminem is a good example of an up-and-coming white artist who's gathering some attention. Then again, Snoop Dog, Dre, and Tu Pac sell very well in the white market. This recording studio that's going up for sale is going to be a big deal." He stopped. "I'm sorry, I get a bit too enthusiastic sometimes." He was a little embarrassed.

"I like enthusiasm," she confessed. "How much do you need?"

"At least fifteen million bucks, probably twenty million. The truth is, we can't consider that deal. It's where we see ourselves in maybe a couple of years. Right now, we're looking at a much smaller deal where we can learn the ropes of dealing with record companies and learning our trade. Baby steps. We're very confident of pulling this off with investors seeing a good return over five years or so.

We'll put up our money and sweat equity and the type of operation we envision will work for everyone. In fact, we just met with a likely investor."

"You have a business plan?"

"Of course. I have an MBA, so I know if you don't have a business plan, you don't have shit. Excuse my language."

"Can I get a peek?"

"I don't see why not. You'll see we've established a solid reputation through our DJ gigs. We're looking at live rap acts overlooked by the recording industry, mostly because of racial prejudice. By selectively recording these acts we'll sell a few hundred thousand CDs if the song catches on. That can be a good living with the right setup, publishing and what have you."

"What's in it for me if I can get you an investor for the twenty million?" Sarah blurted out this offer thinking, *this might be a way of getting into Leon's and Dixon's network.*

Dewayne was incredulous. "Are you serious? Can't you see the fly in your ointment? We don't have enough money to swing that deal. You shouldn't waste your time." He squinted at her. "You have contacts?"

"Just remember price is a matter of terms. There's lots of different items that determine price. Maybe it's tax savings. Structuring the deal so he gets his price while we get our terms." She waited, letting him absorb her concepts, then patted his arm, "I'll make some calls and see what I can do. No promises, but I do have contacts who may be interested."

"Well, believe me, we'll look at anything, but I'm not enthusiastic about doing a deal that has too much debt. A smaller deal would be much better."

Sarah laughed as she made her decision. She liked Dewayne and would have taken him to bed at another time, but Joshua was too much on her mind. Standing up, putting her glass down on a nearby table, she said, "Listen, much as I'd like to spend more time with you, would you excuse me for a couple of minutes? I apologize for being rude, but I promised to call the person who invited me here."

"No, problem. I hope it's an investor," Dewayne said cheekily. "I'll make my way inside and see you there."

She took a cellphone from her purse and punched in the number that Glenda had given her. After a couple of rings, it went to voicemail. She left a message thanking her for the invitation and suggesting she would see her for coffee sometime during the following week.

Dewayne had disappeared. Looking around, she spied him cavorting on the dance floor with a blonde bimbo. She was disappointed. He saw her, shrugged, and waved. She smiled in resignation. It turned out, as the evening progressed, by accidentally running into each other, they managed two dances together.

In the normal celebrity fashion for tardiness, fully an hour and a half later than advertised, Star, with other musicians rapping and riffing, brought a high level of excitement to the room. Up until this time, Sarah had mostly been on her feet dancing. The superb band had done the trick in terms of allowing her to mix and chat. Numbers of different men found her attractive; her dance card was full. She tried to take part in slow dances, pleading she was "sitting this one out" to potential partners on the faster-paced numbers. From the conversations, as they slow danced, with an expert fraudster's eye, Sarah quickly assessed her various dance partners' revenue potential. She accepted business cards from a couple of prospects, storing them away for a future time. She wanted no distraction from Kirov and Leon.

Although the lights on the patio were dimmed, the pool remained fully lit. Sitting down on the steps leading from the ballroom, Sarah gave a sigh of relief; her feet were killing her, and she was sure she had sweated through her blouse. In the ballroom, Star was singing a slow blues number from her recent album, dancers swaying in time to the music.

"Would you like a lift home?" Dewayne loomed out of the darkness.

"Thank you. Did you forget I have a car?" she laughed. "Do you have a business card? Let's see about doing business."

"Of course," he said, and fumbled through his wallet searching for his business card for the DJ business. Handing it to her, he said, "Are you seriously suggesting you can find us an investor?"

"I think there's a good chance." She examined the card and put it in her inside jacket pocket.

"Do you have a card?"

"No," she answered coolly. "I'll call you." Her smile took the sting out of the words. "Let me make a couple of calls, and I'll be in touch."

He leaned forward and gave her a light kiss on the cheek. Taking hold of her arm and pulling her close, he whispered in her ear, "Why don't you let me take you home?"

She gently pulled herself free. "You can't take me home. I have a car. Even if you did take me home there's nothing at the end of it. You'll end up with blue balls."

He burst out laughing, "You mean as opposed to black ones? No, I get it, where do you live?

"Santa Monica. How about you?"

"Baldwin Hills." He saw her puzzled look, and said, "It's sorta that way," pointing in a vague south-westerly direction.

"How about a kiss goodnight?" He was nothing if not persistent.

Her driver had seen her and pulled the car forward. "That's me," she said, ignoring the question. They walked down the steps, giving the driver time to open the back door for her.

"You're very likable," Sarah smiled up at Dewayne as they stood beside the open door. "I'd like to postpone the pleasure part until we've done business. I'm sure you understand. I'll be in touch." She stood on tiptoes, quickly kissing him on the cheek. He was so startled he couldn't gather his wits in time, just watched while the driver closed the car door behind her. The car pulled away leaving him standing on the driveway with his arm raised in farewell.

Monday, August 12

Two days after the party, Sarah received a call on her cellphone from Glenda who screamed into her ear, "Thanks very much, bitch. You really screwed me over."

"What do you mean?" she protested.

"What do you mean? What do you mean?" Glenda repeated herself in a whiny voice.

"Tell me what I've done wrong. I thought we were friends."

"We're not friends. You stay out of my way from now on. I got hauled over the coals for giving you the invite. Dixon would have forgiven that misdemeanor, but what he wouldn't forgive is overhearing you telling another guest that he's on his way out."

"I was telling someone a joke. There was nothing to it."

"There was as far as Dixon was concerned, and I have an interview with HR to deal with now. I'm so pissed off at you. Keep out of my coffee shop, I don't want to ever see you again." There was a click as she hung up.

Sarah stared at the silent phone in her hands. "Too late." she gloated. "I got what I wanted from you. So, screw you."

–––––––––––

CHAPTER 6

Sarah gets an idea, but Leon is ambivalent.

**Los Angeles, California
Tuesday, August 13–Wednesday, August 14**

On the night of the burglary, Joshua watched as Sarah entered Dixon's lair while he sat in the van patiently keeping observation. He monitored the alarms and passersby, seeing everything. It seemed like an eternity before Sarah's voice crackled over his radio. He turned the volume down as she told him not to expect any contact while she worked. Sarah was about to discover her abuse of Glenda the day before did not go unnoticed by the cosmos. Karma has a funny way of leveling life out.

A short while later, Joshua saw something that made him sit up straight in his seat. The cleaning crew had arrived.

Where the hell is she? She should be out by now.

He spoke into his radio mouthpiece. "You have company, they're standing by the front door." There was no reply.

Fuck. She can't have turned her radio back on.

He kept calling but there was still no reply. He watched the three cleaners standing by the front door, talking among themselves. One reached in her pocket, brought out a cellphone, dialed a number, and put it to her ear.

What the hell's going on?

He called Sarah again but still didn't receive an answer back. Then a police car pulled up. *At least it doesn't have its emergency lights going.* More attempts to reach her went unanswered. *Damn. They're going in.* He watched as the cops entered the building and could only sit and wait, convinced this would end badly. More time passed. Joshua squirmed in his seat as he grew more frantic. Suddenly, the cops ran from the building and jumped in their car. The lights flashed red, white, and blue as they roared off into the night, siren wailing.

Where the bloody hell is she?

A few seconds later, Sarah exited the front door, walking quickly towards the van. Opening the door she said, "Let's get the fuck out of here." She sat back in her seat, closed her eyes, and sighed with relief, "I got the stuff from the safe."

Joshua pulled away from the curb and grinned back at her, delighted by her claim of success. Then he saw her face was pale and stressed and quickly grew somber.

"Are you OK?"

"I just had a near miss. Almost arrested. I'm shaken up is all."

"What can I do to help?"

"Don't ask me what happened. Let me collect my thoughts. I'll let you know when I'm ready. Get back to the hotel, sharpish. I have to use the bathroom."

Her stress remained palpable. Nothing more was said as Sarah decompressed. Joshua headed to a small hotel on Main Street in Venice which they were using as one of several alternative safe places. Once in their room, Sarah retreated to the bathroom where she stood in front of the sink, running cold water over her hands and looking at herself in the mirror.

"God." She closed her eyes, breathed in deeply, let it out slowly and rolled her shoulders, repeating the process until her body felt relaxed. After a few minutes passed, she opened her eyes and stared at the ghost reflected in the large mirror over the double sink. The lines across her forehead, a certain tenseness in her jaw, and clenched teeth, spoke of the stress she felt. Desperate to dismiss recent events, she took a few deep breaths, ran her fingers through her hair, and opened the bathroom door with a bravado she didn't feel.

Joshua had already filled an ice bucket from the machine down the hall. Sensing her anxiety, he grabbed a handful of ice cubes and dropped them in a glass standing by the sink.

"Gin good?"

"Shit, yes. Make it a double."

He made for the minibar and poured two small bottles of Gordon's Gin and a bottle of tonic water over the ice cubes. He finished off by squeezing a lime into the drink and handing it to her. Sarah took a large swallow, the refreshing taste failing to calm her nerves.

"That was the closest call ever." Her voice trembled as she spoke. "I was scared shitless. Knew I was going in the bag for sure." Shuddering as a nervous chill swept over her, she took another swig of gin.

He selected a bottle of Bacardi with a can of Coke for himself. Pouring the Coke into the rum and taking a contemplative sip, he added a touch more soda. They sat at a table in front of a window overlooking a courtyard with the blinds closed so they couldn't be seen from outside.

Joshua gave his version of events quietly, giving her a chance to recover.

"I saw the cleaners all standing around and wondered what was going on. I called and called but got *nada*. What the hell? Next thing I knew the police arrived. It pissed me off because there was no way of helping you. I felt like a spare prick at a wedding. What happened in there?"

Sarah took another big gulp from her drink, sat back in the chair, and told him the whole story.

"I did good although I did forget to turn my radio back on."

Joshua started to interrupt. "But..."

"OK, that was a big mistake, but your idea about the expensive duds and the doctored pass all worked like a charm. The cops bought my explanation after I flashed my dazzling smile and showed them my ID. They told me the cleaners saw flashes coming from the second floor and were frightened to go inside. I told them I didn't know anything about flashes and was dropping off a report for Dixon. They made me hang around while they did a search, but a radio call made them leave in a hurry after apologizing for the inconvenience."

"A lesson learned the hard way," murmured Joshua.

"No shit. I wasn't thinking of the flash, the curtain was partially pulled." She scowled. "On top of that, I spent too much time on his desk. I was expecting the safe to have only files but there was a Tiffany piece probably worth a 100 K and a derringer in there too. I left them alone. As for the files, I managed to photograph all of them as you'll see when you develop these." She handed him the Minox.

"Great. I picked up some trays and chemicals at Rite Aid earlier and have a dark room set up in the bathroom here.

Why don't you relax? I'll develop the film. Then, if you feel like it, we'll have a look at what you got."

"Good idea. Wake me when you're done. I've just had a big scare, and I'm dead meat now that the adrenalin rush has gone."

Getting up from the table, she brushed her hand across his shoulder in a sign of affection as she passed him. *So . . . he worried about me.* He smiled at her in return.

"Have you chosen a bed yet?" This room had two California king-size beds, a separate room had not been available, so they shared a double room.

He turned to watch her, answering, "No, take the one you want."

She threw herself down on the one nearest, got under the top cover still fully dressed in her business suit, and fell asleep almost instantly. Joshua leaned over to tuck her in. Sarah opened her eyes, sleepily smiled up at him, then closed them again.

He smiled back down at her, aware of the hollow feeling in the pit of his stomach.

God, I'm glad she's safe. She looks so beautiful.

His intuition told him the butterflies in his stomach were more than the usual anxiousness but resisted the temptation to kiss her. *Stick to business. Forget the kissing; you'll only regret it.*

Joshua walked into the bathroom, closing the door behind him. He switched on the red light, examined the trays containing the necessary chemicals and, satisfied, began the process of developing the film. An hour and a half later, pleased with the seventeen negatives that yielded seventeen large-scale photographs on glossy photo paper, he started with his analysis of the information on the prints.

Wednesday, August 14

Sarah woke up at seven the next morning to find Joshua already up and dressed, "Want a room service breakfast?" he asked, as she peeked over the covers.

"Denver omelette, orange juice, coffee, and a croissant with marmalade," Sarah answered as she sat up and groaned, "My God, I slept all night in my clothes."

"Yes, you did. There's no room service so you'll have to settle for bagels and cream cheese with a cup of instant coffee, but you hit the jackpot with the safe. Go shower and change. We need to talk."

He turned back to his computer screen and heard her scramble out of bed.

"Oh, by the way, I made a bit of a mess in the sink developing this stuff."

She made no comment, just closed the bathroom door and turned on the shower.

An hour later, feeling a little more human despite the meager breakfast, Sarah, dressed casually in jeans and a T-shirt, walked over to Joshua and sat beside him. There was a stack of photographs on the table which he selected one by one, giving his analysis of the data they contained.

"There's no trace of Kirov anywhere in these photos. There's nothing on Dixon's computer nor the company's server. No email, no nothing."

"How about Leon?"

"Let me finish. Leon is a much different kettle of fish. He's in bed with Dixon who acts as his attorney. Together they're bringing money in from the Cayman Islands disguised as loans and buying up real estate on Leon's behalf. It looks like a classic money laundering case."

"Dixon's an accountant, isn't he?"

"He's also an attorney who drafts all the agreements. Any clue as to where we go from here?"

"Not yet. Apart from Kirov, we seem to have hit all the right buttons. We have the advantage in that they don't know we have access to Dixon's computer. In fact, they don't even know you exist. I think I'll go back to my hotel, take in the sights, and relax a little. Give me some quiet time to think. There's something in the back of my mind that keeps nagging away."

She gave him a quick buss on the cheek. "I'll see you later."

Sarah had been gone about fifteen minutes when Joshua called Sonny from the lobby payphone.

"I've just developed the photos of files from the safe and will get them over to you shortly. Lots of incriminating stuff against Leon only. Nothing on Kirov. Expect a FedEx delivery."

"Good work. That confirms some of our suspicions. What's your next move?"

"Anything on Matthew yet?"

"Nothing other than what I sent you."

Joshua signed off. "I'll be in touch."

He accessed Dixon's hard drive and spent some time going through files and emails but could see nothing new or significant.

Sarah strolled along Santa Monica Pier on a beautiful typical sunny Southern California day. The breeze blew cool enough to make her nipples stiffen as she sat on a nearby bench, gazing over the ocean towards Malibu, her face blank, taking in the peacefulness. She started to feel normal again when an unexpected memory of her near capture flashed through her mind. The thought caused a shiver to run through her body, and it took a few moments to regain her composure.

A nearby bumper car attraction reminded her of the party with Dewayne and she smiled at the memory. Then a song blasting over the speakers electrified her. *Of course! The break-in fiasco made me forget.* She continued to explore the possibilities in her mind, her smile growing wider, *that will work if I can get everyone to play ball.* She found a phone booth and called Joshua.

"I've got something. Let's meet." They arranged to meet at her hotel in a couple of hours.

Grand Cayman, Cayman Islands

That same day, while Joshua and Sarah plotted against him, several time zones and nearly 2,500 miles away, Leon sat behind the desk of his private bank near the Caribbean Club on Grand Cayman. As the president and founder of the Imperial Bank of Panama, he retained a majority share with the remaining shares owned by his brother. He was a tall black man in his 60s with a closely shaved bald head and week-old manicured salt and pepper stubble beard. Slim and fit, he cultivated a look that said money, and the black Bentley Arnage standing in his personal parking spot did nothing to dispel that image. Today he wore a silk Tommy Bahama shirt showing dark blue palm trees subtly etched against a lighter blue background. A snakeskin belt held up black pleated pants with the silver buckle matching the trademark bars on the front of the Ferragamo loafers. He was married to a beautiful woman who was his childhood sweetheart; they had three boys all under the age of ten, ostensibly the perfect family.

This façade was not believed by most of the people in the know on Cayman. It was a small island, and the word was Leon could be most accommodating if you wanted to shelter profits from criminal enterprises. He wasn't your stereotypical bank president, not that his clients cared. Going to his bank was like buying a car, there are all kinds of additional features and extras available for a fee. Being an original native of Cayman had its advantages. It was a favored location for people seeking confidentiality on deposits of monies from illegal activities or sheltering money from the tax man. His career had started as a teller with a large multi-branch US bank where he earned rapid promotion and learned how the bank's system catered to large suspect cash deposits.

His start in the drug trade came when he saw the ease with which millions and billions of cash changed hands with a little effort and imagination. Initially, he got his stake from small but very lucrative drug boat runs to the Florida coast. A few trips were enough to finance the bank where his brother ran the day-to-day operations while he took care of the money-making side of the business, the illegal part. Nowadays, most of his income came from organizing and laundering a flow of money between a select group of clients engaged in one criminal enterprise or another.

He was his own biggest client but Anthony Nunzio, the same Nunzio who owned Studio Z studios, was a big contributor to his bottom line. Illicit cash from Mob operations was flown in once a week in big suitcases, somehow always passing unhindered through customs. Leon, chosen because of his illicit banking contacts in the black and brown communities, moved Nunzio's money around the world.

The money received was first divided into much smaller amounts and each was wire transferred through a variety of dummy accounts, blind trusts, and shell companies until it was untraceable by even the most dogged detective. The newly cleaned cash was returned to his banking operation minus a percentage for his and others' fees. Offloading the paranoia of being monitored by US authorities was not so easy. He kept his dealings at a lower level, trying to hide in a sea of larger and nastier creatures who attracted most of the attention of the DEA and the FBI.

Leon was rich, a multi-millionaire who was discreet in his spending. He invested in art, precious metals, and US real estate, concentrating on Southern California. The Imperial Bank of Panama wasn't subject to the same onerous restrictions, regulations, and reporting requirements on banking operations as in the United States. His future was rosy, providing contributions to the right political connections continued.

Among fellow smugglers, he boasted, "I make enough on one run to the North Carolina coast to last me a lifetime, and I've been doing it for lots of lifetimes now!" This success didn't prevent him from skimming ten million a year from Nunzio using sophisticated accounting and fake expenses. If caught, the penalty, as he well knew, was being tortured to death in a gruesome fashion.

Maybe, it's time to retire from all this, he reflected as he gazed out of the window at the blue sky, puffs of white cumulus looking like artillery bursts before they grew into towering cumulus nimbus. Thunder rumbled and he watched the blue sky turn black under the clouds as a heavy shower of rain fell, the palm trees bowing as they caught the increasing wind gusts. The air conditioning blew a cool breeze, shivering the papers packing a tray on his desk.

Leon's private line rang. He picked it up.

"Who is this?"

"Hello. Am I speaking with Leon?" The female voice was pleasant but not familiar to him.

"Who is this, please?" He was deliberately terse, not liking unexpected calls on his private line. A line known only to a few handpicked people.

"I'm Sarah. We've not met but we have a mutual acquaintance in Ivan Kirov. Hopefully, that name rings a bell."

"So, what can I do for you?" Leon was noncommittal.

"Ivan recommended I call you for help with a loan situation. He said your bank was always looking for the right opportunity to loan money."

"Sarah, tell me how you know Ivan. I don't recall him mentioning you."

"I wouldn't pretend to know him well. We've socialized a few times at his house in Antibes. He gave me this number. Told me it was your direct line. Said you specialized in dealing with offshore money and I should call you and mention his name if I ever needed help with money."

Leon said, "I'll have to call you back, say half an hour. What's the best number to get hold of you?"

Sarah gave him her room number and the hotel's telephone number.

"I'll call you back in a few minutes." Leon terminated the call.

Sarah was disappointed. "Who knows if he'll call back?" she said to Joshua.

They waited in silence while Sarah paced around the hotel room waiting, peevishly hoping Leon wasn't blowing her off.

Joshua was sanguine. "Be patient," was all he said.

Twenty minutes passed. Her phone rang. "Yes," she answered shortly.

"Well, Sarah," Leon's voice was somber. "The word on the street is that Ivan is laying low. I've tried all my contacts, and I can't get hold of him to vouch for you. If you have some other name perhaps? Someone else I can call?"

Sarah decided to use a sympathy close. Putting emotion into her voice. "No, I don't have anyone else. This was just a chance Los Angeles real estate deal that came my way. It was a stroke of luck when Ivan said to call you. I didn't expect him to be missing but completely understand you passing on this opportunity. So, no harm, no foul. What's the deal with Ivan anyway? I've been trying to get hold of him for a few days now to talk about my deal."

Leon coughed, "Excuse me," he said, "Ivan seems to be under investigation about some arms deal or other, and it looks as though he's got to lay low until it's settled."

"That explains a lot. Listen, would you like to hear my pitch anyway? Take less than thirty seconds and you can decide if we can do business and if not, we'll both go on our merry ways. By the way, Ivan told me that it was likely that you had large amounts of cash waiting to move into investments in the U.S. You know what I mean." Sarah sat back in her chair and raised one arm with her fingers crossed, waiting for an answer.

There was silence for a couple of moments. Sarah had hit the nail on the head. Leon now understood that Sarah knew of his involvement in money laundering. *Thank you,*

Ivan, Mr. Big Mouth. Leon was annoyed, but said, "Yes, I'll hear what you have to say but it doesn't mean I'm obliged to do anything."

Sarah brought her arms down, her hand curled into a fist, "Yes," she mouthed to Joshua. To Leon, she said, "Let me put my cards on the table. The borrowers won't qualify for a traditional loan from a bank although they do have some collateral in cash and the father owns a trucking company. We're looking for twenty million to purchase a commercial building and business in LA. You see, it's clear that—"

"What type of business and where in Los Angeles?" Leon interrupted her.

"The details will remain confidential until you and I have a non-disclosure agreement in place. I can say it's a great opportunity for someone to move some offshore cash." She waited several seconds for this to sink in before continuing. "Let me be frank, neither my clients nor I are naive, Leon. We don't care where the money comes from and know enough not to ask too many questions. The clients have a certain amount of cash and want to see if there's an investor in the offing who will come up with twenty million dollars. If you're willing to loan the money, the security is a nice piece of Los Angeles real estate."

Tapping her fingers on the table, she saw a tiny chip in the polish. *Damn, another manicure.* "If you think such a deal is feasible, we should meet and get to know one another."

"You'll have to come to Grand Cayman."

"And the money? I don't want to come out there on a wild goose chase."

Leon played the story through in his mind, greed and distrust arm wrestling in his head. Greed, as it often did, eventually slammed distrust's fist to the table. "Well," he said, "I guess we can consider doing business, you're a friend of a friend. Who's the buyer?"

Sarah was ready for this question, answering, "All in good time. I'll bring the buyer out with me so you can judge for yourself if the deal is worth chasing. Let me call you back so we can coordinate schedules. Would early next week be a good time to meet?"

"Yes, let's look at Monday. I'm available to you for the Tuesday as well. Give me a call when you're ready. Bye."

She was about to reply but the phone went dead in her ear.

Following Sarah's call, Leon took a few minutes to decide on his next course of action before picking up the phone and dialing a number.

"Matthew, I've just had a call from someone claiming to be a friend of Ivan. Her name is Sarah and I have her telephone number here. Can you chase it down for me? She may be coming for a visit, and I'd like to know whatever you can find out."

The voice on the other end had a thick Irish accent, pleasant on his ear but difficult to understand.

"Give me her name again and the number. I'll find out what I can."

Any difficulty with the accent was a small price to pay for having a good hitman on board. Not that he had any choice. Matthew was recommended by Nunzio which was like receiving a royal command.

Los Angeles, California

We're on, she exulted. *That went as well as could be expected. If Kirov doesn't show his face, we're on. Now I'll call Dewayne and get the ball rolling.* Sarah dialed a number and left a voicemail.

"Josh, I think we have a shot at pulling this deal off. Leon seems to be on board and there will be no holding back Dewayne and his kin. We could pick up a nice fee for getting the loan and bring down Leon and even Dixon at the same time. Have you talked to Sonny yet about those records from the safe and what a bonanza they turned out to be?"

"Only briefly. I've sent the photos by FedEx but haven't heard back."

"He can't still be mad about our little escapade in Brussels. Getting those bank records for him should give us absolution, surely?"

"You don't know him like I do. He wasn't happy and mentioned the thousands of euros."

"So, what," she snorted. "Forget him. We're not working for free and, remember, Leon is going to be a much bigger payday than Goossens and his friends."

Her phone rang. It was Dewayne. They made an appointment for the following day, and she hung up.

Joshua said, "Swanning off to Caribbean islands with dusky men. I might get jealous."

"Yeah, right. That would be a fine thing."

"What, you don't think I'd get jealous if someone I liked made advances on someone else?"

"I don't see you as the jealous type. You might envy them."

"Very profound. We'll take this up when I see you making out with Dewayne."

She laughed, "Well, he's not unattractive."

"Now I'm jealous." They laughed together and the conversation turned to the upcoming meeting with Leon.

CHAPTER 7

Sarah arranges a meeting and Leon acts.

Los Angeles, California
Thursday, August 15

The traffic congestion on the I-5 Freeway was heavy, allowing Sarah the time to recall her conversation with Dewayne about his father's company. At Star's party, while he sipped champagne, he mentioned his father had picked Commerce for their garage and offices.

"Commerce?" she had inquired.

"Yes, it's a small unincorporated city of warehouses, about five miles east of downtown. It's also the main distribution center for the Long Beach dock's shipments in and out of Asia."

"Bit of a schlep from West LA, isn't it?"

"As it turned out, yes. But, if the mail delivery contracts are ever threatened, we're well positioned to start shipping from the docks and beyond. We have multiple freeway choices which allow easy access to everywhere."

After spending close to an hour surrounded by trucks in stop-and-go traffic, she was dubious about Dewayne's claim and sighed with relief when she left the freeway at Bandini Blvd. A few minutes later she turned into a lot with the sign *Henry's Trucking* on the front of a single-story concrete block building.

She thought, *Looks like everything rolled into one: garage, workshop, and office.*

To discourage unwelcome visitors, the lot boundaries were marked by a chain link fence topped with rolls of razor wire. The entry gate wore similar attire. Two trailers were parked on the front half of the paved lot with the rear half being gravel.

Sarah parked her van next to a new Ford F150 truck. The other parking spaces were vacant. Through the open garage door, she could see two truck cabs, one a Peterbilt and the other a Volvo, perched over service pits, their hoods up. There was no sign of anyone, not even a Rottweiler on a chain. Pushing open the door marked OFFICE, she found herself behind a chest-high reception counter looking at three desks.

Adjacent to the desks were offices and a meeting room separated by glass-paneled walls. A big screen TV in the meeting room played CNN, the sound muted by the closed door. Lighting was courtesy of harsh fluorescent tubes glaring white light aggressively down from the ceiling, but, overall, it was much smarter than she expected. The only visible occupant sat in a comfortable-looking chair behind a desk in the larger of the offices, a grey-haired black man who, upon seeing her, got up and approached her, smiling.

"Can I help you, young lady?"

"Yes, I'm Sarah and have a meeting with Dewayne and his brothers. I was expecting them to be here."

"Ah. As you can see, they're running a few minutes late and will be here shortly. I'm Henry, the boys' father and owner of this company." He waved his hand vaguely around. "Why don't you step on through here." He opened the gate, indicated she should follow, and led her through the reception area, skirted the office furniture, and entered the office he had recently vacated. She sat down on a hardwood chair in front of the desk where Henry had retaken his seat. On the wall behind him hung a painting showing a younger version of Henry together with a woman Sarah presumed to be his wife. A printer and a computer stood on a small table alongside a series of well-used green metal filing cabinets. The desk itself was messy, file folders and paper littered the desktop, partially hidden by a large computer monitor and keyboard.

Sarah had done her homework and knew that every year for the past twenty years, Henry had a contract with the Post Office to carry mail between Los Angeles and San Francisco. With guaranteed freight both ways, even with the low rates the Post Office paid, he'd done well. His earnings afforded him a nice bungalow in Baldwin Hills with stunning views over West LA.

"You've been very successful in a competitive business. How have you managed it?"

"The first years were very difficult, a real struggle. Long hours, dealing with all the paperwork. Frankly, doing anything to keep my family fed. It wasn't until my contacts started helping me out that my income climbed. We had just started to enjoy some success when my wife suddenly died."

Sarah drew in a sharp breath. "I'm sorry. It must have been hard raising three boys."

Henry turned and looked at the painting behind him, "That was done about fifteen years back. She's the force behind our achievements. Her mother left us a house in the Adams district, so we didn't have a mortgage to pay. That helped a lot. She insisted on private education for the boys, so they've all ended up with degrees from good universities. I'm very proud of them but we'd be nothing without her. I miss her terribly." He sat for a moment, lost in contemplation. "Getting back to the reason you're here, I understand you're arranging a loan for my sons' business venture."

Sarah nodded affirmatively.

"Everyone's excited. Is that what you do, arrange loans?"

"I connect people who can help one another. That's what I'm doing now. Dewayne and his brothers want money, I know someone who's in that business and is willing to look at the deal." Sarah pursed her lips; she hadn't expected an interrogation from the father.

"What about fees?" Henry got right to the point.

"Yes, there will be upfront fees that will be disclosed when we make the deal," Sarah said sharply.

Henry tilted his chair back and gave her a withering look. "Look, I'm just trying to make sure my boys aren't going to get ripped off. We've all worked too damn hard. Jayden, the eldest, he's twenty-seven, and Dewayne, who's two years younger, both drive for me. Jamal, who's twenty-three, works in the office doing paperwork and getting the hang of how everything works."

"From what they told me, they don't want to be in the trucking business."

"No, they don't," said Henry, thinking back to the conversation during a recent family meeting. "They told me the trucking business was my dream, not theirs."

Sarah was sympathetic. "You're looking at a younger generation with different ambitions."

"I know. I know," Henry said gruffly. "They seem to be putting more concerts together and it seems to be paying off."

"Dewayne said that some of the rappers were interested in your sons producing their music and getting recording contracts."

"Hip hop," Henry scoffed. "They need to be promoting Ellington, Peggie Lee, and musical greats, not this rap shit. Excuse my language."

Sarah laughed, "It's a generational thing. Your music had a tremendous following at one time, but your sons told me there's no money in that style today. They also said rap is only going to get bigger."

There was a lull in the conversation with each considering what to say next. Sarah broke the silence.

"Henry," she said quietly, "you have to be realistic, popular music is the music of the young."

"I suppose. The boys do have more energy and drive when it comes to music, I'll give you that."

"From my understanding, they wanted to rent studios before I came along and offered the possibility of buying a studio. You're proud of them and rightfully so. But, according to Dewayne, they can't both drive and do music. They're thinking of you and letting you know they won't be around to drive for you forever."

Henry said wearily, "I can't say I'm not disappointed. Frankly, I could see this coming. Trucking has given me a comfortable living but it's a tough life and I won't stand in their way." He collected his thoughts, continuing, "Three trucks reflect a success I couldn't have achieved without them. We've all made good money and been smart enough to stash it away. It looks like the next phase is me having to hire new drivers. If that becomes too much of a hassle, I'll just sell the business and retire."

He was interrupted by the sound of voices growing louder as they approached the front door. Sarah saw the hands of the clock stood at just after one o'clock.

The three brothers came in the door with shouts of welcome directed at Sarah who stood and welcomed them with a big smile, shaking hands with Dewayne who introduced his brothers Jayden and Jamal. "I see you already met Dad."

"Yes, I was just getting the third degree." Sarah laughed.

"He'll do that to you," said Jayden knowingly. Everyone laughed, even Henry.

"There's more room over there," Dewayne said, pointing to a small conference room where six people could sit comfortably around a table.

They each took a seat except Henry, who said, "Look, boys, this is your deal, I'll sit this out. If you want my opinion on anything, just ask. OK? Nice meeting you, Sarah. Come say goodbye before you leave." As he walked out the door, he called over his shoulder, "I'll be out in the garage, looking under the hood of that Peterbilt, if you need me."

Sarah opened the meeting. "Let's summarize the facts. There's an opportunity to buy a recording studio and building but it needs something in the vicinity of fifteen to twenty million. There's no way you can qualify for a loan from a lender so you must drum up the money, probably from an investor. Now, how much money can you come up with to close this deal?"

Dewayne pursed his lips. "Seven hundred and fifty thousand max."

Jayden agreed. "As you know, we weren't considering Studio Z as even a remote possibility. We just don't have that kind of money."

"I'm going to be upfront with you." Sarah eyeballed the three brothers. "There's a good possibility there's offshore money available, but it's a loan not an investment. The advantage is that it's a cash deal for twenty million to get you your studios. The costs will be close to $400,000 upfront."

Dewayne was outraged. "That's unbelievable. We'll have a one-hundred-percent mortgage. It will be nigh on impossible to have a positive cashflow for at least five to seven years."

Jamal chimed in. "Look, guys, this is a great chance. If we don't take this opportunity now, we may regret it the rest of our lives. I know we need an investor and not a loan, but let's get the loan, get up and running, and we can get the investor or investors as we go along."

"That's actually a good approach," said Jayden.

Dewayne reflected. "Let's see, I don't need a calculator to tell me that we'd have to have fantastic conditions to be able to manage this deal. The cash going out each month will kill us very quickly and put a lot of pressure on us to have hits immediately. Revenue production will be hit by the natural delay in getting the business going. That, along with refurbishment costs, will see our reserves depleted."

Jayden said, "Yes, but on a positive note, with twenty million, we're getting enough to fix the place up and have a serious reserve allowing for that negative cashflow. I mean we could probably stand to lose a million a year for five years. Are we saying we cannot produce a couple of paying records in five years? If so, I'm out of here."

Sarah smiled and interrupted the boy's excited chatter, wanting to keep the meeting as short as possible. "Are you all in agreement to move ahead? Any disagreements?" There was silence. "Good. I'll go to the Caribbean to meet the lender and firm the loan up. I'll expect my expenses, hotel, flight etc. to be paid by you. I won't charge you an hourly rate."

"Can we come as well?" Jayden asked. "We're putting out a lot of money and ought to be sure of the players. I'm just not giving anybody any money without knowing who's involved."

Sarah frowned. "Here's the thing. I can't have everyone traipsing over there. That would make things too complicated, and I want to keep things as simple as possible. I'd say either you, Jayden or you, Dewayne. You can meet the lender, make sure everything is kosher, and report back to your brothers. As soon as you have signed contracts on the Studio Z deal and we open escrow, the upfront fees will be wired. I'm not sure how the escrow will be handled, and the lender will have a big say in that. Let's get you comfortable with the lender first."

Jayden sat back in his chair. "Wait a minute," he said. "I'm just thinking about this. We're taking your word on this guy. We know it's a fishy deal from the start because as Dewayne says no one is lending us, and I mean us three, that kind of money and that kind of leverage without good reason. What's the game here? Tell us a bit more so's we know what we're getting into. Who's lending us the money? Where's the money coming from?"

"First of all, it's a loan secured by real estate and a going business, so there's the security for the lender. Secondly, it's a loan from a bank that invests in Southern California real estate. It's located in the Caymans for tax reasons. Thirdly, what the fuck do you care?" Sarah stated each point patiently and without rancor. "You're going to find that the Studio Z people won't care where the money comes from, just that it's green and spendable."

"Yes, but it's our green and spendable that's going in upfront," Dewayne said defensively. "Where's the guarantees?"

"There are no guarantees other than most of the points get paid when the deal closes. To answer your question directly, Jayden, I suspect the money is drug money that's been laundered and is looking for a place to invest. What's a better investment than a loan against real estate in the United States? One of you'll get to meet the lender on the trip so you can make your own assessment of the risk."

With a puzzled look on his face, Jamal spoke up, "Do we have any liability if it is drug money?"

"If, and that's a big if, this is drug money, the way it usually works is by the time the money is ready to be loaned to the United States it's so clean you could use it as a band-aid. The Feds call it layering and it's a complicated affair where the money is shifted around the world until it's too difficult for even accountants to say it's illegitimate. You, on the other hand, are just obtaining a loan from a legitimate overseas bank so you have no knowledge or liability."

The room was quiet for a moment as each brother considered the gamble they were making. Finally, Jayden broke the silence, "Who's going to go, how long will they be gone, and when do they leave?" The three faces turned to him. He went on, "I say Dewayne goes. What do you think, three or four days to get things done?" He looked inquiringly at Sarah.

'I'd say two or three days at the most, probably leave on a Sunday and come back late on Tuesday or Wednesday. That depends on flight times and the availability of the lender."

Dewayne looked like the cat that ate the canary. "Thank you for that vote of confidence, it only takes Jamal now to make it unanimous."

"I say, brother, go make us a deal."

The brothers stood, shook hands, and hugged, excited and apprehensive all at the same time.

Sarah took note of the time and, not wanting to push her luck, said, "Let's break this up, it's time for me to go. Dewayne, book us first class flights to the Grand Cayman; let's go on Sunday." She accessed her calendar. "Yes, let's leave the 18th and come back on the 20th, that's a Tuesday; early flight going, late flight coming back. Is that good for you?"

"Any time is good for me."

"That should give us enough time to put this deal together. I'll call my contact there when you give me the flight times. Let's stay at a decent hotel, there's the Oyster Shell on Seven Mile Beach, book a suite for me."

She stood up, reached out and shook hands with everybody and was about to leave when Henry stepped back in the room.

"Ready to leave?" he asked Sarah.

"Yes, on my way."

"Deal done?"

"The first step is done. Dewayne and I will be visiting the lender shortly. After they've met, you can make up your minds whether you want to go ahead or not," Sarah said matter-of-factly. "I've got to be going so I'll bid you all goodbye." She shook hands with Henry and left, calling out, "We're on our way, gentlemen, and, Dewayne, don't forget to call me with the flight times."

Leon was moving money between two corporations for Nunzio when his phone rang.

"Hi there, it's Sarah. Is this a good time?"

"Actually, you'll have to give me a couple of minutes if you don't mind waiting."

"No problem." Sarah sat in her hotel patiently waiting until Leon broke the silence.

"Ok, I'm ready, where are we?"

"I'm arranging to come over on this upcoming Sunday, we have a stopover in Miami and should arrive just before 11:30 pm before flying back on Tuesday, late afternoon. I'm bringing one of the prospects with me. We're staying at the Oyster Shell. Perhaps you and I could meet on Monday and then the three of us can meet on Tuesday morning. Does that work for you?"

On the other end of the phone, Leon yawned. "I have nothing doing that can't be rearranged."

"I'll call you early Monday morning to set up a time for a meeting, perhaps around 10.30, or is that too early for you?" Sarah was treading carefully; she wanted this meeting in the worst way.

"No, not at all. We can meet at my bank. You have the address? No? Here." He read off the address and said, "Any taxi knows us; we get many overseas visitors. I'll wait for your call on Monday, and just let me know if you change your plans."

"Very good, Leon. I hope we can do business. I'm looking forward to meeting you, and we'll speak on Monday morning. Bye now."

Grand Cayman, Cayman Islands

Leon put the receiver down and assessed the situation. Kirov was still missing. Not being able to verify Sarah's connection with him was a minor irritation but an irritation, nonetheless. The street rumors had Kirov talking to the Feds, but he doubted it. *There's no way he's cutting deals. Kirov has too many political connections. I think I'd better up the skim from Nunzio to make up for the lost business from Kirov. Then there's Sarah. Hmmmmm. Better be careful just in case it's a set-up.*

He considered his position. His motive to complete the Sarah deal was solely to solve a temporary cashflow problem. Not a cash shortage problem, quite the contrary. He had too much cash on hand for a small bank and although the authorities were lax and even corrupt at times, he didn't want excessive reserves to attract any more attention than necessary. *Offloading the cash to Sarah's deal is the ideal way forward.*

After calling Matthew and telling him to come visit, he ushered him into his office and closed the door.

"Thanks for coming quickly."

Nunzio had told Leon that Matthew's reputation was that of a specialist for hire with talents including safecracking, burglary, explosives, and murder. His rumored preference saw him taking his victims down in a *mano-a-mano* fashion. An expert with all manner of firearms, he had even trained in Libya with Spetsnaz, the Russian special forces. Leon recognized Matthew was there to protect him, but also knew he was perfectly placed to keep an eye on Nunzio's business interests. Fortunately, Matthew lacked a financial background, so he wasn't a threat to the skim.

"Matthew," began Leon, "what did you find out about that telephone number I gave you to check?"

"Still working on it, boss. The number is a hotel in Santa Monica, but we know that because you went through the switchboard to get her room number. I haven't pinned it down any more than that," answered Matthew defensively.

"A few minutes ago, Sarah called me again from the same number and announced she's coming here on Sunday, arriving 11:30 at night." He handed Matthew neatly handwritten notes. "She'll be with a dude named Dewayne and they're staying at the Oyster Shell until Tuesday afternoon. We're looking at making a big deal and she says she knows Kirov, so I'm considering it. I'm nervous because he hasn't turned up. You haven't heard anything, have you?"

"Nothing at all, just unlikely rumors. Word on the street is that he's hiding from either the DEA, the FBI, or even the CIA, take your pick," advised Matthew.

"I wish he would show up. I'm always nervous when someone disappears and then someone strange comes in with a deal. I don't like coincidences. This Sarah and Dewayne could be a sting. If it is, I want to know. You're my first line of defense." He spoke with a stern face and emphasized each point. "I want to know everything, and I mean *everything*, about this pair and any other partners. They fly back on Tuesday. Keep me informed and I'm going to want you to go to LA and check them out there as well. Understand?"

Matthew took Leon's notes with a grunt and studied the flight times. Leon continued, "Do you remember Connie?"

"I do. She's on reception at the Oyster Shell. We've used her in the past, as I recall. Nice looking local girl, very pleasant."

"That's right. Well, Connie will let you in their rooms and I want you to bug them. They're due here on Sunday for a meeting with me on Monday so you should have no problem getting into the rooms. You'll have to rely on Connie keeping the coast clear. Got any questions?"

"No, I'll get Connie to tip me the wink when they check in." Matthew stuffed the paper inside his jacket pocket. "Will that be all?" he asked in a flippant manner.

Catching the veiled disrespect, Leon hardened his voice. "Yes, keep me informed. OK?" He watched as Matthew walked away thinking, *Insolent piece of shit. If it weren't for Nunzio, I would take you out deep and feed you to the sharks.*

Closing the door behind him, Matthew walked out to the car park where he climbed into his spanking brand-new Mercedes S500, black with black-tinted windows over a cream interior. Leon, who figured it was always wise to keep Nunzio's man happy, had ordered his brother to give up his pride and joy when Matthew was around.

He decided to have a chat with Connie and, after retrieving some equipment from home, made the short drive to the Oyster Shell hotel. Knowing Matthew tipped well and recognizing the car, the valet service jumped to attention when the black Mercedes swept into the hotel forecourt.

"I won't be long, quick errand. Keys on the seat."

He walked into the hotel foyer and saw Connie managing the front desk. He loitered within her peripheral vision long enough for her to finally see him. She gave a nod of recognition and Matthew strolled forward to meet her.

"Hi, Connie, how's things?"

"I'm all right. How can I help you?"

"Two parties, Dewayne and Sarah, checking-in on Sunday. Can you tell which rooms they have booked?"

"Yeah, sure." She went to the computer and typed a few keys. "Here it is. Let me print it out for you."

"I don't need that, what I do need is to book rooms with an adjoining wall for the length of their stay. I don't want them cleaned or entered during that time. OK?"

She nodded, "Sure, I'll take care of that myself."

"Could we check the rooms out now? I'd like to set everything up so we're ready for when they arrive."

"OK." Connie hesitated. "I'm due a half hour break. Meet me by the elevators in five minutes."

"Sure, thanks." Matthew took his time strolling over to the elevators, arriving at the same time as Connie. They stepped into an otherwise empty elevator to the fifth floor in the east wing. Connie led the way as they walked briskly from the elevator to the suite door.

"I'll keep these rooms for them. Believe me, with the ocean views, they're not likely to object and want to change. Do you want to book these other two rooms until Tuesday?"

"Yes, send the bill to Leon at the bank."

She nodded, pulled out her keys, opened the door to the suite, and let him in. "This will be Sarah's suite. I don't want to know what you're up to, so I'll stay outside here until you're finished, OK?"

Once inside, Matthew saw a large picture hanging on one of the adjoining walls which attracted his attention. He carefully measured the wall. Closing the door behind him, he motioned to Connie to open an empty adjoining suite. Leaving her outside, he drilled a tiny hole into the suite reserved for Sarah. He returned to Sarah's suite and made sure the hole was hidden by the picture. He swept up a few grains of drywall and returned to the empty suite. Here, he planted a pencil-thin microphone in the hole, sensitive enough to pick up conversations in any part of Sarah's suite. The listening device was wired to a voice activated tape recorder. He completed the surveillance set up, tested it to his satisfaction, and repeated the process in the room adjoining Dewayne's suite.

"One last thing, are you on duty Sunday night?"

"Yes, we have three couples registered, including your couple. They're coming in on the late flight from Los Angeles. It's a long shift for me, so I'll be here until well after midnight before they're all put to bed."

As they walked towards the elevators, he leaned over the railing and surveyed the ground floor far below. He pointed out a small bar and restaurant. "I'll be there, probably nursing a drink, where I can keep an eye on the people checking in. I don't think our couple will be hard to spot but maybe you can tip me a wink."

"Not a problem, you're going to be in a perfect position to see them as they head to the elevators. The porter will have their baggage, and I'll be escorting them to their rooms."

"Great," said Matthew. "I think that's all, see you on Sunday." He handed her an envelope containing a couple of Benjamins.

"More to come," was all he said, as she thanked him profusely.

Leaving the hotel, he exchanged a crisp US twenty-dollar bill for the keys to the Mercedes. It paid to take care of people in key positions in the tourism business; it was how things got done.

CHAPTER 8

*Sarah and Dewayne do business while
Matthew observes the proceedings.*

**Grand Cayman, Cayman Islands
Sunday, August 18–Tuesday, August 20**

Matthew had been in position for thirty minutes when the
airport bus pulled up outside the hotel and six passengers
and their luggage spilled through the hotel's front door.
When Sarah and Dewayne checked in, they found their
room assignments were on the same floor but in different
parts of the hotel. This arrangement suited Sarah perfectly,
providing her space without Dewayne peering over her
shoulder.

They were easy to spot, any signal from Connie being
unnecessary. On the chair beside Matthew, effectively
concealed from sight in a leather travel bag, a video camera
recorded through a pinhole mesh. The angle was such that
he caught excellent front, profile, and back views of Sarah
and Dewayne walking past his position on their way to
the elevators. They were escorted by Connie who, while
providing a running commentary on the hotel facilities,
gave Matthew a quick wink as she passed him.

He waited a few minutes after their elevator door
closed, then took an alternate elevator to the same floor.

Cautiously stepping out of the elevator to avoid a chance meeting, he quickly went to the room adjoining Sarah's suite. He plugged in the headphones monitoring her room and heard a female voice thanking someone, followed by the sound of a door closing.

Probably Connie leaving, he concluded.

The tapes silently turned as they recorded; stopping and restarting as sounds and silence were interspersed in the natural order of someone moving around the hotel suite humming a tune. Matthew took a quick walk down to the room beside Dewayne's suite to make sure the recorders were working properly. The sound of him singing in the shower tripped the recorder which worked perfectly. It switched off with the silence that followed. Matthew waited patiently until it tripped again, capturing Dewayne singing as he moved around the suite. Satisfied, Matthew returned to the suite beside Sarah's to monitor her activity live.

"If anything about the deal is a setup, she'll be in the thick of it," he reasoned.

As he listened in on Sarah, he ran the video of Sarah and Dewayne in the camera's viewer, looking at their body movements, walking style, and, of course, their faces. Sarah particularly.

I don't think this one's hiding anything, nice tits by the look of it. An observation Sarah would have loved to hear. *Looks conservative, kind of pleasant. Nice nose.*

He rewound the video and turned his attention to Dewayne who lagged behind Sarah on the way to the elevators. She stopped, turned, and said, "OK?" It was said in such a way that left nobody in any doubt that Sarah was saying, "Hurry the fuck up."

Matthew's cellphone rang. "Yes," he answered.

"What's happening with the lovebirds?" Leon wanted an update.

"Parties recognized and the rooms are set up. We'll see what the tapes show but my bet is they're kosher. I don't think they're lovers, but we'll see about that over the weekend. Looking at the body language and voice tone, I'd say she's in charge."

"Is that it? Not much to go on, is it?" Leon said acidly.

"Give me a chance to finish," Matthew said soothingly and quickly went on. "This pair don't act big time. Experienced players?" He made a disapproving grunt into the mouthpiece, saying, "I don't think so. They look harmless."

Leon said, "We'll see what the tapes say. I'm interested to see if she looks for the bugs. Tomorrow is a key day. I expect there will be a lot of action when she reports back to her client after meeting with me. I'll leave it in your hands. Call me if anything significant comes up." The phone went dead in Matthew's ear.

Prick, Matthew thought. *I'm kind of surprised he agreed to a meeting without being able to verify with Kirov. Still, that's his lookout.* He took another soda from the mini bar, sipping it while rewinding and replaying the footage, listening in on Sarah who appeared to be getting ready for bed.

Off to bed already? She must be tired. So much for any involvement with Dewayne.

Monday, August 19

The following morning, Sarah poured cream into her coffee while greeting Dewayne who joined her for breakfast.

"Good morning, I hope your room was comfortable." Sarah gave him a welcoming smile as she poured cream into her coffee.

"I slept well, thanks. You?"

"Heavenly. I was very tired and went to sleep instantly." Sarah smeared strawberry jam on a piece of croissant and thrust it quickly into her mouth. Blotting her mouth with her napkin, she raised her finger as she finished chewing, a sign she wanted to speak.

"Yummy," she exclaimed. "I hope you found something to amuse yourself because, as I told you, I'm going to be gone most of the day meeting Leon." She raised a questioning eyebrow.

"Yes," he said, "I'm just having coffee then relaxing for a couple of hours before heading out for some snorkeling."

"You get to snorkel while I get to work. Nice. I'll call you when I get back and we can talk about how the meeting went."

"I wish I was coming today, but I meet this lender tomorrow. Right?" He was slightly miffed that he wasn't going with her today and suspicious that he wasn't included.

Sarah pursed her lips in disapproval, hoping Dewayne wasn't going to turn out to be a jerk.

"Of course, you're going to meet him. As I told you on the plane, it's important that I negotiate a deal with the lender so I can bring it to you for your approval. Don't forget I'm representing you, not him. I'll see what areas we agree on and what areas are open for negotiation. Then, when I come back to the hotel, we can prepare for our meeting tomorrow without wasting time on stuff on which you and he agree."

They made small talk for the rest of breakfast and Dewayne wasn't sorry when Sarah announced she was leaving to meet Leon. She had rebuffed his advances once again while holding out the promise they would get together when the deal was done. It left him feeling frustrated and he decided to try and relax, maybe take in a movie, then go snorkeling.

Maybe the concierge knows where I can get laid. The prospect cheered him up no end.

Sarah called Leon to confirm their appointment and, promptly at their appointment time, she found herself being ushered into his office by his secretary.

"He'll be with you momentarily," she said, closing the door.

This left Sarah to choose from one of two tufted wingback chairs placed in front of a small desk at the end a large room. The sunlight streaming into the two huge windows shone on books occupying the built-in shelves behind the desk. Sarah stood reading the titles on the spines of the matching leather-bound books with authors such as Shakespeare, Dickens, Poe, and other literary giants. She concluded Leon probably bought in bulk to create an impression.

A booming voice with a slight Caribbean accent called out from behind her.

"Some nice first editions there, if you're interested." She had obviously underestimated him. She turned to see Leon; hand extended in greeting, walking towards her.

"Sarah. So nice to meet you." They shook hands. She assessed his grip. *Firm but not brutal.*

Leon continued, smiling broadly. "Decent flight?"

"Yes, everything's comfortable, hotel's great. I left the client there, by the way. You'll meet with him tomorrow to finish up."

Leon sat down behind his desk and invited her to sit down.

He didn't mince his words. "Listen, when did you last see Kirov? He's still not surfaced."

Sarah was surprised by his bluntness and her jaw clenched in a sign of disapproval. "That's an easy one, we met on Valentine's Day this year. He had a party and I think . . ." she took a moment to give him the impression she was being helpful, "yes, I went to his house several times after that, so probably saw him last towards the end of February, maybe beginning of March."

"And you don't know where he's at now?"

"No, I didn't even know he was missing." She was defiant and acted annoyed, sensing his questions had an attitude. "Like I said before, Kirov and I were talking about accessing investment money and your name came up. He told me that you were solid and gave me your telephone number. Completely by chance, this commercial property came my way and that's the reason I'm here today to do business." Sarah sat back in her chair, having said her piece.

He sensed her frustration, "I'm sorry. To be honest with you, not knowing about Kirov has me on edge. I know he's got trouble, and Russians can be awfully fucking sneaky."

She was surprised by his obscenity. "Can he cause you problems?"

"No, nothing like that. He's been a good client. I just hope he's gone to ground and isn't in jail or dead."

"I'm sure he'll turn up." She made it sound as if she was tired of talking about Kirov. "Let's talk about this deal and make sure we actually have something to negotiate."

She pulled out her notes and handed him several folders she had prepared, showing details of the property. Dewayne had put together five-year projections of business revenue and net profits. These numbers were educated guesses to be validated when the books and records for Studio Z were inspected. One of the folders outlined the net worth of the three partners along with their business experience.

Five hours later, the details of the deal were hammered out. Essentially, Leon's bank would loan twenty million dollars to Dewayne, Jayden, and Jamal's new yet-to-be-named company. The loan was to be paid back on an interest-only basis for seven years when the loan would become due and payable. The last part of the negotiation involved forgiveness of mortgage payments for the first three years. It took three hours and many spreadsheets to overcome what was a sticking point for Leon. Finally, Sarah conclusively proved how the concession would benefit him in the long term, and he resignedly agreed.

"Now the important part," said Leon, "our fees." He pulled a calculator a little closer. "Let's see, we don't want to spoil the deal by being greedy. Why don't you and I split five hundred grand in upfront fees. Let's do a . . ." he slowly stroked his chin, "I'll be generous, so let's say a seventy-thirty split in my favor."

"I'm bringing you a deal where you get to move your cash into US real estate. You know I'll have to be really creative with documents to successfully put this deal together. Plus, I've got more expenses than you. With respect, I see this as a fifty-fifty deal," Sarah declared firmly.

"Based on what you've told me, I'm the only game in town. You want a quick close and your deal goes away if I don't fund it. Me, I'll find someone else to shift my money if you don't want it." He gave a little shrug, eyeing her, calling her bluff.

Unintimidated, she said, "I'm here and now and frankly haven't accessed any other sources. Ivan told me you offered a fair deal, and your proposal is not reasonable. Make it fifty-five per cent to you and forty-five to me and you've got a deal." She reached across the desk, and they shook hands.

The mercenary Sarah now showed her claws. "What about points on the back end? At close of escrow."

Leon said, "Let's not give anyone reason to gripe. How about two and a half points? Gives us another five hundred grand at the same split. Deal?"

They shook hands again.

"I'll bring my client in tomorrow to confirm the details and get signatures on a letter of intent. What's a good time to meet up?"

Sarah hadn't mentioned the seller would also pay her commission on the sale of the building and the studio business. That would be another two hundred grand to her. Here was a perfectly legitimate deal where she and Joshua stood to pocket over half a million dollars.

"Let's meet early morning here at the bank, say 8:00 a.m.; it will be very quiet then." He gave her a sly glance, "Why don't you keep the real estate commissions on the buildings and business. Too complicated for me to be picking peanuts out of horseshit."

"Thank you. You might like to know there's something else to consider," began Sarah confidently. "How would you like to own a trucking company with a proven track of delivery between Los Angeles and San Francisco?"

"Go on," said Leon, frowning as he concentrated, thinking, *that's an intriguing suggestion.*

"My client is part of a family-owned trucking company based in Los Angeles. Been in the business of running routes between LA and San Francisco seemingly since the dawn of time. The owner may be ready to retire. I wondered if you might want to think about buying that company as part of our deal."

Leon was cagey. "Look, I appreciate your offer, but I'm not sure that a trucking company is the way I want to go. Leave me the numbers but take it off the table for now. It's probably a no go for me."

This was an unexpected development for Sarah who had calculated the purchase of the trucking company would be a big attraction for Leon. She tried not to let her disappointment show.

"I don't have the financial details yet but, frankly, it seemed like a good opportunity. FYI, getting paid commissions for the business and the real estate is complicated. The licensing rules are horrendous, and that commission may go by the wayside. At least getting half the loan points up front makes sure our time is paid for." She hesitated, "I do wish you'd give more consideration to buying the trucking company."

"No," said Leon. "One step at a time."

She glanced at her watch, "It's getting late. I should get back and consult with my client."

"Don't worry. Based on what you've told me, we have a deal. I only have one other item, its non-negotiable. Dixon of Whitlock, Katz, and Dixon in Santa Monica puts the contract together and processes the money in the deal."

Sarah played dumb. "I don't know them. That's your escrow company?"

"Dixon's my attorney and his company handles my finances for real estate deals in California. They're a big company and you're getting a legitimate loan from an overseas bank. These loans can be complex, but Dixon knows the procedures to make it a smooth process. All monies will be handled by wire transfer and processed through Dixon's escrow."

Sarah said, "Seems straightforward enough. You'll draw up the letter of intent and fax a copy to the hotel for my attention?"

"I'll get it to your hotel later today," said Leon. "We'll get our upfront fees from your clients when they sign the deal with Studio Z. Is there anything else we need to discuss prior to our meeting tomorrow?"

"No, the whole reason to come here is to set up the financing and go back with the commitment. Then we can make the deal."

"Are we still on for 8:00 a.m.?"

"Can we make it mid-morning? I need to explain the deal plus he'll have to confer with his brothers. There's also the time difference."

"Sure. Finally, you should disclose the front money is passed through immediately on opening of escrow and is nonrefundable. The other five hundred grand is to be passed through when they close the deal."

"I don't know how they will take a million dollars in fees. It could be a deal breaker, although my bet is that they will just protest loudly and create a bunch of noise. I'm sure they'll go through with it in the end."

"The fees are non-negotiable. It's the way I do business. They won't get a loan under these conditions otherwise and, let's face it, they don't have enough money. The clincher for me is it looks good for a long-term investment. If they default and I have to foreclose, so much the better. See you at eleven tomorrow. Just hold on a minute and I'll have someone call you a cab."

Leon had no intention of giving up the trucking company idea but wanted to mull the idea over. *Might be a nice deal for distributing product between LA and San Francisco. That Sarah's a canny bitch, playing the dumb card. I'm not sending them any money until I find out more about her. Not taking the trucking company was the right play. Made her think twice.* He was wary, his defences on full alert for signs of a set up by a US government agency.

While Sarah was on her way back to the hotel, Leon spoke to Nunzio in New York.

"I've just had someone in my office who's looking to buy your recording studio, Studio Z. I have a client willing to put up the money for the loan. I'd like your OK to move ahead."

Nunzio said, "I don't think you've met either Ben Weiner or Ara Danielian; they represent me out in California. They're dealing with it. I told them just a couple of days ago to move ahead with a sale. Who are the buyers?"

Leon considered how much to tell Nunzio. "Three brothers who are into hip-hop music, you know, rap, if you can call that music. I think they'll make a go of it based on the presentation made to me and my client."

"Any reservations?" Nunzio meant was there any chance of him being compromised.

"No. I'm having them thoroughly vetted. Matthew's been monitoring them here in Cayman. Nothing to report so far. He thinks they're above board. He's on their flight back to LA and I told him to keep a close eye on them and make sure they're clean."

"What about the ten million for that deal we spoke of last week?"

"All in hand, should be ready in a couple of days."

"Yeah. Get it transferred to Dixon's escrow account. He'll advise you on what he needs in the future. Anything else?"

"No," said Leon, "I appreciate your time and I'm glad I called. Hopefully, we'll put this deal together quickly and smoothly."

Nunzio knew he was being greased and didn't like it. "Ben and Ara are running the deal. Call Ara. His offices are at Studio Z, the number's in the book. Just tell him you spoke with me and keep me in the loop." Leon found himself cut off.

Ara's office phone rang. Charlene said, "There's a Leon on the phone. He mentioned Mr. Dixon. Should I put him through?"

"Yes, Charlene, put him through. *I wonder if this is about the ten million dollars for the airport deal.*

"Ara, we've not met. It's Leon and I own Imperial Bank of Panama in Cayman. I just got off the phone with Nunzio. I'm calling about Studio Z."

"Leon. Your name is familiar to me. Dixon speaks highly of you. Now, how can I help you with Studio Z?"

"I have approval to make an offer from Nunzio. It's coming from three aspiring producers. My client's guaranteeing the loan that these brothers are using to buy the building and business."

Ara was shocked. "Tell me about the buyers."

"It's the lender who's important here. He's a client of mine putting up the money as a loan through my bank. I'm letting you know whatever price you settle on for Studio Z, the buyers have loan approval."

Ara's eyebrows went up. "Leon, you know we're looking for ten million."

"Yes, thank you, Ara, you won't be disappointed."

"Well, this is good but surprising news. I'll await further results."

Ara considered this latest news. *If they're working through Leon and Dixon, we should get a favorable result.*

After meeting with Leon, Sarah rode back to her hotel where her first task was to make a drink, kick off her shoes, and plump herself down on the comfortable chair. She wriggled out of her bra without taking off her dress and heaved a sigh of relief. She finally relaxed, poured a Tanqueray and tonic, squeezed in a Mexican lime, and took a sip, reflecting that it made the perfect refreshing drink. After confirming dinner with room service, she put her feet up, closed her eyes, and dropped off to sleep. An alarm rang on her phone just before it was time for Dewayne to arrive. She freshened up, poured herself another stiff drink and answered the knock on the door. Greeting him warmly, holding the door open, she waved him into the suite.

"I know wine isn't your favorite, but I've got bottle you may like to go with dinner. Maybe you'd like something more potent first? Take the edge off? Cocktail? Gin and tonic? Beer? Whatever you fancy. Here, sit down over there." She indicated a very comfortable chair in front of a fireplace where a faux log fire burned.

"Gin and tonic sounds great." He walked around her suite. "Wow, this is nice. Mine's pretty good but I think yours is better."

He walked over and opened the door to the balcony. The light net curtains billowed into his face when the stiff breeze hit them, the night outside was very black. He closed the window, grimacing, "Not such a good idea."

Sarah laughed. Hearing ice cubes hitting the glasses, Dewayne turned and faced her, watching her measuring the drinks into the glasses, the tip of her tongue poking between her lips as she concentrated on squeezing the maximum amount of juice from the lime.

"What was Leon like?"

She didn't answer immediately, but put a slice of lime into his drink, carried the glasses over to the fireplace, gave him one, sat in the adjoining chair, and held out her glass to clink a toast. "*Salud, pesetas y amor y tiempo para gozarlos,*" she intoned.

"A Spanish toast." Dewayne was familiar with the saying.

She moved a coaster and placed her drink on the table between the chairs, crossing her legs as she did. Hands clasped together in her lap, she said confidently, "Leon's a cool cat. Certainly got his head screwed on. My bet is that he's been in the game a long time, which is good for us because he'll have experience, less likely to make mistakes."

"You mentioned a letter of intent; is that what we're going to sign?"

"To get the process started, you and he will sign a letter of intent, that's the reason I had you and your brothers execute a power of attorney. You're legally signing on their behalf."

There was a knock on the door. "That's room service," Sarah said. "I've ordered us the conch stew that we talked about earlier." She opened the door and admitted the waiter who wheeled their meal into the suite on a trolley.

"Just leave it on the table, we'll handle it from there."

They sat across from one another at a table. "What did you do today?" She spooned the chunky seafood stew into his bowl.

"Had a great time. I'd forgotten about flying and diving within short time periods and decided not to chance it. Played nine holes of golf instead. Lotta fun, it wasn't too hot either. Came back here, had a nap, took a shower and, *Voila!* here I am." He didn't mention an encounter with a hooker in the bar downstairs who entertained him for an expensive hour.

"Good, I'm glad you found something to do. Let's eat our meal, then we can discuss this loan offer."

Dewayne nodded his appreciation. For the rest of the meal, they made small talk comparing their experiences of travels to other exotic places. With self-preservation kicking in, Sarah let him do most of the talking.

After finishing the meal, Dewayne sipped his wine and considered her over the glass. "What do you get out of this deal?"

"I know wine isn't your favorite, but I'm saving the champagne for the deal closing." She gave him a smile, "Let's go over to the couch and go through the paperwork from Leon."

They sat on the comfortable couch next to one another where she showed him several pages of type on Imperial Bank of Panama letterhead. "This is the letter of intent," she explained. "There's two parts to the deal. The first part is the purchase of the building, and the second part is the actual business of Studio Z. You make the deal with Ara and Leon guarantees to fund your twenty-million-dollar loan within five days of opening escrow."

"We'll have a hell of a job paying back a loan that size," he objected.

"Stop being so pessimistic. Hear the rest of the deal first," she said firmly and over the next hour outlined the structure of the transaction.

"What do you think?" she said, as she concluded her summary.

Dewayne busied himself crunching numbers to compare his business plan revenue projections against the deal offered by Leon.

"You've done a great job." He congratulated her. "The forgiveness of payments for those first few years makes this a very attractive proposition. I'm glad we don't have to depend on Studio Z's financial statements because we're looking at a different business model. We know the studios and there's a pent-up demand for their use by our clients. Last point. How much is it going to cost us?"

"I'm not going to hide it from you, the costs for you to get this loan are very reasonable considering the circumstances. Only five percent. That's 500K up front and 500K on the back end when the loan funds."

Dewayne said nothing; he looked glum.

"What are you thinking?" she asked, irritated.

He sat with the letter in one hand gazing blankly at her. "How are we going to pay Ara. He'll want upfront money when we make our offer. We're spending nearly all our money just to get the loan. With all due respect, Sarah, my dad would say this looks like a classic con. I think we'd better forget the whole thing."

Sarah said, "I'll handle Ara. Let's call the others, explain the deal to them, and let's hear what they have to say."

The call to Jayden and Jamal was difficult with lots of shouting between the brothers but it didn't take long for them to realize that although the fees would nearly exhaust their current cash, they would still have millions of dollars to bridge the gap. They agreed that Dewayne could go ahead with the deal providing he approved of Leon.

The call over, Sarah yawned and stretched.

"Just to remind you, we're to meet for breakfast downstairs at nine in the morning. The meeting with Leon is set for eleven. I suggest you not party tonight, you need to be very sharp tomorrow. Now, please, leave me to my work." She opened the door and embraced him as he was leaving.

"Be patient," she said, but he left shaking his head.

Sarah went back to her room, saw the time. and thought, *Fuck it, I don't know what time it is in LA or what Joshua's up to, but I need to hear if there's any updates about Leon.*

She undressed and put on a bathing suit under an oversize man's blue striped shirt. She dropped her laptop into her purse, carried a towel loosely in her hands, and slipped out of her room using the nearby emergency stair exit to access the beach.

Despite the moonlight, it was very dark away from the hotel. The air was warm and humid, pleasantly so. Several couples were enjoying paddling in the surf, too distant to be of concern. She walked to a nearby phone booth, made sure there was nobody in the vicinity, unscrewed the lightbulb and stood in the darkness for a few moments, checking her surroundings. Positive there was no one watching, she coupled the payphone to her acoustical modem and using multiple internet proxies sent an instant chat message to Joshua's computer.

"Price $20 million with upfront payments of $500,000 in fees and another 500 thou on the back end. After the split, we'll enjoy about four hundred grand to us with no risk."

He messaged her back. "Great news. I have good news too. I managed to get access to Leon's computer. One of his bank staff fell for the FTC letter and the malware is installed, waiting for me to activate it. Where do you go from here?"

Sarah outlined her plan in one sentence and Joshua chuckled on the other end before sending his response.

"No surprises there. You're coming home tomorrow. Do not underestimate the opposition. No visiting Leon after hours either, he's looking well protected at both the office and house."

Sarah was irritated at Joshua's apparent rush to stop the chat.

"You're forgetting something. Use our Swiss banks to set up alternative accounts and I may need a safety deposit box too."

"Consider it done. Bye."

She was upset, the contact with Joshua made her realize how much she missed him. *What's up with him? Doesn't he miss me?*

The surf continued to rumble and spread a white blanket of foam over the sand, hissing as the tide advanced. Alert for someone watching, Sarah slowly made her way down to the surfline where she paddled in the warm water. Her bag slung over her shoulder, walking slowly, head down, deep in thought, she weighed up the risk and reward of the different strategies she could employ. Before long she found herself at the side door used to leave the hotel, it was locked. She looked down at her feet, still wet and covered in tiny grains of sand. *Damn. I've got to walk through the hotel to my room looking like this.*

She made her way through the brightly lit lobby, thinking, *so much for a discreet walk.* Her senses suddenly became aroused. *Someone's following me. Who and where?* Sarah made her way to the elevator, pausing to window shop in one of the high-end stores, using the reflection to watch for anyone following her. She reminded herself to act less suspicious of her surroundings and more like a loan broker. Certainly not someone looking for a tail. On her way to the elevator, the corner of her eye caught a shadow moving off in the direction of the shops, offering her just a fleeting glance, a vague impression of size and shape.

"God, did he see me making the call to Joshua?" Sarah muttered to herself, sure but not one-hundred-percent positive the suspected watcher hadn't been in the vicinity. *Probably picked me up when I came in the lobby,* she mused.

Getting off the elevator at her floor, she strolled to the railing overlooking the atrium that ran through the center of the hotel for its twelve floors. She was trying to play tourist, enjoying the view as she sought out anyone obviously loitering. Sarah gave up this endeavor as futile a few minutes later and made her way back to her suite convinced but not surprised Leon had someone following her.

Meanwhile, in Los Angeles, Joshua continued to monitor Dixon's email. His persistence was rewarded when a ping announced an email from Leon to Dixon. Joshua read the contents out loud to himself.

"I have a potential twenty-million-dollar loan coming up secured by LA property. When the deal is in escrow, we'll use your same appraiser to make sure the value of the building and the business come in at twenty million."

He let out a whoop of joy that subsided as he read the last paragraph. "I wish Kirov would show up. I've got Matthew checking her out. We should sign a letter of intent tomorrow and then they must put the deal together in LA. I told them five days to fund. You have access to my private account numbers, and we'll use those reserves to fund the deal."

Joshua sent Sarah an encrypted chat. "You're being monitored. 24/7. Be careful."

CHAPTER 9

*Sarah and Dewayne get a result
and Joshua delivers a gift.*

**Grand Cayman, Cayman Islands
Tuesday, August 20**

Very early the next morning, Matthew called Leon. "There's nothing much to report. The tapes from the room reveal that they're very happy with the deal. They called the brothers in LA and after a touchy moment over the projections, she pulled it together. Everything is cool. Last night, she went down to the beach for a stroll, and I saw her wading in the surf by herself. As you know, it's very hard to follow anybody down there without being spotted. I didn't want to get too close but, all in all, I'd give them both a clean bill of health."

Leon was not satisfied. "The only way we're going to find out more is if you go to LA and make sure they are who they represent themselves to be. I told you about the trucking company which I'd like you to check out while you're there. I'm meeting Sarah and her client shortly, but it will be a quick meeting because they're booked on a return flight later today. You have the details. Did you manage to get on that flight?"

"Yes, I have a reservation in economy. I figured with them being in first class it was unlikely they'd know I'm following them."

"We're set then. Call me tomorrow night with progress. You might be in LA for a few days until we get this deal settled, so pack accordingly. Stay somewhere convenient but nice. Expenses are no problem. If there are no other questions..."

He left the question hanging in the air but wanted to move on quickly. Ahead of him lay a lengthy telephone call with Nunzio to explain, once again, the reasons for the delays in accessing his laundered funds.

Mathew got the not-so-subtle hint. "OK, boss, Hollywood it is. I hope there's no earthquakes. Bye." He left the office and put pedal to the metal on his way to his apartment to pack.

At nine the following morning, Sarah had seen Joshua's message and shrugged it off. They had both expected Leon to take precautions. She was biting into a croissant when Dewayne arrived. The smell of coffee made his mouth water as he put his overnight bag under the table beside Sarah's. They intended to take a taxi to Leon's bank and although they hadn't yet checked out, there was still plenty of time for a leisurely breakfast.

"Sleep well?" Sarah served herself a second fresh, warm croissant. She cut it open and, licking the fingers on one hand, reached for the strawberry jam. "Any worries?" Sarah continued, looking at Dewayne who poured himself a cup of coffee from the flask.

He raised the cup to his lips and took a large sip. With closed eyes he appraised the quality.

"Hmmmm. Very nice."

"The meeting's at eleven. We'll check out of the hotel and leave our luggage with the porter. Taxi over to Leon where he'll go through the deal we discussed last night to make sure you understand. Then you and Leon sign the letter of intent. Our mission accomplished, we hit the road, having just enough time to catch our flight back to LA."

After finishing his breakfast, Dewayne checked his watch for the umpteenth time. A glance over her shoulder to the reception desk revealed five people in line awaiting check out. More people were coming out of the elevators heading for the same line.

"We should check out." He brought his overnight bag from underneath the table.

Sarah paid off the cab in front of Leon's Imperial Bank of Panama while Dewayne stood to one side with his back to her. He was admiring the impressive single-story building with dark glass windows hiding the interior. Set on a large lot, there was plenty of parking and the suitably tropical grounds were well manicured.

"Impressive," he said, in admiration.

"You better believe it. Come on. Let's go."

She walked up the steps and pulled open the large glass front doors. It was like any other bank with one teller in attendance behind bullet-proof glass, the three other teller windows were vacant. The rest of the bank was styled open plan, the more senior and experienced bankers having offices and the peons in cubicles. Everyone was glued to their computer screens.

A banker in the nearest cubicle saw them enter and approached them. "You were here yesterday, I believe?" The accent was broad Boston.

"Yes," Sarah answered, "Sarah and Dewayne for an appointment with Leon. We're a little early but perhaps you could let him know we're here."

"Oh, certainly," said the banker, scuttling off to a nearby office where she knocked on the door and, holding it open, spoke to an unseen person. They heard a voice reply and the Boston accent turned and waved for them to come to the office.

Dewayne took a good look at Leon as he emerged from behind his desk, a large smile on his face. He greeted Sarah with a kiss on both cheeks. "Nice to see you again."

"And you must be Dewayne." Leon turned to face him. "I'm very pleased to meet you." He shook hands and Dewayne noted his direct eye contact.

"Sit down. Please." He indicated two chairs in front of his desk. He pulled one chair out and held it while Sarah sat down. Dewayne took a seat alongside and Leon settled into his chair looking first at Dewayne and then at Sarah, a welcoming smile on his face.

"Comfortable? Can I get you a drink, water, coffee, tea? Whatever you want." He was very gracious.

They glanced at one another, each shaking their head. Sarah said, "No thanks. I don't mean to be rude but we have a flight to catch this afternoon so we should probably get down to business."

"Very well." Leon said. "But," he gave Dewayne the once over, "tell me a little about yourself. We're lending you a lot of money and I'm interested in why you think your business will succeed."

Dewayne made his pitch and did well. He exuded confidence as he launched into how he and his three brothers operated as DJs. They could see which young artists they should promote and felt they were good at picking talent.

He concluded, "Jay-Z, Tupac, Snoop Dog, LL Cool J, Ice Cube. These names and many more probably mean nothing to you but they're all very successful artists making millions of dollars in the world of music, rap music. All came from disadvantaged backgrounds and started at the bottom, waiting for that chance of discovery. Having our own recording studio will allow us to tap into that large pool of unknown artists who have a lot of talent."

He showed Leon excerpts from videos on his computer, showing clips of several artists performing their rapping styles at their DJ events. He commented, "These guys have big local followings and just need more exposure. I'm sure you saw the potential in our business plan."

Leon was impressed. "I read through your profit and loss statement together with the budget and marketing plans. Meeting you has me more convinced than ever that this will be a successful transaction all around. We'll commit to making the loan when you make your deal with Studio Z." Leon put his hands on his desk and leaned forward.

He studied Dewayne closely. "Do you have any questions?"

"We're obviously most concerned about the nonrefundable upfront money. Can't we do a normal deal where the loan points are part of the closing costs? I mean, it's a million dollars altogether."

"Well, first, let me tell you a little bit about the bank. I've been the owner of this bank or at least the majority shareholder for the past fifteen years. This is our only branch. Cases such as yourself are our sweet spot because we're prepared to take on more risk than our counterparts in the US. To offset our risk and costs we must be sure of commitment by our borrowers. That's the reason we insist on nonrefundable deposits to get the ball rolling. If this is a deal breaker for you then let's not waste each other's time." Leon waited for Dewayne's answer.

"Well, what about a discount? Maybe knock 250 grand off the costs?"

Leon smiled. "I'm sorry, but the fees are non-negotiable. I think Sarah obtained a great deal for you. The forgiveness of payments, for instance. If you don't want the deal . . .?" He left the rest unsaid.

Dewayne rubbed his face. "No, I guess we're in agreement."

"You're clear on all you're committing to?" Leon contemplated them both.

"Yes, agreed," said Dewayne.

Leon leaned forward, "I understand you have a power of attorney for your brothers?"

Dewayne reached into his briefcase and slid a four-page document across the desk. Leon read it through carefully.

Leon pulled a grey folder from his desk drawer and removed documents from it. "This is the letter of intent for the loan. I believe Sarah's given you a copy. Initial where indicated, sign and date the last page." He held out a pen and Dewayne initialed and dated each page and signed with a flourish. Leon then signed on behalf of the bank.

"I'll have my secretary make both of you copies. I'll keep all original signed documents and forward copies to Dixon."

"So, we're cool?" asked Dewayne.

"We're cool."

The journey had begun. Amid the congratulatory handshakes and back slapping, Leon stood back, separating himself. He reminded them they would lose everything if they defaulted on the agreement.

Sarah responded, "I don't think making the deal will be a problem now that we have your loan commitment."

Their task now complete, they made their farewells to Leon and caught their flight back to Los Angeles in an exultant mood.

Los Angeles, California
Tuesday, August 20

After a stopover in Miami, Sarah and Dewayne caught their flight to Los Angeles but, almost as soon as the fasten seatbelt sign went off, Dewayne's prattle became boring. His conversation went in one ear and out of the other and she was grateful when, somewhere over West Texas, he finally fell asleep. Sarah pulled out her book and fell asleep shortly afterwards. An announcement to fasten seatbelts and put seats in an upright position awakened her. She pulled up the window shade, outside it was early evening; the sun had just set.

He spoke quietly, "You slept through the meal but to be honest, you didn't miss much. How are you getting home?"

"My transport's in parking so I'm good. The next step for you is to find a good real estate broker to negotiate the Studio Z deal. He'll realize the letter of intent signed between you and Leon shows you mean business and be able to communicate that to the seller."

They retrieved their luggage from baggage claim and walked out onto the arrivals' concourse. Dewayne's brothers greeted them effusively with back slaps, big grins, and hugs all around. They had parked in the red zone and ignored the ongoing speakers broadcasting loud threats about illegal parking. After a few minutes, Sarah parted company, promising to be in touch the next day.

Matthew only had a small carry-on wheelie suitcase and was deliberately slow getting off the plane. He kept a careful eye on Sarah and Dewayne, watching them retrieve their luggage and head onto the concourse. Fortunately, three flights had arrived almost simultaneously, leaving the baggage claim area swamped with impatient passengers. It wasn't hard to be inconspicuous.

The driver of his preferred ride, a Lincoln Town car, met him at the gate. As they made their way onto the concourse outside of baggage claim to pick up the car, he saw two black guys parked up in a white Cadillac Fleetwood.

That will be their ride, he reasoned. *Must be his brothers, I'd lay money on it.*

He watched from a distance as Sarah and Dewayne spoke briefly, embraced, and she walked away while they drove off with Dewayne in the rear passenger seat.

"Here's something for your troubles." He handed the driver a crisp C note. "What's your name?"

"Paul. Paul Garabedian." He pointed to his license on the dashboard.

"Paul. I want you to wait here. I'll be back in a couple of minutes."

"Give me a break, the cops are really strict here. They'll ticket me if I don't move."

"I'm in a rush. Here's another hundred. Now shut up and be here when I get back." His tone brooked no argument.

Sarah timed the pedestrian light to the parking lot nicely while Matthew caught the red light. He waited impatiently for the light to turn green and almost lost her.

He was lucky; his movements were concealed by the large numbers of people arriving and departing, many pushing handcarts topped off with layers of suitcases. He saw her unlock the door to a small van, noted her parking space and license plate number along with its proximity to an exit and sprinted back to his car.

His driver said, "Thank God, you're here. The cops have been all over me to move."

"Just a few more minutes, I'll let you know when to go." He was sure her destination was in Santa Monica but kept a careful watch of the passing traffic, counting his blessings the one-way system mandated she would drive past him.

"See that small black van in the third lane over? Follow it."

"What is this, a movie?" The driver asked sarcastically, then realized he might offend a fare who'd already given him two C notes and might be good for more.

"No, nothing like that. I'm a private investigator and it's part of an investigation. There's another hundred in it if you don't lose them, just don't get too close."

As the driver pulled away from the curb, he glanced at Matthew in the mirror and said, "There better not be anything funny going on here. I have my license to think about."

"Trust me, your license is not at risk. Just don't lose them."

"I won't. That extra hundred's on top of the fare, right?"

"Of course."

Sarah's van drove through the airport to North Sepulveda then turned onto Lincoln intending to follow it all the way into Santa Monica.

"The 405's jammed. That's why she's gone this way," explained Paul.

Thirty minutes later, Sarah unlocked the door to her hotel room and breathed a sigh of relief. Dog tired from all the flights and time zone changes, it took a brief shower to freshen her up. Slipping into jeans and a T-shirt, she called Joshua from a pay phone in a nearby grocery store.

"I think your suspicions on Matthew might be right. I'm sure I'm being followed," Sarah said. "It's just a feeling but it doesn't usually let me down."

Joshua concurred. "Your suspicions are correct. I was at the airport and saw Matthew follow you to the airport parking then to your hotel. He's staying at the Miramar Hotel on Ocean close to you in Santa Monica. I'm positive Leon thinks you're setting him up and just as we expected, he's checking you out. These are rough players, and your life won't be worth spit if they find you out."

"There's nothing to find out yet. I'm boring and straight. I've told them I've just moved to Los Angeles and had a chance meeting with Dewayne. I'm working for fees as far as everyone is concerned. I mean there's no crookedness involved, and we can make half a million legally. Of course, they don't know we're passing on information to Sonny."

"Got to go, be careful where you call from; Matthew may try to bug your room."

"I'll be good. I'm not in the hotel right now. I'm hiding around the corner in a store."

"I'll keep monitoring Leon's hard drive. Oh, and by the way, I left a little present for you in one of your drawers. We'll talk soon. Bye." He chuckled to himself at the thought of what Sarah would discover back at the room.

Sarah returned to her room, opened the drawer where she kept her T-shirts, tops, and underwear. It appeared undisturbed but she found a box concealed beneath her very racy underwear. Groaning, she said to herself, "Now, he'll be imagining what color thong I'm wearing every time we speak."

Using a knife that appeared almost by magic, she sliced through the tape binding the box shut, opened the lid, and revealed a Sig Saur P229 with three extra full magazines. She released the magazine from the butt and ejected the round in the chamber to make sure the gun was completely empty. Snapping the full magazine back into the handle, she chambered a round, engaged the safety, and weighed the gun in her hand.

I love these Sigs, they feel so comfortable but what the fuck does Joshua think this is, World War Three? She put the gun in her purse along with the extra magazines and went to bed.

CHAPTER 10

The Mob gets involved.

Matthew watched Sarah enter her hotel, satisfied he had located her so quickly. He hadn't followed up on Leon's instructions to trace her phone calls and failed to realize she was staying at a different hotel. He said to the driver, "OK, now I know where she's staying. Take me to the Miramar Hotel, it's very close to here."

Arriving at his hotel, he gave the grateful driver another crisp one-hundred-dollar bill and a good story to tell his mates.

After registering at the desk, the hotel porter, a friendly young black man, was dispatched to carry his bag the short walk to the private bungalow Matthew had booked.

"Stayed here before, sir?"

Matthew wasn't in the mood for conversation and said curtly, "Yes, in this same bungalow."

The porter unlocked the door and put his bag on a luggage rack which stood by the television console. He hovered a second or two, waiting for his tip, and he grinned his appreciation when Matthew handed him a twenty for his troubles.

"Thank you, sir. Let me know if you need anything." He departed, closing the door behind him.

After unpacking his few necessities, he had a quick shower. The last few days had been nonstop with little sleep, so he popped a small dose Benzedrine tablet to give him a boost for an hour or so. After changing into a black T-shirt over black slacks with a leather jacket for comfort, he met the Lincoln Town car he'd ordered and settled into the rear passenger seat diagonally from the driver.

The slim, balding chauffeur closed the door behind Matthew and got behind the wheel. "Where will we be going, sir?"

"Hi there, what's your name?"

"Blake, sir."

"Well, Blake, I'm in town for business and haven't been here for a while. I just want to get the lay of the land. Let's have a cruise around Santa Monica up towards and including Westwood, Brentwood, and Santa Monica itself."

"Very good, sir. Sounds like you know your way around. Is there any set route or should I just cruise and let you direct me as we go?"

"I like the cruise idea. Let's go. Perhaps a run up Wilshire to start."

For the next couple of hours, Blake drove a tour of the general West Los Angeles area while Matthew commented on the architecture and design of buildings and the changes to the various neighborhoods. It wasn't by accident that one stop included the building housing the offices of Whitlock, Katz, and Dixon. On the way back to the Miramar Hotel, he requested Blake drive the roads and back alleys in the vicinity of Sarah's hotel. At last, feeling at ease with the lay of the land, but suffering from a Benzedrine headache, Matthew called it a day.

Matthew tipped Blake generously on top of the fare and, smiling at the very attractive female manning the reception desk, returned to his room.

Wednesday, August 21

The following day, Leon called Nunzio in New York. "We're working on the Studio Z deal, but I have a situation in LA and need some help. Got anyone I can use?"

"It'll cost you. Call Vincent at *La Cucini di Papa* and he'll help you out."

Leon read the name back.

"Yes, it's in Van Nuys." Nunzio hung up.

Leon called Matthew and after giving him the address and name of the restaurant told him who to see and to make sure he mentioned Nunzio's name.

"Now we're getting somewhere," exclaimed Matthew. "I'm still betting she's no threat."

Leon said disapprovingly, "We're just making sure. I hope you're right, now get on with it."

An hour later, Matthew was at the wheel of a rented Chevy Chevelle SS with a V8 454 engine heading towards Van Nuys and his appointment with Vincent. He was using Van Owen Street, connecting Burbank and Woodland Hills and one of the main drags across the floor of the San Fernando Valley. As the traffic thinned, he accelerated, speeding past the numerous apartment buildings lining the street, looking for all the world like good soldiers standing at attention. Coming to a stop at another red light, he reflected on changes to the neighborhood from a few years back.

This was all orange and walnut groves forty years ago. Now it's strip malls with 7/11s, donut stores, and nail and hair salons. All run by fucking immigrants.

The light changed and he drove off, shaking his head at the sight of a huge billboard advertising an ambulance-chasing attorney. *Even the signs are in Spanish,* he thought indignantly.

He spotted *La Cucini di Papa*, the last in a line of retail businesses, just west of Van Nuys Boulevard, and pulled into the cul-de-sac, accessing the parking lot at the rear of the restaurant. He walked briskly to the entrance, opened the door, and saw four men playing cards at a table strategically placed to intercept anyone entering. Immediately, one got up.

"This is a private club."

The greeting, deliberately cold and menacing, was given to any stranger inadvertently mistaking the place for a regular restaurant. This rather large man with a distinctive broken nose had a strong East Coast accent and stared at the briefcase in Matthew's hands.

"Who are *you*?" He put heavy emphasis on the '*you.*'

"I'm Matthew. Vincent is expecting me."

Vincent's name produced a welcome result. The big man nodded, his chiseled features relaxed with a hint of a smile about his mouth, his teeth showing Pepsodent white. He gave Matthew the once over, but his eyes weren't smiling; they were hard like flints. Without volunteering his name, he said, "Vincent's through here. Follow me."

Matthew quickly assessed the other clientele as Flint Eyes escorted him through the main restaurant. The three remaining card players glanced over with a 'who the fuck is this civilian' type look as he walked past. It reinforced his feeling of being an intruder. Three more felons were engaged in an animated discussion on baseball odds over sports pages scattered on a corner table. The conversation stopped as they took notice of Matthew, their argument resumed in quieter tones after he had passed by. A haze of cigarette smoke hung in the air. These guys were the last to worry about the nonsmoking regulations. The décor, cream stucco with fake brown beams, had a distinct air of neglect.

This is where the Mob hangs out? It's a bit dingy. Mind you, it's an ideal setup for Vincent and his crew, a safe place to hang out while they figure out their next caper. He saw the windows were draped with heavy net curtains, effectively screening the occupants from prying eyes.

He followed Flint Eyes towards an office door with a center glazed window, the words 'PRIVATE' in black letters pasted unevenly on the glass. After knocking, he pushed open the door without waiting for an invitation. The office had no windows; the double overhead fluorescent tubes glared a bright white light down onto a table serving as a desk. The walls were cheaply clad in an overcoat of light brown imitation walnut panelling that did nothing to improve the looks of the place.

Matthew took a quick glance around. Boxes, probably restaurant supplies, stencilled with unintelligible markings, were stacked in one corner. A modern flat screen monitor stood to one side of the desktop, a keyboard and mouse in front. A multi-line telephone with speed dial and speakerphone stood on the opposite side. A separate table stood alongside the desk with a printer on top and the computer underneath. The mass of cables connecting all the electronics couldn't be hidden, making it untidy, grubby even. Vincent, sitting in a large vinyl office chair, had gangster written all over him.

Flint Eyes left, quietly closing the door behind him.

"Don't believe I've had the pleasure. Anthony says hello." Matthew reached out his hand, looking Vincent in the eye.

They shook hands, Vincent nodded an acknowledgment. Tall and slim with a cruel hard face, his shoulders nicely filled out his sports coat, a black T-shirt underneath emphasizing his muscular physique. A tanned complexion, good looks, and black wavy hair couldn't hide the distinctly feral look which made him a magnet for the ladies. Women who liked bad boys liked Vincent. He was the poster boy for bad boys: tall—six feet, Matthew guessed—and looking like he kept up his gym membership.

"Get you anything? Drink? Whatever you want." Vincent was being very hospitable, knowing that Nunzio had sanctioned Matthew to operate in his territory.

Matthew sat down and shook his head. "Nothing, thanks. Appreciate your time. Uhm," he gathered his thoughts. Leon had told him not to disclose the reason for the telephone tap. "I presume it's OK to talk business here."

Vincent said, "Yeah, yeah. We sweep all the time but just an outline of what you want, no details."

"I'm working on a deal and not sure of one party." Matthew pointed to the telephone and then to his ear. "Tap," he mouthed.

Vincent understood immediately. "I've got just the guy. I'll have someone take you to him, tell him what you want, and it will get done."

"Thank you. As a courtesy, Leon sent you a present." Reaching down he picked up an elegant ostrich hide briefcase and put it on the table. Vincent pulled it open and peeked at the wads of Benjamins. He nodded with an appreciative look on his face.

"Thank you, I appreciate the respect, and good luck with your endeavors." He got up from behind the desk and took Matthew into the main restaurant where he waved Flint Eyes over and introduced him to Matthew.

"Bruno, take this man where he wants and give him what he needs. Thank you, Matthew." They embraced. "I look forward to seeing you again."

Bruno and Matthew made their way to the parking lot at the rear of the restaurant. He gave Matthew's Chevelle a look of disgust. "Let's go in my car."

Matthew climbed in the black Cadillac Fleetwood Brougham. The soft leather seats oozed comfort but were hot from the sun beating down; he squirmed as the heat burned through his trousers. Bruno put the air con on gale force, pressed a couple of switches, and the black-tinted windows whispered closed, obscuring them from any curious bystanders. They rode in comfort towards the San Diego Freeway and after a few minutes he lowered the fan to a cool breeze.

Bruno glanced at Matthew, "What's the job?"

"I have a hotel where I need a telephone tapped."

"No problem, our contacts in the telephone companies can get you anything you want."

"Can we get records of calls made?"

"Like I say, anything you want. Where's this hotel?"

"Santa Monica."

This was working out better than he anticipated. A peek at Sarah's telephone records might be very revealing.

"Santa Monica, Santa Monica, let me see."

Bruno scrolled through his phone memory, glancing down as he did, causing the car to veer. He corrected the steering. "Got it."

He dialed the number and drove one-handed, holding the phone to his ear with the other hand on the wheel. "It's Bruno. I need to meet you in Santa Monica. What about that place we met last time, you know the one I mean?" He took a breather as the other party spoke at length, then countered, "I don't care, meet us an hour from now. See ya." He put the phone down, saying to Matthew, "Even with LA traffic, we'll get there in plenty of time."

The air conditioning kept them comfortable as they hit the San Diego Freeway. Matthew handed Bruno an envelope. "I appreciate you running me around like this. Here's a grand for your time. How much to settle with this telephone man we're about to meet?"

Bruno expressed his thanks, "I'm not sure about the telephone guy, depends on what needs to be done." Bruno was not much of a conversationalist, the radio was off, traffic noise was muted, and it was quiet. *A little too quiet,* thought Matthew. To break the ice, he asked Bruno what he did for relaxation.

"I put the homeless out of their misery," he said with a serious face. Then he laughed. "No, just kidding. I go shooting quite a bit."

"So, what's your favorite gun?" asked Matthew.

"Now you're talking. Well, I favor . . ." and went on to extoll the virtues of his favorite automatic pistol, revolver, rifle, and shotgun. Matthew couldn't get a word in edgeways other than an obligatory grunt that meant almost anything. He groaned as Bruno's voice droned on when the traffic slowed to a crawl while passing a fender-bender in the Sepulveda Pass. Their destination, Sal's Deli, was within a thousand feet of Dixon's building.

Antonio sat in a booth at the rear of Sal's Deli. He was balding with a two-day growth of beard on his sallow and pitted complexion, his arms were muscular, and hair peeped out of the top of the T-shirt worn underneath his white worker's overalls. His company photo identification hung around his neck, and his name and company logo were on his breast pocket.

Ripping pieces of ciabatta bread from a loaf in the middle of the table, he dipped them into the mix of olive oil and balsamic vinegar on the plate in front of him. He slipped the pieces into his mouth, letting them sit on his tongue like communion wafers, relishing the fresh bread. Over the top of his glass of red wine he saw Bruno's bulk walk in the door. Antonio didn't know Bruno's companion but assumed he could be trusted.

As Matthew and Bruno walked up to Antonio's booth, he stood up and greeted Bruno with a hug and a kiss on both cheeks.

"*Ciao,*" said Bruno.

"*Ciao,*" acknowledged Antonio.

"Antonio, this is Matthew, a friend of mine."

As an associate he didn't warrant the customary back slapping and kiss on the cheek, just a head bob and a searching look by both parties of the other's face.

"My pleasure," said Antonio.

Matthew grunted a response in return. They sat down with Antonio facing Bruno and Matthew. The proprietor appeared as if by magic, dressed in a white shirt with a crisp white apron. There was a rapid exchange of Sicilian with all three joining in a burst of laughter. Matthew, not understanding a word, sat silent with a bemused smile on his face. The proprietor served them extra plates together with more olive oil, balsamic vinegar, and warm ciabatta bread. Two more glasses of red wine were poured.

"Tell him what you want," Bruno said to Matthew, nodding in Antonio's direction.

Matthew set down his wine. "This woman Sarah has booked into a room at a hotel on Santa Monica Boulevard." He pushed a piece of paper across the table with the address clearly written out. "Can you bug the phone and get me records for her room at the hotel?"

"It shouldn't be a problem. My inside man will conceal the tape recorders at the telephone company, they'll be voice activated." He shrugged and examined the piece of paper. "Wow. Tracing cellphone calls as well. That could be a big item. I'm an engineer and have to create a program for that. It's not that hard, to be truthful, but you might not be pleased with the results."

"Why? You're the telephone company."

Antonio offered a lengthy technical explanation. "If she's doing anything suspicious, she'll be using different SIM cards on cloned or stolen phones and getting rid of it after a single call. On top of that, removing the battery when the phone's not in use makes it untraceable. If, and it's a big if, she's using the same phone with different SIM cards we might be able to track it by its ID number. It'll be hidden among the other phones in use on the network, and it's like looking for a needle in a haystack of needles. All this being said, I'll have to pay a couple of guys on the inside, could be a day or so time wise, and I can't promise anything."

Matthew scoffed, "There's no problem with cost. Can't you track her cellphone?"

"There's no guarantee we'll find her calls even triangulating it with the cell towers. My boss was talking the other day and he said that in the near future we'll be able to track someone's location within a few feet and in seconds. We don't have that capability right now."

"How about getting her emails?"

"She just moved into town, so I'd imagine she's using the hotel's internet. We'll use the provider and I'll have a contact there who'll be able to get copies of her emails. Just so you know, I won't get anything if she's connecting to internet proxies."

Antonio's reply made Matthew mostly happy. "We'll find out if she is what she says she is. Work on those cell calls because I'm sure she'll be using a cellphone. Then her emails, phone records, and recordings of her calls. That should do it nicely."

Bruno looked meaningfully at his watch. "Are we finished?"

In the short time they were together, he had already demolished the bread and sopped up the olive oil and vinegar. Now he drained his glass, ready to leave.

"That's it for me," said Matthew, opting to leave his rather harsh-tasting wine unfinished. "When will the hotel phone be bugged?"

"I'll have it all put in place by tomorrow morning. Soon enough?"

"Soonest is best," said Matthew, pulling a white envelope from his inside pocket and sliding it across the table.

"How will I get the tapes to you?"

They agreed Antonio would deliver the recordings, and a machine to play them, to Matthew's hotel. If Matthew was out, he would leave the tapes at the front desk and pick up an envelope with any payments due.

Bruno turned to Matthew. "Ready?"

Not waiting for an acknowledgment, he slid out of the booth. "Do a good job," he grunted to Antonio as they did the ritual back slap and hug. He walked off without a backward glance.

Matthew smiled at Antonio, said, "*Ciao,*" and followed Bruno out of the door.

CHAPTER 11

*A real estate offer comes together,
and Sarah avoids problems.*

**Los Angeles, California
Wednesday, August 21**

Braking to a stop at the red light on Ventura Boulevard,
Marcus groaned aloud. His air conditioning had failed that
morning. With no time to visit a mechanic, his shirt was
already wet on the back. He leaned forward against the
gut-buster seatbelts to ease the stickiness, but it made little
difference. Putting his foot down but wary of motorcycle
traffic cops, he decided to go the scenic route over
Coldwater Canyon to Mulholland Drive to get to the 405
Freeway.

Cruising west, Marcus had the windows open and
KLOS blasting Zeppelin's "In My Time of Dying."
Prophetic, as it turned out. He gently nudged the
accelerator and the 302 V-8 engine in the '68 Mustang
coupe answered with a satisfactory growl as he pulled
forward. Now he was second in line and should make the
green. He hated people moving into the intersection at the
last second, leaving him stuck at another red light.

The Mustang was now over twenty-five years old, the
Columbo of cars, battered but having performance where

it counts. The new exterior standard green paint job
attracted admiring looks but the interior left something
to be desired. Conversations with occasional passengers
consisted of apologies for the uncomfortable seats, a
missing door panel, and the worn carpet. Otherwise, the
body was straight, the gauges worked, and everything
mechanical had been rebuilt. The rebored engine gave it
some serious bite when needed, and a decent set of rims
and radials set off the exterior look. Best of all, the blinkers
in the louvered hood worked, giving Marcus an obscene
amount of pleasure; he didn't know why.

"Ara and Weiner, eh?" As he turned down the radio,
Marcus spoke out loud in disbelief as he reflected on the
meeting with Jamal, Jayden, and Dewayne a few minutes
before. They had gone into a Studio City real estate office
telling an agent they wished to buy Studio Z, a recording
studio in Beverly Hills. As an expert in commercial
property, Marcus had been brought in to represent them
and steer the transaction to a satisfactory conclusion.

During the meeting, they established the owners of
the Studio Z, Ara Danielian and Ben Weiner, were asking
ten million dollars for the purchase of the studio and the
building it occupied. They scoffed when he mentioned
Ara's nickname of Iron Arms and his connections of a
dubious nature. They weren't worried and told him they
had connections in the black community should there be
problems. He kept an open mind as to whether these three
young black men had the ten million dollars necessary
to buy the studio. After all, they hardly looked like multi-
millionaire businessmen.

To avoid wasting everyone's time, he had politely
demanded proof they had the funds to close the deal.
It was the mention of Whitlock, Katz, and Dixon who

Marcus knew to be high-powered representatives to the entertainment world that convinced him these budding entrepreneurs were serious. Now he was on his way to meet their loan broker, Sarah, in Santa Monica, where the transaction would be supervised by the partner, Dixon. He anticipated the meeting would provide him with the necessary written verification he could present to Ara.

He picked up his car phone and called his partner, Sharron.

"Marcus, I'm starving, how about lunch?"

"Not now. Gotta pen? Great. Call the title company and have them fax you copies of all the docs for Studio Z recording studios in Beverly Hills. The business, the building, the whole schmear. We'll need comparable sales records too. Did you get that?" She repeated his instructions back to him.

"Good," Marcus said. "I'm on my way to West LA for a possible ten-million-dollar deal. See you later and keep your cellphone handy."

Sarah was fully prepared for her meeting with Dixon as she arrived at his offices but not ready to meet an angry Glenda hell-bent on revenge. The automatic entry door swung open, and she walked hesitantly into the lobby, carrying a slim alligator briefcase containing a copy of the documents signed by Leon.

She announced herself to the receptionist and waited, on edge, impatient to move somewhere less exposed, fully expecting retribution to appear at any moment. The receptionist made a telephone call, stood up, and said pleasantly, "Follow me and I'll take you to a conference room for your meeting with Dixon."

The maze of cubicles she'd last seen the night of the burglary looked different in daylight. It was noisy for a start and full of people with headsets looking at computer screens, engaged in conversations with invisible customers. Offices on either side seemed mostly unoccupied. The receptionist stopped and stood at an open door, her arm extending an invitation to enter.

As Sarah walked towards the door she caught a glimpse of a woman's profile in an office on the opposite side of the cubicles. In that split-second, Sarah thought, *Oh God, that looks like Glenda. She looks upset. Who's she with? She mentioned HR.* The woman took a tissue from her purse to blow her nose. *Shit. That's her all right. Now what?*

"Please take a seat. He's running a little late and will be with you shortly." Masking her stress, Sarah smiled at the receptionist and took a seat at the table making sure she was facing away from Glenda.

"I'm also expecting a real estate guy by the name of Marcus to join us. He should be arriving any minute. Perhaps you could show him in here too?"

"Yes, Mr. Dixon mentioned he was expecting you both."

The receptionist gave a parting smile, closed the door, and left Sarah alone.

Glenda was bewildered at the turn of events. Here was Nancy Braithwaite, one of her best friends and the firm's head of human resources, lecturing her. She only half listened as Nancy droned on, finishing with, "This came from Dixon. He wants you to take a month off with half pay, but you can keep your full benefit package."

"But why?"

Nancy interrupted her. "Look, I've already explained it once. You know why. He's not happy you gave away an invitation to Star's party to someone not employed by this firm. That's frowned on but that same person had the audacity to spread disparaging rumors about Dixon to another guest. The rumors could only have come from you. It was Dixon who overheard the conversation. He's lost confidence in you and wants you to take time to consider your future with the company."

She leaned forward, showing empathy. "Personally," she continued, "I'd take the time off and come back refreshed and ready to take up where you left off." She jerked her head towards the upstairs. "Dixon's been in a funny mood these past few days."

"So, I'm not fired?"

"No. Only suspended. He's adamant that you are not fired. Too much time left on your contract is my guess. He probably wants to avoid a big pay out. My advice is not to be tempted to come around and we'll see you back here in a month. I won't suspend your security pass, it's too much trouble to get it reinstated. Now, if there's nothing in your office you need?" Nancy looked at her across the desk.

"Just my keys in my desk. You know, this almost feels like a reward more than a punishment. I don't understand it. At the same time, a month off sounds good right now, even on half pay."

On the other side of the offices, Sarah's nerves were taut. *Christ, I hope she can't see me. Can't afford a scene with her in front of Dixon. That would really queer our pitch.* She sighed. *I'll just have to be patient and sit this out.* She swung round in her chair and gazed at the artwork on the walls thinking over the events of the past few days. *We're going to have to be ready to react and adjust. Matthew is a threat and now there's Glenda. Does it ever end?*

She checked the time, *Where's that broker and where's Dixon? They're late. Let's hurry up and get this going.*

Her thoughts were interrupted by the receptionist ushering Marcus into the office.

"And you would be Sarah, I presume," he advanced, reaching out a beefy hand which she shook, saying, "Yes, pleased to meet you. You must be Marcus."

"Correct." His London accent sounded strong to her ear. He sat down in one of the chairs opposite her and smiled. "Do you have the letter?"

"Yes. We're waiting for Dixon, he's a partner in this company." She checked the time. "He seems to be running late."

Marcus made no reply, he was busy swinging around in the plush leather chair that both swivelled and reclined. Unfortunately, and unexpectedly, the chair reclined suddenly, almost spilling him onto the floor. Sarah tried to conceal her amusement as his arms and legs flailed frantically while regaining his balance, but Marcus grinned, granting her permission to laugh out loud. They both turned serious as the door swung open and Dixon walked in the room.

Sarah hadn't quite known what to expect of Dixon. He was in bed with a notorious drug and arms smuggler, and this led her to expect a burly thug type. Quite the contrary. He dressed like many financial people of that era: Armani suit, yellow suspenders, matching silk tie, white collar on blue striped shirt, gold cufflinks, and expensive highly polished shoes. *Looks younger than his late forties, she thought. Tall too, maybe six feet, and handsome with it. Overall, a clean-cut guy.*

Introductions and business cards exchanged, Dixon took control of the meeting. He picked up and examined Marcus's business card.

"You're the real estate broker in this deal?" He gave Marcus a penetrating stare.

The answer came with confidence. "Correct. I understand you have the proof that your clients," a nod to Sarah, "have the money to buy Studio Z together with its real estate. The sellers are influential, and I don't want to bring unqualified buyers to the table."

Sarah pushed her copy of the signed letter of intent across the desk to Dixon. He shuffled the papers together and put them to one side.

"Our client buys, sells, and finances real estate on a regular basis. We have a procedure for international funding that ensures a smooth passage for all concerned." He handed Marcus a letter. "This outlines the financial commitment you need to negotiate the Studio Z deal. I've signed it as a partner of the company. The transaction will be conducted through our escrow sales office and that is non-negotiable. We are a worldwide corporation who represent many multi-million-dollar entertainment celebrities. When we put our name on a document, we're putting our considerable reputation on the line. OK?"

Marcus took the letter. "Excuse me. I'll just give this a quick look over." The room was silent while he carefully finished examining the documents.

The speaker phone in the center of the table rang. With a gesture of disgust and an "Excuse me," Dixon picked up the handset, listened for a few moments, and said, "Let's have as little fuss as possible. I'm very busy but tell Glenda I'll try and see her after I'm through here." He put the handset back on its cradle.

Sarah was dismayed at Dixon's phone conversation. *It's going to get ugly if I bump into her.*

Meanwhile, Dixon was moving on. "Marcus, go structure the deal and everyone will be satisfied. Now, I don't want to be rude, but I'd like a word with Sarah about the loan, would you excuse us?" He motioned to Sarah to sit down, then stood up to shake hands and dismiss Marcus.

After Marcus left the conference room, Dixon stroked his chin and looked at her thoughtfully. His first comment took Sarah's breath away.

"I've seen you before."

She kept her nerve. "I doubt it. I've only just arrived in town."

"Were you at Star's party by any chance? I think that's where I saw you."

"Yes, I was there. An invitation came out of the blue."

"Ah, now I remember. It was Glenda who gave you the ticket. Yes. Very much against company policy, I'm afraid. How did you come to meet her?"

Sarah shifted uncomfortably in her chair. *This is going tits up,* she thought.

"I'm staying around the corner and the coffee shop over the road was convenient. I met Glenda there completely by chance, we went to a bar, had a drink or two, and she offered me the invitation. I wasn't going to turn down that opportunity."

"OK. And now you're here with an offer on Studio Z. Quite a coincidence."

Sarah, her insides in turmoil but outwardly calm, answered, "Yes, well the buyers are clients of Marcus. I'm handling the financing through Leon."

Dixon was cordial but guarded. "Yes, Leon told me about you. He mentioned Kirov being your sponsor. How did that come about? He's pretty careful who gets in the front door."

Dixon sat with his arms folded on his desk, his head cocked to one side, making it clear he expected a response to his statement.

Sarah studied him for a few moments, her face expressionless, looking him directly in the eyes, challenging him.

"Not careful enough, apparently."

"You mean about him going missing?" Dixon showed his interest, leaning forward in his chair.

"Exactly. No one seems to know where he is, certainly not me."

"You've no idea, eh? How did you happen to meet him?"

Using her first line of defense, she said, "My parents died young and left me a considerable fortune. I've been bumming around, mostly Europe, lots of Med. That's how I met Kirov," she said blandly. "Me and a friend were walking in Cannes and bumped into him. He liked the look of my friend and invited her to his house in Antibes. She would only go if I went along. I remember it only because it was Valentine's Day."

"Is your friend around? Maybe she knows where he is."

"Hardly. He had too many women around for her taste, so she never went back. She left for Barcelona a couple of days later and I think she's in Australia right now."

"What about you?"

"What about me? Oh, I see what you mean." She thought for a few moments. "I guess overall I went there a half dozen times or so. He liked me but it wasn't physical, just a casual friendship. There were always a ton of people at his parties. A couple of weeks later, I had an obligation in Rome and that was the last time I saw him."

Dixon decided to test her. "I'd like you to consider using my banking facilities. Perhaps we could set up an account for your commissions?"

Sarah chose her words carefully. "I'll stick with my bank in Zurich for now. They're most accommodating and we have a long-term relationship." She looked at Dixon and said sweetly, "You see, Mum and Dad banked there, and I have unlimited credit. Any funds from the deal will be deposited in my personal spending account."

"And where is that?"

"D & R Bankengruppe. They're in Zurich. You'll be notified in due course of the account numbers."

After her rebuff, his mood seemed to change, the questions grew shorter and more pointed, the tone almost accusatory.

"Tell me about your family. You say your parents passed away?"

"Yep. Big accident. Car crash. Both dead, I'm afraid." She went on the offense and gave a wry smile. "Look, Mr. Dixon, meeting you is the culmination of a series of lucky circumstances. I can't explain it, I can just take advantage and keep rolling the dice. Making connections and meeting Dewayne was a perfect example of how I put people together. Sometimes it makes me money, mostly, it's a favor."

Dixon was wary. "With Kirov missing, you can understand our reasons to be doubtful. You turn up out of the blue with this deal claiming his recommendation yet nobody else seems to know you. Then you meet and socialize with one of my key employees who wasn't aware you were about to do business with us. You see, government agencies are always trying to access our clients' financials and frankly it all looks too coincidental. You could be a plant."

Sarah went on the attack. "You're wrong in your assessment of the situation. First, Kirov did not recommend me. He made a general statement mentioning Leon might be able to help me finance any future deals I came across. Second, I only came up with the deal after I used Glenda's invitation to attend the party. That's where I met my prospect. I didn't know if I could help him but offered to make a couple of calls. That's the reason I'm here today."

"From my perspective it's a coincidence too far." Dixon was blunt.

"Then don't do the deal," she said pointedly, calling his bluff and reaching down for her purse and briefcase.

Taken aback by her brazen approach and with visions of both Leon and Ara's wrath if he blew the deal, Dixon relented. He rose to his feet to dismiss her, saying curtly, "OK, don't be so hasty. I guess that's all for now. Get the deal done and let's make some money."

Sarah said, "now that's out of the way, here's the loan documents that Leon gave us to complete. Perhaps you can have your escrow officer hold on to them until I call and let them know we have a deal with Ara. It will save some time and, from what I understand, it's purely a formality from Leon's standpoint."

Dixon was short and to the point. "I'm glad you're so confident on making the deal with Ara. I'll give these to Francine, our escrow officer. She'll be waiting on your call."

As they stood to make their departure, she saw the office occupied by her former friend was empty. *Where the hell has she gone?* Despite Dixon being aware of the invitation fiasco, Sarah remained eager to avoid any confrontation.

Glenda had returned to her upstairs office to retrieve her keys. Arriving back on the ground floor, she met up with Nancy and together they made their way to the exit. She'd given up on meeting Dixon. As they turned into the general office area, maybe fifty feet ahead of them, Glenda saw him, accompanied by a woman, about to enter the lobby. *Is that Sarah?* She frowned and increased her pace a little. *From the back it looks like her. No. It can't be, surely not. And with Dixon? God, it would be great if it was her, I'd clean her clock.* As Dixon and the woman disappeared from view, she thought, *Dream on. It can't be.* She slowed down and allowed Nancy to catch up.

Sarah had been unaware Glenda was in hot pursuit until she turned the corner into the lobby and caught a glimpse from the corner of her eye, recognizing her instantly. Keeping her cool, she walked brazenly alongside Dixon to the exit where they shook hands and he wished her luck.

Sarah walked quickly along Wilshire Boulevard and turned the corner onto a nearby street. She saw no sign of being followed and relaxed her vigilance a little on her way back to her hotel. The cool breeze off the ocean helped cleanse her mind of Dixon and Glenda, for the time being at least.

As they left the café, Matthew turned to Bruno, "Let's see if Sarah's around. It's only around the corner. We can drop by 20th and Wilshire; she's doing a deal with Dixon and could be there. Then we can go by her hotel. It's a hell of a long shot, I know, but we're in the neighborhood anyway and maybe we'll get lucky."

They cruised by both buildings but there was no sign of Sarah.

"There wasn't much of a chance, but you never know. It was worth a try, now let's go pick up my car."

Bruno waited at the traffic light to turn onto Wilshire when Matthew said, "Hold up. That may be her. Go around the block."

After her near miss with Glenda, Sarah was nearing her hotel when she sensed something wasn't right.

Her first thought was, *Did I miss Glenda following me?*

She couldn't figure it out until she saw the black Cadillac turn at the traffic light and drive away from her. The dark tint stopped her seeing the occupants but the hair on her arms stood to attention. She knew, just knew, that they had an interest in her. The rest of the walk back to her hotel was a nervous one, every moment she expected the Cadillac to reappear. She reached the hotel entrance and looked back just in time to see it cruise past.

God Almighty, if it's not Glenda, it's Matthew. That was him for sure.

She made for the safety of her room, locked the door, and sat on the end of her bed, nursing the Sig P229, not expecting trouble but prepared for it all the same.

Meanwhile, Dixon returned to his office where he instructed his secretary to refuse any meeting with Glenda. Then he emailed Leon.

Dixon: "I don't know what to think. It's up to you to make the decision here. There's nothing overtly wrong but don't you think her timing is suspicious?"

The reply from Leon came almost immediately. "I thought so too at first, my default reaction, but I figure it's not likely a sting. The Feds have much bigger fish to fry."

Dixon: "I confirmed today that I saw her at our party at Star's place. I must say she had a plausible explanation for everything."

Leon: "You're convinced she's OK then?"

Dixon: "From what I've seen and heard, yes. I've moved ahead, sending the broker on his way with the letter. It's a sweet deal, maybe too sweet. Are you sure you want to move forward?"

Leon: "No, I'm not one-hundred-percent sure, but it's worth the risk. This deal alleviates any problems from the authorities here in Cayman. I've got Matthew keeping watch on her and, believe me, at the slightest sign of a problem, Sarah and her mates will wind up filling a hole in the desert."

Monitoring the exchange from the Beverly Wilshire, Joshua grimaced when he saw the emails between Leon and Dixon. He used an internet relay chat to message Sarah.

"Everything going according to plan but they're nervous. Watch your back for Matthew."

Bruno drove Matthew back to Van Nuys to pick up his car. The return trip back to Santa Monica proved to be a nightmare, nose-to-tail traffic all the way, an almost two-hour trip. At the hotel, he poured himself a beer and dialed Leon. There was no answer, so he left a voicemail. Flopping down on the bed, feeling dog tired, he practiced that old soldier's knack of falling asleep instantly.

———

CHAPTER 12

*Francine reveals secrets and
Leon comes to town.*

**Los Angeles, California
Thursday, August 22–Wednesday, August 28**

The following morning, Matthew had still not heard from Leon, so he decided to check out the truck company he had been asked to investigate. He used the Thomas Guide maps to find his way to and from Commerce and later that evening again called Leon from the Mirabelle.

"Over the past couple of days, I left voicemails but got no return calls. Where have you been?"

Leon's reply was harsh, "None of your business. What about Sarah?"

"No activity as far as I could see. Vincent was very helpful in getting her hotel telephone bugged. The first batch of tapes are innocent enough, just calls about the deal with you. I think she's a solid citizen."

"We'll see. Dixon agrees with you. They met yesterday and he was impressed."

"I met up with Bruno's tech guy in West LA. We were just down the road from Dixon's offices so knowing she was in the area we took a drive-by. Caught sight of her walking into her hotel. We left her alone and went back to Vinnie's restaurant."

"The bugging devices at the hotel are most important. They might reveal something yet. Keep an eye on her because I'm willing to bet she's got at least one partner. Have you checked out that trucking company yet?"

"It's clean. It's a small operation with a yard and offices in a big industrial area with fucking miles of warehouses and rail lines. They're well located for easy access to a bunch of freeways. Henry Brown is recorded as the owner. I parked a little way down the street and watched for a while, but there was nothing going on. I expect the trucks were out doing deliveries."

"Good. Let me think about it. Nothing else then?"

"No, that's it. I'll call you if anything changes."

After days of monitoring her calls and doing some personal surveillance, Matthew learned Sarah lived very quietly. He reported back to Leon on her movements.

"No nightlife despite the multitude of possibilities here in Santa Monica. No boyfriend. Shops and eats out locally, usually on Montana, an expensive neighborhood. Walks a lot, doing sightseeing and shopping. The tapes recording her conversations are innocent enough and all about the Studio Z deal, same with emails. There were a couple of very flirty calls with Dewayne, but I think she's leading him on."

"Sounds almost too innocent. What about cellphone use?"

"I saw her using a cellphone and Antonio managed to trace it, don't ask me how. He gave me a list of numbers called, they were mostly to the trucking company or a cellphone listed with Dewayne. Several to a real estate office in Studio City and more to brokers here on the Westside. Nothing to be alarmed about."

"No sign of a partner?"

"No. None at all. The calls to the real estate offices made sense because she's been looking at some places in Westwood. Twenty-story jobs. Maybe she's looking for something more permanent than the hotel." Matthew sniffed, his nose was stuffy and runny. *Damn allergies*, he cursed to himself. "Hold on, I have to blow my nose."

Leon heard a loud sneeze followed by the honk of a nose being blown. Then Matthew continued. "Her hotel is a boutique job, expensive, very discreet, and she's just moved in. Perfectly placed for Dixon's offices. According to the latest tapes, she's waiting for a courier to deliver her copies of some legal papers."

"This all seems to confirm your thoughts that she's an upright citizen."

In his hotel room, Matthew shrugged. "I dunno. She busted me following her today. She was taking her time in an adventure type store, and I lost sight of her. Next thing we bump into each other. She smiles at me and says, 'You look familiar, have we met?' Took me right off guard, I can tell you. I denied everything, of course, but you know, it's not a bad thing. She must know where the money comes after meeting you through Kirov. She's acting accordingly. I think she's smart."

Leon was astounded at Matthew's thinking. "You think she knows we're suspicious and following her? You're contradicting yourself. One minute you're convinced she's the genuine thing and the next you're saying she's suspicious. Which is it?"

"It's just my instincts. She's behaving exactly how I expected her to behave except for her fronting me out today. She's not stupid. She told you she didn't care where the funds came from. That tells you she knows the funds are suspect. Didn't she say Kirov told her you're laundering cash in the telephone call? And what did you find out about her banking?"

"She told Dixon she banked at D & R Bankengruppe in Zurich for her commissions. We're looking into it now, but you know how the Swiss are about money, even with our connections. The fact that it's a private bank makes it even more difficult and takes time, probably too much time in this case, we only have a couple of days."

The line went quiet while Leon pondered the situation. "Just keep the light surveillance going. If you want help, I'm sure Bruno's available. I think I'll come to LA to supervise this deal personally. Stay in touch." He left Matthew holding a silent telephone.

Joshua and Sarah now limited communication to emergency-only status. They were confident Joshua was their ace in the hole and unknown to the opposition. Sarah was nervous while waiting for the deal to close. Once the action started, she was fine, but now her thoughts were dominated by the things that could go wrong. Most of all she was lonely. Her emotions swung from high to low, nothing in between; she was out of balance and knew it. Joshua's absence made her long for his company. Getting out looking for an apartment was good cover and took her mind away from negative thoughts.

Joshua maintained a schedule of monitoring Dixon's and Leon's computers. He concentrated on Grand Cayman business hours which ran three hours ahead of California time. It didn't take him long to see the actual running of Leon's bank was left to David, twin brother and closest confidante of Leon. Typically, Leon issued commands by email.

"Move one million dollars to Max."

David was connected to the bank's network, allowing the malware Joshua had installed to read everything on his computer in much the same way as he could read Leon's.

He's using a different computer to make the money transfers, Joshua reasoned. He had been unable to see, let alone hack, this other computer. *Whatever's on this other computer is gonna give us Leon's innermost secrets.*

He messaged Sarah, "We need to meet at the other place."

Sarah understood this to mean the Venice Apartments on Rose, in Venice, just south of Santa Monica, another of several alternative hotels and rooms they'd booked as a safety precaution.

At the hotel, Sarah and Joshua embraced, hugging each other hard to rid themselves of the stress they both felt.

"I've missed you," Joshua said as they pulled apart.

"Me too. I've been starved for company." Turning back to face him, her eyes were wet with tears. "It's not till now that I realize how lonely I am."

Joshua took her in his arms and whispered words of comfort in her ear. A short while later, they stepped back from one another, still holding hands, emotions running high, the atmosphere in the room electric. Joshua acted first, reluctantly loosening his hands from hers, saying, "We'd better not start anything we'll be sorry about. This deal is too important."

Sarah interrupted him with a knowing smile. "When it's over, can we resume this conversation?"

"Definitely. Yes." Joshua agreed, his eyes sparkling. The anticipation fueled a thrilling feeling, a glow in his heart that dissipated the hollowness occupying his stomach.

Sarah asked, "Do we have anything to drink here?" Adding casually, "Oh, and by the way, Matthew followed me today."

"Soft drinks in the fridge. You were followed?"

"Yes. I caught him right out too. I always go to the mall because that's the easiest place to shop and see a tail. He's good but it's hard for just one person to do the following, even disguised with different hats and jackets. At first, I never got a good look at him, but sensed he was there. You know, you get that feeling."

"How did you shake him?"

"This will blow your mind." She explained her daring tactic.

"Well, it's no surprise. We know they've been checking you out since Cayman and I saw him follow you from the airport. Are you carrying that piece I left in your room?"

She opened her purse and showed him the Sig nestled in a side pocket.

"Good. Make sure you've always got a weapon handy. We'll have to watch out for another tail because they may replace Matthew. I'll have to help out on watching Dixon's building, you're too exposed. There's a lot to discuss and not much time. Let's get started." He sat down at his computer, and she sat alongside as he typed in his password.

"I've been monitoring Leon and his brother David's computer. Here's the picture." He went on to analyze their options, moves, and counter moves.

"It's a fluid situation and we must be able to adapt and react as circumstances present themselves. For instance, David is using a different computer for money transfers. I've got a solution, but it's drastic."

Friday, August 23

Marcus sat facing Francine, a statuesque blonde, and noted the name plate on her desk identifying her as head of Dixon's real estate escrow department. She created the contracts and legalese necessary for properties to be bought and sold. In California, these were known as escrow instructions. Her office was handily located next to Dixon's, not half as large or pretentious, but benefitting from large windows opening out to the same terrace. She was highly experienced, dependable and had prepared the Studio Z escrow instructions.

"It's nice to be doing business with you," he remarked as they greeted one another.

Francine hesitated. There had been a time when she and Marcus had a wild relationship, but it ended badly. Even so, their professional relationship survived, time healed, and they became friends again. She flashed a wide smile, a big attractive mouth with perfect white teeth, very Monroe.

"You're looking good. I can see why Dixon employed you," he remarked, giving her an appraising look.

She looked him in the eye. "I got this job on merit. Don't you forget it," she said severely. Then, leaning forward in her chair, she pushed her oversized breasts together until they almost popped out of her V-neck sweater.

"Having these didn't hurt the selection process." She laughed and relaxed. "Now sit there and be quiet. I've got to look at this other file first."

Marcus did as he was told while mulling over the events of the past couple of days. It had been a rush to get the contracts signed by all parties. A whirlwind of events where he dashed between Ara's offices, his home office, and Henry's trucking company negotiating the deal for the three brothers to buy Studio Z. Offers, counteroffers, even a counter-counter offer, the travel and the traffic made a tiresome deal more so because Marcus insisted on delivering the paperwork personally. Everyone bitched and complained about concessions while Marcus kept a cool head, a moderate tone of voice, and a pen ready for signatures.

He had delivered the sales contracts signed by both buyers and sellers to Dixon's office in the late afternoon of the previous day. Francine had worked her wizardry to produce the escrow instructions in record time, and Marcus had picked them up that morning. Ara signed his copies and Marcus left him gloating in anticipation of a hundred thousand simoleons hitting his account as soon as the buyers signed their escrow instructions.

Francine's voice brought Marcus abruptly back to the present. She was reviewing the folder containing the Studio Z transaction.

"This is a big show bizzy deal. Meet any stars yet?" she asked with a quick smile, stroking her hand across her face to brush away a stray hair.

"Not yet. I hope there's going to be good contacts in the future."

She seemed genuinely pleased for him. "Well, you'll get to see the inside of that world anyway, pretty exciting."

She continued to turn the pages in the thick folder of legal papers. Were signatures notarized where appropriate? Was each clause initialled? Were the instructions signed in the right places? With her administration skills, attention to detail, and the ability to focus, it was easy to see why she headed the department.

"Has Sarah dropped her escrow instructions off yet?" Marcus asked, trying not to look at Francine's vast cleavage, only partially succeeding and confident she knew it.

She didn't look up. "Meeting the buyers here in half an hour."

Marcus saw the time, "Damn. I can't hang around; I have another appointment as soon as you tell me Ara's instructions are correctly executed. I would have preferred to be here when the buyers sign their instructions and the earnest money changes hands."

Francine finished reading the file and looked up at him. "Ara's signatures are good and in all the right places. Drive carefully," She spoke to his back; he was already halfway out the door with a wave of acknowledgment. She laughed and shook her head in a mixture of humor and resignation. *He'll never change.*

Sarah entered Dixon's building on her way to the escrow offices, still apprehensive at the prospect of running into Glenda. An assistant appeared to guide her to the office, and it turned out her angst was in vain. A stray comment, made when passing two women in conversation, produced a huge smile on her face. Glenda was on a plane bound for Athens for a three-week vacation.

The sound of laughter coming from Francine's office came from Jayden, Dewayne, and Jamal who had arrived before her. She let out a huge sigh of relief upon being greeted with hugs and cheek kisses by all three brothers. Francine introduced herself and appeared to Sarah a thorough professional. Everyone shook hands and they got down to business.

Earlier that day, to cover the fees they'd agreed to pay to Ara and Leon, Dewayne arranged a wire transfer of funds to Francine's escrow account. While Sarah and the buyers sat in front of her, Francine turned to use a computer sitting on a table beside her desk. Sarah's eagle eye noticed the screen was missing the security shield designed to permit only the operator to view the screen contents. Francine pulled a sheet of paper showing rows of typed letters and numbers from beneath the keyboard.

My God. She's got a cheat sheet. How am I going to get ahold of that?

Sarah shifted her vantage point, standing up and walking over to examine a painting on the wall, commenting, "Nice office."

Francine seemed blissfully unaware that Sarah, from her new perspective, could see her computer screen. She started to type in her password and Sarah almost choked. The password setting showed the actual text and was not hidden by an asterisk.

Wow, someone up there's looking out for me. Glad I came prepared. A miniature camera sat under her blouse, nestled snugly in her bra, the lens cleverly concealed as a button. The shutter was activated by a lead that ran under her clothing and through a hole in her skirt pocket to a push button. There was no rhyme or reason for the last-minute decision to bring the camera. It was because she was going to be in Dixon's building and brought it "just in case."

Francine began entering the information from the cheat sheet to set up the wire transfers, tracking each number with her forefinger. She moved first across and then down the page, her lips moving in unison. Sarah captured it all in a series of photos.

When the wire transfers of monies to all parties was completed, Francine shuffled the paperwork into a neat pile on her desk.

"The accounts should balance by Monday, August 26. Just remember, a wire transfer cannot be recalled even though, technically, the money might not yet have arrived on the respective bank's books."

Jayden grumbled. "Let's hope that half a million bucks and a lot of hard work didn't go down the drain. It had better pay off." He wasn't feeling the joy yet, just the risk. The others were just as serious.

Sarah brought them back to reality. "Cheer up. Come on, you guys," she said, play fighting Jemal and Dewayne. "Francine will send your loan documents to Leon, just a formality really. She'll handle all the funds and coordinate the closing from here on out."

Twenty minutes later, Sarah stood with the brothers outside of the building.

"It's up to Marcus to arrange the rest of the contingencies with Ara, inspections, the financials, and the like. I'll focus on the loan. Call with any questions. You know how to get ahold of me. Dewayne has my cell number." With that, she shook hands and had a hug with each of them as they parted.

A short while later, using the phone booth at a local store, Sarah called Joshua. She was breathless with excitement.

"We should meet ASAP. The two hundred grand commission is in Zurich and, better than that. I've got shots of Leon's account numbers and passwords."

"Calm down. What?"

"I've got pics of Leon's passwords and account numbers. We should meet."

"Wow. Fabulous news. I won't ask how you came by that. Look, I can't meet right now, I'm right in the middle of Leon's stuff. In fact, we'd better not meet at all. You'll have to develop the photos yourself, send them to me, and then we'll chat."

In Beverly Hills, Joshua decided to confirm the two hundred thousand dollars in loan commissions had arrived at D & R Bankengruppe in Zurich. He picked up his Nokia to make the call only to find the battery had died and decided to let it fully charge. He made a call from his room telephone to the bank, something that would later put his life in danger. *They know about Sarah, but they don't know about me.* He justified the security breach as he waited a few minutes before Herr Richter at the bank confirmed the deposit.

Two hours later, Joshua received a fax of three JPEG images on his Nokia. He loaded the images onto his laptop and then magnified them to the extent they were blurred but still decipherable.

Fifteen minutes after sending the fax, Sarah used a payphone in another grocery store to call him.

"Did you get the photos I sent you?"

"You've captured a gem. Nice job. We now have details of Leon's clients and all their banking information. Looks like some are law abiding but it's mostly villains and he's laundering their cash." Joshua was very excited. "This makes it imperative we hack the dedicated line at Dixon's they're using to send their SWIFT instructions."

"SWIFT, I remember that from Belgium. Isn't it messages and codes between banks with instructions on money wire transfers?"

"Exactly. Your wonderful pictures included all the relevant bank codes. That will save me any problems with SWIFT authentication. It's not a particularly difficult hack but I'm going to need access to the right line, and I already know their lines are still analog and not digital.

"When are we going to do this?"

"What about tomorrow? I think it's a solo job; you've got Matthew to worry about."

"You sure? *I'm* supposed to be the burglar."

"Positive. I'll be dressed as a telephone repair man. Easy peasy. I'll have the Printer doctor up Glenda's cloned pass with my photo and ID instead of that New York woman. I'll use it to go through the parking garage entrance."

"What if the pass doesn't work?"

"Good question. I was hoping to avoid disabling the alarms, but I'll have my laptop in the worst-case scenario."

"I should get back to my hotel. I haven't seen any sign of Matthew, but he may be lurking somewhere. Good luck tomorrow. Let me know how it goes."

Sunday, August 25

It was Sunday, an ideal day for a break-in and, as he expected, the parking garage to Dixon's building was empty. The Printer had worked his magic, replacing the description on Glenda's security card with Joshua's photograph and description. For added cover, *Jake: AT&T Telephone Maintenance* was sewn on his overall pocket. Joshua tentatively swiped the card through the parking gate reader, there was a pause, and the gate rolled up. Giving a quick prayer of thanks, he ducked under the opening gate and made his way to a door marked MAINTENANCE.

The door was secured by a simple Yale lock which yielded to his picks in seconds. Stepping inside, he locked himself in and scanned the interior with his flashlight. He was inside a large storage room with floor-to-ceiling shelving dividing the space into selected areas, plumbing, electrical, and so on. A few moments of searching revealed an interior door at the end of one aisle that opened to a small room containing all the telephone equipment.

Joshua went to work. He searched for and found the terminals and junctions he needed. He used an external Sportster modem which he connected to his laptop's serial port. He then connected the modem to the telephone line using a cable with crocodile clips. When he was satisfied, he took a deep breath and connected to Leon's bank. He was quickly prompted for Francine's username and password which he entered. He waited, the hourglass symbol on his screen seemed to last forever and made him hope he wasn't being traced.

He checked the time; the seconds became minutes before the screen lit up. Suddenly account numbers appeared on the screen. He scrolled down to the first account number, outlined it, and requested access. Prompted to enter another username and password, he consulted a copy of Francine's password list and entered the matching information. Granted access, it didn't take long for Joshua to understand he had a sensational intelligence coup on his hands.

Leon's using a host of banks to launder billions of dollars internationally for individuals, known and unknown.

It took almost an hour for Joshua to finish making a copy of the files containing Leon's financial empire to his laptop. He exited the building by the way he entered, walked quickly to his car on a nearby side street, and drove back to the Beverly Wilshire Hotel.

In his hotel room, Joshua first made a copy of the files to a CD. Then he set about methodically combing through Leon's bank accounts. The downloads showed monies flowing from Leon's bank to his worldwide contacts in astonishing amounts. He identified the initials on the spreadsheets from Dixon's safe as accounts in Haiti, Zurich, and Monaco.

He pored over the results, eventually uncovering a correlation between money coming from accounts belonging to Nunzio and other accounts owned by Leon. He grinned when he saw there was a systematic and sophisticated skim of Nunzio's money by Leon who, in a joint venture with Dixon, used the skimmed money to invest in real estate.

Joshua timed his entrance into Sarah's hotel lobby perfectly. He passed her in the lobby, purposefully bumped into her, and spilled papers from the file he was carrying onto the floor. She was startled to see him.

She loudly protested, "Please be more careful and look where you're going next time."

Why is he here and not at the safe hotel? raced through her mind while falling into character, apologetic and fumbling, she tried to help him pick up his papers.

"I'm in room 238," he said quietly.

The encounter over, Sarah left the building and took a five-minute walk to a nearby grocery store to pick up some fruit. She returned to the hotel and went straight to room 238 and knocked on the door.

Joshua looked through the peephole in the door and saw Sarah was alone. He let her into the room, closed the door behind her, and uncocked his gun.

They embraced. Joshua kissed her firmly but quickly on the mouth, pulled away, and asked, "What are we like for time?"

"Not enough, I'm afraid. I'm nervous being out of the hotel room for too long. I like them to think they know where I am."

"Come and look at this."

Joshua opened his laptop, plugged in a device, and Sarah watched an image of his computer screen projected against the hotel room wall. Using a power point presentation and a laser pointer, he showed Leon sitting in the middle of a web of bank accounts like a big fat spider.

He said quietly, "It's going to take an accountant to sort all of this information out."

"What's Leon doing?"

Joshua demonstrated the way Leon had taken almost ten million dollars from Nunzio over the last year.

"That's only one year's record. I was able to go back and now have five years' records. I don't know how long he's been Nunzio's key guy, but I'd bet we're looking at big numbers over time. We're already at ten million for last year alone. Maybe as much as fifty or even one hundred million overall."

Sarah sat looking at the illustrations on the wall. She was flabbergasted.

"Look at these two accounts." Joshua used the laser to point out two accounts. "These are just two of the accounts he uses to transfer money to Dixon. One account has twenty million dollars recently deposited in Leon's name. Now follow the flow of money carefully." He used the laser to show the money moving around different accounts. "It's obvious this money has been embezzled from Nunzio. Leon's using it for the loan on Studio Z."

Using the laser pointer again, he said, "Here's another account with ten million dollars that's been laundered. The difference is this money hasn't been stolen and Nunzio is probably planning some kind of investment."

Sarah remarked, "Wasn't there an email somewhere that mentioned buying a company at the airport? That might account for the ten million."

"I don't recall. To recap then, Leon's lending twenty million to the three brothers to buy the recording studio. To accomplish that, Leon's using funds he's embezzled. Nunzio doesn't know it yet, but his money is being used to buy the studio he's selling. They must have a bent appraiser on the books for these loans to pass any scrutiny. The purchase price on the studio and building is ten million and the buyers are keeping ten million for reserves. That means a twenty-million-dollar appraisal. No way, unless you own the bank which, of course, Leon does. If this comes out, and it will, Dixon and Leon are going to end up in a hole somewhere."

Sarah was downcast. "Maybe you should have hacked the money while you had the chance."

"You'll see the reason I didn't in a moment." He advanced the slide saying, "Here's the interesting part."

"Wow." Sarah was impressed with Joshua's analysis. "That's daring. Nunzio will have a shit fit. Isn't it interesting that Ara has done business with Dixon for years. You'd think he'd be suspicious of Leon loaning money on a deal that Nunzio already owns."

"Leon certainly has *chutzpah* but then again Nunzio isn't his only client, and the account is not one to which he has access. Why should Ara be suspicious? Ready for the best part?"

"Haven't you already covered that?"

Joshua said smugly, "No, I said 'interesting' part. This is the best part. Look." Joshua advanced the next slide. It was an action plan for Joshua and Sarah and detailed their steps on the yellow brick road to a huge payoff.

"Here's what I think we should do." He went down the list point by point.

Sarah shook her head in admiration at the audacity. Her only comment, "It'll require luck and good timing, but it's doable."

Their roles planned; it was time to go. Embracing fervently, they said their goodbyes, reluctant to separate. He opened the door to check the corridor was clear and ushered her out of his room. He waited, watching the corridor until she went in her door, three rooms down. He heard her deadbolt lock click and with a final corridor check he closed his own door.

Tuesday, August 27

The day before the studio deal was due to close, a deposit of twenty million dollars was wired into Dixon's trust fund from one of Leon's accounts. This was followed by a second deposit of ten million dollars from another account.

Francine checked the paperwork once more. *The twenty million is the Studio Z deal. He wants me to keep this second ten million in the trust account. Something about Nunzio buying a business at Whitman airport.*

"That's there, and that's that, good," she muttered to herself as she riffled through the papers. She finished. *All there. Just the recording now.* She gathered up the deeds for hand delivery to the County Recorder's Office where Ben Weiner had wangled a special recording for the next day, Wednesday.

The next event that day saw Leon fly into Los Angeles on an evening flight to personally supervise the Studio Z funding from Dixon's office. He knew the money had already been wired into Dixon's trust fund but was vigilant for any mischief. His concerns lessened slightly when he reviewed Sarah's behaviors over the past few days. Bugging her phone revealed nothing of consequence. Losing Matthew's surveillance a couple of times was no big deal, Matthew himself admitting he hadn't wanted to get too close. The loan fees had passed through as promised.

I'm small fry when it comes to drug dealing. The Feds aren't going to spend a million to try and catch me.

It was his intuition. In the same way Sarah could smell a tail, Leon thought he could smell a threat. The fact that she socialized with Kirov told him she was not the innocent she would have him believe. She kept dangerous company, but Matthew, who listened to the tapes and watched her, was still of the opinion she was new in town, innocent, and exploiting an opportunity.

Leon was still anxious when he called Matthew after settling into his suite at the Breakers Hotel in Santa Monica. "I want you and Bruno to follow Sarah tomorrow. If there's any shenanigans it will be when the money is at close of escrow. If you want me, I'll be there."

"What do you mean? What are you expecting?" asked Matthew.

"I don't know, do I?" snapped Leon. "The money is exchanged tomorrow. I think that's when she'll likely attempt to fuck me and disappear. Stick to her like shit to a blanket. Got it?"

Matthew grunted in the affirmative and ended the call.

CHAPTER 13

Celebration time for some.

**Los Angeles, California
Wednesday, August 28**

The week before that Wednesday had been a busy one
for buyers, sellers, and brokers, respectively. Finally, all
contingencies having been met, Wednesday dawned, the
day the loan would fund and the deal close. The sellers
would have their ten million dollars, less fees, charges,
and commissions. The buyers would own the building and
Studio Z, with ten million dollars in reserves, minus fees
and charges.

It was hot and they were nervous. At Henry's house,
where they were sleeping over, the knowledge they were
risking all made sleep hard to come by for his sons.
Until midnight, they'd occupied time together, playing
video games and monopoly until gradually, with eyelids
drooping, Jamal first, then Henry, went to bed. By three
in the morning, they were all in bed, tossing and turning
on hot sheets, endless possibilities flowing through their
respective minds. In many ways they were like kids waiting
for Santa except they were all out of cookies and milk.

The day began with a huge Henry's trucker-style
fried breakfast, chicken fried steak, and corn beef hash

omelettes. The *chili verde* dressing was a nice extra touch. The conversation was animated, the food dealt with quickly. Their several trips to the studios had allowed them to sharpen their construction and alteration budgets. The last couple of days spent fleshing out their business plan proved they were ready to hit the ground running. The three sons clinked coffee mugs with Henry who toasted, "Success!" Breakfast over, they went to Henry's Trucking in Commerce, settled down, and waited for destiny to call.

Henry was their rock, sitting in his office, reviewing some papers, and smoking his pipe. He watched as his three sons fidgeted. They were up, walking around, then they sat down, then up again. They came into his office several times on some pretext or another, and he would chat to them in a calming tone.

Got ants in their pants, Henry chuckled to himself softly. "Hey," he called over to Jayden, "what time is Sarah arriving again?"

"She said she'd be here just before the deal recorded."

"When this deal closes, I want that girl on the payroll. She knows Roscoe's and everyone knows that's good eating."

In the Danielian residence, Ara sat down to breakfast. A large carafe of freshly brewed coffee stood within reach, ready to top up his half-empty cup. The smoking jacket was a gem from the 1920s. Bright yellow with a wide red silk collar. Red silk cuffs on the forearm-length sleeves, and the tops of the waist-high front pockets were augmented by a red sash. The yellow was tempered with sepia-colored birds and animals in hunt scenes. Truth be told, he looked like a pimp. An elegant pimp maybe, but a pimp, nonetheless.

He paid little attention to the television playing CNN with the sound off, the ticker news tape style in text format at the bottom of the picture relaying the latest bad news. The Wall Street Journal sat neatly folded by his elbow, unread. His concerns were only about the two deals, Studio Z and Whitman Airport.

He was somewhat nostalgic about moving on from Studio Z but excited about the Whitman deal with Nunzio as a silent partner. Ara was scheduled to arrive at Studio Z later that morning where he would wait for Dixon's phone call confirming the funds had arrived. In the meantime, he opened his newspaper and busied himself looking through the headlines.

Marcus started his day with a drive down to Du-pars restaurant on Ventura Boulevard just east of Laurel Canyon in Studio City. He waited for Sharron to arrive and passed the time reading the menu and sipping his coffee. He'd made up his mind to order the house specialty when Sharron walked in the door. Her appearance was especially fetching this morning, showing off her tanned legs and firm brown arms in a blue, sleeveless, figure-hugging, knee-length dress. Sliding into the booth opposite him with a bright smile lighting up her face, she said, "Good morning, sunshine. Today's the day."

Marcus pondered. "It's an odd deal all the way around. Then again, what do we care, we're making nearly half a million on the deal. Let's eat up and get back to the office to wait for the deed recording."

Sarah started her day worrying about Joshua and this next break-in. She had argued with him right up to the last minute, pointing out she was the experienced one in these highly dangerous encounters while he was the behind-the-scenes guy, the computer whiz. It made more sense to play to their strengths. He had countered that Matthew was watching her and not him, and this was a daylight job where she might be recognized. Most of all, the job required his computer skills.

"Believe me, I don't want to go, but it's time to get my feet wet."

After reluctantly giving in, she readied herself to leave the hotel as soon as possible after the deal closed, making sure there were no odds and ends to be cleared up.

In all the households affected by the Studio Z transaction, eyes never strayed far from the time that seemingly dragged by. Ara frequently checked his Vacheron Constantin. At Henry's Trucking, the clock in the office chimed every fifteen minutes, adding an edge to the proceedings. Marcus and Sharron, despite their intense conversation about a property listing, continually glanced at the time. Sarah was never far away from her watch, and Joshua, his game face on, watched cartoons on TV. It was his big day. He'd slept well, eaten a hearty breakfast, and planned to leave for Dixon's building shortly.

Dixon stood and welcomed Leon into his office as a friend, partner, and co-creator of their criminal enterprise.

"Leon, I'm surprised you came. Is there a problem with the Studio Z deal?"

"No, but as you know, Kirov hasn't surfaced, and I wouldn't normally do this deal but for this upcoming audit. Sarah remains an unknown factor. I'll believe all is well when everyone has the money they should have. Then I'll call the dogs off."

"The deal is about to record so your timing is good. When we get notification from the recorder's office, the money changes hands via wire. We'll get an acknowledgment the money has been delivered to all the banks in question."

At eleven that morning, Francine received notice that the deeds had been recorded. After accounting for escrow costs and commissions, she balanced the books by wiring the appropriate amounts to ATJ Enterprises, a holding company buying Studio Z and to Ara as the seller. She also wired Sarah's account at D & R Bankengruppe her share of the loan commission. She then called the principals in the transaction, Ara, Marcus, and Sarah, to let them know the deal had closed and also sent all the principals an email confirmation.

She walked into Dixon's office where he and Leon were enjoying coffee. "Studio Z is done and recorded, and the funds paid out," she informed them while handing Leon a copy of the closing statement. Leon carefully studied the document, a huge smile lighting up his face when he finished.

"Good job. Thank you."

Francine said to Dixon, "I called Ara to let him know we've recorded. I also sent him an email. Do you want to talk to him further?"

"Yes, I should talk to him myself, maybe later. A sweet deal, you did a good job. Put the file over here." He gestured towards a wooden tray on his desk. "Yeah, on top. That's it."

"I'm gone for the day," Francine said.

"See you tomorrow." Dixon waited until Francine closed his office door. Turning to Leon, he said, "See, I told you there was no problem. We don't want the wrong sort of attention, the staff putting a face to a name on a document for instance. I wish you'd stayed in the Caymans."

"That's easy for you to say, your share is just five million. I've got fifteen million dollars at risk," retorted Leon. "I was wrong about Sarah. OK? Now we're done, let me get out of your hair and thanks for accommodating me. I'm at the Breakers Hotel for a couple more days and then back to Cayman. Tomorrow, I may visit Studio Z to see our new investment." He rose and stuck out his hand to Dixon, who shook it vigorously. "Everything good?"

"Yes, perfect," said Dixon. "We're in great shape."

To Ara, Studio Z was just another deal. Sure, it had brought quite a few stars and starlets his way, but overall, he'd rather be running his restaurants and socializing. The studios and the musicians tended to be a difficult lot with the drugs being just one complication. The airport trucking company proposition intrigued him. He pulled the file towards him to check the penciled numbers one more time.

Marcus and Sharron sat in the Van Nuys office drinking coffee and swapping war stories when the phone rang. Marcus picked it up.

"Yes, how are you? Good."

There was a pause as he listened intently. He punched the air, a big grin spread over his face, but his voice was calm as he repeated what he heard.

"Studio Z closed, and our commission hits the bank tomorrow. Thank you, Francine. Yes, soon."

He put the phone down and said to Sharron, "We just made about a quarter million dollars apiece. We'll pay Harry his share, then let's go to Hawaii."

"I'm there," agreed Sharron enthusiastically.

Sarah sat with Henry and his sons, waiting. Her cellphone rang. Henry turned the television off, and the room went silent. It rang a second time. Everyone looked at her expectantly, the atmosphere almost explosive with anticipation. Smiling, the center of attention, Sarah looked at the time, just after eleven. The phone rang a third time.

"For fuck's sake, answer the phone!" Jayden and Jemal shouted in unison.

"Hello."

"Sarah, this is Francine. Congratulations. Your clients now own Studio Z. The closing statements will be available tomorrow."

"Yes, are you going to be in the office for a while? Maybe I could stop by, there's some other business I have in mind. No. I completely understand. No problem. When are you back in your office? Tomorrow? OK, I'll be in touch. Bye."

Sarah turned to the room and said, "You are now proud owners of Studio Z studios and have a twenty-million-dollar debt to pay off."

Jayden stood up yelling, 'You mean it worked? We got the loan, and we own the building and the studios?"

Sarah grinned. "Like I said, the deed is recorded, and the money has transferred to your MTJ company. You can transfer it to Blag Records when you're ready. Your first payment on the loan will come in year four. How about them apples?"

The scene at Henry's Trucking became bedlam. Jayden, Jamal, and Dewayne, naturally elated, jumping up and down, rapped nonsensical words nobody could understand. Henry walked around, a big grin on his face, immensely proud of his sons. When things finally calmed down, Henry and his sons decided to go to Studio Z. Sarah put on a happy face but worried about Joshua being in harm's way. She made her apologies, excused herself on the pretext of another appointment, and said she would drop by the studio later that day.

Once in the car, she used a cloned cellphone and texted the words "CLOSED" to Joshua before removing the SIM chip and battery and throwing the phone into a nearby vacant lot. He was in the coffee shop occupying the seat Sarah had used to watch Dixon's offices. The text meant the Studio Z commissions should be in the Swiss account. It also meant that Francine was away from the building.

The text prompted Joshua to leave the café and move his van from the meter on a side street to a spot outside of Dixon's building immediately in front of a Lincoln limousine. This time he'd gone all out. The van was rented, and the Printer had taken a mere hour to turn it into a bogus AT&T company vehicle. He turned off the engine with butterflies in the pit of his stomach. The last assignment had been a nice quiet Sunday job. This was more dangerous, being in the middle of a working day, with Leon and Dixon known to be in the building. His nervousness was understandable, his upcoming hack might alert them in some way.

Conquering his fears and confident of his disguise as "Jake," a telephone repairman, he took two bright orange traffic cones and, with a friendly smile and a nod to the waiting driver of the Lincoln, marked out his van's parking space. Satisfied, but a little jumpy, he walked to the parking gate, swiped the cloned card through the reader, and the gate rumbled open.

He made his way to the telephone equipment room, opened the panel, found the right connections, and tapped into Dixon's wire transfer line using the same methods he had used on his previous visit. Prompted for identification, he entered Francine's username and password. On his screen he selected the first in a list of Leon's accounts and, courtesy of Francine's password cheat sheet, gained access. Having the correct bank codes allowed him to transfer eighty million dollars from these accounts to a bank in Jersey, U.K. controlled by Joshua using a P.O. box address. The funds were then automatically transferred to a blind trust in Haiti and from there in a series of complex, automatic, and undetectable transfers to several different accounts in a holding bank in Luxembourg.

From another of Leon's accounts, Joshua deducted thirty million U.S. dollars while avoiding the temptation to take much more. This thirty million was filtered through a much more complex series of similarly untraceable automatic transfers. Joshua expected nineteen million dollars would be credited to their account at WRN Bank in Geneva. He split off eleven million dollars which was scheduled to show up within about a week at D & R Bankengruppe in Zurich. This would join the money earned from the commissions on the loans. It took over an hour of frantic activity, on the fastest connection available, before Joshua was satisfied. In every case the wire transfers were authenticated and passed the SWIFT sniff test.

Finished, he replaced the panel, wiped down everything he had touched, peeked out the maintenance door, saw it looked clear, and left by way of the gate. All the while, thirty feet over Joshua's head, Leon was saying. "Very smooth operation, I must say." A sentiment with which Joshua was in total agreement.

The Lincoln parked outside Dixon's office belonged to Salvatore Vitale, one of Vincent's crew who owned a limo hire company. The passenger door opened, and Leon was about to get in when he saw Joshua leave the parking structure by ducking under the gate.

"Hey. You!" he shouted, waving to get his attention.

Joshua had no choice other than to bluff it out. He walked towards Leon with a quizzical look on his face.

"What's up?"

Leon scrutinized the van and the telephone company overalls. *He looks genuine enough.*

"Why are you using the parking exit gate to leave the building?"

"It's what I always do, just use my swipe card to get in and push a button to get out."

"Can I see your ID, please?"

Joshua lifted the ID card hanging around his neck and showed him, thankful the Printer had doctored Glenda's cloned pass to make it resemble an AT&T identification. "I was checking on the lines. Routine maintenance."

Leon looked at him through narrowed eyes thinking, *This guy looks very nervous.* Observing beads of sweat on Joshua's forehead, he thought, *Why's he sweating?*

He said, "Hmmmm. How come you're working in the garage?"

"I was in your central telephone room; it's part of a storage unit in the garage. We're behind on replacing some analog equipment and I got an order to check out this building today. Is there a problem?"

Leon's antenna was up. He was unable to get over the fact that 'Jake' used the exit normally used by cars, alongside his obvious nervousness. He couldn't put his finger on it, but something nagged away in a remote part of his brain and the message was, *Something's not right.*

Leon had to let it go. "No, OK. There's been a lot of break-ins lately. I was just checking." He handed back Joshua's ID, nodded to him, and went back to the limousine.

Joshua watched the limo drive off, leaving him time to let out a long breath. *That was a close call. I wonder when he'll put two and two together.*

Leon called Dixon. "Have you had any problems with your phones? I just talked to a repair guy coming out of the parking garage."

"Don't know anything about it but that's not unusual. I wouldn't normally deal with that mundane stuff. My understanding is only the telephone company people have access, but I'd have to check with the building's management company."

Leon hung up. His paranoia was getting the best of him. "Do a U-turn," he commanded Salvatore. "I want to have a closer look at that telephone van."

Meanwhile, as Joshua was packing up, he saw the brake lights flash on Leon's limo not more than a couple of blocks away. He decided to get out of Dodge while the going was good. He made an immediate and convenient right turn before driving at speed to the nearest public parking. It took him five minutes to rid the van of the AT&T stick-on logos. Now driving a plain white van, he pulled out of the parking structure but didn't see the Lincoln cruising through a nearby alley.

"That's him," exclaimed Leon as he got a clear look at Joshua's face. "Cheeky bastard. He's changed vans."

Joshua kept a close eye on his mirrors the whole way to the rental agency where he intended to return the van. Traffic was heavy but Salvatore was experienced and equal to the task. They continued to follow him after he dumped the van off and made the short walk to the Beverly Wilshire Hotel. Joshua was blissfully unaware of their presence.

As Sonny remarked later, "I'm amazed that two experienced operatives couldn't spot a tail, and not just once either, and don't get me started on the Zurich transfer."

Finding an obscure corner off the hotel lobby, Leon called Dixon. "Your telephone repair man is staying at the Beverly Wilshire. Does that sound kosher to you?"

"I don't understand. What do you mean?"

"Check the money and make sure everything's OK at your end."

"You were here when the transfers came in, so all the money transferred correctly. I don't understand how a telephone guy affects the deal."

"You don't have to understand. I'm telling you there's something fishy going on and I'll bet that bitch Sarah's in the middle of it. We're going to have a little chat with our friend in the hotel to find out more."

He sat back in his seat and thought for a moment, dialed his brother David in Cayman, and let the phone ring continuously until voicemail picked up. He hung up and tried again but there was still no answer. There was no answer from his cellphone either. Cursing, he was forced to leave a voicemail on both phones, requesting an immediate call back as soon as his message was picked up.

While Leon contemplated his next move, Matthew and Bruno sat in a vacant lot about 150 feet from Henry's Trucking, waiting, and watching for Sarah. Matthew believed the Cadillac stood out too much, and much to Bruno's disgust they were using the Chevelle. They had followed her taxi from Santa Monica and were sure she hadn't rumbled them. Matthew reasoned this trip to the buyers was probably to celebrate the deal closing. They had prepared for a long day of it with sandwiches and flasks, one of coffee, the other a mixture of coffee and bourbon.

Bruno's phone rang. It was Leon. "Bruno, that you?"

"Yeah. We're at the truck place. Sarah's inside."

"She's still there?" Leon sounded puzzled. "I'm surprised. Something's going down. I don't care what you have to do but don't fucking lose her. And keep in touch." He hung up.

Bruno put the phone down. The phone call had disturbed Matthew who kept his eyes closed, deliberately ignoring the conversation, he was too comfortable.

"Hey, wake up." Bruno nudged Matthew in the ribs. "Leon called."

Matthew pulled himself up in his seat, yawning. He scratched his balls and dismissed any thoughts of a nap.

"What's up?"

Bruno looked at Matthew distastefully. "Sleeping on the job. Leon wouldn't like that."

Matthew laughed. "Well, he ain't here, is he? You're keeping watch so why're you getting up in my face?"

"That call was from Leon. He thinks Sarah is a problem. We've got to make sure we don't lose her."

Matthew interrupted him. "What kind of problem?"

"How the fuck should I know? I don't want any aggro from Leon. Let's just follow orders."

Not two minutes went by before a yellow cab turned into Henry's Trucking. Five minutes later, it left.

"There she goes now," said Bruno. "I saw her in the back of that taxi."

They followed the taxi as it headed north on the 405 Freeway. In heavy traffic, it took the exit west to Santa Monica.

"You'd better get over or you're going to miss the exit," barked Matthew.

"I'm trying but this asshole won't let me in." The asshole in question was driving a VW Beetle and gave them the finger as they drove alongside, refusing to move over and causing Bruno to miss the exit.

"It's OK," he told a raging Matthew, "she's going to her hotel. *Vaffanculo!*" Bruno blew her a kiss and waved as she soared above them on the overpass.

"I can't believe you lost her. Take the next exit, I think it's Olympic, and head for her hotel. We're cooked if we can't find her."

Sarah returned to her hotel having planned her escape with care. Five minutes after arriving, she used the elevator to access the parking garage and left the building via the rear exit doors. Nothing in sight, nothing to observe her leaving. Relieved, she walked quickly down the alley at the rear of the hotel. A couple of blocks later she used a side street to go to Wilshire where she went into a McDonalds. There she acquired the key to the restroom and locked herself in the single cubicle.

Stripping off her business suit, she opened her backpack and pulled out jeans, sneakers, a black hoodie, and a Dodgers baseball cap. She stuffed her suit into the backpack and checked herself in the mirror, straightened her cap, and made the backpack comfortable on her shoulders. Giving herself a final glance of approval, she exited the restroom.

The length of her head start was dependent on the time the balloon went up and Leon discovered his cash was missing. *Could be a day, more likely a few hours.* Quickening her pace, she headed to the 1981 Chevy G 20 Campanero purchased for cash the day previously from an eBay advertisement. Taking the key from a magnetized holder under the rear bumper, she drove away, confident no one had followed her.

Meanwhile, Bruno and Matthew had arrived at Sarah's hotel and found she had checked out. Leon was apoplectic when told.

"What the hell do I pay you guys for? If there's money missing, and I'm sure there is, you won't just answer to Vinnie. No, it'll be Nunzio who'll be pissed, and you know what happens when he loses money." He sighed in frustration and said resignedly, "Come to Beverly Hills and let's see about our friend there."

CHAPTER 14

*Sarah makes a phone call and Leon
receives some bad news.*

**Los Angeles, California
Wednesday, August 28**

In his hotel room, Joshua made a copy of ninety-five
percent of the files on Leon's accounts on a CD. He left out
details of the accounts from which he'd syphoned off the
multi-million-dollar transfers earlier. The front desk of the
hotel had a FedEx pick up scheduled and he was just in
time to send the CD off to Sonny. Returning to his room,
he went back to his computer to examine and map Leon's
money transfers to get a better understanding of money
flow. As he started to delve through the files, he was struck
by the thought, *This is complex shit and it's been going on for
years.*

Sarah sat relaxing in a condo on Pacific Coast Highway
just north of the pier in Huntington Beach. The lease
belonged to a South African corporation, and she was
confident her hideout was secret. She watched the surfers
cut graceful arcs across the rolling waves through the net-
curtained windows and thought about the future. Neither
she nor Joshua were aware their covers were certainly
blown.

Sarah had no interest whatsoever in mapping Leon's money. Her antenna was quivering in anticipation of a huge payday with a great exit strategy. After rehearsing her script, she walked to a nearby store and used a payphone to call Marcus. Cordial greetings and mutual congratulations were exchanged. Then she revealed the purpose of her call.

"I'd like you to call Ara on my behalf. Tell him I know who's been skimming millions from his boss over the past few years. Tell him I also know where the money is hidden."

"What are you talking about?" asked Marcus, frowning in disbelief, a look of puzzlement on his face.

"You must have heard the rumors about Ara and the Mob. Well, Ara's boss, a certain Nunzio from New Jersey, has been screwed out of millions of dollars by certain individuals. I want to cut a deal with him."

"You expect me to go to Ara and tell him this story. He'll cut my balls off."

"He'll cut your balls off if you don't. I have proof."

"What kind of proof?"

"Eighty million dollars proof in bank statements? Satisfied?"

"Well, no, not really." Marcus felt a trickle of sweat run down the middle of his back. "Christ Almighty." He gritted his teeth at the thought of a problem with a deal involving the Mob.

Sarah spelled out the terms of the deal to Marcus, instructing him Ara had until 5:00 p.m. to make the deal.

"What news, young Marcus?" Ara's dulcet tones betrayed nothing.

"Are you sitting down?"

The line went silent then Ara said irritably, "Marcus, don't fuck about. Come to the point. What's going on?"

Marcus said nervously, "I received a phone call from Sarah a few minutes ago. She told me she knew someone has been swindling millions of dollars from your boss, someone called Nunzio from New Jersey. Ring any bells?"

Ara took the news in his normal unflappable manner. "What boss? I'm a restauranteur. Nunzio? What the fuck are you talking about, Marcus?"

"Here's the clincher, Ara." Marcus was growing more nervous by the second. "Sarah said, if Ara invests thirty million, he'll get eighty million back. More than double his money. On top of that, she'll throw in the name of the person who's looted the money over a long period of time."

"She's mad. This is just preposterous." Ara started to lose a little of his famous cool.

"Don't shoot the messenger," Marcus said, immediately regretting the unfortunate phrase. He blundered on, "She's given you until 5:00 p.m. today to come back with any interest at all. Says she has proof."

"What kind of proof?" Ara asked, aware his bluff was being called.

"Bank statements, she said, and asked me to negotiate a deal based on her receiving a thirty-million-dollar finder's fee with you receiving eighty million in return. She was specific about the dollar amounts. I'm in the same boat you are, Ara. There's no further information. I took the phone call five minutes ago and called you first. I haven't even called the buyers yet. If you like, I'll put her directly in touch with you or Ben. That way, you make your own deal and I'm out of it."

"Marcus, you have nothing to worry about, you're brokering the deal. The buyers brought this Sarah to the deal, didn't they? You weren't or aren't connected to her in any way, are you?"

"Ara, I've had no contact with her apart from one meeting and a couple of phone calls. All deal related."

Ara saw the time. "Let me make a couple of phone calls and I'll get back to you. I want you to come to my office at Studio Z and take the call from Sarah there. OK? Come by yourself. There's no need to bring Sharron." With that, he hung up without waiting for Marcus to answer.

Marcus sat back in his chair, his face showing apprehension as he considered the nasty possibilities awaiting him if he walked into the lion's den. Sharron sat opposite him, a look of consternation on her face.

"What's going on?"

Marcus outlined the conversation he'd just had, closing with, "He's probably on the phone to Weiner right now."

"That sounds about right."

Marcus got up and stretched. "The question is, what are we going to tell the buyers? This could mean a lawsuit."

Sharron had been expecting that comment. "Tell them nothing," she began coolly. "I don't think we should make any moves until we see what Ara has to say about Sarah's deal. Otherwise, it's premature to speak to the buyers. The deal's closed and everyone has their money."

"You're right. Boy, I wish I were a fly on Ara's wall right now." He shrugged into his jacket. "I'd better go. Sarah will call my direct line and I've forwarded all calls to Ara's office. You wait here and I'll call as soon as I get a lay of the land. See you later."

Matthew and Bruno made good time getting to the Beverley Wilshire Hotel where they found Leon and Salvatore waiting in an area scattered with sofas and armchairs for guests to relax. Leon was anything but relaxed as he vented his anger at their losing Sarah, concluding, "Moving on, we found out our mystery man is in room 334." He paused to collect his thoughts.

"What do you want us to do?" asked Bruno.

"What I don't want you to do is to screw this one up. Now, this spot is as good as any to watch the lobby. Me and Sal are the only ones who've seen him. He's sure to come through the lobby at some point. Even if he doesn't, I'm confident she'll appear. In either case, your job is to follow them and bring them down to my warehouse without making a scene."

"After that, I'd—" He was cut short by Salvatore.

"I think that's him, the one in the white shirt by the counter."

Leon raised a newspaper to shield his face while giving a quick look. "Yeah, that's him all right."

Leon watched as Joshua handed a brown envelope and some papers to the hotel desk clerk. *I'd give a year's profits to know what's that's all about,* he thought.

"Sit down, sit down," he urged Matthew and Sal as they started to make a move. "We're too late for the package and we can't have any fuss here, it's too public. Would you recognize him and not make a mistake?"

Matthew gave a quick glance over his shoulder. "Yep." Bruno nodded his head, affirming he too could identify this stranger from room 334.

"Good, then take him in his room."

Joshua spent a few minutes hanging around the front desk until the clerk handed him his papers back. He made his way back to the elevator, the doors closed, and they saw the indicator show the elevator stop at the third floor before continuing its journey.

Leon was about to issue instructions to Matthew when his phone rang. He saw his brother was calling.

David was apologetic. "Sorry I missed your call. Listen, I've been busy checking our balances. Have you been changing the accounts around at all?"

Leon grew serious and sat up straight. He pointed a finger at Bruno and Matthew, forcing them to be quiet.

"Why, what do you mean?" Leon recognized the sinking feeling in the pit of his stomach as a harbinger of bad things to come. He listened for a few seconds, propping the phone against his neck between his head and shoulder.

David continued. "The good news is the Studio Z deal got done. The sellers have collected their ten million. The buyers have possession with the loans against the building and the business also recorded..."

Leon interrupted him. "Yes, yes, I know all that. I was there. Now, get on with the account changes." His complexion had acquired a greyish tint.

"Well, only you will be able to see what's really going on, but it looks to me there's a mix up on several of the accounts. The totals aren't adding up and there's about a 100-million-dollar error."

Leon exploded. In the hotel lobby, unable to shout or even speak loudly, he was forced into a hoarse whisper. Machine-gunning his questions at David, not waiting for answers: "What the fuck! A hundred million? Are you kidding me? You're telling me these accounts have been cleaned out and we don't know where the cash went?"

"You didn't authorize any wire transfers to a bank in Jersey?"

"No. Get on to the bank, we must have friendly contacts in Jersey."

"Not that Jersey," said David bluntly. "The island between England and France. It's a tax haven. You must have come across it before. The money will have been moved on from there, that's certain. Of all people, you know how the system works."

Leon was about to shout down the phone at his brother when he caught himself. *That's not going to accomplish anything.* He tried to stay calm as he took several deep breaths.

"Get ahold of Rudolf at Pan Pacific Bank and see if we can't put a trace on the funds and stop the transfer. Do whatever you have to do. I'm not able to check this out right at this minute. I'm going to Dixon's office; probably get there in," he consulted his watch, "maybe twenty minutes. Then he and I can see what's really going on."

He hung up. Then glared at both Matthew and Bruno.

"Go to room 334. I want him, anybody with him, and any computers. In fact, bring all of his stuff down to my warehouse. I don't want him damaged too much either; he's got to answer a lot of questions. Think you two can handle this?"

The unhappy pair nodded affirmatively.

He turned to Matthew and handed him a slip of paper. "Here's the room number, Sal's taking me back to Dixon's."

Matthew thought for a moment, "We're going to need a van. We don't want to be putting him in the trunk in broad daylight. Bruno can drive the van and I'll follow him."

"The guy from the room used the van rental place around the corner from here," volunteered Sal.

Leon was somewhat mollified by their sudden enthusiasm, which he interpreted as respect, important to Mob members.

"Matthew, you take charge and I'll leave you to sort everything out. Don't disappoint me. See you at the warehouse after I've finished my other business."

While Leon discussed his future three floors below, Joshua called Sonny from his Nokia 9000.

"Don't you ever call at a decent hour?" Sonny grumbled, sitting up straight in his armchair, willing himself awake. "I was sleeping."

"You've got to see this. I just sent you a fax. Go look at it and call me back."

It took Sonny five minutes to return Joshua's phone call; he was salivating. "Is this outline true? Where's the detail? This is the best intelligence I've seen in a long while."

"I've just sent you a CD by FedEx so you can start a forensic accounting when you get it."

"What are you getting out of it, apart from the fee?" Sonny asked suspiciously.

"We want five million dollars for the detailed information."

"No," Sonny said. "Come on, if this is true, it's only worth two million for the whole file. Deal?"

"Five million and we have a deal. You don't have everything, you know." Joshua said with a knowing smile on his face. "I'd say the CD only contains eighty percent of the material we got from Dixon's office."

"You're holding out on me again?" Sonny said acidly.

"Yes, I'm not giving up all the cards until we get paid something near what it's worth. This was a risky deal. You won't be sorry you paid the price because the information is well worth it."

"OK. I believe you. I won't argue. I'll send funds to your Geneva account. You get results but I'm not happy about the extracurricular activity. We'll see what the future brings but don't contact me. I'll contact you."

Joshua never found out how the two men with large guns got into his hotel room without his knowing. One moment he was looking at his computer screen, the next he felt metal touching his ear. He jerked away and began to turn his head.

"Move and you're a dead man," said a deep voice.

It all happened so suddenly. Bound, gagged, hooded, put in a laundry basket, and covered with his own bedsheets, he was wheeled down seemingly endless corridors to the parking lot. There, he was unceremoniously dumped into the back of a van. As it drove off, Joshua found himself totally disoriented. Any estimate of time, distance, or direction was lost in his confined state. Escape was impossible. In this confused situation he had only two questions. *What gave me away? Where's Sarah?*

He was bumped, jostled, and horribly uncomfortable on the metal floor of the van until it finally came to stop. They had arrived at a truck workshop and warehouse located on East Olympic Boulevard in Los Angeles. Part of Leon's deal with a Mexican cartel provided him with this valuable stopover where cocaine, heroin, and methamphetamine were smuggled in from Mexico. They were parceled into smaller loads and distributed to a network of dealers in the LA area. Bodywork specialists were employed to fit hidden compartments in vehicles for moving drugs and cash across the international border between the US and Mexico. Right now, the warehouse was empty.

As he heard the van doors open, Joshua was roughly pulled out. Still hooded and gagged, he stumbled as he was pushed from behind, his footsteps echoing in the stillness, the metal barrel of a gun hard against his back. It was cold and damp in what he guessed was a warehouse. His captors made no conversation as they forced him into what seemed to be a small room. Here, although already handcuffed, he was duct taped to a chair. They left him alone and he heard a distant door close, leaving him in silence. He listened carefully. Was that his imagination or were those muffled voices arguing?

In the manager's office, Bruno answered his cellphone.

It was Leon. Bruno listened to his question before answering, "He's not going anywhere. Where are you?" He waited before replying. "At Dixon's. So, you'll get here in what?" he listened. "OK, you're not sure, probably early evening." He paused again, listening before answering. "Yes, we have a computer. Loads of other stuff as well: guns, passports, cellphones, IDs. This guy's a pro." After listening to Leon again, he said. "Good. We'll be here waiting. What do you want me to do if the girl calls one of the cellphones we've got here?"

Leon didn't hesitate. "Tell her she'd better come in or it's a chainsaw for her partner."

At Dixon's offices, with David on speakerphone, Leon frantically tapped his passwords on his keyboard, looking at his various bank accounts. Dixon leaned over his shoulder while they reviewed the damage.

"How can this be?" Leon wailed. "What's going on?" He knew in his heart of hearts he'd been conned but there might be a tiny chance that what he was seeing and hearing was wrong.

Later, after contacting other associates in the money laundering world and getting nowhere, his brother David squashed his last hope. "Just to confirm, if you're looking at the accounts on your computer you can see they didn't touch $75 million in the account ending 4122. I don't know the reason for that. They deducted $30 million from the account number 5175. A further $80 million was taken from accounts 3159, 4863, and 1217. That's a $110 million dollar loss. We're lucky we've got plenty of reserves in other accounts, hopefully the insurance will cover the loss."

"I think we have the culprit here. He'll be getting the waterboard treatment shortly."

"OK. I'll call you later," said a quiet and suddenly respectful David as Leon hung up.

Leon closed his eyes and clicked the speakerphone off with exaggerated deliberation. "We have to get the girl," he murmured to Dixon. "She could go running to Ara and we'll end up dead. I'd have the guy taken care of now but need to talk to him myself. Either one of them goes free and we're finished."

"How are you planning on finding her?"

"A lot depends on the motherfucker we took to the warehouse. Maybe he'll talk or maybe she'll try and contact him. We'll see the numbers he called on the cellphones too. Either way, we have a good shot at taking care of them both. I'll let you know where we stand as soon as I know myself."

CHAPTER 15

*Sarah makes a phone call and
Nunzio plots revenge.*

**Los Angeles, California
Wednesday, August 28**

Marcus was running late and the people he was meeting
didn't like to be kept waiting. He drove the Mustang over
Beverly Glen, avoided the bottle neck at Sunset, and half
an hour later drove into the parking lot of Studio Z. He
admired the superb lines of Ara's parked Bentley which
dwarfed other cars in the lot in size and sophistication. He
smiled ruefully as he passed by, his complexion showing a
slight tinge of green.

He was greeted with Cristal-filled champagne flutes
as he entered Studio Z. To celebrate, Dewayne, Jayden,
and Jamal had started their first day of ownership with
an impromptu party. Unfortunately, Marcus had to defer,
protesting that he had a meeting with Ara. Henry feasted
his eyes on the scene, a beaming smile on his face as close
friends, acquaintances, and a few celebrities flocked to
support his boys. Several stars of the screen had already
stated they would be coming by with their congratulations.
Raucous party? Maybe. But nothing Studio Z hadn't seen
many times in the past.

The door to Ara's office was open and he stepped in. He didn't recognize Ara's visitor, but their conversation stopped as they both looked at him.

"Close the door behind you please, Marcus. It's getting a little noisy out there."

Ara greeted him in his normal gracious manner and introduced Vincent, describing him as a partner in several joint business ventures. Marcus quickly assessed him as a gangster.

"Want anything to drink? Coffee? Water? Tea? I know you English like your tea."

"Nothing for me, thanks, Ara."

"OK. Let's get started." Ara was perfectly relaxed as he began to speak. "Let me explain some things to you, Marcus. Someone has embezzled large sums of money from a client who has hired Vincent and me to settle this matter privately. No authorities. Do you have a problem with that?"

Marcus considered his reply carefully, "Confidentiality is not a problem as long as there's nothing illegal."

"Not illegal. No," confirmed Ara. "Our client doesn't want to bring a lot of unwanted attention on himself and his family."

Marcus chuckled inside at Ara's use of the term 'family,' knowing in Nunzio's world it was organized crime. "As I said, as long . . ."

Vincent broke in, "Tell me what the fuck you know about Sarah! That's what I want to know. How come she's controlling our money?"

"Hold on, Vincent," Ara said firmly, his arm outstretched, his palm facing Vincent. "I vouch for Marcus, he wanted to hand this over to us and back off. I asked him to assist us after Sarah made the first call to him. There's a lot of money at stake here. Let's keep level heads and not start a blame game." He turned to Marcus. "First of all, will she call your number so we can negotiate the rest of the money?"

"Yes, we're on call forwarding," Marcus confirmed and continued, "but..."

He didn't get any further as Vincent interrupted. "What's the fucking *but*?"

"She wants me to negotiate the release of the rest of the funds after I fax this agreement with your respective signatures. The name of the embezzler will come later."

Ara was taken aback. "This is new. I thought she wanted us to negotiate on the phone."

Marcus saw a flush spread up Vincent's neck to his face but before he could utter a word, Ara, seeing the rage, leaned across the desk, and said, "Calm down, Vince. Big picture, OK? Look at me." Ara used a glacial stare, willing Vincent to comply.

In the face of Ara's look, Vincent blinked. He took a deep breath, calmed himself, glared back at Marcus, and said, "Go on."

"I'm just going by what she's telling me to do." Marcus was upset by Vincent's outburst, but saw Ara had control. "Look at the positive. She's willing to give up eighty million and just wants to feel safe with the business agreement. She fears retribution, legal or otherwise."

As he thought it through, Marcus realized Sarah had made an intelligent step in creating an agreement to be signed by Ara and Weiner. *It legitimizes the process. Mostly they want their money back, that's their number one objective. Sarah taking a percentage as a finder's fee instead of keeping the money was the right decision. They'll look at it as the cost of doing business. In the old days she would have never made it off the 'hit' list. How can she guarantee there won't be retribution?* Marcus almost immediately put it out of his mind. Sarah surely must have taken precautions to prevent the possibility.

Ara wasn't happy with the turn of events plus he was still worried about Vincent's reaction. "I was hoping we'd have a negotiation to settle this matter. She's left no room for discussion with this fax business."

Marcus said, "She's in the driver's seat. There's the promise of a lot of money to come as well as the name behind the embezzlement. Is her finder's fee the problem?"

Vincent interrupted Ara who was about to answer the question. "No, it's the way it's been done. There's no respect. It feels like blackmail, and I don't like it. She stole from us, and I won't have it." He leaned back in his chair, his face impassive, white, as cold as marble.

Ara laughed to ease the tension. "I'm sure our friends and partners aren't as worried as much about respect as about eighty million dollars or so. Vincent, don't get hung up on principles; let's get the money back."

He turned to Marcus. "Go ahead, tell Vincent everything you know about Sarah."

Marcus purposely deliberated a few moments. "I think you know as much as I know about Sarah. Practically nothing."

At this Vincent rolled his eyes. *Fuck me,* he mouthed.

Marcus summoned up some courage, and said, "If that's a criticism of me, I'd like to remind you that no one on your side of the deal had any problems, did they?" He continued, "You were all very eager to take the money paid to close the deal." He felt nervous challenging Vincent, but fortunately Ara saved the day.

Waving his hand in dismissal of Vincent and his criticism, he said, "Carry on, Marcus. No one's blaming you."

"Here's what happened," Marcus said, and went on to detail the transaction as it had happened from his perspective. He pointed out that one of the main participants, Dixon's bank, was someone with whom Ara already had business experience.

"No suspicions then?" inquired Vincent, giving first Ara and then Marcus the once over.

Marcus stated emphatically, "Yes, of course. But not about Sarah. The deal smelled from day one. Look at the buyers? Successful, yes, but enough to get a multi-million-dollar loan? No way. Drug money?" He shrugged. "It did cross my mind, but I dismissed that idea when I got the loan approval letter on Dixon's letterhead. A company like that wouldn't want to take on the liability unless it were true. The letter, the deposits of a hundred grand or so that passed through to you guys. Come on, I'm telling you, at that point, my chips were all in. I think yours were too, weren't they Ara?"

"Well, the money paid to us to keep the property off the market and a five-day close made a sweet deal."

"They also paid Sarah a substantial fee up front to get the loan," Marcus asserted. "Let me repeat my question: Vincent, Ara, did you see anything suspicious in the deal? Did I mislead you in any way?"

"No one's making that suggestion, Marcus," answered Ara quietly. He caught Vincent's eye. "You saw the terms, Vincent. In fact, you were quite enthusiastic."

Vincent's face lost a little of the stony look. "Yeah. I'm just trying to learn more about Sarah." He shook his head in disgust. "Do the buyers know where she is?"

"Sarah left their offices just after close of escrow. They always contacted her on a cellphone, or she went to the trucking company. Up until this stunning new information today, it was a normal deal that closed on time. And the deal did close, you got your ten million dollars."

"Quite right too," agreed Ara. "What have you told the buyers?'

"Nothing until I know something concrete."

"Any other questions, Vincent?"

"No, I'm satisfied." Vincent was anything but satisfied, the saucer of cream had turned sour, and he wasn't liking the taste.

Ara shifted in his chair and praised Marcus. "Good work. As the old saying goes, 'Treat 'em like mushrooms, keep them in the dark, and feed 'em shit.'" He laughed as Vincent regarded him with a stony look.

"This isn't the time for fucking jokes, Ara," he said, his eyes like daggers.

"Calm down, Vincent. This is exactly the time for some humor. Releases the tension. Allows you to make wise decisions." His voice was soft, but there was no doubt that Ara was running the show.

A wary Marcus hesitated before deciding to make a statement that summed up what was obvious to him. "Ara, you can't make a decision until you know the rest of Sarah's demands. Then you either sign off or not. Let's face it, she's promised to give back eighty million in two payments and the embezzler's name. I'm not on your side of the fence but wouldn't you agree this is a no brainer?" He checked his watch. "You don't have too much time to make up your mind, she'll be calling any minute." Marcus shrugged and gave them a questioning look.

"It's your show," said Ara. "Let's hear what she wants." Vincent leaned forward, taking more interest as Marcus outlined the deal proposed by Sarah.

The phone rang. Ara took a gander at the screen, and said, "Marcus, this looks like your ID and number. This may be Sarah." He checked his watch and handed the phone to Marcus.

Vincent said to Ara, "Antonio?"

"In place," replied Ara, who had authorized Antonio to bug Marcus's phone in the hope of tracing the call made by Sarah.

Marcus was puzzled. *Who's Antonio?* He knew better than to ask questions, so he took the receiver to answer the call.

Sarah was sure Ara would demand proof of the embezzlement which would require her to fax documents to him. She decided upon using an acoustic coupler, her Nokia 9000 and a payphone would mean the connection, though secure, would be too slow. An advertisement in a local paper directed her to a small furnished office in a multi-story building just off the 405 in Long Beach. This was ideal; she was able to sublet it on a week-to-week basis and the building entrance had a keyed lock. Ara's Mob contacts were likely to trace the call's location quickly, but the availability of a power connection meant a faster fax transmission through her Sportster modem. Her intention was to keep the call short and leave before the arrival of unwanted company.

She inserted the phone line into the jack on the Sportster external voice and fax modem and used a cable to connect it to the serial port on her laptop. Plugged in and powered up, with a comfortable headset in place, she was ready to make calls.

She dialed Marcus's number and after a brief hesitation heard him say, "Hello."

"Is that you, Marcus?"

He grinned at her sauciness. "Yes, it's me, Sarah."

"Do we have a deal?" Sarah's voice echoed down the line.

"I don't know, but the man who does know is present in this office. Do you want me to put him on speakerphone?"

"Oh, Ara himself, no doubt. Yes, put him on."

Marcus directed Vincent to press the speakerphone option.

"Hi, Ara. Do we have a deal?" Sarah said boldly.

Ara leaned forward to speak into the mic, saying, "We need some proof. Get us some proof and maybe we got a deal."

"Give me your fax number and I'll send you proof."

"Hold on a minute."

Sarah sent the fax. At Ara's office, the fax machine whirred in the corner.

"Hold on. It's coming through now." Ara retrieved six pages, sat back down, and began to go through them one at a time.

Sarah said. "Got the fax?"

Ara was reading the fax over. "You'll have to excuse me taking time, but this is a lot of information."

Marcus's peripheral vision enabled him to see Ara holding what appeared to be several bank statements. Halfway down the last page was a diagram with circles and arrows.

There was no nervousness in Sarah's voice, it was all business.

"Let's cut to the chase, Ara. Over the last year alone about ten million dollars has been embezzled from your bank. Right now, the accounts used for embezzling your money contain a total of eighty million dollars, give or take a million or so."

Ara perused the fax. "This means nothing without more information," he said tersely. "We need to know who."

"Look, I'm preserving that until I know I'm safe. I'll release forty million dollars to any bank you choose as a sign of good faith. What have you got to lose? I'm not asking you for money, my fee is already in the bank. I'm asking to keep that fee, give me a guarantee of safety, and in return I'll supply the other forty million. On top of that, and of more value, is the name of the person or persons who've been skimming you rotten for years now. That comes with the second forty million. How's that?"

Ara asked, "Why should I pay to get my own money back?"

Sarah laughed. "Quit stalling. You've lost ten million this past year alone, at least eighty million altogether, maybe more. You've missed this hand in your pocket despite audits, even surprise audits. What makes you think you can find it now?"

"Why aren't you taking the whole eighty million then?"

"Because I don't want all the New York families breathing down my neck for the rest of my life. You're all smart businessmen. Here's a unique opportunity to get eighty million bucks you didn't know existed until I came along. Come on, Ara," she continued, "put on your big boy pants and make a decision."

Ara sighed. She was right. She held all the cards. He said, "What do we do next if we go through with this?"

Sarah was cool as a cucumber. "Here's my suggestion. Have you and Weiner sign the finder's fee agreement that's part of the package I've just faxed to you. Basically, I'm to be paid thirty million dollars up front and nonrefundable. In return, I'll supply you with information to allow you to recover eighty million dollars embezzled from your companies. It will spell out how and when you get the first forty million dollars with instructions on the release of the second forty million."

"I'm giving you permission to keep thirty million nonrefundable on the chance that I'll get eighty million back?"

"I suggest you get a move on. The clock's ticking. I'll give you another forty-five minutes to sign or the deal is off. I'll call back shortly with a fax number for you to send a signed copy of the agreement. When I get the signed agreement from you, I'll arrange the necessary documentation for you to collect your forty million dollars. All nice and legal. Deal?"

Marcus and Ara exchanged glances; there was a momentary silence.

"I can't hear you, gentlemen." Sarah interrupted their mental gymnastics as they tried to come up with a way to outwit her.

Ara indicated to Marcus to mute the phone and turned to Vincent. "What do you reckon?"

Vincent had a grim look on his face. "Crafty bitch has us by the short and curlies."

Unmuting the phone, Ara asked wearily. "How long have we got?"

Sarah was firm. "After you receive the fax number from me, you'll have five minutes to get the signed document back to me and I'll sign and fax a copy back. I'm moving around because I know you're lying when you say you don't have a trace on. I'll be in touch shortly. Bye for now."

"Cool cat," observed Ara as the call ended. "Got her shit together. This is a well-planned and sophisticated operation. Marcus, would you excuse me, I've got to make a couple of calls. Vincent will show you where to wait."

While Marcus waited in the reception area and flirted with Charlene, Ara called Antonio. "Any luck on tracing the call?"

"She was calling from an office building in Long Beach. I sent a couple of people down there, but I expect she'll be gone by the time they get there. I've done the best I can."

Marcus's fly on the wall would have heard Ara outlining the deal on the phone to Weiner from the Studio Z.

"How long have we got?" Weiner inquired.

"She's moving around, and we have five minutes to fax the signed agreement when she calls back. She knows we're trying to trace the call."

"What did you think of this evidence she sent you?"

"The bank accounts she faxed me were pretty damning, but she made sure it didn't show who was responsible."

Weiner was in shock. "What's this all about? Who's gone off the reservation?"

Ara made no reply. Weiner said, "Give me five minutes and I'll let you know what we're going to do."

Seven minutes later Ara's phone rang. Weiner was on the line.

"We've got a deal but first of all does anyone know of this Sarah's whereabouts?" The tone in Weiner's nasal voice took on a menacing tone. "This Marcus. You know I don't like him. A right limp dick. Think he's involved?"

Ara didn't hesitate. "We know she called from Long Beach. I haven't heard back yet but I expect she'll be long gone. Marcus just brokered the deal. My understanding is the buyers brought her to the table."

"What have they got to say?"

"I don't know. Marcus will call them when he hears what we have to say."

Weiner interrupted him. "I want you to be the lead and communicate directly with the woman. We may be able to catch her if we have her call your number at a set time. Get our 'phone guy' on the job."

"I told you, Antonio traced this last call to an office building in Long Beach. She's not going to use the same place again. I don't want to frighten her. We stand to recover a hell of a lot of our money," reasoned Ara.

"Keep him on it anyway," ordered Weiner. "You never know, we might get lucky."

There's been a screw up somewhere. Someone's going to get clipped, thought Ara as he rejoined Marcus and Vincent who were holding drinks. The party at Studio Z was noisier than ever with more people arriving as word spread.

"Come on, you two, we still have work to do. This is no time to be drinking." Ara smiled. "That can come later. Let's get back in here before we're swallowed by this crowd." He waved at Dewayne who was guiding friends around the individual studios, showing off the gold records decorating the walls. Marcus also waved a cheery greeting to him before they retreated into Ara's office.

Newark, New Jersey

Nunzio walked back to his club from a nearby payphone, pondering the call from Weiner. He was consumed by both rage and curiosity. *Who the fuck could steal that amount of cash? It's gotta be Leon in Grand Cayman, Zhang in San*

Francisco, or Dewey in Spain. He walked in the door of his club and headed for his office, waving Carmine to join him.

"Carmine. Carmine! Get in here, will ya?"

Not a *consigliere*, only the family boss had a *consigliere*, Carmine was his right-hand man. Anthony relied on him for good advice, but, more than that, he trusted him. In a life where trust was not a watchword this said a lot about their shared values of loyalty and honor. Sitting alone at a table, his chair pushed back with his legs stretched out and crossed at the ankle, reading the "Racing Form," he was deciding how much to bet on Blagger's Choice in the fifth race at Del Mar. He had a tip from a jockey who owed him a few thousand dollars. *Still, gotta be careful with horseracing, even with a fix in, it's still possible to lose.*

Nunzio's call interrupted his concentration. He shook his head in disgust. *Fuck, I'm right in the middle of an earner and he fucking calls me. It had better be good.*

He put his newspaper aside, took a swig of cold coffee, grimaced, and stood up. A big man, he was probably six-four and mostly muscle. His mere presence was enough to have a debtor's ass twitching in fear. Over the years, he had lasted in a profession where mistakes meant family justice, usually a one-way trip to the landfill, often in pieces.

Carmine walked in the open door with a light step for such a big man. Uninvited, he took a seat facing Nunzio across the desk.

"What's up?"

"Let's take a walk." They left the club by the back entrance and walked briskly towards a local coffee shop. Nunzio told Carmine what was going on in Los Angeles. They spoke in Sicilian, careful to cover their mouths with their hands when talking in case they were under observation. The Feds had been known to use lip readers.

"This so-called loan officer in the Studio Z deal wants to make an exchange."

"What do you mean, an exchange? I thought the studio was sold."

"It was. But . . ." He went on to explain the deal Sarah was offering. "By rights the money's ours, but we didn't know about it. That's her point. She's saying she should get a finder's fee. Apparently, she's already taken that thirty million. Spirited the money off to another account where it's long gone by now."

"Where's this loan officer now?" Carmine scratched his head.

"Nobody knows. She put a call into the real estate broker's office today and told him she wants to strike a deal and return the funds. The broker got in touch with Ara and gave him the message. Then she called Ara and Vinnie to try and close the deal. Ben Weiner got involved and called me. I gave the go-ahead."

"We'll give her a deal all right," Carmine scoffed.

"No, she claims one of the crew or an associate has taken eighty million dollars of ours over a long period of time. Now . . ."

He opened the door to the coffee shop and stood back to allow an elderly woman to leave. She smiled her thanks, brushing by them as Nunzio and Carmine smiled back. Despite being an infrequent visitor, Nunzio was recognized by the owner, a handsome widow in her early forties, originally from Palermo. He greeted her with a smile and a friendly, "*Buongiorno.*" She smiled back, quite beautiful, her gleaming white teeth a startling contrast to her dark tanned skin.

"*Salve,*" she replied, as she waited for him to order.

"*Dui caffe ristretto e dui cannoli, pi favuri.*"

"To go or eat here?" she said, avoiding his gaze, looking down.

"We'll eat here, if that's OK."

Pulling her cardigan closer at the neck, she turned back and said pleasantly, "Of course."

Nunzio offered to pay. She shook her head. "There's no charge." She returned his smile coyly, and said, "I'll bring them over to your table."

Carmine led the way to a small round table for four, covered by a white tablecloth. Nunzio took the seat nearest the aisle and Carmine nearest the wall. This allowed them to cover both the back kitchen and the front door. Anthony used this coffee shop infrequently and wasn't worried about his conversation being monitored. He figured the Feds couldn't bug everywhere.

Mrs. Russo deftly set coffee and a small plate with a cannoli in front of each of them. Nunzio thanked her, took a sip of coffee, and waited until she was out of earshot. Leaning forward, he said, "I want you to get set to travel. I'll let you know where you're going and what I want done as soon as I hear something. Make sure your passport's handy. Not sure where yet, could be Caymans, Spain, or San Francisco. You can pick up appropriate clothing, if needed. The jet is at your disposal. It's already gassed up and ready to go."

"That's vague enough," observed Carmine.

"I ain't in the fucking mood for jokes," Nunzio said harshly. "This is about millions of fucking dollars of my money that's been scammed. It can only be one of three people, Zhang in San Fran, Leon in Cayman, or Klaus in Spain. Who's your money on?"

"That Zhang is a very slippery piece. Him and his fucking triads." Carmine spoke contemptuously of their San Francisco heroin connection.

"Hmmm. That's interesting. What about Alicante or the Caribbean? No suspicions there?"

Carmine took a bite of his cannoli, chewed it carefully, and swallowed. He wiped his mouth with the napkin.

"I always got along with Leon. Like all middlemen he's probably skimming a bit and owning a bank certainly makes it easy. He's not my bet though. As for Spain, we've never had a problem with Klaus. No, my bet would be Zhang. When do we find out?"

"As soon as I get a call," Anthony checked his watch. "Let's finish up here and get going. You get whatever you need and head out to the airport. I'll call you when I have more information. *Capisce?*"

Seal Beach, California

Sarah packed away her equipment, left the Long Beach building, and drove about seven miles to Seal Beach where she used another short rental office to repeat the process. Once again, using the Sportster external modem and her laptop, she adjusted her headset and reconnected to Ara.

"Is that you, Sarah?"

"Yes, Ara, here's the fax number." She read off the telephone number she was using. "I'm giving you just one minute to call me back." She hung up.

Her phone rang a minute later with Ara on the line.

"I see you're moving around."

She interrupted him. "Just fax the agreement, you don't have a lot of time."

Ara had signed the agreements after obtaining Weiner's approval and now faxed them to the number she was using. Sarah read them through, signed her agreement with the terms, and faxed the documents back to Ara.

She asked, "Can you confirm you received the fax?"

"Yes, everything's in order."

"Good, I'm now sending a fax containing the bank codes, permissions, and addresses you'll need to recover the forty million dollars. I know I can't count on you not trying to trace this call but be careful, I have copies of everything located in a very safe place and they will be released to the media on my premature or unusual death. You'll get the other half of the money when I feel completely secure. My fee has already been paid. Gentlemen, are there any questions?"

There was silence. Ara scanned the room. There were no questions, they were stunned by her audacity.

"What about the name?" he demanded.

Sarah giggled. "Keep your shirt on. You really don't have a clue as to who it might be? No guesses?"

Ara was irritated and it showed. "Let's not play games, Sarah. You're on thin ice as it is. Give us the name so we can all move forward."

"Ouch," she replied. "Don't threaten me, Ara, or you won't get the other forty million and I'll take my chances. The name comes with the second payment."

Ara saw Vincent was about to explode and clapped his hand over his mouth to stop him answering. "There's no threat, we recognize you're doing us a big favor. That's why we've paid you thirty million dollars."

"I'll be magnanimous and do you a favor. You obviously know Leon and Dixon. They're your problem."

When Ara was satisfied that the funds were in place, he called Weiner, telling him Sarah had followed through on her part of the deal, the money was secure. He saved the bombshell about Leon and Dixon until the end of the call.

"Nunzio's not going to be happy," was Weiner's only comment.

Ara called Antonio. "Any luck on tracing the call?"

"Another office. This time she was in a Seal Beach building. Our guys were nearby and got there quickly, but, again, she was gone, and it was empty. Also, it looks as though she's stopped using the cellphone we linked to her earlier. There's no trace of it anywhere."

Ara sighed and called Ben with the news.

Newark, New Jersey

Nunzio and Carmine were about to leave when Nunzio's phone rang. He gave Carmine a grim look, flipped the phone open, and took the call.

"Yes?"

As he listened his face grew darker. "Thanks, I'll take care of the matter from here." Irritably, he terminated the call.

"Hang on, Carmine, nature calls. I'll be right back." He made a quick trip to the toilet.

When he returned, he put Carmine in the picture. "Wheels up for LA. Leon's our man. He's been working with Dixon, the attorney. They've been operating a skim and Dixon has managed to conceal it from us. It could have been going on for years."

"You're joking, right?"

Nunzio glared at him. "Listen to this. You know about Studio Z in LA that I told Ara to sell? A week or so ago, Leon called me to let me know he had some rappers who wanted to buy it. I didn't give a fuck. He was funding the loan through his bank. I didn't know he was using my fucking money. Money they skimmed from me, the fucking parasites."

"How do we take them out?"

"I'll leave that to you. Just take care of them both. You know Matthew? That guy I stuck in Leon's operation to keep an eye on things?"

"Yes, he's the independent we used to clean up the Moneybags fuck up."

"Use him and Bruno from Vinnie's crew. I'll leave you to supervise things. Dixon's prominent in the Malibu crowd so make it look like an overdose or an accident, perhaps both. Keeping this quiet will be the problem. I'm sure some fucking police rat will notify the press about Dixon's connection to Leon and the shit will hit the fan. Perhaps we should take him out in the Caymans?"

"Let's just whack him out at the first opportunity and have the body disappear," commented Carmine. "Leave it to me. What do you want done with this Sarah and her partners?"

"Give them a pass. She earned it. She gave us Leon and half the money. We're supposed to get the other half when she's happy. Ara's sorting that out. The guys who got the loans for the studios with my money also get a pass. The loan is an asset of Leon's bank which is about to become my bank, so I'll keep that in place. We may be able to leverage the loan to get control of the studio at some point but I'm not getting into a fight with some *moolinyans* over it. We're better off buying that business at the airport."

Carmine nodded his assent. "I should go," he said. "It's a seven-hour flight but I'll pick up three hours as it's West Coast time, so I should be there by this evening. I'll plan everything out on the plane."

Los Angeles, California

"What a turn up for the books," said Ara. "Can you believe we're getting over eighty million back?"

Vincent stared at him, a brooding look on his face.

Ara continued, "More importantly, a big hole got plugged. That Dixon was a slick operator. I bet Nunzio blew his stack when he got the names." They both laughed at the idea. He continued, "Yeah, and he was hooked up with Leon of all people."

"We've still got to collect the other forty million," Vincent reminded him.

"Even so, it's found money, plus what we saved on future fraud. By the way, is Carmine coming to town?"

"Yeah, he's going to make sure what Nunzio wants, Nunzio gets. You can imagine what he wants, and Carmine's coming here to make sure the 'i's are dotted and the 't's are crossed."

Vinnie's cellphone rang, and he answered. "Yes?"

A heavy Brooklyn accent said, "It's Carmine."

"What's going on?" asked Vincent.

"I'm on the jet and we'll arrive at Van Nuys airport in about an hour, pick me up there. Find out where Leon is but I don't want him to know I'm in town. Got it?"

"Got it. I'll be ready."

"Things are moving along," said Vinnie cryptically as he put the phone down.

Ara ignored the comment, knowing it never paid to ask a lot of questions in their line of work. He checked his watch. "Look at the time, I'd better be on my way. See you later."

Vinnie grinned resignedly. "And I get to spend the evening in the charming company of Carmine. No disrespect, but you have the better deal here." They stood, briefly hugged, patting each other on the back, and Ara promised to be in touch.

Someone's about to get clipped, crossed Ara's mind for the second time that day as he climbed into his Bentley. He dismissed the thought and, with his foot pressed firmly down on the accelerator, the engine responded, purring as it surged effortlessly on its way to his home.

CHAPTER 16

Sarah pays a visit and Bruno disobeys orders.

**Los Angeles, California
Wednesday, August 28**

Bruno took his phone from his pocket when it rang. A nasal accent snarled in his ear, "Do you know where Leon is?" It was Vincent.

"Yeah, we're at his warehouse. He said he'd be here in a couple of hours."

"I'm on my way to pick up Carmine at the airport so we should arrive at the warehouse right about the same time. If he gets there before us, tell him he should wait for me to arrive with info on a big score. Don't tell him Carmine's coming. Is Matthew there?"

"Yeah," said Bruno.

"Have him go over to East LA. You know the place I mean?"

"Yeah. Yeah." The subject of their conversation was a scrap metal yard where disposal of bodies and cars were a specialty.

"Have them ready to receive a couple of packages."

"Got it. What about the missing money? We've got the *stugots* here. If he's connected to the girl, she knows we'll put his head in a vice and squeeze his fucking eyeballs out. She'll give herself up then. Wouldn't you?"

"With all that loot on her hands, maybe not. We don't know what their connection is yet. Are they friends? Are they business partners? Are they fucking? It all depends. But, Nunzio said hands off. You got that?"

Bruno said, "I got it, but it seems simple to me. We could split millions."

Carmine said menacingly. "For starters, it's Nunzio's money. He's made a deal, so nothing better happen to them. Untouched, OK? Do what you're fucking told."

A chastened Bruno put the phone back in his pocket. He gathered his thoughts. "Matthew, here's the deal. That was Carmine and he's on the fucking warpath. He wants you to go to East LA. You got a pen? Write this address down."

"Let me guess. I was there a little while back. Is Ritchie still the man?"

Bruno was shocked and showed it. He hadn't expected Matthew to be so well-informed. Seeing his puzzlement and to gauge his reaction, all Matthew said was, "Moneybags."

"You were on that?" asked Bruno, his eyes widening, clearly eager for more details, but Matthew just smirked.

"What happens to our jailbird in there?" Matthew changed the conversation and tilted his head in Joshua's direction.

Bruno stared back in silence, gathering his wits. "Carmine wants me to stay here and look after numb nuts until you get back. Tell Ritchie there will be a couple of packages later this evening but more likely tomorrow morning. He's to be prepared either way."

"Is Ritchie still not using the phone?"

"No. He's squirrely since that wiretap bust. Deliveries from our crew must be in person and payment up front."

Matthew chuckled. "Glad to see time hasn't changed Ritchie Boy. OK., I'm out of here. How long a round trip from here, do you reckon?"

"Hmmmm. Maybe an hour and a half. Don't hang around chatting up Ritchie either. You know how he likes to gossip."

Huntington Beach, California

In Huntington Beach, Sarah spoke to Sonny, keeping it brief. "This is Sarah. Joshua missed a call and I'm concerned. It's not like him. I have no idea where he is. Got any ideas?"

"Give me some time and I'll call you back."

Sarah paced the condominium impatiently, only the worst case scenarios played out in her mind as she waited on Sonny. An hour and forty-five minutes later the ringing of the phone startled her.

"I had a couple of my people go to Joshua's hotel room posing as FBI agents. The hotel manager claimed the occupant had vandalized the room and left without paying his bill. When they gained access to his room, they saw it had been thoroughly searched. They questioned a maid and she saw two men in white overalls wheel a laundry basket onto the service elevator. She saw the light on the floor indicator go down to the parking garage, presumed it was the laundry collection, and thought no more of it. My guys told the manager it was probably a civil matter and, in any event, not their concern."

"Leon?"

"Well, it certainly looks that way. I don't know. You tell me. Is there anyone else? Someone from Belgium, for instance? What reason would Leon have to kidnap Joshua? The deal with Studio Z went through, didn't it?"

"Yes, I don't know the reason yet," Sarah lied. "What about his computer? Guns?"

"Nothing left behind except some personal effects, razor, toothbrush, that kind of stuff. What have you two done to piss Leon off so much that he would resort to kidnapping?"

"I don't know. Nothing. Let's look at possible places where Leon could be holding him. Any ideas?"

"I know you're not telling me everything." He spat the words into the mouthpiece, remembered it was Joshua's life at stake, and said, "The only likely place is a warehouse we suspect Leon uses. If he's taken Joshua, my bet is you'll find him there. It's a longshot and we're operating with a lot of unknowns." He read off the warehouse's street address. "I'm trying to gather the cavalry but they're on another job and unreachable. I'm afraid you're on your own. Help is at least a couple of hours away."

She gazed through the net curtains at the ocean. *No surfers today; the gusty wind has flattened the waves.* "It's definitely worth a look. I'll be in touch." She disconnected the call.

A few minutes later, Sarah checked herself out in a full-length mirror. *Not bad.* Turning to look at her profile, *all I need is the mask, cape, and PVC, and I could double for Catwoman.* The Sig Saur, oiled and cleaned, lay in pieces on the table. She remembered a couple of months back when Joshua saw her reassemble the nine millimeter. "You look like you could do that blindfolded," he'd noted.

She'd appropriated his maroon cashmere scarf and invited him to blindfold her. After doing so, she proceeded to disassemble the automatic, reassemble it, and draw fire from a combat position. She chuckled as she remembered his shock at her all-star tactical skills.

While having these thoughts, she unconsciously and deftly finished reassembling her Sig by screwing a custom suppressor to the end of the barrel. The additional length made for a clumsy quick draw, but she wasn't expecting to walk into a *High Noon* main street-style shootout.

East Los Angeles, California

Sarah parked the Chevy Contempo on a side street in East Los Angeles. She was in a spot where the dark tinted windows allowed her to study Leon's warehouse entrance gate unseen. Examining the premises through binoculars showed the entry gate opened and closed on a rail using a chain-driven engine. *Slow and noisy. Automatically closes when it reaches the end of the track.*

God Almighty, that forecourt is lit up like a Christmas tree. She zoomed in on two security cameras monitoring the front of the building then lowered her head, closed her eyes, and let out a silent scream of frustration, *Josh better be here or its all wasted time. Razor wire and cameras everywhere. Only way in is through that front gate. I just have to be patient.* She calmed herself with a succession of slow, deep breaths.

She stopped the deep breathing when an excruciating pain ran across the bottom of her rib cage causing her to close her eyes and hold her breath. *Not now. Please don't let that start,* the voice inside her pleaded. She rapped the bullet proof vest under her hoodie. "Don't leave home without it," she muttered to herself, loosening the Velcro waist straps, and moving her shoulders to ease the eight pounds' weight. The spasm departed as quickly as it had arrived, and she started breathing again. *Thank God, that's over.* She wound the window down. The breeze caressed her cheeks. *Ohhh, so refreshing. Great, the sweat's drying up.*

She thought back to Sao Paulo. *Jeez, I was lucky there. All over nothing. A .45 slug right at my heart from less than twenty feet. Felt like I'd been slugged with a baseball bat. Without a vest, I'd be dead.* She groaned. *Here we are, six, seven months later, and I still can't laugh or cough without pain.* Fuming quietly at the world, Sarah drew the hood over her baseball cap, pulled the peak low over her face, her binoculars scanning the warehouse for the slightest sign of movement.

Time passed. "Come on," she muttered. "Gimme a break." To her amazement, her prayer was answered by a light from underneath the warehouse door growing brighter and larger as it rolled upwards. She couldn't see the driver, but she recognized the car as a 1970 Chevelle, the 454 V8 growling as it pulled forward to the main gate and sat, engine throbbing, as it waited for the gate to rattle its way open. The warehouse door rolled shut behind the car. Impatiently, Matthew drove through the gap before the gate finished opening, turned up the street and put his foot down.

The moment she saw the Chevelle emerging, Sarah, having disabled the dome light, rolled out of the van on the passenger side. She peeped around the rear fender, drawing back as the headlights swept over her van. It roared past, leaving behind a hint of red taillights receding in the distance. The gate reached its maximum opening distance and halted briefly before beginning its journey home. Using this golden opportunity, Sarah sprinted across the road.

Matthew glanced in his rearview mirror as he drove off at speed. He frowned as he saw a shadow flit across the road. *Was that someone running across the road?*

The momentary distraction almost caused him to rear end the truck in front of him. *Jesus Christ.* He jammed on his brakes as he saw it signal for a right turn at the last second.

"Nice late signal, asshole," he shouted out as the Chevelle's stopping distance got a workout. His cellphone, wallet, and an opened packet of Milk Duds flew off the passenger seat onto the floor. To add insult to injury, the Milk Duds spilled out, rolling in the grooves of the rubber floor mat.

Scarcely avoiding a collision, his heart beating faster than usual, he forgot about shadows and sped on to Ritchie's metal yard. It wasn't until later that he realized its significance.

Sarah made the safety of the sparse concealment offered her by the bushes and small trees growing along the warehouse wall. The gate clanged shut as she lay in the shadow of a gardenia bush, quietly appreciating the hint of coconut in the scent of the blooming flowers. The next few seconds were spent catching her breath and assessing her surroundings while she planned her next move.

Inside the warehouse, Bruno bent over Joshua, making sure the knots were tight and the masking tape secure. He recalled the instructions that Carmine had given him that the captive not be harmed. He pondered the consequences and decided to risk it. *This kid is the key to millions. What's the harm in a couple of questions?*

The hood was ripped off Joshua's head and a leering Bruno sat facing him astride a reversed chair, leaning forward, his arms resting on the back, head resting on his linked hands.

Joshua looked him in the eye. *The pupils are a black nothing. No soul there.* He noted Bruno's flawed complexion with its pockmarked skin. The broken nose, compacted knuckles, and cauliflower ear spoke of the noble art. He was huge, broad shouldered, all muscle. Jersey might be black leather jackets and Brioni suits, but Bruno's been living the California dream. XL Tommy Bahama shirts, chinos, and Bally loafers worn without socks. There was a big laugh at a meeting of the Family's captains when Bruno's name came up. Carmine saying, "Herman Munster goes Hawaiian." Bruno hadn't been present, but it became his nickname in the crew and even police files named him as Bruno (Herman) Russo.

He spoke softly, "I'm going to take your gag out so you can answer some questions. Don't fuck around and think about trying to escape. I want to cut a deal with you. Give me what you've taken, and I'll let you go. You know how to work that computer over there." He jerked his head in the direction of the office where Joshua's belongings were spread out. "What do you say? Just nod *yes* and I'll take the gag off."

Joshua thought quickly. *What do I have to lose? If I can buy time and somehow get my hands free. He's on his own.* He shook his head vigorously, indicating he was ready to talk.

Bruno left the handcuffs and the duct tape in place but unbuckled the ball gag, sat back in the chair, and swung it by the straps.

"I need the computer," said Joshua.

Bruno glared at him. He clapped the gag back in place, pulled the hood back over Joshua's head and left the room. Joshua struggled to get free, but Bruno returned before he could get anywhere. With the gag and hood removed, he faced Bruno once more. "I'll need my hands free to operate the computer."

'What do you think I am, stupid? Tell me what to enter and I'll put it in."

"How fast are you on the computer?"

Bruno was dumbfounded. "Whadda ya mean?"

"When's your pal back?"

"What's that got to do with anything? Cut out the funny stuff."

"Look. I'm much better than most on the computer, and, at a stretch, I might do it in an hour. I don't think you plodding away with those sausages you call fingers will get it done before your mate gets back. It's up to you."

Bruno wasn't the smartest kid on the block, a trait carried forward to present time. He replaced Joshua's gag and hood to take a minute while he figured things out.

While Bruno worked his mental gymnastics, Sarah had worked her way quickly along the front of the warehouse, trying to use cover to shield her from the cameras. *They can't be monitoring them.* She turned the corner, the wind hit her in the face as she eyed the situation. A loading dock, serviced by six roll-up doors, ran the width of the building. A security camera pointed in her direction. *No big deal, I'm already on the front cameras.*

Two overhead lights suspended from the roof shivered in the wind, making dark shadows dance across the dock. The glint from the brass face of the Yale lock caught her eye. *Not twenty feet away. It must lead into the main building.* She ran up the steps on the side of the dock to the door, completely exposed to cameras and anybody monitoring them. She picked the lock in seconds, pushed the handle down and gingerly cracked the door open. It was pitch-black inside. She slipped through, gun in hand, closed the door behind her, and activated her night vision glasses.

The eerie green glowing light through her glasses illuminated details of the distribution point for the loading docks. Rows of wooden pallets with boxes, stacked about ten feet high offered narrow corridors between them. Nothing stirred. She could hear the silence.

How much of this is cocaine? she wondered, looking at the quantity of boxes. *Quite a few kilos, by the look of it.*

A hectoring voice interrupted her thoughts, disturbing the quiet. *That's coming from the main warehouse.* A faint light showed from under a nearby door. She flicked off the power to her glasses and pushed them up on her forehead. Pistol ready, in a combat stance, she advanced towards the light. *Let's hope there's only a couple of bad guys.*

Looking through the plastic porthole in the door, she could see into the main warehouse with rooms and office branching off.

Where's that voice coming from? Yes, over there. Sounds like he's pissed. Satisfied the rest of the warehouse was empty, ready to shoot anything that moved, she crept along the wall to an open door.

The voice coming from the room beside the open door had adopted a more threatening tone. She dared to peek around the door frame and saw a hooded figure lashed to a wooden office chair. A giant squatting on a chair with his back to her, partially blocked her view.

Joshua. What kind of a mess have you've got yourself into?

The room was dazzlingly bright, the walls and floor covered in white ceramic tiles, the light hostile to the pupils. An overhead shower delivered a slow drip of water onto Joshua's hood every fifteen seconds or so. It wasn't Chinese water torture, just a worn washer.

Directly beneath him was a central drain. Sarah instantly understood the plans for Joshua's fate.

That's where they wash away the blood. Mine too if they catch me. So much for Ara's promises.

Sarah stepped forward, "Take the fucking hood off of him and move to the back wall there or you're a dead man."

Bruno swung around at the sound of her voice, *Who? What the fuck? A woman?*

"Make another quick move like that and I'll put one in your fucking head. Got it? Sit down facing that wall and be snappy about it." She pointed the gun and waved it in the direction she wanted him to take.

Bruno could see the gun was cocked, safety off, and the look on her face meant business. The silencer and the night glasses pushed up on her forehead said professional. He did as he was told, sighing, *Carmine's going to have a fit.*

He refused to give up the handcuff key until Sarah poked his ear none too gently with the silencer on the end of her gun. He sat wallowing in misery as she freed Joshua. Stiff from being tied in the same position for hours, he rubbed the circulation back into his limbs while she watched Bruno closely, glancing every now and then at Joshua.

A few minutes passed. Joshua flexed his legs and arms. "We can't sit here all night waiting," he said. "Give me the gun. I'll cover him while you tie him up."

Securing Bruno was no easy task, but using a spare roll of duct tape and the handcuffs, he was trussed up like a Thanksgiving turkey. The hood and the ball gag were added for extra discomfort and maximum humiliation as he was left fully conscious, red faced, and raging through his hood.

"Let's get our stuff and get out of here," said Sarah.

They left through the open warehouse door, Joshua hobbling in pain while his circulation and cramping lessened. Sarah trotted ahead, pushing a handcart stacked with the property seized when Joshua was captured. She stopped at the gate, surveyed the street, all was quiet. She ran back, saying as she got level to him, "Deal with the handcart. I'll close up."

She returned to the warehouse and punched the button to get the gate to start opening. As soon as the opening was big enough, Joshua pushed the handcart through and started hobbling across the road. Meanwhile, Sarah hit the button to close the warehouse door, sprinted under it, and made a mad dash for the security gate. Nearly there, she tripped and sprawled on the concrete while the gate continued its unrelenting closing journey. Recovering her balance, she limped to safety with a badly skinned knee.

While Sarah drove, Joshua searched through their recovered property. He completed his inventory. "Yes. It's all here. We've got enough to go wherever we want. Cellphones, multiple passports, all our IDs, not forgetting the precious laptop. Let's dump the H&K, you keep the Sig, and I'll keep the Glock." He slid it into his hip holster.

Ten minutes later, Sarah turned onto the 605 Freeway heading south on her way to Long Beach airport, anonymity, and a life off the grid. Neither talked about the elephant in the van, the forty million dollars originally destined for Nunzio now destined for a Luxembourg bank a few days hence.

I-5 Freeway, Burbank, California

Big Vinnie picked up Carmine from Van Nuys airport and started on their way to deal with Leon. As he drove, Carmine said, "Listen, never mind what Nunzio said. I'm confident these dirtbag hackers will talk. When we get our money and the records back, they disappear. It's a matter of principle."

When Vinnie was around Carmine, he liked to demonstrate his Sicilian heritage which came through his grandfather. "Ara's a fucking *camurria*, him and his agreement. *Madonn*, we'd look like a right bunch of *cazzi* if we let them off the hook. The *moolinyans* would love to hear we're that weak."

Carmine scowled. "Nunzio passes instructions to Weiner. Ara handles Studio Z and we're the back-end muscle when needed and right now, we're needed. This is too much money to keep stupid promises. We'll get the information from this mook even if I have to cut him up a little."

"Matthew?" Vinnie was covering all the bases.

"Matthew can go too, he's a friend of Leon," said Carmine.

"Are you sure about Nunzio? He didn't want anyone touched."

"We'll blame Leon. We'll say we got the information from him after he killed Matthew and the mook. Besides, when he sees his share of the *scharole*, he's not going to be worried about how we got it." He saw Vinnie's puzzled look. "What? I thought you spoke Italian. Money. When Nunzio sees the money. *Capiche*?"

"Yes, I *capiche*."

"You mutt, you know nothing."

They lapsed into silence for the rest of the journey.

710 Freeway, Cudahy, California

Having concluded business with Ritchie, Matthew was on his way back to the warehouse. The traffic was light and the Chevelle was eating up the miles when his cellphone rang. It was Leon.

"It's hit the fan, Matthew. The shit has hit the fan."

"What's up? What's the problem?"

"Bruno is dead." He was almost shouting into the mouthpiece. "The hacker's missing and must have killed him."

"What are you talking about? I only left him less than an hour ago."

"I don't know. He's dead. I saw him with my own eyes just now. Listen to me. I know you work for me, but you also freelance with those people out of New Jersey."

"What of it?" Matthew's voice was cold.

"They might be thinking I've been skimming off them. Matthew, that's a death sentence. My family. You must help me."

"What do you want me to say? Big question is, did you do it?" No answer was forthcoming. "I'll take that as a yes."

"Matthew, Matthew, I can make everything right. I swear. I'm begging you. I just need a little time. Help me."

"Money always talks. Can you make restitution and a big fine?"

"Talk to them for me. Find out what it takes."

"Give me a number to contact you."

Leon rattled off a number. "You can trace the first call but after that you'll have a problem."

"That's your private number at the bank."

"Yes, but that's not where I'll be. No one will know my whereabouts."

East Los Angeles, California

Matthew hit the button to close the warehouse doors behind Carmine and Vinnie's Cadillac. He waited as they got out, the sound of the doors slamming echoed around the quiet warehouse. He stood silent, a serious look on his face as they approached. They glanced at each other, puzzled.

Not liking the eerie undertone, Carmine broke the silence. "Hey, Matthew, everything OK?"

Matthew said quietly, "You've got to see this to believe it."

He led them to where Bruno lay tied up, gagged, his face contorted, eyes bulging, bloodshot and wide open, staring without seeing. He was quite dead. A black woolen hood lay beside his head.

"What the fuck happened here?" asked Carmine, looking down at Bruno.

"I found him like this when I got back from Ritchie's place. I left him alone with the dickhead we lifted from Beverly Hills. He's gone and so has all his gear."

"Everything's gone?" An unhappy Carmine was dangerous, and he was very unhappy.

Vinnie stood silent, recognizing the signs and ready for anything.

"Yeah. They dropped his driver's license. Probably fake but it gives us his photo. We've got shots of her from the security cameras so at least we have their pictures. Leon badly wanted the computer. Speaking of Leon, on my way back here I got a call from him. He was all in a panic. He came here, found the hostage gone, and Bruno dead. I told him to wait around but he wasn't having any. He told me to contact him in the Caymans. That was it. I got back here and found this mess."

Carmine was disgusted. "*Porca puttana*. How could this happen? This fucks up all my plans. We have a dead man, the hackers on the hoof with our forty million, and Leon hiding in the fucking Caymans." He nudged the corpse with his foot. "What killed him?"

Matthew knelt by the body. "He's bound up like an Egyptian mummy. There're no bullet holes. Even now, he's warm to the touch. There's about an hour between me leaving him and Leon's finding him dead. If you ask me, he suffocated."

Vinnie interrupted him, "What are you, a fucking pathologist?"

"In my line of work, you see death up close." Matthew said matter-of-factly, his tone warning Vinnie he was treading too close. He pointed at Bruno's face. "If you look in his eyes, you see they're bloodshot. Lots of broken blood vessels caused by the gag suffocating him. I don't think they meant to kill him; this was an accident."

Carmine said, "It's of no consequence. Take this," he prodded the body again with his foot, "and get rid of it."

"The van's outside but I'll need some help to move him, he's a big boy," said Matthew.

"I'll take care of it," said Vinnie, and he made a call.

A short while later another of Vinnie's crew, Giuseppe, arrived. He greeted Vinnie and Carmine with the ritual cheek kissing and hugging. Matthew was introduced as an independent associate.

Carmine said, "Good, now me and Vinnie will take off." He addressed Matthew. "Come by the restaurant when you're finished, no matter the time."

They put Bruno's body in the van wrapped in a rug, "Looks like a python that ate a goat," Giuseppe said, and laughed.

Dumping the body turned into a fiasco. Ritchie's scrapyard, designated to destroy the van and the body, was a hive of police activity, a raid in progress. Matthew could hear a chopper overhead, red, blue, and white lights everywhere, radios crackling. Apart from the disposal of cars containing dead bodies, Ritchie operated a chop shop with an active sideline boosting cars.

Matthew could see Ritchie and his employees silhouetted against the police spotlights, lined up, sitting on the curb, hands cuffed behind their backs. Ritchie recognized him and desperately tried to make eye contact, but Matthew drove on, looking straight ahead, the world on either side nonexistent. *What are we going to do about Bruno now?*

Giuseppe saved the day. In the early hours of the morning, Matthew followed him along Angeles Crest Highway on the way to Mount Wilson. They were looking for a turnout Giuseppe had used previously.

The two-lane road, narrow by California standards, made him nervous. A car passed going the other way in the downhill lane, its headlights illuminated his face, sweat glistening on his forehead. The van's soft suspension wallowed around the sharp, twisting bends like a hippo in a mud pool. Out of his passenger side window, he could see a black nothing interrupted by glimpses of civilization's lights twinkling far below.

His headlights swept over an outcrop of rock as he rounded a corner, followed a second later by a vista outlook road sign. Simultaneously, the turn signal on the car ahead started blinking and its brake lights came on. Seconds later he made the same turn and stopped behind Giuseppe. Thick undergrowth, Douglas fir and Coulter pine, hid them from the road. His window hissed down as Giuseppe approached.

"Better be quick about it. Pull over there." He pointed out a spot. "Be careful, there's no barrier." He shone a flashlight and the beam settled on a four-inch-high concrete curb. "That's the only thing between you and a five-hundred-foot drop. After you're in place, I'll put my motor behind and when you get out, give me the signal and I'll push it over."

"I'll leave the engine running, put it into neutral with the parking brake off."

"Exactly."

"Go ahead," he said to Giuseppe as he stepped clear.

A crash echoed up the canyon signifying the van hitting the bottom, disappearing into the chapparal and trees hundreds of feet beneath.

"Good job," said Matthew, taking his seat in Giuseppe's car. "Now, take me back to the warehouse so I can get my car."

CHAPTER 17

A cocktail for Dixon, and Leon takes a boat trip.

**Los Angeles, California
Thursday, August 29**

After Giuseppe dropped him off, Matthew spent two hours driving the Chevelle in stop-and-go traffic; the morning rush hour was in full swing. The delay allowed him time to ponder the Joshua and Sarah situation. *Where could they have gone? How can I find them? What's going to happen to Ara's agreement now? Will Nunzio lower the boom on them? Will he give me the contract?* These, and a thousand other hypothetical questions with very few answers, rattled around his brain. He turned into the parking lot at *La Cucini di Papa*, empty apart from two Lincoln Continentals parked up by the restaurant's back door.

He knocked, and the muscle who opened it said, "You're expected." He pointed to a door. "They're in the back office over there."

Warily, his nerves tingling, senses alert, he felt the reassuring weight of the Glock on his hip as he knocked on the door and opened it. He was relieved when both Carmine and Vinnie greeted him cordially.

Carmine released his grip and said to Vinnie, "I'd recommend Nunzio open the books up for this guy except he's Irish. Good job."

"Yes, well done, Giuseppe spoke highly of you," acknowledged Vinnie.

Carmine said, "Let's sit down for Crissakes. You want something to drink? We're waiting for a call from Nunzio."

"No, nothing for me, thanks. He's not going to be happy about Bruno," Matthew commented dryly.

"He's not going to give a fuck about Bruno. He's worried about the cash," Carmine retorted sharply. They sat in silence for a few moments; the phone rang.

"That'll be Nunzio for you," said Vinnie, handing Carmine the phone.

Cradling the phone between his ear and shoulder, Carmine listened carefully as Nunzio's heavy Brooklyn accent sounded loud and clear through his earpiece.

"That you, Carmine?"

Carmine got right to the point. "Yeah. We're betting on Jamaica for Leon. He has contacts with a bunch of hoods there, family in Montego Bay, and a big boat. He told Matthew that he was going back to Cayman, but we think he's scamming us so we're looking for him in the wrong place."

"We do business with someone who knows the scene down there. If Leon turns up, we'll have the locals solve the problem. Keep you out of it. Any news on the other two?"

"We're working with one of Vinnie's crew to trace the calls. Still waiting on word."

"This is a real fuck up, Carmine. You and Matthew go to Van Nuys airport. The jet's fueled and ready for the Caymans. Matthew knows the people there. Get hold of Leon's brother, David, and use him to take control of the bank. I'm sending a couple of accountants from here to help straighten things out."

"When will they get there?"

"The four of you are expected tomorrow at the bank. I want them working day and night to get this sorted. Make sure David knows who's running things."

"Do you want the bank closed?"

"Business as usual, but stall any suspect transactions until they can be verified. Second, Vinnie will stay and take care of business in LA. See to Dixon personally."

Carmine said, "With the time difference and dealing with Leon, it might be too late to handle Dixon. He's probably been warned off by Leon and done a runner."

"We'll find him anyway. Meanwhile, do as I say, put the frighteners on Leon's brother and straighten out the bank." There was a click as Nunzio disconnected the call.

"Score one for us. All because of you," Carmine said to Matthew, grasping his cheek and squeezing it gently, patting the other cheek with the palm of his hand. "Good information on Leon's boat."

Santa Barbara, California
Friday, August 30

The following morning, Vincent dropped Carmine and Matthew at the airport for their flight to the Caymans. Afterwards, he'd driven to Santa Barbara where he reconnoitered Dixon's house and found he could observe the property without the possibility of interference from nosy neighbors.

Just before noon, the electric gates opened, and Dixon's Aston Martin emerged. Vincent followed the distinctive car back to the Biltmore where a grinning valet took delivery. Dixon went into the hotel where he sat at the crowded bar. It was well stocked with many fine brands of liquor, and he took his time deciding.

"Give me a large Glenmorangie. No ice, just straight up." He slapped a fifty down.

"I see you know your single malts, sir," the barman replied cordially. He took a bottle from behind the bar and carefully poured a generous double portion of the eighteen-year-old Scotch.

"Nectar of the Gods," replied Dixon, who took a mouthful and swished it around his mouth before swallowing it with a sigh of appreciation.

He doesn't seem worried. I don't think Leon's been in touch. I wonder why? thought Vincent. *He must be expecting someone because he's scanning the door every time it opens.*

Vincent dressed casually formal to fit in with the Biltmore crowd. With an expensive salt-and-pepper wig, matching beard and mustache, his own mother wouldn't have recognized him. His jacket was reversible so he could switch color from brown to green to throw off any pursuit. He looked around and secured a place at the bar just two stools down from Dixon. Like any ambush predator, he waited patiently for the right moment to strike.

In an unfortunate twist of fate, Dixon left the bar to greet the arrival of friends while his drink stood alone on the bar, momentarily unattended. Vinnie left his seat and stood behind Dixon's empty seat. He leaned forward, resting on the bar beside Dixon's glass, squinting as if short sighted as he appeared to examine the labels on the spirit bottles behind the bar. A syringe concealed in the palm of his hand contained an undetectable poison. Using this ruse, he deftly squirted a lethal dose into Dixon's drink.

Even a sip was fatal, symptoms replicating a heart attack occurring within a few minutes.

Vinnie returned to his seat at the bar and sat quietly finishing his Heineken. Meanwhile, after returning to the bar, Dixon entertained his friends by purchasing a round of drinks and offering a toast to his guests. Vinnie watched Dixon drain his glass, waited a few minutes longer, and left the bar. As he walked through the exit door, there was the crash of breaking glass accompanied by a scream. He turned and saw Dixon lying on the floor clutching his chest, already unconscious and not breathing. Several of his guests crouched over him, one giving chest compressions.

Someone shouted, "Call 911!"

Vincent ignored the ruckus and made good his escape. He knew traces of the poison would have disappeared from the body before an autopsy. This would leave the coroner no option other than to record a verdict of 'natural causes.'

Montego Bay, Jamaica
Friday, August 30

The voyage from the Caymans had taken eleven hours and dawn had broken by the time *Candyman* moored in a guest berth at the Montego Bay Yacht Club. For the last twenty miles they had endured thirty knot winds and a six-foot swell in choppy seas, all driven by a low-pressure system south of Puerto Rico. Rough going even in the Bertram. One of the diesels developed a rumbling noise for the last quarter of the journey, forcing him to drop speed. With his nervous family aboard, the boat rocking and rolling, and his kids throwing up, Leon was highly relieved when they finally tied up alongside the dock.

They had cleared customs and were met by his cousin George who lived at nearby Doctor's Cave Beach. From a secret cupboard in the engine compartment, Leon took a duffle bag full of hundred-dollar bills wrapped in five-thousand-dollar bundles. He counted out twenty bundles and stuffed them in a white plastic shopping bag. *That'll take care of things with George until I can get Nunzio sorted.*

He went on deck, locked up, and walked down the dock, past the Yacht Club, and into the parking lot where George was loading the luggage into a black Cadillac. Leon's wife, Cassandra, stood beside the passenger door, the girls in their seats watching their parents but waiting quietly. He went to either side of the car and kissed them goodbye before turning his attention to Cassandra.

He held her tight. "It might be a while," he whispered. "I'm in a little bit of trouble and need to sort it out. It could take a couple of weeks."

"You will be careful, won't you?" Her eyes welled up and a tear trickled down her cheek, spoiling her mascara. He never discussed business with her, but she knew he had dealings with dangerous people.

He kissed the tear away, and said, "Here's a hundred grand," handing her the shopping bag. "You pay George five grand a month out of that to make sure you're safe. If I'm not around, David's holding money in an account under your maiden name. I don't know how long it will take to get the boat fixed, but I'll take off when it's done. You wait here for me to contact you."

"Can I count on David?"

"Yes. He's still running things at the bank. There will be other people involved but you're another customer with a large account. Everything's in your name, everything—the house, cars, the lot. Don't forget the gun safe by my desk. You have the combination. There's cash in there too. You're set."

Cassandra received another hug and a long, lingering kiss. He handed her a tissue.

"Hold on, looks like George is ready to go. I'll be in touch. Love you."

She got in the passenger seat, he closed the door behind her, and the Cadillac started to pull away before she could lower her window. Her last view of him was hazy, the tinted window blurring the image of a much-reduced man, the weight of the world on his shoulders. She sobbed into the tissue, waving her arm to dismiss the children who were asking why she was crying. Leon waved them goodbye and watched until they turned on to Sunset Drive and disappeared.

As he walked slowly back to the boat, depression swept over him. He didn't know when he would see his family again. *Is Matthew helping Nunzio?* he wondered, stepping over the taffrail and walking down the ladder to below deck. *I'm stuck until I can get someone to look at that port engine. Won't be anyone around for a couple of hours yet. Think I'll have a snooze.* He climbed under the duvet, stretched himself out, and fell asleep. He awoke a short while later, made some coffee, and walked up on deck. He checked his watch. *Still too early for the mechanic.* He stood up and stretched, enjoying the early morning warmth while settling back on a locker, waiting, sipping his black coffee, and thinking of his next move. *Flying out from here is going to be too easy to trace. They won't anticipate me going to Haiti.* He smiled in satisfaction.

At the Montego Bay Yacht Club, Winston Green walked purposefully down the dock. Everything about him said grease monkey, from his dirty fingernails to his oil-stained denim overalls, blackened on the rear end from wiping his hands. He was muscular, easily handling the weight of a red metal toolbox. He gave the dock the once over. It was quiet, the only sounds coming from fishermen a couple of slips away laughing and joking, tipsy already. A figure farther down the dock sat on a locker, waiting. *That'll be Leon.* As he approached the slip he called out. "You the one needs a mechanic?"

"Yeah." Leon stood up, waited a few minutes until Winston got close. "Welcome aboard."

"What's the problem?"

"I'm not sure. We developed a rumble that seemed to be coming from the port engine."

"Let's start it up and get a diagnosis going. Show me where you think the noise was coming from."

Leon went to the bridge and started the engines, causing a slight vibration throughout the hull as they throbbed away. They descended a ladder into the engine bay where Leon bent over the engine, his head pointed away from Winston as he listened for signs of trouble.

Winston said, "Hang on, I'll get a better light and a stethoscope to see what's going on." With his back to Leon, he opened his tool chest and pulled out a drawer of tools. In the compartment beneath lay a sawed-off pump action Remington shotgun and a nine-millimeter Baretta with a silencer attached. Winston's problem-solving skills provided a permanent and guaranteed solution.

Picking up the Baretta, he turned and shot Leon twice in the back of the head using expanding bullets. A mixture of bone, blood, and brains spattered the engine and engine compartment. Almost headless, the body slumped over, sliding to the deck in a trail of blood and gore. Being careful to avoid the blood pooling beside the corpse, Winston pocketed seven hundred dollars and some credit cards from Leon's wallet. He took several polaroid shots of Leon's disfigured body before switching off the twin diesels and beginning his search of the boat from stem to stern.

While Leon was destined to become another number in the unsolved murder statistics for that year, Winston strolled back down the wharf, easily managing his toolbox in one hand and a large canvas bag in the other. Weighing in at nearly seventy pounds, it contained close to three million dollars in crisp one-hundred-dollar bills.

Grand Cayman, Cayman Islands
Friday, August 30

The S-Class Mercedes was conveniently parked a couple of paces from their hotel. With a grunt, Carmine settled in the soft leather back seat with Matthew seated alongside him. There wasn't much conversation. The trunk lid closed with a thump, the driver's door opened, and he took his seat. Squinting over his shoulder, he said, "Imperial Bank. Right?"

"Yes."

Twenty minutes later, Carmine sat across the table from Leon's brother in Imperial Bank of Panama's boardroom. The two accountants sent by Nunzio weren't invited, they sat out of hearing, silent, suited and booted, two lurchers sniffing the scent of rabbit.

Carmine said pleasantly, "David, we seem to have a difficult situation. Nunzio, that's Mr. Nunzio to you, sent me here to help clear up the mess caused by your brother."

"What mess are you talking about?" David said bravely, making his first mistake.

Carmine's face grew cold and dark. He didn't look at David—he looked through him, his voice flat, menacing, and direct. "Are you telling me you don't know where Leon's hiding with the millions of dollars he's stolen from us? You'd better wake up because I'm not here to fuck around."

"I thought he was in LA. If he's not, I have no idea where he is."

"When was the last time you spoke?"

"Couple of days ago. I told him someone had hacked our bank accounts, but I haven't heard from him since. I handle the public and merchant banking end. He handles the private clients' accounts although, on occasion, I have transferred funds as necessary under his direct supervision. I didn't question anything, just followed his instructions."

"See, here's the deal. You're going to work with those two accountants out there and we're going to go through your records. Very quiet. Very discreet. Very thorough." He cocked his eyebrow as David interrupted him.

"That's impossible. I can't do anything without Leon's approval."

Carmine sighed. "But you don't know where he is, do you?"

"No," David stammered, "but the clients' information is confidential."

Carmine sat back in his chair, folded his hands in his lap, stared at the ceiling and sniffed. Leaning forward, he said. "What about the millions of dollars these two hackers stole? What about the hundred mill Leon stole from Nunzio?"

Carmine pulled out a .357 Magnum. All David could see was the very large hole pointing at his head. "Well..." his voice trailed off. Beneath the Louis XV writing desk, his legs began to shake as he unsuccessfully tried to stem the urine trickling down his leg.

Carmine calmly leaned across the desk and smacked David with the gun. Blood gushed out of a gash on his eyebrow.

"Here's how it's going to be. We're taking over the bank now. You're responsible for Leon's debt and those two accountants outside are going to work here full-time. You'll keep your position, and everything will be normal as far as the staff, customers, and the law are concerned. We'll be behind the scenes running the operation. Everyone gets paid. You got that?" He rapped the gun on the desktop.

David cowered, his face ashen, a tissue held over his wound failed to stem the blood. It ran down the side of his neck onto his shirt, staining the collar a deep crimson. He sagged in his chair, a picture of abject submission.

"Yes. Yes. Whatever you want." His voice cracked to a whisper. "Please, put the gun away."

"That's better." Carmine sneered, putting his gun back in his waistband. "Do as you're told, and everything will be cool. Fuck me around, and you'll get more of the same." He picked up a box of tissues from the desktop and threw it at him.

"Here, clean yourself up."

He picked up a framed photograph from the desk.

"Wife and kids?" he asked.

"Yes, please, please..." David was begging.

Carmine was having none of it, he put his forefinger to his lips, shushing him. "I'm sure you'd do anything to make sure your family's safe. We all would. Don't disappoint me." He shook his head and put it back in place on the desk.

"Now the first thing I want is the master keys and anything else needed to get what we want done. Let's meet your IT people ASAP. We need to go through the computers for traces the hackers might have left and this place needs to be swept for bugs."

David had no option but to cooperate and had given all the help he could before retreating to the bathroom. Involuntarily shivering, he crouched on the toilet, weeping from the motivational pistol whipping.

Carmine turned to Matthew. "Let's search through Leon's office. I doubt he's left any clues, but we can tell Nunzio that it was done."

As predicted, the search proved unsuccessful. Afterwards, Carmine gave instructions to the accountants. Matthew wasn't included in the conversation, so he took the opportunity to wander into the lobby of the bank where he took a seat at an empty desk. He was about to make a dangerous move and wanted to be sure he was unobserved. Keeping his phone below desk level, he quickly tapped out an encrypted relay chat message to an address book name of Harry Rood.

"Leon needs help. Has lots of cash. Only you can help him."

Matthew checked his watch. "Hey, Carmine," he called out, "I need to call Antonio and see if he found any phone numbers for us."

"Right. While I look through the bank's client lists, you call him and find out what he has to say."

Matthew called Antonio.

"It's the same person you bugged in the hotel in Santa Monica and her partner. They've done a runner and could be anywhere, maybe even overseas. Any chance of locating them by their phone use?"

"These people are sophisticated. We did find the one cellphone, but she's stopped using it and it's disappeared off the network. She used two different rented offices on the calls to Ara and was gone by the time we got there. We're still checking everything, and I'll let you know."

"Yeah. Call me with anything you get."

"Don't rush off. Ara told me to check the Beverly Wilshire for any calls from room 334. During the time your man was in that room he made one call that will interest you. It was to a bank in Zurich."

"Which bank?"

"The number's registered to a D & R Bankengruppe. I just got off the phone with Ara who told me four hundred grand was sent to that same bank as part of a deal."

Matthew put the phone down and went to tell Carmine the good news.

Tel Aviv, Israel
Saturday, August 31

Sonny was frustrated and worried. *Where the hell are they? Are they safe? What's going on?* The previous evening, the two fake FBI agents who had been at Joshua's hotel room completed their more urgent assignment from the Israeli embassy and called him. He immediately dispatched them to Leon's suspected warehouse. After breaking-in, they found it to be empty. The only sign of recent activity were strips of duct tape strewn on the floor, ominous clues someone had recently been held captive.

Sonny considered. *Joshua must have been abducted from the hotel and taken to the warehouse. If Sarah rescued him how come they haven't checked in? Are they still alive? Prisoners maybe? More likely dead, bodies never recovered.*

He shivered at the thought and spread the word around his vast network. Nothing turned up. It was as if Joshua and Sarah had never existed.

CHAPTER 18

*Sarah metes out justice and Herr
Richter shows his true colors.*

Zurich, Switzerland
Tuesday, September 3

Joshua paid off the taxi at the hotel entrance shortly after
arriving from Zurich's Hauptbahnhof. He checked in at the
hotel reception.

"Any messages for me?"

The clerk searched for his name but came up with
nothing. "I'm afraid not, sir."

"Thank you." *She's supposed to be here by now.*

The bellhop opened the door to his room, placed his
suitcase on a small stand, and walked around the suite
extolling its virtues. The five-star Dolder Grand sat like a
majestic old lady atop a hill with stunning views over Lake
Zurich and distant mountains. Smiling frequently, Joshua
was tired and not paying attention as the net curtains were
opened, revealing the views over the hotel's golf course.
He'd been travelling constantly, backtracking and covering
traces of his movements. It was almost as if, instead of
laundering money, he was laundering himself; different
identities, disguises, and passports all designed to keep
Nunzio off his trail. His caution was well placed; he had no
illusions about the long reach of the Mob. He handed over

ten Swiss Francs, ushered the bellhop out, and sighed with relief as the door closed behind him. He undressed and showered, letting the hot water play on his neck for fifteen minutes or so to ease the tension before he went to bed.

He slept for a couple of hours and, waking, picked up the phone, called reception, and found Sarah had still not checked in. He lay there, unsuccessfully trying to calm the negative thoughts flooding through his mind. *What's keeping her? She's not normally late. No calls on the cell.*

After leaving the warehouse, they had driven to Long Beach where a contact of Joshua's was a pilot for a private jet service. In a stroke of luck, he was leaving for Atlanta the following morning. For a price, he agreed not to list them on the passenger manifest. On arrival in Atlanta, Joshua went his way and Sarah went hers, agreeing to contact one another only in an emergency but with the arrangement to meet in Zurich on September 3. And here he was, waiting. *What are we going to do about the Mob's money?*

Meanwhile, Sarah was fighting for her life on a train bound for Zurich. She was in an empty carriage and had been enjoying the panoramic view of Lake Zurich as the train skirted its shores. The noise of a carriage door sliding open behind her interrupted her reverie. A young man lurched through the gangway between the seats. He caught sight of Sarah sitting alone and leered, his face flushed. She could smell his boozy breath as he stood in the aisle, leaning over the back of the seat adjacent to her.

"Want some company?" he asked in German.

She gave him a stony look, and said, "*Nein, danke*—no, thank you."

No sooner were the words out of her mouth than the train lurched sending him staggering as he lost his grip on the seat. His awkwardness made her laugh, something she instantly regretted as his face grew dark in a drunken rage.

"Stuck up bitch, eh? We'll see about that." He jumped on her, thrusting his hand between her legs, his other hand around her throat.

Sarah's self-defense training kicked into action but her first punch missed its target, succeeding only in enraging him further. Fortunately for her, he made the tactical mistake of putting both hands around her throat to strangle her. It left his nether regions fully exposed to her knee which she jerked upward with such savagery that it ruptured his right testicle. His mouth gaped open in reaction as the first wave of excruciating pain surged through his groin. Swift karate chops to the vagus nerves on either side of his neck followed. He slumped down on her, unconscious, weighing her down.

Her heart was racing as she struggled to free herself from under him. Finally, standing up and breathing hard, she adjusted her clothing and straightened herself out. The crumpled heap of humanity in what had been her seat was still breathing. She heaved him into a sitting position and leaned his head against the window in a hunched-over pose. Other passengers would assume he was asleep. Picking up her backpack, she took a seat several carriages down the train where there were other passengers. Facing the door, she waited, ready for anything.

The train slowed to a stop at Ruschlikon where she saw her assailant limp over to a bench seat. He sat hunched over, his head face down between his knees, his suit and shoes liberally spattered with the contents of his last meal. Then, as the train was pulling out of the station, the sight of him retching again caused a smile to cross her face. She heaved a huge sigh of relief. *Soon be in Zurich with Josh.*

Then it hit her. *Christ, what are we going to do with the extra forty million?*

Dolder Grand Hotel, Zurich

The telephone rang in Joshua's room. "Yes?"

"What kind of answer is that?" It was Sarah.

"Thank God, I've been worried."

"Why don't you slip up to my very nice double deluxe room? It has great views, and we can enjoy a drink before dinner."

"Give me your room number and I'm there."

Her peal of laughter was loud in his ear, and true to his word, a few minutes later, he knocked on her door.

They hugged and she kissed him lightly on the cheek. He kissed her back, then they were kissing hard, tearing at each other's clothes, the near miss with Goossens, the Mob, and her attempted rapist, fueled emotions. Knives, forks, spoons, and dishes were swept to the floor as they found relief in frenzied sex on the table.

Both were panting, sweating, and laughing as Joshua pushed himself off her, reaching down to pull up his underpants and trousers. Sarah sat up and pulled her dress down.

"If you'll please hand me my underwear."

She was still wearing her bra, which had been pulled up over her breasts, and she was missing a button on her blouse, which gaped open. She adjusted herself while he handed her a purple cotton thong.

"If only I'd known," he laughed.

They kissed and held each other tight. She whispered in his ear.

"That was incredible. Come to bed with me. Let's enjoy the closeness we have while we can."

Their arms around each other, they went to the large bedroom where they climbed beneath the sheets, nestling in each other's arms on the eighteen-hundred-count Egyptian sheets. This time their lovemaking was slow and deliberate, each exploring the other's bodies with both eventually exploding in ecstasy. Afterwards, they lay entwined, feeling the strain of loneliness and despair of the past weeks dissipate as they fell asleep.

Wednesday, September 4

The following morning, they ate a room service breakfast and planned out the day.

"We have to visit Richter at the bank and arrange for the bearer bonds," said Joshua. "No appointment needed, so we can collect them whenever we want. That might be a good time to contact Marcus and settle Ara's forty million."

Sarah frowned in disapproval.

"I don't think Ara double-crossed us. It was probably Nunzio, and we don't want him and the rest of his friends chasing us forever. After we settle that issue, we can go wherever we like."

"Hmmm. I like the sound of wherever we like. Not that this is shabby." She admired the luxurious room. "Why don't we have a day off and I'll do some shopping. When I get back here, I'm going to have a spa treatment. Maybe we can pick up the bonds tomorrow. After that, let's start planning our next move."

After he heard about the call to D & R Bankengruppe, Nunzio instructed Matthew and Carmine to go to Zurich and leave the accountants to supervise David and banking operations in the Caymans. They had flown on American Airlines in the first-class cabin using stolen tickets supplied by the ever-enterprising Sal "Tickets" Russo who lived up to his nickname. It was late evening when they checked into the Hotel Doppelzimmer on Neumuhlequai in old town Zurich where the concierge confirmed the D & R Bankengruppe was within easy walking distance. It was decided that a quick stroll would allow them to get their bearings and maybe visit a couple of watering holes.

"Cobbled streets," said Carmine with a smile. "Brings back memories."

"For me too," Matthew echoed. "It's hard to believe the large number of cobbled streets left in London."

"I was thinking New York."

"Can't help you there."

"Packed with people," Carmine commented, as they elbowed their way through the throng. "Looks like a farmer's market."

"Yeah. I forgot about it being so busy this time of year. It's a bit more than the farmer's market you're used to back home. I think it's a street party called *DÖRFLIFÄSCHT*." Matthew's accent showed off his fluent German. "Rubbish bands and lots of folk art that the locals wouldn't touch with a bargepole. The food stalls are usually good, especially if you like brats, sauerkraut, and schnitzel. They love their meat here."

Carmine checked out the surroundings. "Look at all these clubs. I wonder who's providing protection?"

"Making a killing by the look of it. Look at all the customers. Where in the hell is this bank?"

They continued their walk until, arriving at a square, they saw, tucked away on the corner, a two-story stone building with a sign over the entrance: *D & R Bankengruppe.*

Carmine said, "That wasn't hard. Now we know where it is, we'll come back about ten tomorrow morning and see what we can find out. In the meantime, fancy one of these clubs? Pick up some company."

Matthew cried off, "Nah. You go ahead. Knock yourself out. My ass is dragging, and I want to get some rest. Why don't we meet up in the morning for coffee or breakfast?"

They bantered back and forth as Carmine tried to get him to go clubbing. To preserve the illusion of fellowship, Matthew finally relented.

Thursday, September 5

Matthew woke up the following morning with classic hangover symptoms and made his way to the hotel café, waiting for Carmine to appear. He ordered black coffee and a stack of Kartoffelpuffer to get something in his stomach. After dipping the crispy pancake in apple sauce, the messy morsel was almost in his mouth when Carmine shouldered his way through a line of people and sat down at his table.

"How'd you make out last night? I saw you leave with that dark-haired number."

Matthew chewed his mouthful slowly, making Carmine wait while giving him a hostile look.

He swallowed. "Well, good morning to you too. If you must know, I just walked her back to her hotel and told her I'd call her after we finish our business today."

Carmine was eager to share the sordid details of his own previous night's conquest and relished in the telling. Matthew inspected him with a detached air. All the bluster went in one ear and right out the other as Carmine rambled on. *You are the most ignorant person I've ever had the misfortune to meet. Why do I always get the assholes?*

He finished his pancakes with a sigh, pushing the plate away, and nudged the coffee a little closer. Carmine had finally finished his lurid tale and after taking a swig of coffee said, "Ara called me last night. There's someone coming to meet us to help with this bank. I think this is her now."

He waved to a small bespectacled woman who had just walked into the café. Matthew turned to give her his full attention. Frau Fischer was in her late forties and had been in the private banking business for the past twenty-five years. Dressed formally, she was wearing a two-piece skirt suit with a grey wool jacket over a black skirt. As she sat down, her jacket fell open, and Matthew caught a glimpse of the Givenchy label. She was attractive in a mousy sort of way, and he noted the gold wedding band with what looked like a four-carat emerald-cut diamond ring.

She spoke beautiful English with only a slight accent. "Good morning."

She turned to Carmine, "You would be...?"

He took advantage of the hesitation. "Carmine," he supplied.

She turned and said, "So that makes you Matthew."

"Correct," he answered.

"Ara gave me the details of your problem. Let's go to the bank and see if the director will help with this embezzlement. Don't get your hopes up. The secrecy laws here are serious, and supplying details on clients could send you to prison. I'm here because I have Swiss citizenship and have served on the banking commission. I know Herr Richter so that might help. It probably means nothing because you don't want the authorities involved, but with my presence we'll be taken seriously. Do either of you speak German?"

"*Ein wenig*," said Matthew. "Sufficient to understand and be understood."

"I didn't know you spoke German," Carmine said.

"Yeah, enough to get myself into trouble so I keep quiet most of the time."

A brisk walk later, they were ushered into the offices of Herr Dieter Richter, the managing director of D & R Bankengruppe. Taking the lead, Frau Fischer spoke German to explain the presence of her two associates along with the circumstances that brought them to the bank. Matthew followed every word while appearing to study the framed print by H.R. Geiger on the wall behind Richter's desk. It featured the profile of the alien from the movie of the same name.

"Herr Direktor, I was hoping you could help the situation along by explaining the call from Beverly Hills and the reason it came here," Frau Fischer finished.

Richter sat back in his chair and surveyed the unlikely-looking trio in front of him. *Frau Fischer, a respectable woman. What are you doing with these two thugs?* He spoke out loud in English, "Frau Fischer, I appreciate your request but the banking regulations . . ." He shrugged and spread out his hands, courting sympathy. "My hands are tied."

Not to be outdone, Frau Fischer produced photos of Joshua and Sarah. "These are two suspects." She produced a business card. "Please call me if they contact you." Fixing him with a steely glare, she said, "Herr Richter, I was hoping for more cooperation. We know one another from banking circles, and I thought our relationship," she emphasized the word, "would have allowed for a little relaxing of the rules. We are talking fraud on a massive scale, not to mention a seven-figure reward." It was a clear offer of a bribe, but Richter remained loyal to his clients.

"I'm sure the police would grant a search warrant. I'd obviously have to comply," he suggested.

"My clients want to keep this matter confidential for the moment. If the matter is not resolved in a timely fashion, the police may become involved," she lied unashamedly.

"Then I regret to inform you, we have nothing further to discuss." He must have pushed a hidden bell because as he stood up, Marie, his secretary, opened his office door, ready to usher the visitors out.

Matthew could see Carmine wanted to slap this fool silly and watched him struggle to contain himself. Herr Richter sensed the danger and was about to summon security when everybody rose and, after politely exchanging handshakes, left the office, muttering thank yous and goodbyes to Marie as they passed her.

Standing outside of the bank, Carmine turned to Frau Fischer. "Where do we go from here?"

She opened her Hermes Birkin handbag, retail value over $3,500, and produced a slip of paper.

"I'll push on the old boy network from my end. Things move slowly here, so be patient. Should I get information, I'll be in touch. Here's the best number to get me." She proffered her card with a Zurich telephone number.

Leaving Sarah shopping on the Bahnhofstrasse, Joshua walked back along Neidendorfstrasse to the square where D & R Bankengruppe was located. He stopped abruptly on seeing three figures standing outside the bank entrance. It was too far to identify features but there was something about them that triggered his adrenalin. *Is that Matthew?*

He stepped into a handily located coffee shop, ordered a latte, and sat at a table from which he could view the whole square. He pretended to look at his phone while he observed the trio outside the bank. They walked across the square diagonally towards the coffee shop. *Fuck. Yes, it is Matthew. Who's the other guy? And the woman?* He had a moment of panic as they approached. *Are they coming in here?* A quick glance over his shoulder showed a back way out if needed. Deciding to hold his ground, he turned his attention back to the trio now standing outside the coffee shop's large bay window.

Joshua thanked his lucky stars he'd chosen a seat where other patrons shielded him from their view but allowed him to watch them closely. He groaned, *Matthew's dangerous enough on his own. Now we have another goon to worry about.* He paid close attention to them, memorizing facial expressions as Matthew did most of the talking. *His German must be good.*

After a two-minute conversation, the woman went on her way. For a moment Joshua thought the two men were coming into the coffee shop and he prepared to abandon ship. Fortunately, they went elsewhere while he considered his next course of action. He texted Sarah.

"Saw Matthew and one other. Go back to hotel and wait for me."

He finished his drink, feeling the warmth of the coffee spreading through his chest, and decided to pay Herr Richter a visit.

Herr Richter, knowing him by an alias, responded to Joshua's question matter-of-factly.

"Herr Boynton, yes, we've had visitors inquiring about your business today." He leaned forward with a serious expression, "I was obligated to quote the law. Nevertheless, one of the people here today was Frau Fischer who is very influential in banking circles. She showed me a photograph that identified you as 'Joshua.' The other photo was of your companion Sarah, who I've seen just once. I was informed you are both wanted for fraud."

"Herr Richter, you've seen my passport, approved our other banking relationships, and deemed everything satisfactory. The names on these photos are clearly incorrect and causing confusion. I'm afraid this harassment comes from a lawsuit I'm pursuing. Unfortunately, the plaintiffs are being very underhanded. This isn't the first instance either."

"Yes, if it was fraud, I found it curious that they were not pursuing this as a police matter."

"Exactly," answered Joshua, wanting to leave the matter as vague as possible.

"Herr Boynton, you should be careful. I didn't like the look of the two men accompanying Frau Fischer. She introduced them as Matthew and Carmine, do those names mean anything to you?" Richter's expression was bland as he waited for a reply.

"No, they're not a party to the lawsuit."

"Forgive me, but I thought they were gangsters. Frankly, I was surprised they were in Frau Fischer's company."

"As I said, I don't know any of these people."

"Herr Boynton, our transactions have been perfectly legal but closer examination might bring about a tax investigation, especially with Frau Fischer's influence. You've been an excellent customer and I'm not anxious to lose your business. However, under the circumstances, you might avoid any unpleasantness by moving your deposits to another bank, perhaps even to another country."

"Truthfully, I'm not worried but I'll follow your advice and close the account. Let's transfer the balance to another entity, I think it's just over eleven million. When that transfer goes through, of the remaining balance, one hundred thousand euros will be paid to you in any manner you choose. Of course, this would be in addition to any commission you earn on the transfer. In return, I hope that any inquiries about me, my companion, or my account will be met with as much delay as possible. Also, I anticipate resuming business with you in the future after this lawsuit has blown over."

They shook hands on the deal and Joshua left the bank after making sure he was not being observed.

Carmine and Matthew made their way back to the hotel with Carmine voicing his dissatisfaction with Richter all the way. He finally came to a halt.

"I've had it with that son of a bitch. I'm going back to give him a slap and teach him to have some respect."

"You can't do that," said Matthew.

They were blocking the sidewalk as they stood arguing and attracted the attention of other pedestrians forced to walk around them.

"Don't try to stop me," threatened Carmine, who turned around and began walking back towards the bank.

"Come on, Carmine, we don't want any problems with the Swiss cops. We're not in New York now. These fuckers will lock you up and throw away the key."

Carmine was having none of it and left Matthew trailing in his wake.

As he made his way along a crowded Neidendorfstrasse, Joshua suddenly came face to face with Carmine. They both stopped, shocked. Carmine managed to grab onto him with one hand, but Joshua's reactions were quicker. It cost him his jacket, but he escaped into the crowd and Carmine threw it to the ground in disgust and raced after him.

Rather than run, Joshua chose to walk briskly, knowing that running in a crowd would cause a stir of complaints easily seen from behind. He could hear Carmine shrieking instructions.

"He's here, Matthew. Joshua is here. Towards the big church. You go that side and I'll cover this side. He's in a blue shirt. Don't let him get away."

Holy shit, not again thought Joshua as he slipped through the crowded street, picking his moments to move quickly between people with apologies and minimal physical contact. Carmine and Matthew were like coonhounds on the scent, pushing and shoving their way through the crowd, jumping up, necks straining, ignoring complaints, trying to catch a glimpse of a fleeing blue shirt.

An out-of-breath Joshua hurried into a large clothing store. In fifteen seconds, he boosted a pair of sunglasses, a black baseball-style cap, and a brown suede bomber jacket. His jacket zipped up, hat pulled forward and wearing the sunglasses, he reversed course, deliberately walking back towards his pursuers. The crowd was dense, and he came within three feet of Matthew who didn't see him until the last second.

Before he could react, Joshua administered a swift kick to Matthew's shin with his steel reinforced toecap shoes. A scream of pain turned into a gurgle with the follow up, a devastating punch to his Adam's apple. As he started to collapse, Joshua grabbed him, lowered him to the ground and shouted out in German, "This man needs medical attention." Matthew was in no position to argue, gasping for air, both hands holding his throat as people gathered around. Joshua slowly backed away through the crowd and made good his escape.

Carmine, suddenly aware of a commotion on the other side of the street, glimpsed Matthew lying on the ground as the crowd drew back to give him space and air. He rushed over and struggled, cursing and shouting, to push his way to the front of the onlookers. He saw two men had propped Matthew up in a sitting position and got down on his knees beside him with his ear close to Matthew's mouth.

All he heard was said in a hoarse whisper, "Joshua. Brown bomber jacket." He nodded his head in the direction of the Grossmunster, a huge twelfth-century church whose twin spires dominated the Zurich skyline. "Went that way. Go. I'll be all right in a minute," he stammered and coughed. "Got me in the throat."

Carmine raced off down the street, leaving more angry faces and shouts behind him, as he pushed and shoved his way in the direction Matthew had indicated.

Joshua was breathing easier. He made his way cautiously along Marktgasse towards the river Limmat and Rathaus transit station.

Whew, close call, too close, but I think I've lost them he thought as he turned a corner. *Fuck. I don't believe it.*

There was Carmine, not thirty feet away, gazing blankly around, looking lost. He saw Joshua and with a roar of rage started running towards him. It was fortunate for Joshua that the Mob lifestyle was not conducive to physical activity. With Matthew out of the picture, Joshua had no problem putting distance between himself and Carmine. He last saw him maybe seventy-five feet back, stopped, hands on knees, gasping for breath. Furious he didn't have a gun, Carmine pointed at his eye and then at Joshua.

The meaning was clear. *I'll see you again, motherfucker. Our business isn't finished.*

Joshua hurried on, keeping a firm grip on the Glock in his pocket until a tram at Neumarkt took him away from the area and he was able to relax a little. He changed trams several times to make sure he wasn't followed and finally arrived at Romerhof, where he took the incline railway to the Dolder Grand.

Sarah waited patiently in her hotel room, furious at recent events. The message from Joshua warning about Carmine and Matthew was devastating.

We shot ourselves in the foot with the money. Never should have used the same bank.

"Stupid, stupid," she shouted out loud as she nervously paced the room, waiting for Joshua to appear.

It's always the little details. One of these days we'll fuck up once too often.

The phone rang; it was Joshua calling from the lobby phone, letting her know he was coming to her room. A few minutes later, there was a double knock on her door followed by a pause and then another double knock. It was Joshua's signature. Taking up her gun, she rushed to the door and used the peephole to confirm he was alone. Opening the door, she greeted him.

"Carmine and Matthew? Here? Are you kidding me? We fucked up. They obviously traced the call you made from Beverly Hills. Why didn't we send everything to the Geneva account? What a pair of morons."

He ignored her running commentary as he brushed past her. "We had nearly a half-million sitting there from the commissions, so we had to go there anyway. We've used Richter before to get bearer bonds and I guess I wasn't thinking."

"Where did you come across them? At the bank?"

He took off his coat and threw it on the bed then sat in a nearby armchair.

"I spotted Matthew and Carmine as they left the bank with a woman I didn't recognize. I hid inside a coffee shop to watch and nearly had a heart attack when I thought they were coming to get coffee. I was ready to run out the back door but got lucky when they stopped outside for a chat. After about five minutes they left. The woman took Niederdorfstrasse, and they went in another direction."

"What happened then?" Sarah asked nervously.

"I did think about following the woman but decided to see Richter again."

"You went back to the bank? Why take the risk?"

He ignored her question. "Richter told me the woman is a big wig in banking circles and the guy with Matthew was introduced as Carmine. Now, I happen to know that name. He's another of Nunzio's hitters. Before we talk further, I need to get on the computer and shift the money in Richter's bank to our laundering operation. We're giving him a hundred thousand euros to stall unofficial inquiries, probably a waste of money. He'll fold like a cheap suit when Carmine and Matthew get ahold of him. Fortunately for us, by that time the money will be untraceable."

"What do we do now?"

"I haven't told you the best bit yet." He related the foot race through downtown Zurich and how he had outwitted Carmine and Matthew.

"My God." Sarah held the palms of her hands against her face, her mouth open and her eyes wide, as she listened. He finished, and she said, "We've got to get out of here. This is a small town."

"We're heading for Paris. I'm arranging for the eleven million to turn up at the bank on Rue Beaubourg, not far from Notre Dame. Once there, we'll get the bearer bonds I was hoping Richter was going to supply."

"Should we call Ara and see if we can make a deal?"

"I say not yet. I don't understand why Ara didn't stick to the agreement. After all, there's forty million at stake. Maybe Nunzio got involved, I don't know. The final piece of the money puzzle will be in place when we collect the bearer bonds in Paris. Then we can work on getting the Mob off our backs. First, let me get the money transfers done. When I've finished, we'll check out and take a road trip."

On Niederdorfstrasse, Carmine rejoined Matthew. "What the fuck happened to you?" he demanded.

Matthew's voice was still gravelly. "I saw him at the last minute, and he kicked me in the shin. Caught me completely off guard. Fucking hell, that hurt." He pulled up his trouser leg to reveal a bruised, red, and angry swelling the size of a large egg.

"Look at that." He paused. "But it was the punch in the throat that put me down. OK, I've had enough of this Richter. Let's go to the bank and yank his chain."

Carmine grunted in disgust. "It took a good hiding to convince you."

Herr Richter was nervous. He wanted a security guard present when he saw the two American goons, but Matthew forestalled him.

"We need a private chat. He can go."

Frightened by the menace in Carmine's glare, Richter thought it advisable to dismiss the guard and now faced them across his desk.

Matthew opened the conversation politely. "Herr Richter, this afternoon we had a run-in with your client Joshua. He had obviously been to see you."

"I can neither confirm nor deny the presence of the client you call Joshua."

"We're talking about this man." Carmine put a small photograph of Joshua on the desk in front of Herr Richter who gave it a quick glance and made the same reply.

Carmine's short fuse was lit, and he was in danger of exploding when Matthew stepped in to try and save the day. It was classic good cop, bad cop.

He spoke in German. "We appreciate your position, but we represent a powerful individual of Sicilian heritage whose reach is extremely long. We're trying to avoid all the bureaucracy, delay, and costs incurred trying to recover a large sum of stolen money. This is where you can help us by cutting through the red tape. We're very grateful to those who help us and as you can see from the attitude of my companion here, a different reception for those who won't listen."

"How grateful would your powerful friend be?" asked Herr Richter who saw opportunity in an otherwise no-win situation. The prospect of collecting from Joshua and from these gangsters would be dangerous but a nice bonus. *A double dip to top up to my pension.*

"How about fifty thousand euros?" offered Matthew.

"One hundred thousand sounds better," countered Richter. "When I receive the money, you'll be told where eleven million euros was sent."

Mathew translated the conversation to Carmine who huffed and puffed but recognized the inevitable. In New Jersey he would've hung the banker out the window by his ankles if not by his neck. In Switzerland, the police were noted for their lack of humor and strict attention to the law. There was no choice but to agree to the terms and Carmine made a call to Nunzio.

At the Dolder Grand, Joshua went back to his room where he spent twenty minutes sending money around the world to different entities, some of which were new and others he'd used before. The ultimate destination was in Paris where the instructions to the bank were to release the deposit in Eurodollars.

Sarah was ready to leave by the time he'd finished and packed up.

"All done?" she asked.

"Yes, I requested we pick up bearer bond certificates in Eurodollars when we get to Paris." He joked, "Let's not lose them, we'd really be up the creek. The ownership isn't registered and whoever has possession becomes the owner."

They had a taxi take them to Museumstrasse where they deposited their luggage in a storage facility. Another cab ride saw them visit a Renault dealer in Opfikon where they purchased a used 1996 Renault 4. After a squabble as to who was going to drive first, Sarah got her way.

"We're on our way." She settled back into the driver's seat, and they started back to Museumstrasse to get their luggage. After that, they planned to make their first overnight stop in Strasbourg.

"We shouldn't have too much trouble not exceeding the speed limit in this piece of shit," Joshua said.

Sarah protested, "It's a lovely car. I wanted the Aston Martin, but you said no. Tell you what, let's stop in Basel for a break and then on to Mozart country. We can only do 75 max on the motorway and this thing should stagger up that high. Maybe we'll swap this out when we get to France."

"No, we've," he corrected himself, "*I've* made enough mistakes. Let's stay beneath the radar and try not to attract any more attention."

Friday, September 6

The following morning, at the D & R Bankengruppe bank, Carmine and Matthew sat in front of Herr Richter who wrote an account number on a piece of paper which he pushed across the desk. They called Nunzio who, using Imperial Bank of Panama in the Caymans, directed David to transfer one hundred thousand euros into the designated account.

Richter began earning his money right away, a model of cooperation.

"Your money was transferred to an account at the National Union Bank in Vaduz, Lichtenstein. The account holder is The Kobe Mining Co. of Pretoria, South Africa. It might have been transferred on from there. I don't know. The transfers were made just yesterday by this man," he pointed to the photograph, "you call Joshua. We know him as James Boynton, a South African citizen with mining interests. We've done a number of transactions for him. The last, a few months back, was small, maybe eight hundred thousand euros."

"Where did that money go?" asked Matthew.

"Durban, South Africa, as I recall."

"How much was this transfer today?"

"He came here today to close their account, about eleven million euros."

He allowed them to view the customer cards showing signatures and details of the account holders. "James and Joan Boynton," read Matthew. "Have you met the woman?" he asked Richter.

"Not enough to recognize her photo, but a young woman, as I recall. Nothing detailed comes to mind."

Matthew made a note of the address and telephone number on the client card. He stood up and waved his finger directly at Richter and spoke German. There was no denying the threat.

"You'd better not be lying, or we will be back."

Reverting to English, "Come on, Carmine."

Rather than walk back to the hotel, they decided to take a taxi. As they took their seats in the cab, Carmine said, "Was that worth a hundred grand? I don't fucking think so and neither will Nunzio. When this is sorted out, someone's going to be paying Mr. fucking Richter a visit."

"It's worth it to us. A nice, relaxed trip to Lichtenstein. I like being in Europe."

As they started out, Matthew called out the address to the driver and said, "Let's check out this place Richter gave us, but I'll be shocked if it leads anywhere."

"They made mistakes on the bank deal. They'll make more. Mark my words."

The address and telephone number turned out to be an answering service where messages were taken and picked up periodically. The manager admitted servicing the client for the past three months. Pressed for details, he referred them to the owner who was not forthcoming, refused to discuss details, and threatened to call the authorities.

Carmine stifled his resentment until they left the building.

"Boy, these Swiss are something else. If this was Jersey, I'd ice that piece of shit. Let's hit one of the clubs and worry about Lichtenstein tomorrow."

Matthew's voice remained hoarse from the blow to his neck, and his leg felt like it had been kicked by a mule.

"Twist my arm. A single malt will go down real smooth right now. But I ain't up for dancing, I'll leave that to you."

CHAPTER 19

Plotting in Paris

Paris, France
Monday, September 9

Three days later in Paris it was a dull day, hot and humid. Clouds hung low enough to occasionally decapitate the Eiffel Tower. Occupying three stories of a building in the fourth *arrondissement* and constructed in the mid-1800s stood La Banque Centrale d'Istanbul. Squeezed between two larger buildings of equal vintage, it lay off a narrow side street leading from La Rue Beaubourg. Thunder rumbled in the distance and a rain shower spattered the sidewalk beside the two imposing wooden doors granting access to this private street. Rambuteau Metro was a five-minute walk away.

Privately owned by a Middle Eastern group, the bank's biggest profits came from funding company mergers and acquisitions. Many of the individual customers' portfolios were in the hundreds of millions while more than three had fortunes that began with a 'B.' Hawala, the money brokering system used extensively through the Middle East, Africa, and India, comprised a significant part of the bank's profitability. It functioned in complete secrecy, relying heavily on honor and trust and was widely considered impenetrable by Western authorities.

Six steps led up to elegant wooden doors which, when opened, revealed a vestibule where an ever-cheerful Natalie reigned supreme behind an antique desk. Known as "La Guardienne," she jealously defended access to the bank's inner sanctum comprised of meeting rooms, private offices, stairs to other floors, and, most importantly, a large vault. There was no elevator. An armed security guard sat on a wooden chair close by.

Farshad, who was the largest shareholder and CEO of the bank, spoke with his brother Farid. "I understand the RLBC bank in Moscow has transferred over eleven million euros for deposit into an account owned by Geneva Holdings, one of our Swiss customers."

"That's correct. In the past this customer has requested the money be transferred to another bank in Zurich. This time there is a request for the eleven million to be collected in Eurodollars."

"Eleven million in Eurodollars? Personally collected? That's like carrying around millions in cash. A little odd. No?"

"Maybe, but these are customers with irregular habits, if you get my meaning. It allows us to collect maximum commissions and fees; just over three percent."

"Five-day turn around?"

"No, three business days is the norm."

"Very well. I'll leave you to deal with it."

Hafeez, Farid's assistant, was tasked with preparing the necessary paperwork for the purchase of the Eurodollars. The account holders were due to sign the paperwork authorizing the purchase later that morning. *They've used Farid before. He'll skin me alive if there's a mistake.* As he reviewed the completed paperwork a recent phone call from his previous boss, David, at Imperial Bank in the Caymans, sprang to mind.

Be on the lookout for any money transactions that don't look quite right. We've been hacked and the money is being laundered as we speak. We're sure it's a woman, Sarah, and her partner, Joshua. They're expert hackers. We're offering a seven-figure reward to the person turning them in.

He sat at his desk, examined the paperwork he was preparing, and wondered what to do. *This couple could be the two mentioned, but it'll cost me my job if I'm wrong,* he thought.

At 11 a.m. on the dot, the CCTV cameras at the bank showed a man holding an umbrella to shelter himself and his female companion from the rain. He pressed the bell for admittance; Natalie activated her microphone.

"How may I help you?"

Looking directly into the camera, the man said, "We have a business appointment with Farid."

She buzzed them in. The security guard got up from his chair as they entered and gave them the once over. He was in his sixties with white hair stuck out from beneath his cap, obviously a pensioner making a few euros on the side. He wasn't much of a threat, even with his gun.

Hafeez, anxious to see the couple signing for the Eurodollars, contrived to walk past as Joshua and Sarah were ushered into Farid's office. He got a frown of disapproval from Farid and a good look at the couple.

In an effort to get another look, Hafeez ran up the stairs to the next floor. Here he found an empty office with a view of the street below and waited for the couple to leave. He was disappointed. Between the rain drops and rivulets running down the windows, all he could see were two black umbrellas. He returned to his office and was at his desk when Farid came in through the open door.

"Those clients made an appointment to pick up the Eurodollar certificates at eleven this coming Thursday morning. Normal wire transfer clearances and bond issuances will be completed the day before. Make a note of that appointment. Let me know when they're ready, and I'll keep them in my office safe."

Once alone, Hafeez collected his thoughts. He couldn't silence the voices in his head. *Should I contact David? I don't want to look like a moron. It's a long shot but I think I'll take a chance. Who knows? Maybe get my hands on the reward. Ha! No chance. Fuck it.* Despite his misgivings, he sent the email anyway.

The reply came immediately, electrifying him. An email with two photos, one of Sarah and the other of Joshua.

"Yes," he emailed back. "They have an appointment on Thursday to pick up Eurodollars. Do you want me to call the police?"

His private line rang, the screen showed David calling. He picked up. "Thank God. What do you want me to do?"

David sounded subdued. "Hafeez, we're on a conference call with Carmine. He's on the line from Lichtenstein."

Carmine chimed in, "Hi."

Hafeez thought, *Who's Carmine?*

David continued, his voice weak, almost a whisper. "You and I have always been able to deal with certain deposits without the authorities getting involved. My brother Leon has unfortunately passed away causing us to trade our ownership of the bank to a New Jersey customer. With his organization's help, I'm continuing to run our banking operations for the foreseeable future. Their interests are represented by Carmine, and I urge you to cooperate. I'm handing the call back to him now." His voice trailed off. The phone went silent.

Hafeez thought. *There's only one customer from New York, he was a gangster, what was his name again? Nunzio, that's it. What was the name of the man who brought Nunzio's weekly drop to Leon's office? Russo, Sal Russo. That's it. Leon said his nickname was "Tickets" 'cause he had all Broadway theatres sewn up. Carmine must be part of Nunzio's outfit.*

Carmine's voice came over the speaker. "Tell me about this couple."

"They match the photos you sent. They've left now but they're coming back."

Exhilarated, Carmine pumped his fist. *Got them.* "Do you know where they're staying?"

"No, sir. One of the owners is dealing with them. I just prepared the paperwork to purchase the bonds. They're picking them up on Thursday at eleven o'clock, Paris time."

"Do you have copies of their identification, passports, etc.?"

"No. Everything's locked in Farid's office safe. I can't open it."

Carmine said, "You've done a great job and good things are coming your way. We'll be in touch."

As he hung up, Hafeez overheard Carmine's voice say, "Plenty of time to get there."

Matthew put the extension down as Carmine turned to him. "Waddaya think of them apples? For the first time ever, I'm grateful for a rat."

"We get to go to Paris?"

"Yes, my Mick friend, we get to go to Paris. I'll call Nunzio and give him the good news. Just in time; Lichtenstein was a bust."

Nunzio wasn't as happy as Carmine expected. "I thought we had a deal with this woman. At least that's what I was told. Now I'm hearing all sorts of tales and forty million of my money is in the wind. I want them taken and questioned. These bonds are only worth eleven million. I want the other twenty-nine million plus their finder's fee. You and Matthew do whatever it takes to get the money. I'll reach out to our friends over there to help you out. Let me know where you're staying when you get there." The phone went dead. Carmine looked at the receiver in his hand for a moment, replacing it on the cradle with an expletive.

Tuesday, September 10

Carmine and Matthew checked into La Maison Genevieve, a boutique hotel on Rue Saint Martin, about a thousand feet from the Pompidou Building. It was a three-story building, offering luxury suites for ten guests with an overall capacity of thirty-five rooms. The tiny elevator barely took Carmine, his luggage, and the hotel porter. Matthew, feeling the need to stretch his legs, elected to take the stairs and was waiting on the third floor when the elevator creaked slowly to a stop. The double suite was well laid out with each having a lounge, a dining area, and king-size beds. One novelty was the recently introduced satellite service for the TV.

Carmine opted for the room with a view of the street from ceiling-high windows running down one side of his suite. Matthew chuckled when he saw Carmine's selection. The street below was jam-packed with traffic, noisy even by New York standards. Fortunately, the suites were separated by double doors for privacy. His view took in neighboring rooftops but with the doors closed and the elevator on Carmine's side, he knew he would sleep well.

After unpacking, they decided to check out La Banque Centrale d'Istanbul. It was a short walk along the Rue Beaubourg with bustling sidewalks and nose-to-tail traffic. The ever-present scooters weaved between cars at suicidal speed, passersby spoke in tongues, the language incomprehensible. Carmine was like a fish out of water. They walked past retail shop fronts and came to the oversized wooden doors guarding access to a private street. A brass plate on a nearby wall showed the bank as a resident.

"Let's see if there's a rear entrance," suggested Matthew.

"Fine by me."

Continuing their walk, they turned on a narrow cross street, Impasse Berthaud, and followed it a short distance until it broadened into a courtyard with buildings on three sides. An alley, only wide enough for a small car and pedestrians, ran off the courtyard and behind the retail shops fronting Rue Beaubourg. It was flanked on one side by walls and on the other by a high spiked railing protecting a thick growth of conifers in a private garden. Prospecting further, they found their way barred by a similar railing with a gate that was padlocked shut. From what they could see, another bank of railings about sixty feet beyond prevented access from the other end of the alley.

"Eight-foot railings, look at those spikes. Getting over this would be no picnic. We'd need a mattress," commented Carmine.

Matthew assessed the distance to the further railing with a practiced eye. "I think this ends just after the bank.

We could pace it out on the pavement on the street. That will give us an idea anyway."

"Yeah, you're right. We'll talk with Hafeez about the rear entrance; he's got to know."

"The fire regulations would probably make them have a way out other than the front entrance."

"We'll have to rethink this whole operation if there's no back door." Carmine chewed a nail nervously. *Taking them after they've left the bank is going to be tough. Nunzio is not going to be understanding if they escape.*

Returning to Rue Beaubourg, they paced off a guesstimate of the distance and arrived at the wooden doors once more.

"Spot on," said Matthew.

He pressed a bell beside the brass plaque. The gates automatically opened inward to reveal a street, just one car width's wide. On either side, retail shops and art galleries were closed, their doors shuttered. Several surveillance cameras were clearly visible. The alley doglegged to the right, and they found themselves in a courtyard facing the steps leading up to the bank's front door. Retracing their steps to Rue Beaubourg, they spotted a typical French corner café, La Station Rambuteau. Matthew suggested they have a drink.

He did the ordering in halting schoolboy French with an assist from the waiter who spoke broken English. Carmine's choice was a red Pinot Noir while Matthew quaffed a Belgian Duvel pale ale. They watched the world go by, each immersed in their own thoughts. The sun came out and lit up the streets, wet from the latest shower, the traffic still backed up. Despite the rain, people were out in strength, providing a multi-colored sea of umbrellas moving in unison like a vast chorus line, crowding under shop awnings during particularly heavy showers.

Matthew sipped his beer. "We'll have to tail them to a quieter location if taking them in the bank's a problem."

Carmine snorted. "We don't know how they will arrive. Do they have a car? Are they on foot? Even taxis are a possibility. Where's the help we were promised?"

Matthew was contrite. "I forgot to tell you, there was a message at the front desk. Someone called Louis will drop by at 5:00 p.m. to get acquainted."

"In the future, make sure I get messages on time," Carmine warned, raising his hand to silence Matthew's excuses. "Louis is from Unione Corse. He's bringing someone with him who's a driver and hopefully some guns. This Sarah and her sweetie are sure to be tooled up. Then it's a three-man job to make sure I don't have to shoot someone playing fucking hero."

When they arrived back to their hotel, they had no problem picking out Louis. He was the only person waiting in the lobby. Youngish, lean and wiry, nondescript, the kind of man people find hard to remember. He looked up, bobbed his head in greeting, and rose from his chair.

Matthew studied him. *What's his game, I wonder?*

Louis said, "Carmine?"

"Yeah. You must be Louis."

"*Mais oui.*" When released from the bear hug, Carmine introduced Matthew, "This is a friend of mine. Louis, meet Matthew."

They shook hands and exchanged nods.

Louis's voice had a French accent tinged with an American twang.

"I went to Harvard. You don't have to speak or understand French," he explained. "It's funny, when I'm in the US, I get mistaken for a Frenchman, in France I'm always L'Americaine."

Returning to the nearby La Station Rambuteau, they set to work planning the kidnapping. The first item was the fourth man who, Louis explained, only spoke French. "He'll be ready when we want him."

Carmine outlined the circumstances of the hacking and those responsible. He deliberately failed to mention the amounts of money involved. Louis had been hired on a fixed fee basis for the kidnapping, and a small house, previously used for a similar purpose, was at their disposal. He'd also take care of any bodies to be dumped.

Louis listened attentively, shifting his gaze from Matthew to Carmine, sipping his Sauvignon Blanc, his face expressionless.

"We had a walk around by the bank earlier." Matthew decided he would speak up. "There's an alley that runs behind the shops. We think the bank may have a rear exit that's not used."

Carmine said, "We've got an inside man. I haven't met him yet or figured out how he can help. We'll need a couple of heaters as well."

Louis said exactly what Carmine had predicted earlier. "Guns, no problem, but how do we handle a kidnap? There's so much we don't know. If it was a robbery that's one thing. These are smart people. We don't have enough people to follow them without being caught. Are they on foot, in a car, using the Metro?"

"Matthew and I talked about that earlier," Carmine interjected. "These jobs are hard enough when you've got all the information. We need a meeting with our inside man. He can fill us in, especially on security. The couple's picking up the bonds the day after tomorrow, so we need to get a move on. I'll call him now to set it up."

"This Hafeez character shouldn't see Louis either," Matthew commented. "The less he knows, the better."

Louis wanted to hear all the latest about New York and they obliged him while finishing off more drinks. Before departing for another meeting, Louis handed Carmine a card. "Call me at this number after you meet your inside man so we can plan this properly."

Later that evening, Matthew and Carmine were buzzed through two doors of a building on Rue Michel Le Comte.

"That's an interesting entryway," remarked Matthew. "You enter and the door closes behind you. The CCTV gives a clear view before you're buzzed through the second door. Makes a nasty trap."

Carmine summoned the elevator and reacted as the door slid open. "Jesus Christ. Look at the size of the elevator. It's a tight fit for just us two. Are they all this small in France?" he asked rhetorically.

They used the narrow stone stairs which wound up and around, their footsteps echoing in the stairwell as, one floor at a time, they checked the apartment numbers.

Anticipating their arrival, Hafeez had left the front door open. He welcomed them into his studio apartment where they saw it was tiny but cozy. A glass-topped coffee table stood on an imitation Persian rug in front of two couches arranged at right angles to each other. The only other furniture was a TV and a stereo that stood on a low table. Matthew judged Hafeez a jazz fan from the Miles Davis and Thelonious Monk CDs scattered underneath. The bedroom was separated from the living area by a shoulder-high lacquered Chinese room divider, and a red duvet cover gave the space a cheery look. A keen photographer, visitors often commented on Hafeez's black and white photographs, framed and hung on the walls, stark against the cream paint. A pair of tall windows, opened slightly, allowed a breeze to unsettle the air, the noise of the intermittent rain somehow soothing.

Carmine stood smoking a Disque Bleu he'd cadged from Hafeez, looking down at the courtyard three floors below. Despite blowing the smoke out of the window, the distinctive aroma of the French tobacco permeated the flat. He threw the half-smoked butt out the window, turned, and sat down to examine a paper spread out on the coffee table. It was a floor plan of the bank.

"I want to be sure I understand you." He pointed to the map. "The reception area has a guard who's armed but will crap his pants at the first sign of trouble. The corridor from the reception area goes to the back of the building."

Hafeez interrupted him, "Not quite. At the end of the corridor is a room for the copiers, computer equipment, and office supplies. There's also a coffeemaker and a snack vending machine but it's not a lunchroom. There's an adjacent storage room with a door leading to the outside and the alley."

"As I was saying," Carmine's look had Hafeez stuttering and mumbling. Using his finger, he outlined the offices on the map. "After these two offices on the left there's a bathroom facing the stairwell to the other floors. On the right is an office, then the vault. They're separated by the stairwell. This office here," he indicated the second office on the left, "is where our target will meet."

"Yes," agreed Hafeez. "Farid's office."

"The door leading to the outside from the storage room is locked and alarmed but never used," Carmine continued. He turned to Matthew. "Do you remember, in the alley behind the shops, we came up against a padlocked gate in a high barred fence. Sound familiar?"

"Yes. A perfect spot to park a van."

Matthew looked at Hafeez, "Can you unlock the door or get us a key?"

"Wait a minute, don't blow his cover. We might need him later." Carmine was resolute. "We don't need a key. This is a three-man operation and a driver. Let me explain the reason." He made his pitch simple and direct.

Carmine scrutinized Hafeez. "OK with you?"

Hafeez was no mug. "I'll explain you were referred by David. That way, they won't know I've taken part. I'm 100% in."

Matthew said, "Brilliant. We're in agreement. That's exactly what we'll do."

CHAPTER 20

Un incidente a La Banque Centrale d'Istanbul

**Paris, France
Thursday, September 12**

At nine sharp on Thursday morning, La Banque Centrale d'Istanbul opened for business. Natalie answered the buzzer for the door. *Mon Dieu. Another busy day.* She recognized Joshua and Sarah on the video monitor and pressed the button releasing the front door electronic lock.

"*Bonjour, Monsieur et Madam,*" she said with a welcoming smile and then frowned. "But you are too early. Your appointment is not until eleven."

Joshua was at his charming best. "We had something unexpected come up and can't make the eleven o'clock appointment. We took a chance to see if we could possibly meet Farid now."

"Take a seat and I'll call him."

They overheard her speaking rapid French with Farid and after she put the phone down, she called out. "He'll be here in 20 to 30 minutes. I can have you wait in his office if you would like."

"That would be great," smiled Sarah.

"I'll have someone show you there." She called Hafeez and requested he come to the reception area. He was openly shocked when he saw Joshua and Sarah.

"B-b-but your appointment isn't until eleven," he stammered.

Natalie rounded on him. "We've been through that. Farid is meeting them in twenty minutes or so. Now, take them to his office, they can wait there." It wasn't a request and made clear Hafeez occupied a much lower position in the pecking order.

"Coffee? Water?" she inquired, smiling, courteous, friendly.

"No. Very nice of you. Thank you." Joshua was equally polite.

Hafeez escorted them to Farid's office without a word being said.

As they entered Farid's office Sarah thought, *Same set up as Dixon, office and comfortable meeting room combined.* They followed an invitation to sit on a couch.

"I'd imagine you're here for the bonds." They both observed Hafeez seemed nervous and out of sorts.

"Yes," answered Joshua.

"I'm so sorry. Unfortunately, Farid has the only access to your bonds which are in the safe right there." He pointed to a small office safe standing by the door.

Sarah assessed the situation in two seconds flat. *And such a nice little safe. Older too. It's almost certainly a three number combination. And it can't be seen from the corridor outside.*

Hafeez was in a rush. "If you're sure you don't need anything, please excuse me, I must go back to my office."

"No. No." Joshua was apologetic. "We're the ones causing disruption. Go about your work and we'll wait here for Farid. Please leave the door open, I'm a little claustrophobic."

Wearing a sickly smile, Hafeez backed out of the door, left the door open, and walked hurriedly back to his office.

Sarah gave Joshua a knowing look. "I'll bet I can open that safe before Farid gets here. What do you say?"

Joshua felt his pulse quicken. "What about alarms?"

"These little old safes rarely have an alarm. You heard Hafeez, our bonds are in there." Her brow wrinkled. "I'm surprised the bonds aren't in their vault. Anyway, we've bought and paid for them. Let's not waste any more time. If you agree, I'll give it a try."

Joshua trusted her judgment and didn't hesitate. "Do it. I'll watch the corridor and warn you if anyone decides to walk this way."

"Have amplifier and headphones, will travel." Chuckling at her own joke she got to work by first locating a nearby plug. *Thank God, I've got a European-style converter.* She found a plug and after powering up the amplifier, she clamped it in place on the face of the safe, close to the lock. She pulled on her headset, made sure the earpieces were firmly in place, and began spinning the combination dial. It was the same method she had used for years now, constantly rotating the dial, listening for clicks and making notes on graph paper.

While Sarah worked the combination and Joshua kept watch, Hafeez put in a desperate call to Carmine. "They're here," he hissed into the phone when it was picked up.

The answer was gruff and to the point. "Who is this? What the fuck are you talking about?"

"Joshua and Sarah are here at the bank. They came early and Farid will see them in twenty minutes. Get over here. Now."

Carmine said, "We'll be there as soon as we can." Hafeez overheard him shouting, "Christ, what a fuck up.

Matthew, get your ass in gear, we've got to leave. They're at the bank." Then the line went dead.

Hafeez was panicked and afraid to let the couple out of his sight. He rushed for his office door intending to return to Farid's office but was interrupted when his phone rang. It was Natalie with one of his regular clients on the line. He had no option other than to spend precious minutes supplying information and answers to the client's concerns. His voice was calm, but his mind was frantic at the thought Carmine would arrive too late.

While Joshua kept watch, he thought back to the day he'd had a conversation with Sarah about the methods she used in cracking safes.

"In movies, you see actors with stethoscopes opening safes. I wish it were that simple. Given the right equipment, most anybody can listen for the clicks as the levers drop into the notches on the wheels. But there's a lot more to it. For starters, you must know what the clicks mean. Then, figuring out the number of wheels creating the combination is another piece of the puzzle. Graphing the results is the absolute key to getting the combination numbers. When everything's in place, you can open the safe door. It's easier for me because I'm blessed with exceptional hearing, my equipment is top notch, and I have a super sensitive touch on the dial."

Joshua came back to the present when he heard footsteps coming down the hall. Sarah was facing him and fully focussed on the task at hand. He managed to catch her attention by taking a step back out of sight of the corridor and waving at her.

"Shit," she said. "I'm almost there." She retreated to the sofa, concealing her equipment with a cushion.

Joshua stepped back into the doorway as Hafeez made his approach. "Hi there, Hafeez is it? You'd mentioned the possibility of coffee. Any chance we could get a couple of cups, please?"

Hafeez took a breath before replying. "Certainly." He sounded and looked exasperated as he retreated to the room where the coffeemaker stood, leaving the door open.

Joshua could hear him grinding the coffee beans as Sarah returned to her task. *Take your time, Hafeez. God, I'm glad the French love their coffee brewed fresh, none of that instant shit.* He waited impatiently for Sarah to finish, hearing her curse only added to his nervousness.

Two more minutes passed. Worried, Joshua peeked over his shoulder. He saw Sarah had already obtained the three numbers of the combination but not in their correct order. Now it was trial and error. She dialed the first series. No dice, the handle refused to budge.

Hafeez left the coffee room carrying two cups. Joshua appeared unperturbed but his heart was beating hard in his chest "Milk and sugar?" he asked innocently as he came close. Hafeez said nothing aloud but glowered for a millisecond, irritated at being treated like a servant. He turned on his heel to go back to the coffee room.

Joshua called out, "Two lumps and cream for both, please."

Sarah tried the second combination, pressed the handle down but the door remained closed. The third combination also failed. The fourth and the fifth? Both failures. *Last chance, baby.* The handle yielded and the safe door swung open. She started breathing again. Inside the safe was a large brown unsealed envelope marked with a black pen in large capital letters, BONDS—JOSHUA/SARAH. Quickly checking the certificates were safe inside the envelope, she slid it beneath her jacket, closed the safe door and spun the dial back to its original setting. Her equipment was thrust haphazardly into her purse, and she resumed her seat on the couch. From start to finish, the whole process had taken four minutes and thirty-seven seconds.

A few seconds later, Hafeez returned to the office with their coffee.

"I do apologize," said Joshua, "but I've just received an urgent call and must leave immediately. We'll return at our appointed time of eleven. Please present our apologies to Farid."

"Are you sure you can't wait?" Hafeez said nervously, his hands full with two China cups of freshly made coffee complete with saucers. He scrutinized Farid's office over Joshua's shoulder, but nothing seemed amiss. Despite his efforts to suppress his fears, Sarah observed the beads of sweat on his upper lip and his apparent discomfort.

Her suspicions aroused, she said firmly. "No, we must leave now. It's an emergency."

On their way out, Joshua greeted Natalie. "I'm sorry but we must leave. I received a very urgent call. Please give my apologies to Farid but we'll return at eleven as originally planned. We'll see you then. *Au revoir.*"

The bank door closed behind them and Hafeez rushed back to his office where he called Carmine's cellphone.

"Where are they now?" Carmine dispensed with any normal greeting.

"They just left. The bonds are still in our safe and they're coming back at eleven."

"Did you see where they went?"

The answer was a brief "No."

Carmine turned to Matthew and related the conversation. "What do you think?"

His reply was matter of fact, "There's no rush then. They don't have the money and will be back at eleven."

Carmine said into the phone, "We'll be there any minute," and hung up.

"Matthew, I think they smelled a rat. That Hafeez probably gave the game away, otherwise why would they leave early like that? I'm not waiting until eleven. They've got to be around, let's see if we can find them."

Joshua and Sarah left the bank and walked towards the nearby Rambuteau Metro station. A taxi came around the corner from Rue Grenier Saint-Lazarre and ground to a halt in the traffic on Rue Beaubourg.

"There they go!" shouted Carmine. "Pull over," he ordered the taxi driver.

"You go after them, let me deal with the driver." Matthew reached in his pocket and spilt change into his hand as he searched for the right amount to pay the fare. Carmine cursed as he hit his knee on the taxi's door, the pain slowing his pace as he started in pursuit.

As they walked briskly towards the Metro entrance, force of habit made Joshua look back. He recognized Carmine limping slightly as he ran towards them while Matthew appeared to be paying off the taxi.

"Christ," Joshua said, "that little shit Hafeez sold us out. Run."

They sprinted into the Metro station at Rambuteau and using pre-purchased tickets avoided the line at the ticket machines. Racing through pedestrian tunnels, down several flights of stairs, they joined the crowd on the platform waiting for the next train to Hotel de Ville. In a desperate effort to conceal themselves they mixed in and behind other waiting passengers.

Matthew had caught up with Carmine and Sarah saw them both appear on the opposite platform. She hissed at Joshua and, trying to remain unseen, they shrank into a crowd of students. The whoosh of air preceding the arrival of their Hotel de Ville train coincided with Carmine pulling on Matthew's arm. He pointed in their direction and, realizing they'd picked the wrong platform, began running back the way they'd come.

The train pulled to a halt, the doors hissed open and throngs of passengers, tourists, and more students, alighted, pushing and shoving their way to the exits. Joshua and Sarah were fully prepared to jump on the train at the last second when the doors started to close. They abandoned that strategy when they saw Carmine and Matthew clatter down the steps to their platform.

"Quick," said Sarah, taking the lead. They followed exiting passengers, scrambling up the steep steps two at a time. Their progress slowed as the crowd thickened appreciably, passengers were making their choices of exit. Their pursuers were not yet in sight but there wasn't much time to lose them.

Joshua called out to Sarah. "They'll be looking for a couple. Let's split up and I'll meet you at Charlemagne's statue. Keep in touch by cellphone." He went out by way of the Rue Rambuteau while she went via the Pompidou Building exit and became one with a crowd of Sorbonne university students.

Once in the fresh air, she headed towards Place Georges Pompidou still using the students as cover. She picked up the pace as the crowd thinned, constantly checking behind her but saw no sign she'd been detected. *Close call, I think I'm home free.* Her relief was premature. The shock of seeing Matthew blocking her path caused her to bite her knuckles to stifle the scream erupting from her throat. She stopped in her tracks, the crowd behind her parting like the Red Sea. She felt a sharp pain in her ribs and looked down to see a gun with a silencer, hidden under a jacket folded across his arm. He prodded her with it to encourage her to keep moving.

"Come with me. Now." The gun made it an order.

He took her by the arm, kept the gun pressed into her side and steered her past the Atelier Brancusi studio. They came to a vacant bench near the ventilation funnels on the Place Georges Pompidou. She felt like such a fool for being taken so easily.

"Sit down," Matthew commanded. "We don't have much time. Carmine's gone the other way."

So, what? she thought, puzzled by the comment.

Although there were plenty of people passing through the square, it was quiet, too early for the street performers normally entertaining visitors. The gun made calling for help inadvisable, so she waited patiently for an opportunity to disarm him.

"Why are we waiting here?"

Matthew produced a cellphone. "I want you to call this number. Just press dial." She did as he instructed and immediately recognized the voice on the other end, almost dropping the phone in shock. It was Sonny. Matthew was grinning like a Cheshire cat.

"Sarah?"

"Sonny? Is that you? What the hell's going on?"

"Matthew works undercover for Scotland Yard. You are safe with him. We've been coordinating a task force to break up Leon's banking operation."

"What about Joshua? He'll kill Matthew given the chance."

"It's OK. I just spoke to him. You must be in a black spot because you didn't answer his calls. I told him about Matthew because I didn't want any accidents with the wrong person getting shot. Now, I'll leave our mutual friend to outline details of the next steps." He grew stern. "We have a lot to talk about but now's not the time. Thank God, you're safe." For the first time Sarah heard genuine emotion in Sonny's voice and was touched.

Matthew arrived back at the Hotel Genevieve later that morning.

"Where have you been?" Carmine asked suspiciously.

Not in the mood to suffer any of Carmine's drivel, Matthew snapped, "I could ask you the same question."

For once, Carmine was apologetic. "OK. OK. Keep your hair on. I lost the guy in the crowd almost immediately after we split up. Did you have any luck?"

"Yes. I followed her from the subway to the Pompidou building. She met up with Joshua near Notre Dame. From there they walked around obviously watching their backs. They didn't spot me and after a half hour hanging around took a taxi. I did the same and followed them to an apartment building on the same street where Hafeez lives."

"Do we know which apartment?"

"Of course. I waited until the coast was clear and asked the concierge about renting a place. She was chatty and told me a young couple had rented the last vacancy, number seven on the third floor. I waited in a coffee shop nearby and as soon as I saw someone about to enter the building, I walked by and managed to score a password as they used the door keypad."

"Chalk another one up for the Limey." Carmine was genuinely grateful. His attitude towards Matthew was now positively benign. "Let's pay them a visit with Louis and his friend."

CHAPTER 21

Un episode sur la Rue Michel Le Conte.

Paris, France
Thursday, September 12

Capitaine de Police Jacques Broussard of La Police
Judiciaire, formerly the Surete, was a bear of a man. Six-
feet-five-inches tall and the best part of three hundred
pounds, he stood, a pipe held clenched in his teeth,
overseeing his team. The sweat marks on his shirt testified
to the heat. It was more like August than September,
hot and humid, the streets steaming after a recent
thunderstorm. He wiped his brow.

They'd set up an observation point in an art gallery
not quite opposite Joshua and Sarah's hideout. He blew
a stream of strong-smelling smoke towards the ceiling
drawing a protest from a detective scanning the street
with binoculars. Accustomed to flout all non-smoking
regulations, Broussard ignored the objection, an expletive
on the tip of his tongue. The detective did not repeat his
complaint, already regretting his outburst's effect on his
prospects of promotion.

Despite his responsibilities for the complex operation,
Broussard showed his attention to detail by example.
They'd set up a remotely operated video camera on the

roof. He was the first person to spot the expected couple when they appeared on the camera feed.

"Here we go. Tell all units. Couple in sight approaching from direction of Rue Beaubourg." The units in question received this broadcast crackling through their earpieces just as a detective from another unit came on the air.

"All units, panel van stopped in street. Driver and passenger appear to be watching the couple."

Several minutes later, Broussard watched on the video as the couple entered their building and disappeared. He cursed, there hadn't been time to tap into the building's interior video.

The observing unit reported the panel van moving. It parked half on the sidewalk outside the entrance to the building. This broadcast caused a general shuffling of feet, a final check of firearms and adjustments to body armour as the police teams readied themselves for violent confrontation.

Carmine was uneasy as he, Matthew, and Louis surveyed the building. They were accompanied in the van by the fourth man, Henri, Louis's crew partner. He was the driver, a role requiring nerve not just for fast driving but for the endless wait while others pulled the job.

Louis said, "Check your guns." He pulled a Skorpion machine gun with a silencer from under his seat.

He had supplied both Carmine and Matthew with 9mm Baretta pistols, both with silencers. They each chambered a round but kept the safeties on until they were ready for action.

"*Alors*, everyone ready?"

"Jesus, I hate this setup." Carmine was jumpy. "See that fucking video camera in the lobby? We'll be all over the six o'clock news if we're not careful."

"*Attendez.*" Louis was unfazed, "I'll take care of the video. Stay here." He checked and saw there was no one in proximity, pulled on a mask, walked to the entrance, and punched the purloined combination into the pad. Once inside, the door closed behind him. He took a couple of steps, reached up and sprayed the camera lens with black paint, disabling it. He retraced his steps to the door, opened it, and beckoned Carmine and Matthew to join him. Masked up, they scrambled out of the van and in single file the three entered the lobby, letting the door close behind them.

"*L'equipe Bleue. Attaque.*" Broussard issued the order leaning forward, watching the video, his pipe held firmly in his fist.

It was timed perfectly. Police motorcycles blocked off both ends of Rue Michel Le Compte from Rue Beaubourg to Rue du Temple. Six uniformed police officers from RAID, an elite tactical unit of Le Police Nationale, burst from their hiding place. In full body armor, they sprinted across the street to the van where one stood on either side with machine guns pointed at Henri. Four other officers quietly covered the outside of the building's entrance.

Carmine, Matthew, and Louis stepped into the lobby where they were met by five RAID officers who stormed out of a storage cupboard pointing machine guns at the trio.

In apartment number seven on the third floor, Joshua and Sarah sat on a couch waiting. Weapons hidden by cushions lay in easy reach. They knew they were bait in a trap and were following the strict instructions issued by Matthew. The noise of a commotion in the lobby made them aware the trap had sprung. Waving Sarah to stay where she was, Joshua disobeyed Matthew's advice, tiptoed to the stairs outside their door and peered over the banister. His view was partially obscured by the building's design, but he was rewarded by a glimpse of three men lying on the ground being searched. He instantly recognized Matthew and Carmine. Two handguns with silencers were kicked out of reach. A third man he didn't recognize was relieved of a Skorpion machine gun that fell from beneath his coat. The officer scowled at him as he picked it up. It appeared the police met no resistance or even protests from the prisoners who seemed bewildered by this sudden turn of events. He went back into the apartment.

"Looks like it's all over. They've arrested Matthew and Carmine, but I didn't know the third man. He had a Skorpion, I'm glad we didn't have to deal with that, would've been dicey."

"So, if they've arrested Matthew, they must be protecting his identity."

"That makes sense. The bad guys don't know he's on the inside and it's better to keep it that way. Let's see what's happening outside."

They pushed the net curtains to one side for a better view and watched as a police van, lights flashing, drove over the sidewalk and parked behind the panel van. A tow truck followed. The excitement brought together a small group of onlookers who gathered on the opposite sidewalk, prevented from getting closer by uniformed cops. The four prisoners, now hooded and handcuffed behind their backs, were bundled into a police van and the doors locked. Accompanied by motorcycle escort, sirens wailing, the convoy made its way through heavy traffic to the Prefecture de Police at the Quai des Orfèvres.

After they had returned from the bank, Joshua and Sarah had concealed the eleven-million-euro bonds above the tiles in the bathroom ceiling. He was pouring her a glass of wine and about to celebrate their lucky escape when the door crashed open. RAID officers poured into the apartment aiming guns and shouting orders. Protesting vehemently, they were handcuffed and ordered to be seated. Their guns were found and confiscated.

Broussard walked into the apartment. "Please be quiet," he ordered in a tone that said *You had better listen, or else.*

They fell silent.

He sat down in a chair opposite them and took his time, making them wait while he lit his pipe and looked them over. Four RAID officers were also present, guns at the ready, alert for any trouble.

He put the spent match in a nearby ashtray, removed the pipe from his mouth, blew smoke out of the corner of his mouth, and spoke.

"Monsieur Joshua and Mademoiselle Sarah, I am Capitaine Broussard of the Police Judiciaire. You will accompany me to police headquarters. We have arrested four armed men in connection with a possible extortion or kidnap attempt on you both. There is also the matter of a European arrest warrant for a technological irregularity at a Brussels bank. The Belgian police want to question you about one of their local hoods as well." He frowned, trying to remember the name, "Ah yes, Goossens. They suspect you know something about his disappearance. I'm obliged to detain you until these matters can be brought before the Public Prosecutor."

An hour later, Matthew waited patiently in an interview cell. The sound of keys unlocking the door announced a visit from Broussard who dismissed the other officer present and pulled up a chair, dwarfing it with his bulk. He listened without interruption as Matthew detailed the joint operation.

"I'm undercover and working the inside but Joshua and Sarah's orders came through Sonny, their controller. He has contracts with Mossad and other private intelligence groups designed to disrupt the operations of people such as Leon and Nunzio. My boss at Scotland Yard decided not to share the fact that I was working covertly because it increased the chance of my cover being blown. Everyone was on a 'need to know' basis. When a life-threatening development cropped up, I was forced to reveal my role to Sarah. You know the rest."

"What can you tell me about the missing money?"

"Before I talk about that, have you been in contact with Commander Stanley at Scotland Yard?"

"Yes, your earlier messages to him resulted in the arrests today. Your cover is secure for now. I've told Carmine that you're being extradited back to the UK on several murder charges. My understanding is Leon was the main target of your operation. You should know he's been killed."

"Killed, you say?" Matthew was surprised. "I sent a warning to Sonny that Leon needed help. Nunzio must have got there first. Do you know what happened?"

"No, and I didn't inquire further, but Stanley said, thanks to you, the operation achieved significant results."

Matthew shrugged. "Nice of him but it was a joint success. Sarah and Joshua flushed Leon out by hacking his bank accounts. I know nothing about the money, other than it's missing."

"Stanley's ordered the investigation closed. The decision is final, you're off the hook. You can return to London after we finish here."

Matthew heaved a heavy sigh. "That's good. It's tempting to continue because of the possibilities with Nunzio's bank and their money laundering, but it's been dicey for a while now. The Mob have contacts everywhere: police, civilians, judges, magistrates, the lot. It's not hard for a paperwork slip to blow your cover and you're whacked when you least expect it. Take Carmine—an hour after wining and dining you, he'd bury you. It's the way they keep people in line."

Broussard used a toothpick to poke away at the bowl of his pipe, and said, "The Belgian police have been notified and are arriving later. They were only too happy to jump at a luxury trip to Paris on the taxpayer."

"Why are the Belgian police interested?"

Broussard glowered at Matthew, "You know the answer to that. I won't dignify it with a response."

"You mentioned earlier some financial issues with a certain bank and a missing criminal."

"Exactly. What can you tell me about the missing money and this Sonny character? I'm trying to wrap my head around all these names and their relationships to one another."

Matthew stroked his chin and collected his thoughts. *Broussard seems like a decent sort. Did a great job organizing the arrests. Still . . .* he made up his mind. "I can't talk too much about it. Like I said, he's some sort of private spook with Joshua and Sarah on the payroll. I don't know anything about Belgium but, according to Nunzio and Carmine, they hacked Leon's bank for a large sum of money, maybe over a hundred million dollars. Truthfully, that's all I know. I wasn't told Sonny had people investigating Leon until after they landed in Los Angeles."

Broussard nodded his head sympathetically. "Very well. What do you know about this arrest warrant?"

"Nothing at all."

"Before our Belgian comrades arrive, let's go chat to our friends and see what we can find out."

As they made their way towards the interview room holding Joshua and Sarah, Broussard's cellphone rang.

"Yes, sir. Yes. Yes, sir." A few more rumblings, the call finished and Brousseau gave Matthew a look of disgust.

"That was the Minister. You won't know Anastasie Bertillon. She's probably the best defense attorney in France. Someone who's made my life a misery on many occasions. It's a crime that she deliberately distracts me with such a fine pair of legs." He sighed, contemplating the thought. "She's now representing Joshua and Sarah. We don't get to see them until she's finished."

For the first time since their arrest Joshua and Sarah were together. They sat in an interview room waiting for an appearance from an attorney. A uniformed police officer stood beside the door, regarding them with a jaundiced eye.

Sarah checked out the handcuffs and leg chains with contempt. *If that guard wasn't here, I'd have us out of this shit in no time.*

Joshua wasn't thinking of being handcuffed. He was wondering if Broussard had found the bonds hidden in the bathroom ceiling. *Weird he hasn't been in to interrogate us. I wonder what's going on.*

At that moment, the door opened and in walked Anastasie. She turned to the officer and said, "Let's get rid of the restraints and then you can wait outside."

The officer, knowing her reputation, hastily complied. After he left the room, Joshua and Sarah quickly embraced, then sat facing Anastasie across a metal table bolted firmly to the floor. She watched their every move with interest as they rubbed the circulation back into their wrists and ankles chafed by the metal shackles. *An unusual case and so much money,* she thought. *Based on Sonny's information, they're in serious trouble.*

She opened the interview by explaining that she had been hired to represent them, together with details of the call she had received from Sonny.

"To sum up my call then, you have to come clean on the forty million and Sonny will make all of your problems in the US, Switzerland, Brussels, everywhere, go away."

Joshua and Sarah glanced at one another. They had prepared for this moment.

Joshua said, "We know the police will have searched our apartment looking for the money we're supposed to have stolen. There's none there. They did take possession of our computer. We recently sent Sonny a CD outlining most of Leon's banking and money laundering empire. On the hard drive of the seized computer there's more detail that Sonny would give his eye teeth to possess."

Anastasie looked from one to the other. "What do you want in return?"

"Complete immunity. We get to keep the referral fee we earned as part of the studio financing transaction. We made a deal with Nunzio's man in LA and already returned forty million to the Mob. That agreement was broken when I was kidnapped, and we were chased through half of Europe. From the remaining forty million, we'll return to Sonny nineteen million immediately from an account in Geneva. Finally, we want assurances Nunzio has been warned off."

"These are vast sums of money. When is the balance available and where is it?"

"He might have to wait but there's eleven million euros in a bank here in Paris." The lie rolled easily off his tongue. "La Banque Centrale d'Istanbul, to be specific. With the nineteen million from Geneva, another twenty five million from Luxembourg, Sonny will receive a total of fifty five million in all. There's another fifteen million currently in transit which reflects our price for the information and the trouble we went through to get it."

"In transit?" queried Anastasie.

"That's all I'm willing to say. It's a take-it-or-leave-it deal. There's no evidence linking us to any crime, and we'll be out of here shortly. Not only that, but we're also sure Sonny wants to avoid any embarrassment concerning our employment."

"You wish to blackmail him now. That's a risky tactic."

"We've done a good job and deserve to be recognized for a great accomplishment. We brought down some significant players with more to come. I'm sure Scotland Yard will give Matthew a medal yet we're here negotiating for our freedom. Do you know we almost lost our asses a few blocks from here? If Matthew hadn't warned us of the plan, Carmine and his cohorts would have wasted us."

"Sonny told me that it was a dangerous assignment."

"Sonny told you it was a dangerous assignment," Sarah said, mimicking her voice. She wasn't in the mood to be taking shit from this overly dressed French bitch. Raising her voice, she said, "What the fuck does he know? He's sat in his cozy office while we're the ones getting kidnapped, tortured, and in fear of our lives."

Anastasie shifted in her seat uneasily, tugging her very short skirt down; she wasn't used to her clients getting in her face.

"Calm down. Being angry with me will do you no good at all. I'm here to help but I don't think you have much choice here." She looked at them sympathetically, "Sonny holds all the cards. He knows you have the forty million hidden and wants the full amount surrendered. You could face significant criminal charges and end up with a long sentence behind bars if you insist on keeping the money."

Sarah was not intimidated in the least. Anastasie was just another authority symbol as far as she was concerned. "Get ahold of Sonny and see what he says. That file is a goddamned goldmine of information. Take your time, we're not going anywhere—for now. Believe me, he's not going to quibble."

"Sonny told me that he already has information from a file that you sent him." She gave Joshua an inquiring look.

His face was expressionless. "This is a more complete file. More information came to light after I sent him the original."

"I see," she said slowly. "And this file is on the computer seized by the police?"

"Yes," replied Joshua. "Password protected and encrypted. Without my help, even a computer whiz will have a problem cracking the code."

Anastasie got down to brass tacks. "You want me to go back to Sonny and tell him to forgive your sins in return for information in an encrypted file. Let me ask you this. What if Sonny doesn't agree and you end up in custody? What's to prevent the police handing the computer over to Sonny? Have you thought about that?"

Sarah lost her temper. "Let's get this straight, shall we? Once and for all. He owes us. Smashing Leon and his associates was a massive coup, and he knows it. If he doesn't get us out of here, and soon, he won't like the shitstorm I'll kick up, believe me."

Joshua took hold of her arm, reassuring her. "It's OK. We've made our point. The ball's in his court now. Let's see what he has to say." He nodded at Anastasie. "Go tell him."

Anastasie met Broussard and Matthew in the corridor adjacent to the interview room holding Joshua and Sarah.

"*Bonjour, Madam la Crocodile.*" Broussard made the insult sound like a compliment.

She knew of her nickname but only Broussard had the *chutzpah* to use it to her face.

"*C'était l'assistant de l'Inspecteur Clouseau,*" she answered with a straight face.

They both laughed. In court, she delighted in shooting holes through Broussard's investigations. Trading insults had inexplicably allowed a professional relationship to develop, each admiring the other's expertise.

He made the introduction. "This is Matthew. He's the undercover officer from Scotland Yard who worked the case. You'll have to speak English, his French is *merde.*"

"That, I understood," protested Matthew. "What's happening with Joshua and Sarah?"

Before she could answer, Broussard said, "We want to have a chat about the forty million dollars they've stolen from a bank with a dubious reputation."

"You didn't find any trace of the money at their apartment then?"

"No," answered Broussard gloomily. "There was nothing incriminating there although we could prefer charges on possession of firearms. Then there's the arrest warrants from Bruges. We have enough to hold them in custody pending further investigation."

Anastasie laughed out loud. "First, I'll have to present during any interrogation, and I can assure you they're not going to answer any of your questions. Secondly, this has become a diplomatic matter with the Minister, our own DGSE, and several foreign intelligence agencies in discussion as we speak. So, based on what I've told you, do you still want the interview?"

Matthew and Broussard exchanged resigned looks causing Anastasie to laugh. "Oh, you poor darlings. I have business so must be on my way. I'll be back in half an hour."

As she turned to walk away, Matthew said, "I have some important confidential information for them. It's something they need to hear. May I have a word with them alone?"

Broussard glared at him and, before Anastasie could answer, snapped, "Come on, Matthew, this is a joint investigation. What are you holding back?"

While Anastasie looked on, Matthew looked him in the eye and continued. "Nothing that affects you. The joint part of our investigation in Paris has finished and was highly successful, thanks to your help. From my standpoint, they were of great assistance in bringing down a notorious drug and arms dealer. The information I have is for their ears only and is considered top secret."

Broussard gave Matthew a searching look while tapping the stem of his pipe against his clenched teeth.

Anastasie broke into the conversation. "I have to make some telephone calls dond when I return, we'll see about you speaking to them alone. OK?"

"Very good," replied Matthew. He turned to Broussard. "I'm sorry, but you know how these undercover jobs are highly secret. My boss at the Yard insisted there are certain points I cannot discuss with you because it might jeopardize future operations."

With a final glare, Broussard said, "Typical Brits." He stalked off and disappeared down the corridor.

"That was awkward," muttered Matthew to Anastasie who laughed.

"He'll be OK in a few minutes. I've seen him huff and puff before. I'll be back shortly. There's a bench to sit on, why don't you wait there for me to come back?"

Joshua and Sarah sat in silence, aware they were probably being observed through the one-way glass window on the wall opposite. Both were thinking about the bonds, wondering if their hiding place had been discovered.

The door opened and in walked a smiling Anastasie. She sat down at the table opposite them.

"Sonny says deal. He received the CD you sent by FedEx and believes what you say. You have been granted diplomatic immunity, so you are free with one stipulation. You must leave France immediately and will be escorted to the airport."

They embraced and, as they released each other, Matthew walked in the door.

He congratulated them. "A quick goodbye. I'll be in touch. You did a great job." He turned to Anastasie. "Per our conversation, would you excuse us?"

"Of course." She left the room.

Matthew sat on the table and said, "We're not being observed or overheard. I made sure of that, cameras are off and there's no one behind the one-way mirror. Now, I have a contact who gave me information about a leak of information from Sonny's company."

Joshua said, "Yeah. When Sarah's cover was blown in Belgium and we were forced to move her. We've been worried about it ever since. When we asked questions, we were told an inquiry was in place but there's been no progress."

"Correct. Well, here's the kicker. It was Sonny himself who passed hints about Sarah's identity to Belgian intelligence."

"Are you sure about this?" questioned Sarah. "Who's your source?"

"You know better than to ask me that. Let's just say the source is impeccable and has a proven track record. It makes sense when you look at the facts."

He used the fingers on one hand to enumerate his points. "One: The arms deal put Sonny under pressure to bring down Leon and he needed to get you on the case as quickly as possible. Two: I think he was pissed off about some financial crimes you are alleged to have committed." He gave them a knowing smile before continuing. "Three: Possible repercussions from the Belgian criminal fraternity. Put it all together and it makes sense."

Sarah was aghast. She turned to face Joshua. "So much for your relatives. He put us in a lot of danger, the scumbag."

Joshua sighed and shook his head. "Let's not get into an argument over it now. Let's get the hell out of here."

They shook hands with Matthew and thanked him profusely.

"You had better be careful with him in the future. Undercover work is dangerous enough without having your handler putting you in danger. That's the reason I had to let you know. Let's keep it between ourselves. Broussard is sulking down the corridor, he's in a bad mood because I didn't share this information with him."

He knocked to have the detention room door opened and Anastasie, accompanied by Broussard, entered.

"I'm going to leave you in the hands of these gentlemen," she said. "You're safe now and have no further need of my services."

She wished them luck, they shook hands, and she left.

Brossard was more succinct. "You are very lucky. Brussels has withdrawn their warrant and there's nothing to keep you here. Carmine, Louis, and Henri will be charged with offenses related to the firearms. Possession of the machine gun will be frowned upon but realistically they will serve two, maybe three years. Carmine will probably be extradited to serve his time in the States. We can't pursue kidnapping or attempted robbery allegations because Anastasie tells me Sonny has refused permission for you to give evidence."

"Can we get our belongings from the apartment?" asked Joshua.

Broussard answered. "Of course. You will be escorted there, you can pick up your stuff, then you'll be taken to the airport."

They shook hands with Matthew, thanked him, and promised to be in touch in the future when things had settled down.

Broussard and two uniformed officers accompanied them back to the apartment which looked as though a bomb had gone off. The sofa cushions had long knife wounds, the polyester fiber stuffing was spilling onto the floor, the back slashed open. Drawers had been half pulled out with various belongings strewn around. The bedroom had undergone the same treatment, a mattress half on and half off the bed showing a gash where it had been searched. The contents of the drawers and cupboards in the kitchen had been emptied onto the counter. Only the bathroom looked unscathed with the cabinet door opened but the contents apparently untouched.

"*Oy vey*," exclaimed Joshua. He looked at Broussard. "Who's going to pay for the damages?"

Broussard shrugged in typical Gallic fashion and made no comment.

Sarah said, "Let's get packed up."

Joshua assisted her in locating their backpacks and suitcases, and they began to sort through clothing and essentials to take with them.

"Well, that seems to be it," said Joshua to Broussard who stood watching the proceedings, surrounded by a cloud of smoke from his ever-present pipe. "Before we leave, I want to use the toilet. Is that OK with you?"

"The officer will stand by the open door while you do so."

Joshua was angry. "You know, we've been treated like *merde* since we've been here. What's the problem with closing the door?"

Broussard made no reply, just strolled over to the bathroom and gave it a once over. He saw Joshua had left a small backpack beside the cabinets under the sink but made no comment. He motioned for the uniformed officer to stand to one side and nodded at Matthew while sucking furiously on his pipe.

"We didn't find any evidence of criminality apart from the guns. Go ahead, I won't insist on the door being open."

"Thank you." Joshua gave a meaningful look at Sarah and went into the bathroom, closing the door behind him.

A few minutes later he emerged carrying the backpack. He held it out to Broussard.

"I forgot this. Do you want to take a look in case I stashed stolen money in here?"

Broussard was no fool. He knew the backpack certainly contained nothing to advance his investigation but decided to call Joshua's bluff. As he suspected, only personal items were discovered. Incriminating items such as multiple passports and duplicate cellphones had been discarded shortly after Matthew's intervention. Broussard gave a sniff of disgust and continued to suck on his pipe while observing them closely.

They prepared to leave when Sarah said, "I have to pee. May I use the bathroom before we go?"

Broussard looked at her, suspicion written all over his face. *It's a reasonable request but I don't trust this pair. I'm sure there's something going on.* He walked over to the bathroom to check it out again but could see nothing alarming. He removed the ever-present pipe from his mouth. *"Eh bien. Entrez."*

Sarah closed the bathroom door behind her and flushed the toilet to hide any noise as she stood on the countertop beside the sink. Slowly and gently, she lifted one of the ceiling tiles and removed the envelope containing the eleven million in Eurodollars. There were eleven paper certificates, each in the amount of one million dollars. She carefully folded each one in half, hoisted her skirt and pushed them down the back of her underpants. Fluffing out her skirt, she pulled the handle to flush the toilet again and rejoined Joshua and Broussard.

She laughed. "Phew, that's better." She nodded at Joshua and said, "Let's go."

Broussard stood by stiffly, wishing he had brought a policewoman to conduct a search of her person. *I'll alert customs before their flight. They can do the dirty work.*

At the airport, they were met by a diplomat from the Israeli embassy who guided them to a hangar where a private plane awaited. Broussard had figured that their being granted diplomatic immunity wouldn't prevent the customs from doing their duty. He was in for another disappointment. The customs officials were uneasy, offending a bona fide diplomat could bring all kinds of shit down on their heads. No crime had been committed in France, so they denied his request. Broussard left them without exchanging pleasantries, returning to headquarters in a huff.

Thirty minutes later they were fifteen thousand feet over the patchwork quilt of the French countryside bound for Israel.

"Home free." Sarah and Joshua sat in adjacent seats, each holding a glass of champagne, the bubbles bursting at the top, tickling Sarah's nose. Finally, exhausted, and relieved at their narrow escape, they made themselves comfortable and fell asleep, holding hands across the narrow aisle.

CHAPTER 22

Sonny makes threats.

It was a smooth flight and a little over four hours later in
the early hours of the morning, they taxied into a private
hanger at Ben Gurion airport. A woman named Dinah
climbed on board and identified herself to the crew as a
senior manager employed by Sonny. She was accompanied
by Israeli customs and immigration officials who were
under instructions from Sonny to conduct a thorough
search of the plane, any on-board luggage, their clothing,
and persons.

"So much for diplomatic immunity," commented Joshua,
as he left the plane and watched their baggage moved to
trestle tables in the hanger.

"Thank God, I didn't put the stuff in my luggage,"
whispered Sarah.

Joshua spoke softly out of the corner of his mouth, "You
mean . . ."

"Yes, still in place."

While their luggage underwent a thorough search,
customs officers took Sarah and Joshua to private rooms
for each to undergo a personal examination.

Just when I thought we were getting away scot-free, Sarah thought as a stern looking female customs officer took her into a room and told her to strip.

"All off?" she asked.

"Yes, everything comes off."

The agent thoroughly searched her blouse, bra, and the pockets in her skirt. The linings of her clothing were carefully examined but nothing incriminating was found.

She stood by in her underpants, watching. "*Fucked at the last minute,* she thought knowing the bonds were about to be discovered.

There was a knock at the door which was opened by another female customs agent. Sarah judged her more senior by her attitude.

"That's it, finish up. We've been told to get her out of here immediately for questioning by Shin Bet."

"But I haven't done a cavity search," protested the first customs officer.

"A million dollars weighs twenty pounds. You think she has that stuffed up her ass? Give me a break. Get dressed," she ordered Sarah.

She almost wept with relief as she dressed in front of the customs agents, being careful to keep her bulging rear end facing away from them.

Exultant, the searches over, Joshua and Sarah were taken by car to a small office building on a nearby industrial estate.

Sonny got up from his desk and embraced Joshua as soon as they were shown into his office.

"Fabulous work." He congratulated them. "First things first. You know Leon has been killed."

"Yes," said Joshua, "Matthew told us. Apparently, he sent a message warning you that Leon was in danger and hoped you could help him."

"When I got it, I acted immediately. I hoped he'd turn informant. Unfortunately, he'd already fled to Jamaica. That was a big mistake. He was dead the morning after his arrival. Looks like a Yardie hit, Nunzio's reach is far and wide."

"What about Nunzio?" asked Sarah.

"The FBI are very happy you got Carmine, his right-hand man. They'll work on flipping him when he's deported. It's unlikely he'll turn against Nunzio, but you never know. The Mustache Pete's era is long gone, *omerta* and loyalty with it. As for Nunzio himself, he's in a Nassau County jail on a bookmaking contempt charge, a small inconvenience. Believe it or not, it's only his second conviction so he'll probably get six months or so and a ten grand fine. It'll be a comfortable time, the Mob has its own wing and run it more like a holiday camp than a prison. Through Matthew, we know he's working from behind bars to wheel and deal at Leon's old bank. It's just a matter of time before he steps out of line and gets caught."

He looked from one to the other. "You've done well for yourselves." They started to protest but he held up his hand. "We supplied you with targets which you have successfully brought to justice, but you pillaged their bank accounts. I want all the money back. I don't know if you read the terms of our contract but as employees you are not allowed to profit from our association."

Joshua was furious. "We are not employees. You contracted with us independently. Besides, we have a deal."

Sonny raised his finger threateningly. "I was forced to make you employees. It was the only way I could obtain your immunity. Your profits are forfeit. That forty million is coming back here. You may keep the fees from the loan you arranged providing the taxman gets his share of the pie."

Sarah still had cards to play. "Let's do an accounting, shall we? We're giving you a total of fifty five million but we're keeping the fifteen million left as our fee."

Sonny sat back in his chair and surveyed them.

Joshua said, "Let's change the subject for a moment, shall we? I have the computer here. Do you want to see the file and tell us it's not worth the money?"

"The last CD was great stuff. I've gathered some financial analysts together but it's going to take time to go through it all. I admit it looks like quite a coup."

"Well, we're glad you recognize the importance of what you have," Joshua said, and chuckled. "But there's more to the story. Sarah suspected you'd pull a fast one. The files on the computer, together with the CD I sent from Beverly Hills, still don't give you the whole picture. The rest of Leon's bank records are on a CD hidden where you'll never find it."

Sonny sat back in his chair, a look of disgust on his face. "I knew it," he said angrily. "There were some entries that didn't look kosher; in fact, I wondered if they were complete."

"You get the last CD only if you agree to our deal. Then we're square." He sat back in his chair, held hands with Sarah, and smiled at Sonny. "By the way, we know it was you who tipped off Belgian intelligence about our identities. What have you got to say about that?"

"Who told you and why would I do that?" Sonny blustered.

"I won't reveal who told us, but it came from someone with no axe to grind who has sources in various intelligence agencies."

Sarah interjected. "I didn't want to believe you would jeopardize the life of your nephew, but our information is absolutely irrefutable. We're letting you off the hook by not talking to your Israeli bosses, but in return we get to keep the money. Putting your agents in harm's way is ..." She stopped talking, lost for words, her face red with anger.

There was a long silence before Sonny reluctantly agreed. "OK. OK. I give up. I deny your allegations but blackmail wins. We have a deal only because of your superb work. If I could prove you committed a crime, we might have a different ending. Analyzing these accounts will take days, maybe weeks, and time is on your side. Leave it with me, I'll convince my bosses that the ends justify the means."

Before they left his office, not wanting to make Sonny an enemy, Joshua arranged the millions in money transfers to satisfy his part of the deal. Negotiations now complete, Sonny shook hands with Joshua, but Sarah ignored his outstretched hand, and they left his office.

Upon arrival at a nearby hotel, Sarah made a beeline for the bathroom. She carefully retrieved the eleven million in bearer bond certificates from her underwear which were now well and truly creased.

"They're a bit crumpled," she remarked, "But still negotiable."

CHAPTER 23

**Paris, France
Friday, September 13**

Later, that same morning, Farid opened his safe to retrieve the bearer bonds. It was empty. Someone had taken the bonds. He called Hafeez to his office and after closely questioning him about Joshua and Sarah's visit, told him to call the police.

Broussard was called in to investigate and wasn't fooled for one second. He knew Joshua and Sarah had somehow spirited the bonds out of France. *Probably with Farid's help,* he concluded grimly. *Forensics hasn't come up with anything. No DNA or fingerprints, nothing, nada, zilch. And the chief suspects are beyond reach in Israel. Bais-Les.* Later that morning, he consulted with his boss who agreed the case would remain open but put on a back burner.

Broussard sat at his desk, incandescent at his failure over recent events. He bit down on his pipe stem, ruining it. Disgusted, he threw it in the wastepaper basket and picked up the phone to make a call to Sonny in Israel. After he heard Farid was denying all knowledge of the theft, Sonny blew his top. He thanked Broussard and immediately called Joshua, demanding he come to his office for an explanation.

Tel Aviv, Israel

Joshua gave a roar of laughter when Sonny offered his thoughts on the missing money. "Of course, Farid's going to say that. The bank uses hawala connections, so you won't find any trace. I tell you, we've been robbed. I'm surprised because we've used him before with no problem. But, you know yourself, it's an occupational hazard. They're bearer bonds. Possession means they're yours to cash, no questions asked."

Sonny sat back in his chair, viewing Joshua through narrowed eyes. *Do I believe you? No. Is there any proof. No. Score to our side, about forty four million in cash formerly belonging to Nunzio. A gun running and drug operation put out of action. A money laundering operation wounded. On top of that, warm relations with the FBI for the information on Nunzio and Carmine. Scotland Yard and MI6 were appreciative of the information on Leon's money laundering contacts. My bosses will be pleased. And there's no come back on my contact with Belgian intelligence.*

"Fuck it," he said out loud, a rare epithet. "I don't care what happened to the money. You and Sarah pulled off a very successful operation and that's what counts. I'll even pay you for the CD with the missing information as long as that's all. By the way, Nunzio's family had a visit from the FBI—regarding you and Matthew."

"Oh?"

"Yeah. He was told in no uncertain terms that Matthew was a British cop. You and Sarah were described as Mossad agents, even though you're not. Any revenge would be met with a strong response. They got the message but keep an eye out. I'm sure there'll be contracts on your lives."

In the weeks following, Sonny played his cards brilliantly. He sent information anonymously to various friendly media outlets identifying Leon's clients. The names included celebrities, politicians, and other less-wholesome types, all avoiding taxes and hiding questionable deposits. The media pounced on those named like dogs on a bone. The subsequent publicity resulted in a huge global scandal with fines, imprisonment, and confiscation of assets for those involved.

The Imperial Bank of Panama closed after inquiries by Cayman authorities investigating the irregularities in the bank's procedures. This loss, with the headlines naming Nunzio as a shadow partner, was a problem for the publicity-shy New York families. He was summoned to a meeting to explain the missing money. Two weeks later, his decomposing body turned up in the trunk of his Cadillac.

CHAPTER 24

**Los Angeles, California
One Year Later**

Sarah and Joshua lay in each other's arms, content in the knowledge that they had enough money to do whatever they wanted, whenever they wanted. Wealthy gypsies, their caravan was a rented Spanish-style mansion in the Hollywood Hills overlooking the Los Angeles basin. Laid out before them, a dazzling display of lights from millions of households lit up the city like an endless series of Christmas decorations.

The baby monitor picked up a faint cry from one of their twin girls, and they turned the television down until she slept again. Turning the sound back up, they were just in time to see artists produced by Jayden, Dewayne, and Jamal win the first of six Grammys. With Studio Z, the three brothers were living their dream of owning a successful recording studio.

Satisfied that good had prevailed, they turned the television off, nestled back together, and resumed their conversation on whether the ends justify the means. It was a long discussion, but they couldn't agree on an answer that made them both happy.

ABOUT THE AUTHOR

Don Spillane was born, raised and educated on the South Coast of England. In the 1960s and 1970s. he served as a young detective with London's Scotland Yard and worked Jack the Ripper's old territory, Whitechapel and Bethnal Green. While helping to investigate murders, armed robberies and other criminal activity, he benefitted from the experience of senior colleagues who arrested culprits for such crimes as the Great Train and Bank of America robberies. His backup was the Yard's famed "Flying Squad" when he zeroed in for the final arrest of his career, a contract killer.

Don has lived in the U.S. for the past 40 years as a dual citizen. With his wife Carol, and their beagle, Lucy, he now lives in Huntington Beach, California where he's worked as a partner, director, and executive vice president in various local, national, and international companies.

Recently, he's found a new and rewarding life writing and creating thrilling novels based on his first-hand encounters with the sordid and unsavory denizens of the underworld. Join him in the exciting international world of courageous intelligence operatives combatting dangerous psychopaths and organized crime.